MW01491217

ERRANT GODS

BLOOD OF THE ISIR
BOOK ONE

ERIK HENRY VICK

Ratatoskr Publishing

New York

Ratatoskr Publishing
2080 Nine Mile Point Road, Unit 106
Penfield, NY 14526

Publisher's Note: This is a work of fiction. Names, characters, places, and incidents are a product of the author's imagination. Locales and public names are sometimes used for atmospheric purposes. Any resemblance to actual people, living or dead, or to businesses, companies, events, institutions, or locales is completely coincidental.

Errant Gods/ Erik Henry Vick. -- 1st ed.
ISBN 978-0-9990795-1-5

For the real Supergirl: mother of my child, wife of my dreams, love of my life, and the lynch pin of my universe.

Go then; there are other worlds than these.

–STEPHEN KING

Contents

ONE

Thou art mad now, Loki, and reft of mind, —
Why, Loki, leav'st thou not off?
Frigg, methinks, is wise in all fates,
Though herself say them not!
—The Gylfaginning

Hunger.

The woman who called herself Liz, despite being named something else, slammed the stainless-steel freezer door and glared at it. The freezer was empty, and she was hungry. Behind her on the worn futon, Luka fidgeted like a small child waiting for punishment. It made her want to choke him.

"We are out of meat. Again." Liz ran her hand through her long blonde hair, trying to force it into some kind of order. She hated looking like a tatterdemalion in front of any man, but even more so in front of Luka. "How long do you expect me to go without? You promised to take care of me, Luka."

"I–I'm…I'm s-sorry, my Queen."

She sneered at the weakness in his voice. "Who sits before me? Surely this petulant child is not Luka *Oolfhyethidn*, feared by so many back home?"

"My Queen, I—"

She whirled to face him, biting back the words that danced on her tongue. Ire coursed through her veins like lava—hot and fierce—and a part of her wanted desperately to let those words fly. "Just stop it, Luka!" she screamed instead. "Stop sitting there acting like that puny little cop beat us! I can't stand to be in the same room as you!"

Luka looked her in the eye for the first time in what felt like an eon. "I wanted to kill him at the end. You forbade me."

Passion burned in his pale green eyes, and she reveled in waking him up again at last. The words she didn't want to say kicked at the back of her teeth like a child having a temper tantrum. She had to say something, or she knew those words in the *Gamla Toonkumowl*—the language of the old ones—would worm their way out. "Who the fuck are you to question me?"

Luka smiled crookedly. "You have embraced cursing in this language, at last, my Queen."

Her anger cooled at once. She had always been labile, but this was something else. Luka knew her so well after all these years in relative isolation. Part of her detested how well he knew her and that his arguments and tactics could sway her thinking. It was the same part of her that wanted to let those words fly—and she fought to suppress that part of herself. "Indeed, it seems I have," she muttered.

Luka's passion faded. As it did, he seemed to deflate, to become less of a man. Her expression hardened, and she sneered at him. "Do you think I asked you, out of all of my courtiers, to accompany me here because I like weak little boys?"

He grinned, but his expression was sour, bitter. He didn't meet her gaze. "I never understood why, my Queen. I just delighted in it."

"After everything you did for me back home? After going to war, even against your own brothers, for me? After killing with such ruthless abandon anyone who stood in my way or who threatened me? How can you not understand, my Luka? After all the things you did, my Champion, this was your reward." She waved her hand down her tall, lean form. With a wide smile, she watched his eyes follow the course of her hand. Their present circumstances had made her thin with brutal efficiency, but she was still beautiful.

The wind outside shrieked, flinging snow at the window of their tiny, one-room apartment. The blizzard had come at the worst possible time. He couldn't hunt in this. It wasn't his fault, she knew that.

But it is his fault, insisted a voice buried in the back of her mind.

Her neighbors in Ontario County would have called it a "white Christmas." She scoffed at the thought. She still didn't understand the point of the holiday—even after all the years she'd spent in this wretched country.

Luka reached into the large side pockets of his black cargo pants and pulled out a foil-wrapped parcel. "Take this, my Queen," he said, holding it out. "I was saving it in case you didn't have enough." He peeled back the foil to show her a piece of meat that was seared just enough to keep its juices inside.

She looked at his emaciated face. He had always put her needs before his own. "You eat it, Luka."

He shook his head. "No, my Queen. I'm not hungry."

"You are so thin, dear one."

"No, my Queen. I am fine. You need this more than I do."

Saliva sluiced into her mouth like spring runoff overflowing the banks of a creek. "The girl was very tasty, wasn't she?" Liz mused.

"Yes, my Queen. I was lucky to find someone so healthy in such a shitty little bar. Usually, they are drunks or worse, but she was young and fresh."

She eyed the package and then tore her eyes away. "You are sure you've had enough?"

Luka swallowed and nodded. "Yes, my Queen. You eat it. I am full."

He was lying, of course. It only took one look at him—bony, haggard, almost cadaverous, in truth—

to see that he needed the meat. She understood his loyalty, his fealty; it was as it should be, after all. In her own way, she loved and honored him, too, and regretted that circumstance and his devotion to her made him look like a man ravaged by a wasting illness.

At the same time, she was hungry. She shrugged and reached for the meat. "If you are sure, my Champion."

"I am sure, my Queen," he said, avoiding her gaze.

"Thou art mad now, Luka, and reft of mind," she whispered, and he winced.

As she ate, her eyes drifted around the little efficiency with forced indolence, lingering on all the things she detested about the place: the peeling, atrocious wallpaper; the stained carpeting; the unstable kitchen table; the broken television—all of it. She forced herself to swallow. "This place…" She pursed her lips, then lifted her arms out from her sides and let them fall, unable to find English words strong enough to express the depths of her hatred for their present state of affairs. "*Thath tyerir mik lankar til ath tayia.*"

He looked at her, the small smile at hearing the ancient language dying stillborn on his lips as the meaning of the words sank in. "Please don't say that, your Grace." Luka's eyes darted around the room. "This place is beneath you, I know. But it's temporary, my Queen. We can pack and leave tonight. Or we can just leave. We can go somewhere else, another state maybe. Or back to Scandinavia. You pick the place, my Queen, and I'll make it happen." His voice rang with some of the confidence and competence she had come to expect from him.

Her eyes locked on his. "You'll make it happen? You promised to take care of me." She waved her hand at the room around them. "Is this taking care of me?"

He withered under her scrutiny, and his gaze slithered away from hers.

"Don't you look away from me," she snapped, mounting fury pounding its staccato rhythm in her temples.

He snapped his head up as if she had slapped him and met her gaze. "I'm…I'm sorry, my Queen. For all of it. This…this place…" He shook his head, looking lost and helpless. "I've allowed myself to grow soft. Everything is so easy here. It was—"

Like some wild beast, anger leapt into her mind, jaws snapping, saliva flying. "You've grown soft? It was too easy? For these…*reasons*…I go hungry?" Her voice boomed, filling the small apartment with her fury. Her breath tore air from the room in ragged gasps. She had to clamp her teeth together to keep from spitting out the words that would scorch Luka like a blistering green fire.

After a single glance at her expression, Luka snapped his mouth shut. He leaned toward her, a seated bow. "No excuses, my Queen. I will go out. The storm isn't as bad as it sounds. Even if it is, what's the worst it can do to me? Make me shiver?"

She shook her head, fury singing its slippery, dangerous song in her blood.

"I can find someone doing some last-minute shopping. I can be quick. I'll be back inside an hour, and the freezer will be full."

The rage-monster departed in an instant. The struggle to keep those words inside had burned the temper out of her, leaving her exhausted and downtrodden. "No, Luka," she said, shaking her head. "We've hunted too much in this town built from dirty snow and rust. We can't risk further exposure. We are still too close to Ontario County. And despite what you did to him, despite the curse I laid on him, that damn cop survives."

"I should have killed him," said Luka with a trace of the bloodthirsty fire he was known for. "I would have killed him, but you said you wanted him to suffer."

She glowered at him. "I did, and I still do." Her tone was biting, glacial, and bitter. "He was impolite. He demanded answers from me. He was so...familiar with me." Liz crossed her arms and suppressed a smile as Luka's eyes darted down for a peek at her breasts. "Too many hunts in one place will lead him to our door again. He still has friends. And seven years of running or not, we are still on his mind.

"Anyway, it's not as if you leave no marks." Her smile was fierce, almost savage, and she quirked her eyebrow at him.

He blushed and looked away like a school boy.

She loved the way he feigned such innocence around her.

Luka cleared his throat. "Then I can go back to the abattoir. I'm sure they didn't find everything."

"No. I just said we can't risk further exposure. That meat was lost to us the moment those two boys found the cave. We can only go back there once, and for one purpose only."

A panicked expression writhed across his face. "I can still take care of you if you'll give me another chance."

"No. This isn't working anymore." She took three long strides across the length of their home and stood in front of him, giving him no choice but to look up at her. She could see how much this conversation distressed him. He'd grown used to being her sole companion. He'd hate going home, and he'd hate sharing her with the others.

Luka gulped like a fish on a hook. His hands fiddled in his lap as if he were conjuring up some clever argument. "Just...just don't do anything rash, my Queen. Don't give up on life. I couldn't go on without you." He touched her arm.

She lifted her hand and rested it on Luka's tense shoulder. "It has been grand, this time we've shared," she said, almost purring. "We've been here a long time, Luka. We have shared so much."

She was surprised to find that she meant every word of it. They fit together, hand in glove. He knew how to please her. He knew how to calm her. He knew how to excite her. She stretched with unbridled lubriciousness, knowing he would resist what she had in mind. She'd always known she possessed the kind of power that made men want to do anything she asked of them, and she used every ounce of it now to twist his will to her own.

Luka's mouth drew a brutal line over his chin, and his hands twitched to a slow stop in his lap.

"But..." she said. The word sounded flat and terrible in the small, ugly space.

Luka nodded, his mouth set in a grimace, his eyes downcast and wet.

"It is time to go home." Her voice was firm but kind. Her fondness for Luka was evident in how she tried to manage her expression, her tone. It was evident in the fact that she hadn't set him on fire, too.

His face collapsed, and he closed his eyes as if it were too much effort to look at her. He shrank in on himself. He opened his mouth, and she wondered if he was going to stand up to her at last. She almost hoped he would.

Luka knew many things—about her, about this silly country they'd lived in for far too long. She mourned the loss of the brash, confident man he'd been before that damn cop stuck his nose in. But above all else, Luka had always known his proper place. "Why, Luka, lea'vst thou not off?" she asked in a whisper.

His gaze fell, and he slid off the futon to kneel with a formal precision at her feet. "As you command, my Queen."

"Take me home, Luka. Let's run the *Reknpokaprooin*, side by side, hand in hand."

A crafty expression stole across his face like a thief creeping through a window. "Before we go, my Queen, there is one more thing I think we should do."

"Kill that cop?" A small, vicious smile played on the edges of Liz's lips. "That could be fun."

9 ⭐ ERIK HENRY VICK

"Better than that, my Queen." His grin was a master painter's study of mischief. "I think we should invite two guests to travel with us. A young boy and his mother, perhaps?"

Liz looked at him with quizzical eyes. "Would he follow, do you think?"

Luka nodded. "Oh, yes, my Queen, he will follow. He's already promised to chase me wherever I may go. Taking his family home with us will just make it more...fun." His eyes twinkled with a good humor that was somehow savage. "What do you think, my Queen? Does it suit?"

Liz laughed. "Oh, excellent, Luka. Your wickedness inspires me." She looked at him for a long moment. "For the fun you suggest, I'm willing to put up with this wretched place a little while longer."

She offered him her hand with a smile and pulled him to his feet when he took it. Hand in hand, the two lovers walked to the futon couch and converted it into a bed. "Inspire me a bit more, my Champion," she said.

TWO

I pushed myself up from the extra-large recliner and grimaced at the streak of white-hot lightning that cascaded through my neck and shoulders. I'd spent way too much time in that damn chair over the past seven years. Sig thumped around upstairs, getting ready for the big night.

"Dad! Where are my teeth?"

I chuckled to myself. "In your mouth, I would hope!"

"Daaad! Not those teeth!"

The last time I felt good, really good, was more than seven years ago. I caught my last case with the

New York State Police early that spring. The case wasn't a long one; it lasted about a week. But it ended with a bang that left me in the hospital.

They called me a hero in the papers, but that's all bullshit. The simple truth is that I failed, and people I cared about paid the ultimate price for my failure. To make things worse, I didn't even catch the pair of psychopaths the media nicknamed the "Bristol Butchers"—Liz Tutor and Chris Hatton.

"Look in your toy box? On the dresser? Up your nose?"

"I did. They aren't there. They aren't anywhere!"

"If I come up those stairs and they are right there in front of you, it'll be tickle-slams on the bed!" No doubt his vampire teeth would be somewhere so obvious it would take me all of two seconds to find them, but such is the life of a father.

I started up the stairs, expecting pain to lance through my legs and feet, but there wasn't any. I laughed at how surprised I was. Thanks to a new cocktail of chemo drugs and biologics—stuff with potential side-effects like cancer and sudden death—I hadn't had to take pain meds in almost three months.

That last case had left me a wreck of a man. For the past seven years, I had been in nearly constant pain. Sometimes it was a thousand bee stings inside my knuckles or an attack of fire ants that squirmed in my hips. Sometimes the pain was a bright, burning fire that raged in my ankles and feet, or a putrefying sick feeling that rotted in my knees and elbows. Sometimes it was all of them at the same time.

The doctors said it was rheumatoid arthritis. I wasn't so sure, since the pain had started after the hoodoo mumbo jumbo Tutor had shouted at me. I called it my Personal Monster™ (patent pending), and I still do.

Sig stood in the middle of his wreck of a room wearing his "vampire shirt" and holding the black cape lined in red satin. Jane had made it for him four years earlier, but it was still in fine shape. His face forlorn, he looked around at the heaps of sticky notes, toys, video-game cartridges and dirty clothes, any of which might hide his precious vampire teeth.

Of course, his vampire teeth were on top of his dresser, right in front of him. I pointed at them.

He smacked his palm into his forehead and then looked at me with a rueful expression on his face.

I couldn't believe seven years had slipped by without my noticing and that he was already so big. The painkillers of the previous seven years and the simple effect of being on disability—of having nothing to mark the passage of time by—had played havoc with my sense of time. Time had lurched around me like a drunken sports fan after a big game.

"You know what's coming, boy."

"Not fair! I'm in my costume already!"

"All right, all right," I said holding up my hands in mock surrender. "But, when you least expect it…"

"Yeah, yeah."

I gave him The Eye and went back downstairs, grinning at this new-found freedom to navigate steps.

Sig would probably spend the evening traipsing through the neighborhood with his pals, ringing doorbells, scoring candy, laughing and scaring the littler kids. There was a pang in my heart. I'd missed the years in which fathers walk with their sons while they trick-or-treat. I hadn't been well enough to have made those trips around the neighborhood with him. I don't remember even answering the door to give out candy. Maybe I didn't.

The weather report was normal for October in Western New York: It was going to be chilly and raining during prime-time trick-or-treat hours. Sig had already worked out how his rain suit could fit under his costume.

He was dressing as a vampire for the fourth year in a row. His idea of vampires did not come from horror stories but from a kids' show he'd watched when he was younger—Max and Ruby. The show was about a brother and sister and their "epic" adventures—many of which involved the brother dressing up as a vampire for some reason only kids could understand.

Even so, when he talked about his costume and fake teeth that squirted cherry-flavored syrup into his mouth like blood, all I could think about was Chris Hatton and Liz Tutor. They weren't vampires, but they weren't quite human, either. The body count they racked up was absurd. They'd had this cave—an abattoir, more like—in which they'd stored bodies for later…consumption. I pushed all that out of my mind. I'd gotten good at it; I'd had a lot of practice.

As evening fell, the weather grew even fouler than expected. The temperature fell to the low forties, and visibility dropped to almost nothing.

"Remember when all he wanted to dress up as was Lightning McQueen?" Jane asked, walking up behind me.

"Sort of." I could remember his birthday parties, bits and pieces of past Christmases and a few Thanksgivings. I guess Halloweens didn't make enough of an impression to penetrate the fog.

"It looks like another miserable Halloween," Jane said.

This year was going to be different, though.

"Yeah. Should we make him stay in?"

"Nothing short of the end of the world could convince our little boy not to trick-or-treat—at least a little." She smiled and picked up the bottle of cherry syrup that was waiting on the counter. "Think he'll go through the entire bottle again this year?"

"Of sugar-infused yumminess? Of course he will," I said with a chuckle.

"If you can answer the door for a bit, I'll take the Sigster and his friends around for a while—at least until it gets too miserable."

"I could go," I said.

"Yes, you could, but then you'd be in bed, gorked to the gills on oxycodone by morning. You should have some real memories of Halloween this year."

"Think he'll have any good memories with me in them?"

Jane put her hand on the back of my neck, something that had not been possible until the previous July because of how much even such a simple gesture would have hurt. "He does have good memories with you in them. You make him laugh so hard Coke comes out his nose. That's got to count."

I grinned and nodded. "I suppose so."

"Hank," she said in her I-am-serious-and-I-will-brook-no-disagreements voice, "you are a great father, despite this stupid disease. What Siggy will remember about this time is your courage in the face of all this bullshit and misery and your commitment to making the best of it."

"I hope so. I'm not sure I'll remember those particular things."

"Psssh! Like what you remember matters. I'm the boss of you, tomato-face, and what I say goes." She gave me a little pinch on the back of my neck and a kiss on the cheek. "Now, quit it before I bust you one in the chops."

"Yes, ma'am! I'll need a big bowl full of candy. Oh, and some candy to give to the kiddies, too."

She laughed and swatted my behind. "That candy is for those kids, Henry. I better not catch you eating any." She looked me right in the eye as she reached into the bowl and took a mini Hersey's dark chocolate bar and put it in her pocket.

I grinned. Jane always made me feel better when it counted. I didn't call her Supergirl for nothing. "Ma'am, I'm afraid I'll have to frisk you."

"Hah! I know what you want, you...you man!"

"For stolen merchandise! Don't worry, I was trained to frisk people."

She looked at me with a sly grin. "If you are good, trooper, I might let you frisk me later." She waggled her eyebrows à la Groucho Marx.

"Ma'am, I think you might be trying to bribe me."

"Give me a few hours, and I'll let you bribe *me*."

"Promise?"

She patted my cheek. "You know it, sailor."

"Eww! No gushy stuff in the kitchen!" said Sig. He was standing in the doorway to the front room, grinning to beat all.

"I'll gushy-stuff you," I growled.

Sig ran into the kitchen, his cape flaring behind him. Underneath it, he wore a black velvet brocade vest over a white shirt. If the splash of red from his favorite hoodie peeking out of his collar, the Nike running pants, and his sneakers spoiled the effect, he didn't seem to notice. Or care.

"Are you really going to wear running pants?" I winked at Jane.

"Yes, Dad. No one cares if my costume is accurate to some horror movie. Anyway, this is what Max wore all the time."

"Are you really going to throw Max and Ruby at me?" He had gotten so tall while I was "away." He came up to Jane's nose—and she was five feet eight inches tall. "If you don't quit growing, you are going to grow out of that cape, O' littlest Jensen."

He shrugged. "Mom will make me a new one if I want."

"That's right," Jane said. "But the next one will be pink and purple."

He looked at her with mock scorn. "That would be silly, Mother. Vampires don't wear pink." He spotted the cherry syrup, and his eyes lit up like fireworks. "You remembered!"

"Of course," said Jane. "I am literally the most awesome person you know."

"You stole that line from that T-shirt Daddy bought me," said Sig as he dug his fake fangs out of his pants pocket. "Fill 'er up, please."

She poured cherry syrup into the fangs' reservoir. "There you go, Count Sigula. Now it is officially Halloween."

"Speaking of which, we'd better get moving, Momma. That candy won't trick-or-treat itself into my bag." He turned and dashed into the front room.

"You'll be okay?" Jane asked.

"Of course. I am married to Supergirl, after all."

She flashed a grin my direction and turned to leave. "Oh, make sure the kids don't take more than two pieces each—otherwise we'll run out."

"Two pieces, aye!" I snapped a salute at her back.

"I saw that, sailor." She gave me a saucy little grin over her shoulder.

I spent the next two hours getting up every minute and a half to answer the door. The candy seemed to be a big hit, especially getting two pieces of it. Princesses, zombies, ghosts, a few vampires, and a metric ton of superheroes—even the Silver Surfer— paid me a visit. The best costumes, however, were the twins dressed as Mario and Luigi.

The temperature dropped from chilly to miserable, and the rain stayed constant. Jane had said that Sig didn't usually stay out for that long but, as he was fond of telling me, he was twelve now, and everything was different. The frequency of trick-or-treaters fell toward nothing as the level of candy in the big black plastic bowl fell toward empty.

I can't say I was worried at that point, but I do remember thinking that it was strange for the Sigster to want to stay out so long.

As the temperature dipped into the thirties and they still hadn't come home, I went out onto our front porch and looked around the cul-de-sac. All the houses on the circle were lit up and full of excitement—except for the Timmens' house right across from us. It was like the missing tooth in a mouthful of shining white teeth. I could have sworn I'd seen them passing out candy earlier, but now it looked deserted. I stayed out on the porch until the cold started nipping at my finger joints. Except for a few cars, the neighborhood was quiet.

I still wasn't actively worried, though. Jane was a capable woman, and she had her cell with her. If something had happened, she would have called. They were probably warm and toasty inside the home of one of Sig's friends.

I stood outside wearing a T-shirt, jeans, and a pair of wool-lined slippers, and it was getting uncomfortable in a hurry—even for a "big, dumb Norwegian," as my loving wife called me at times. I went back inside and sat down on the stairs to wait.

At nine o'clock, I could no longer claim not to be worried. There hadn't been a single pack of skeletons, zombies, or video-game characters ringing the bell for a half-hour, and yet there was still no sign of Sig or Jane. I called her mobile, but it went straight to voicemail.

I couldn't stand to wait any longer. I had to do something. I changed into warm boots and wrote a brief note asking Jane to call me immediately when she got in. I considered going on foot, but one look at the ice-cold rain froze that thought. I got in the truck, cranked up the heat, and turned on all the seat heaters. They would be cold if they were out walking in the night's freezing soup.

I idled to the corner at the end of the street and scanned the road in both directions. Not a single soul moved outside. It looked like the set of an apocalypse movie, all drifting fog and flickering shadows. I turned right and crept around the neighborhood. Sig's closest friend lived on the street that cut our neighborhood into two parts. I stopped in front of his house and climbed out of the truck.

The porch lights were still on, but a single sheet of paper was taped to the door. "No candy," it said in crayon. I rang the bell and waited.

Evan, Sig's friend, opened the door and gaped up at me. He still had some of his Halloween makeup streaking his face.

"Uh...hi, Mr. Jensen. We don't have any more candy. Sorry."

"That's okay, Evan. Are Sig and his mom here?"

Evan shook his head. "They went home when we finished getting candy."

"What time was that?" I asked.

Evan frowned down at his arm where his watch would have been if he'd been wearing one. "No watch," he muttered. "That was stupid."

"It's okay, Evan, your best guess is fine."

"I think it was about an hour or two ago." Evan shook his head. "I don't know. I'm only twelve."

"I know, buddy," I said. "It's okay. That's close enough."

"Okay. Wanna talk to my mom or dad?"

"No thanks. I'd better get home and see if they've shown up yet."

Without a word, Evan turned and ran toward the back of his house, letting the door swing shut behind him.

I got back in the truck and drove toward home. My stomach ached like I'd been sucker punched and my knuckles creaked and snapped on the wheel. As I drove up the road toward our house at the end of the cul-de-sac, something caught my eye in the shrubs near the Timmens' front porch. I twisted the steering wheel, and the truck's headlights and fog lamps swept their front yard clean of shadows.

Something dark was wound around the trunk of the shrubs to the right of their front door. Something black. I got out and hobbled toward it, grimacing as the cold bit into my ankles and feet. I fell to my knees and wrestled with the black cloth at the base of the bush to unwind it. Cold ate into my knees like acid, making the position even more painful than normal. Finally, I worked the cloth free of the bush and held it up. It was Sig's vampire cape. The neck was torn.

I struggled back to my feet and limped to the front door. The house was dark, but I rapped my knuckles against the door's wooden frame. Maybe they'd turned off the lights to signal they had no more candy.

Bobby and Bobbie Timmens thought sharing the same first name was cute. I'd always thought it was kind of stupid, but hell, what do I know? They also wore matching sweaters quite a bit. They were that couple. They referred to themselves as "the Two Bobbies," and so the rest of us did, too.

After twenty seconds that felt like hours, I knocked again and pressed the doorbell several times. No lights came on, and nothing stirred. It felt like I was being watched, but there was no movement—no noise at all inside the house.

"Bobby! It's Hank," I called, ringing the bell again. The house remained silent. Not even Bobbie's dogs barked.

I walked to the garage access door at the end of their porch and peered into the dark garage. Only one of their cars was there; their huge Ford Expedition was gone. Maybe they'd gone to dinner when they ran out of candy.

I tried to convince myself that the cape in my hand wasn't Sig's, but the red lining with its secret pockets said differently. Maybe the wind ripped it off Sig's neck as they walked home. That was garbage, though, and I knew it. The wind was strong, but it wasn't that strong.

I stared across the street, willing my eyes to pierce through the rain and the dark and see people moving inside my house. With a sigh, I got back in the truck, throwing Siggy's cape into the passenger seat, and backed across the circle and into my own driveway.

I should have called the police right away, but I dithered next to the phone, picking up the handset and putting it back down several times. I didn't want to admit that what I feared was a possibility. Finally, I picked it up, put it to my ear, and dialed the local trooper station.

By the time the doorbell rang a half-hour later, I was almost out of my mind with worry and impatience. I had wanted it to be a miscommunication. I had hoped Jane and Sig would stroll in so we could say it was all a mistake and send the troopers on their way.

I opened the door to a uniformed trooper and two cops in plain clothes. "Come in."

"Hello, Mr. Jensen. I'm Sergeant Kamphaus. We met a while back, if you remember. Detective Johnson and Detective Spaulding are with the Monroe County Sheriff's Department." He gave me a little one-shoulder shrug. "Jurisdiction." Johnson was short and heavyset. He had curly hair and bloodshot eyes. Spaulding was tall and rangy, with laugh lines etched into the skin around his eyes.

"Okay," I said. "We can sit in the kitchen."

"Mr. Jensen," said Spaulding after we'd taken our seats, "I understand you believe your wife and son to be missing?"

Johnson had his thumb on the little button that opened and closed his ballpoint pen. He clicked it while Spaulding talked.

"Yeah. They went trick-or-treating earlier in the evening, and they never came home. I was the primary on a case a few years ago...well, I guess it was a bit longer than that. The Chris Hatton serial case."

Johnson grimaced. "I remember. The Bristol Butchers." His pen went *click, click, click*.

"Yeah. Hatton and I spoke on a couple of occasions, and he threatened to 'take care' of my family and to 'take them away from me.' Maybe he's making good on that threat."

"Why would you think that?" asked Detective Spaulding, leaning forward. "After all these years?"

I raised my hands in a helpless shrug. "They're missing."

Spaulding shook his head. "We don't know that for sure, Mr. Jensen. It's only been a few hours."

"No, no," I said. "You don't know my wife like I do. She'd be here, or she would have called. At any rate, it's past my son's bedtime, and we are sticklers about that. Jane especially."

Spaulding glanced at Kamphaus, and the sergeant gave a short nod. "I understand that you were injured in the Hatton case? Some kind of explosion—"

"Yes. Seven years ago. But not by an explosion."

"—that left you concussed. You were in the hospital."

Frustration began to bubble through me, and I shifted position in the chair. "Yes."

"While you were recovering, there was...some kind of incident?" Spaulding acted like he was embarrassed, but he was watching me with sharp eyes that didn't miss a beat.

"Yes. I got my bell rung pretty good." I looked at Kamphaus, and the compact trooper returned my gaze with a bland expression.

"But it was more than that, right?" asked Johnson, still toying with his ballpoint pen, clicking it at random times.

I looked into his bloodshot eyes and scoffed. "If you already know the story, why ask me about it?"

"Come on, Hank," said Kamphaus. "You know they have to ask."

"I know," I said in a low tone of voice. "I don't have to like it, though. Yes, Detectives. I was injured badly that night. I blacked out and woke up in the hospital. I had a concussion and other injuries. I'm told I went off the deep end a bit."

Johnson clucked his tongue and clicked his pen. "Post-traumatic stress disorder, it says here."

I drummed my fingers on the table for a moment and then looked at each of them in turn. "It was a long time ago."

"You've been disabled in the years since?" asked Spaulding.

"Yes. The doctors say it's rheumatoid arthritis."

"My mother-in-law had that," said Spaulding. "It's a horrible disease."

"It's an absolute monster," I said.

"It didn't let my mother-in-law age gracefully." Spaulding looked down at my hands as he said it, but looked up, rabbit-quick and wolf-eyed to catch my reaction.

"Given what it's done to me, I can see how that could happen." To be honest, I was taken aback that he would say something so disheartening to someone suffering from the disease.

"How have you been doing with it?"

"Upright and breathing." I shrugged. "Better than the alternative."

"Have you been seeing a therapist?"

I shook my head. "What's the point of that? If a rheumatologist isn't enough to help me, I don't think talk therapy will be any better."

Spaulding nodded and sat back in his chair, glancing at Johnson.

"You know the statistics on this kind of thing as well as we do, Hank," said Johnson with a grim expression on his face. "You know what we have to do next."

I grimaced. "Yes, I know. Can you do me a favor, though?"

"What's that?"

"Can you start people investigating other avenues while you clear me?"

Johnson pursed his lips and looked at me for a moment. "I don't know that we can do that yet."

"I was a state trooper for a long time—a decade and a half," I said. "Doesn't that buy me some credibility here?" Again, I looked at each man in turn.

Kamphaus wouldn't meet my eye.

Johnson returned my gaze, slack-faced and empty-eyed. "You were, but you've also had a significant amount of stress in recent years. Stress can be tough on a marriage."

"If you knew my Jane, you wouldn't be thinking that."

"And there's also the PTSD business." Johnson was looking down at his little pad—one that was very much like the one I used to carry.

"And your career does buy you credibility," said Spaulding. "We wouldn't even be investigating this early if not for your background. It's too soon, and you know that."

I drew a deep breath and let it out slow. "Okay. I know you have to rule me out."

Johnson pinched the bridge of his nose and then rubbed his temples. I was willing to bet it had more to do with the bloodshot eyes than the conversation.

"How can I help you do that as fast as possible?" I asked.

"Just be honest and have patience with the process," said Spaulding.

I shook my head. "I never knew how that sounded from this side of the table."

"Sorry," said Spaulding, "but it is the truth."

"I know, I know. Ask your questions."

They asked me all the expected questions—where I was earlier this evening, what time I saw them last, who might have seen me driving around, et cetera. I told them about my visit to Evan's house and gave them the phone number and address.

"Let me ask you this, Mr. Jensen. Where else did you drive to tonight?"

"I told you: I went and looked for them in the neighborhood."

"And you drove?" asked Johnson.

"Yes." I gestured impatiently toward the window. "The weather was bad, and I don't have much endurance these days."

After a pregnant pause, Johnson just nodded.

"Okay," Spaulding said. "Is there anything else you can tell us?"

"The Timmens are involved in this somehow."

"Your neighbors across the street? Where you found the cape?"

I nodded. "Call it a hunch."

Johnson glanced at his partner. "Okay."

"Roberta Timmens was a person of interest in the Hatton investigation."

"Suspect?" asked Johnson, lifting his eyebrows.

I hesitated and shook my head. "No. She was a potential witness, but we never got to interview her. She was out of town when it all came to a head. And after that, what was the point?"

"What makes you suspect her now?"

"She was a member of Elizabeth Tutor's bridge circle. She was the only one who wasn't murdered or abducted. I'd think that if the Butchers wanted her dead or gone, she would've disappeared long before now."

Johnson looked at Kamphaus.

"We'll look into that," said Kamphaus.

Johnson turned to look me in the eye. "You know what I have to ask you next."

"Did I kidnap my own family? The answer is no."

THREE

*I*t was 4:30 in the afternoon and the spring air was crisp and bold. I drove my cruiser through the little town of Marion and beyond, enjoying the rural scenery and country bliss that was Thorndike Road. Yet something nagged at the back of my mind—something dark, violent, and hungry.

I was headed to the safe house. The meal Jane had cooked was bumping around in the back seat. If I knew my wife, there was enough for forty or fifty *people. Jane said she wanted us to have a decent supper for once.*

Jane wanted to be nice to Mrs. Layne, and I was okay with that. Melanie Layne was sweet. She was only a part of this because she liked to play bridge. Ms. Layne knew who the Bristol Butchers were, though. She'd played bridge with one of them every week: Liz Tutor, that whack-a-doo woman who lived west of Bristol. Chris Hatton's lover.

The thought of the two serial killers made my blood boil. We'd gotten too close and had tipped our hand. People died because of my mistakes.

I'd be damned if I let them kill Melanie Layne, too. We put her in one of our safe houses with troopers guarding her around the clock. My partner was with her, waiting for dinner.

I turned left into the drive of the safe house, lifting my hand to wave at the old codger sitting on his porch on the right. The man was Richie Duvall, a retired trooper who'd picked up a few shifts helping us guard witnesses by sitting on his porch, watching the road, and drinking coffee.

As my tires crunched the gravel of the drive, the sun dropped like a stone over the horizon. The sky went from late afternoon to full dark as if some mystical stage hand had thrown the breakers for all the lights. A moment later, the moon bounced from the eastern horizon and shot up into the center of the night sky.

The police radio of my cruiser vomited a dollop of static into the car at eardrum splitting volume. It felt like a warning, like someone screaming for me to turn around—to look behind me before it was too late. As the static faded, the radio made a sound like someone was tuning an old AM radio using the dial—a kind of sliding static intermixed with discontinuous voices and music. I reached out to snap the radio off and then jerked my hand back like it had been burned.

The radio was already off. "What the hell is going on here?" I muttered.

The headlights flickered a couple of times and then died, plunging me into the dark shadow the house drew in the moonlight. I hit the brakes and let the cruiser skid across the gravel to a stop. It sounded like a knife blade scraping against bone.

Nothing felt right. Nothing looked right.

Something in the backseat popped like a child's cap gun. I jumped, cracking my head against the driver's side window. I twisted around, grimacing at the pain in my neck and shoulders, right hand seeking the Glock on my hip.

It was nothing. One of the glass lids of Jane's Corelle casserole dishes had slid out of the groove meant to hold it in place. I tried to laugh it off, but I had developed a serious case of the hinkies. I eyed the house, overwhelmed by a feeling that a large predator was watching me—a bear or a lion.

The feeling intensified as I got out of the car. I glanced across the street toward Richie, but he had left the porch, though the lights were blazing inside.

Before I could close the cruiser door, the police radio blared the opening stanza of "The Wheels on the Bus." I slammed the door to shut out the sound, but I could still hear the words, plain as day. I backed away from the car, watching it as if it were alive. As suddenly as it had started, the song stopped, and an eerie stillness wrapped around me.

I stood very still, hand on the butt of my gun, eyes bouncing from shadow to shadow in the dark dooryard. Behind me, the house sat as quiet as a tomb. There was no sound of chatter, no television noise, nothing.

I turned and swept my eyes across the ground floor windows of the house. They were dark, empty. Dead. Something was wrong, but Richie had waved like everything was normal. I glanced across the street again. Now the lights were out at Duvall's house. It looked abandoned.

That couldn't be right. I'd just seen it all lit up a second ago.

I walked up the three stairs to the back door, trying to be as quiet as a big man could be. I pulled the handle of the screen door, wincing at the rusty shriek of its hinges, and propped it open. I pushed the back-door open, and the ominous feeling intensified. The air wafting out of the house was malignant— pregnant with violence.

There was a slimy, coppery smell in the air. It was a familiar smell. Blood.

"Jax?" I called, trying to keep my voice light. "Jane made dinner. Come help me get it in from the cruiser."

The only sound I heard was that of fluid dripping. I pulled my Glock out of its holster and held it ready. I stepped into the four-feet by four-feet mud room and froze, straining my ears to hear in the silence, my eyes to see into the gloom.

I slid into the cold darkness of the house and opened the inner door of the mud room. A dark shape lay on the linoleum floor—a dark shape in the form of an elderly woman. Melanie Layne.

My hand scrabbled near the door frame until I found the light switch. Something deep in my mind screamed that I should leave the light off, but I had to see if she was alive.

Soft yellow light washed across the room. She lay there unconscious and handcuffed to the rusty radiator. There was a small trickle of blood at the corner of her mouth. Her eyes were pinched closed, but her breathing was regular. I shook her gently by the shoulder, but I couldn't rouse her.

With my eyes glued to the gloom in the next room, I holstered the Glock and removed the handcuffs. I stooped and scooped Mrs. Layne up, cradling her like a newlywed bride. I backed out through the mud room, placing my feet with care, and then continued out onto the gravel drive.

The air outside was cool and sweet, and it was only then that I realized the safe house smelled like an animal's den—a meat eater's den.

"That our witness, Jensen?"

I jumped, almost dropping Mrs. Layne, her shoulder length gray hair dancing in the breeze. Richie Duvall stood at my elbow, peering at Mrs. Layne's face.

"She's a hottie," he said.

That wasn't like him. Richie had always been a straight shooter. "Jesus Christ, Richie. Give a guy a heart attack," *I whispered.*

"Gotta die sometime," *he said.*

Instead of his service pistol, Richie held a child's cap gun. "What the hell, Duvall? Where's your firearm?"

Duvall looked at me like I was a nutcase. "Right here in my hand, Jensen. You wigging out on me?"

"I'm not the one acting like a kid, Richie." *I shook my head.* "Can you stand watch out here? I can't leave her alone, and I have to go back inside and find Jax."

"I don't know. I've got a TV dinner in the oven."

"Be serious, Richie! I think Chris Hatton is inside the house."

Duvall shrugged and reached out to caress Jane's cheek, her long black hair dancing in the cool breeze. "TV dinners are expensive on a cop's retirement, Jensen."

"TV dinners, Duvall?! I said I think Hatton's in there. What the hell is the matter with you?" *This was off script—wrong in all the important details... Jane should be at home with Sig.*

He sighed. "I guess I can watch your wife for you. She's a hottie, after all, but you shouldn't go back in there and get eaten. Wait for backup, man. Let them get eaten."

"What in the blue fuck are you talking about, Richie?" *I asked, my voice incredulous.* "Are you fucking drunk?" *This is all wrong.*

"Well, I've got a TV dinner to tend to."

"For fuck's sake, Duvall! I don't have time for your games. I've got to get inside!" I said with a cold disdain.

"'Course y'do. You went inside the first night, too. Don't get me killed this time."

The first night? This time? *None of it made sense. I stared into his soft blue eyes, struck dumb and paralyzed by the strangeness of it all. But there was something familiar about all this. Something my mind wouldn't cough up.*

"Well?" he groused. "You gonna stand here all night making eyes at me or are you gonna get on with it?"

"Stay with her," I said, putting Jane down on the gravel and twitching her bangs out of her face. "I've got to go inside and find Siggy." *Jax was the one inside, not Sig.* "I mean Jax."

"Yep, I'll watch your wife. She's a hottie. But you were right the first time. Siggy's in there with the beast. Jax is years dead."

The feeling of déjà vu gone astray surged through me like a bloated spring river breaking its banks. I couldn't shake the feeling that the only one in this farce who was sticking to the script was me.

As I climbed the steps to the house, my senses kicked into overdrive. The smells of a New England spring evening were almost overwhelming, and the bees buzzed in the woods a couple of acres away. With one last look at Jane's face, I stepped back into the foul-smelling house. I had my gun out again, holding it ready in front of me.

My gaze was riveted on the black space defined by the open mudroom door. Part of me wanted to glance behind me, for at least one more look at Jane, but my head would not turn. As I put one hand out to grab the handle of the screen door, I saw that the utility room light was off again.

I heard the subtle scrape of an athletic shoe on a wooden floor, and my training took over. I snapped into the "move and shoot" stance that I had drilled to exhaustion. I peered into the laundry room, eyes straining to sift the shadows.

As I stepped inside, all sound ceased. It was like being thrust deep underwater, where the only noise was that of my own pulse beating in my ears. I slid forward on the balls of my feet, muscles as tight as high-tension power lines, nerves crackling. I tried to move like a wolf stalking a rabbit, smooth and quiet.

Something clicked, and the kitchen lights flared, momentarily blinding me.

Bloody tracks of athletic shoes trailed across the blue and gray linoleum and two bodies sprawled on the kitchen floor near the sink. The bodies were dressed in NYSP uniforms, and the faces of both troopers were gone. Blood pooled beneath them, dripping and running in tiny rivulets from bites marks and gashes all over them. The bites in their flesh were savage—not the kind of bite and release marks a human might make, but vicious tears and gouges like those made by a ravenous animal.

My shoulders and neck muscles were tight and burning as if they'd been set aflame. I tried to roll my shoulders, but that only increased the discomfort.

Two dark, gaping doors stood across the kitchen from the utility room, beckoning me.

"Don't be timid, Hank," a voice called from beyond the doors. "Come the hell in." The voice sounded like my partner, Jax, but there was a strange quality to it—too gravelly, too full to be entirely human.

I crept toward the doors. After a brief hesitation, I slid my left foot into the darkness. My eyes struggled to adjust. It had been a smart tactic to turn the kitchen light on like that. My night vision was gone, and the darkness of the room was as effective as a blindfold. With my left hand, I felt around the door frame, looking for a light switch.

"You know I'm armed, and you know how good I am with this pistol," I said.

"Oh, Hank, you amuse me so. I would expect nothing less than perfection out of you with your preferred weapon." This time, the voice sounded like my boss, Lieutenant Gruber.

Something shifted in the darkness across the room just as I flicked the light switch on. Bright white light splashed across the bloody carnage on the dining room table in front of me. There was a body on the oval table, broken and twisted, laid out to mimic the gentle curve of the oak. I couldn't seem to stop my gaze from wandering back and forth across the gruesome mess.

The white of exposed bone, the ripped flesh, the partially congealed blood clothing the body on the table, the expression on the victim's face—Jax's face—all told of an agonizing and terrible death.

Chris Hatton was sitting on the opposite side of the table, grinning like he'd just surprised me with a birthday cake.

My gaze crawled back to Jax's lifeless, staring eyes, and I fired my pistol.

Hatton jerked from the impact of the bullet, but he never stopped smiling, never flinched, even as my round ripped through his right shoulder. Fresh blood splattered on the wall behind him as the bullet exploded out of his back.

It wasn't a killing shot—too high and too far off center—but even so, being shot hurts. Humans react to being shot. They cry out, they clutch the wound, they fall down or slouch to the side. The man across the ruin of my partner's body didn't do any of those things.

He laughed.

My stomach felt like I'd swallowed three pounds of lead, and my blood ran cold. Numb from the neck up, I stood there, staring at him in bewilderment. My hands, however, were not confused. They did what I'd trained them to do.

The next bullet smashed into Hatton's torso, just above his solar plexus. That was a killing shot. Even if death was not instantaneous, it should have put him down in a hurry...but it didn't. Another bullet slammed into the base of Hatton's neck, just above the junction of his collarbones. And yet he was still laughing. He hadn't even paused when the bullets ripped into his flesh. He shouldn't have been able to breathe, let alone laugh with such abandon.

The Glock wavered in my hand like I'd never held it before.

"Ah, Hank," said Hatton, wiping at the tears on his cheeks. "This is why I like you so much." His voice sounded like his throat was full of blood. "You act. You don't dither, farting around like a little boy. You don't talk about it, you don't beg or question why things are the way they are. You just act. Where I come from, that is a trait to be prized."

My mouth opened, but I had no words. I just stared at him, feeling slow and stupid, both arms drifting down to my sides like balloons with slow leaks.

He held up a blood-speckled index finger as if asking me to pause for a moment so he could catch his breath.

The blood that had been pouring out of him a moment before slowed to a trickle. I shook my head to clear it. "That's... What in the hell?"

"Nothing so dramatic as that, Hank." As he said the words, the gunshot wounds closed. His voice already sounded better, strong and full, although he looked ghastly—gaunt and ashen, like a man half-dead from starvation. "But I do come from a place that is as beautiful as your heaven."

I stared at him, struck mute or stupid or both.

"You can't kill me, you know," he said. He held up his hands, palms toward me. "Not that I want to go on proving it to you. I do feel pain. You should be more compassionate."

My gaze drifted back to the body on the table. What I saw tore the air from my lungs. It was no

39 ✦ Erik Henry Vick

longer Jax. Now Sig lay there, his face bloody and torn, flesh ripped, bones broken. "You bastard!" I was on the balls of my feet, and the gun snapped up as if I were controlled remotely.

Hatton looked at me and grinned. "He was delicious. Not as tasty as I expect your wife to be. She's a hottie."

This was all wrong. Sig wasn't dead. Hatton had killed and eaten Jax, not Sig. The woman outside was supposed to be Melanie Layne, not Jane! "What the hell is this, Hatton?"

"Just a little snack. I was hungry." He was gloating, goading me.

Violence boiled in my blood. Once again, I was surprised by the movement of the pistol in my hand. The gun was pointed between Hatton's eyes, and at this distance, it would be impossible to miss. I wanted to pull the trigger. I wanted to shoot Hatton in the face like I've never wanted anything else. But I couldn't. It wasn't right. I had to bring him to justice, not impose my own. Killing him would make me like him.

"Ah, Hank, you disappoint me." His voice had changed. It was deeper, torn and abused. "The queen said you wouldn't have the guts."

"Tutor?" I asked in a tremulous voice.

Hatton nodded slowly. "My queen, yes. But you know that isn't her name." Hatton's face stretched, his eyes bulging against his eyelids. "She cursed you to suffer, and suffer you will."

Something was building inside me, something dark and terrible. At the same time, fear dragged icy fingers through my soul. "What in the hell are you, Hatton? What is she?"

"Come find us and find out. Don't take too long, though. We are hungry, as always, and your son looks delectable."

"Are you...are you two vampires, then?"

This wasn't how the conversation was supposed to go. He should have been in handcuffs by now. He should be telling me some delusional crap about being a god.

Instead, he laughed. "No. Not vampires. Gods."

Ah, there it is, I thought.

The darkness building inside me exploded, erasing coherent thought. The gun bucked again and again. When the slide locked back, my hands hurt like they'd been crushed under some heavy weight.

Hatton sat there like a statue, staring daggers at me. "I told you not to do that, Hank. I told you it was futile." Blood ran down his face and neck from bullet holes in his cheeks and forehead. His left eye was gone, and his left deltoid twitched. I knew what was coming, what he was about to become, and I didn't want to see it again.

He reached out with slow deliberation, his arm stretching, growing impossibly long, and took the Glock from my hands. Then, using just one hand, he squeezed the gun, muscles and tendons popping out on his forearms. The composite body of the pistol cracked like ice, and he tossed it to the floor in disgust.

"I told you not to do that," he said, staring at me. His voice was several registers deeper than it had been, like someone had piped it through a vocal synthesizer. "I told you both times we had this conversation." His tone took on a basso quality. "Why don't you ever listen?"

"Both times? Just what in the blue fuck is going on here, Hatton?" Terror pounded in my temples in time with my racing heartbeat. I looked down at the table, unsure if I would see Jax or Sig. It was Sig. I swept his broken body into my arms and turned to run.

Stars and light exploded from the left side of my head, and I was airborne. Hatton roared like a cornered predator. "You can't have him yet," he screamed as I slammed into the plaster and lath wall. "You have to come find me first!"

Then I was through the wall and flying across another room. I smashed through that wall, too, coming to a stop only after colliding with a cast-iron tub.

"Hatton!" I screamed. "You leave them alone!"

Then something in my head snapped, and everything changed.

FOUR

It was around 5:30 in the morning when the phone yanked me out of the nightmare, adrenaline shrieking in my bloodstream. With the dream still fresh in my mind, memories of the actual event flooded in—Hatton's monstrous eyes as he scooped Melanie Layne up off the ground and ran toward the woods, the smell of Jax's blood, the spent cordite, and plaster dust. It felt like I'd gone fifteen rounds with Mike Tyson.

After a few seconds of confusion, I scrambled for the phone, full of hope and dread. "Jane?"

The line fuzzed and fizzed.

"Hello? Jane, is that you?"

Static screeched, but a female voice cut through it: "…hear me? I wanted…"

The voice was female, but it wasn't Jane. Disappointment dragged me down like a concrete life preserver. "If you can hear me, the connection is terrible."

"Is that better?"

The static was still intense, but at least I could make out the words. "Who is this?"

"Well, hello again, Hank. I'm not surprised you don't recognize my voice; you spoke more to Bobby than to me back when we were still neighbors."

"Bobbie Timmens?" I stood and began to pace around the bedroom, shock robbing me of any rational thought.

"Yep, it's me. How are you, Hank?" asked Bobbie.

"I'm fine." The response was automatic—hardwired into my genetics. My mind was awhirl with sleep and the stuff of nightmares. "Are you at home? I found Sig's vampire cape in front—"

"Don't worry about that right now, Hank. Just listen to me. Our mutual friends, the Bristol Butchers, asked me to bring them something. Well, a couple of somethings."

"Bobbie, what are—"

"Just shut up and listen to me, Hank." Her voice was suddenly cold and distant. Something about it brought to mind the morning I interviewed Liz Tutor in front of her house like a hammer to the forehead.

"No, Bobbie, you listen to me for a second. Jane and Sig—"

"Our friends want me to give you a message. Are you ready to hear it? Because I am ready to hang up if you aren't. I'd much rather be with them than standing here in the cold, yabbering at you."

"Who…who are these friends you keep talking about?" Of course she couldn't mean anyone but Hatton and Tutor.

"Last chance," said Bobbie.

There was a kind of promise, as hard and cold as steel, in her voice that caused a shiver to wiggle down my spine. "Don't hang up! I'll listen."

The line crackled—a perfect storm of static. Bobbie was silent, drawing the moment out. "Okay, but I'm warning you, Hank, any more interruptions, and Jane will suffer for it."

"Whatever you say, Bobbie."

"Good. Luka said to tell you hello."

I didn't know that name, but I knew exactly who she meant.

"He wanted me to remind you of a conversation you had with him at Jay's Diner. Remember when you said you'd chase him anywhere? Remember that he said that if you did, you'd have to leave everything behind—your life here, your job, your family, all of it?"

"I had that conversation with a serial killer—a man named Chris Hatton," I said. Now, it was my voice that had gone frosty. "Are you telling me you are…I don't know…in league with Hatton?"

She sighed as if I was the stupidest man she knew. "That's not his real name, Hank. I think you knew that already. Do you remember the conversation at the diner?"

"Of course," I snapped.

"We've made it easy for you. There's nothing left of your life here. The queen took your job when she cursed you. She says hello, by the way. And Bobby and I have taken your family. We're taking sweet Jane and precocious little Sig on a trip."

"Bobbie, why would you do that?" My voice shook with rage. "Why would you throw in with those two? Why would you drag Jane and Sig into this?"

"Because Luka *asked* us to. After the gifts he and the Midnight Queen bestowed on Bobby and me, it was the least we could do. If you were smart, you'd do whatever it takes to get off their shit list. If you only knew what they could do for you, you'd be thanking me."

I had no answer to that; I just sat there boiling and breathing hard.

After a short pause, Bobbie chuckled, low and sensuous. "Luka expects you to follow him. He'll take care of Jane and Sig until you come for them. As long as you chase after him, he will not touch them. Do you understand?"

"I'll kill him. If one hair on either of their heads is out of place, I'll kill him with my bare hands." My voice sounded strange—flat and distant, and at odds with the fist-shaking rage that I felt.

Bobbie laughed like a kid getting candy for lunch. "Luka said you could be quite funny. I see what he means now."

"We still are, you know," I muttered.

"What? We still are what?" she asked, sounding confused.

"We still are neighbors. I'm looking across the circle at your home as we speak."

She chuckled again. "Oh, Hank, you are a dear. That is just an empty building now. Bobby and I are *moving*." She tittered like a drunk. "We'll never go back there."

"Where will you go? If you go through with this, you'll be a fugitive for the rest of your life." I wished like hell the call was being traced.

"Hardly," she scoffed. "I'll have a place of honor where I'm going. Bobby and I will be valued retainers in the Court of the Dispossessed Queen."

"The Dispossessed Queen? Is that supposed to be Elizabeth Tutor?"

"That isn't her real name, either. She has vast holdings on the other side. Her—"

"Other side? What does that even mean?"

"—empire was unrivaled in its time and soon will be once more. We're going with them to reclaim it."

"Don't tell me you buy into their twisted delusions. Bobbie, you have to know deep down that those two people—"

"That's what you don't understand, Hank. The queen and Luka are not *people*. They are *gods*."

"Bobby, it's not too late for—"

"Hank." Her voice was tight and clipped. "This call is dragging on, and I have more information to share. Do you want to hear it or not?"

I shut my mouth with an audible *click*. I recognized the utter futility of trying to talk sense to an insane person. I wondered what a delusion shared by four people would be called. *Folie à quatre?*

"You have to go deep into the abattoir. Find the end of it, down deep. There is a door there. You have to go through it to—"

"He's waiting for me in the cave?" I couldn't keep the astonishment from my voice.

She chuckled again. "No, silly. I just said you have to go through the door and—"

"Bobby, you aren't making—"

She sighed, sounding peeved. "I'm trying to *help* you, Hank. Well, I was. I'm not standing here in this damn cave and wasting any more time with you. Follow Luka, and your family will be safe. If you're smart, you will bring what you need to survive away from civilization. I don't care if you believe me or not. I'm going through now."

There was a noise on the line like she'd dropped the phone onto stone or concrete. "Let's go. Time for a swim, little Siggy," she said.

Faintly, I could hear Jane start to protest, and the sick lethargy that had been spreading through my veins like molasses was burned away in an instant. "Jane! I'm coming, Jane! I'm coming!" I yelled so hard it felt like my voice box was going to break into a thousand pieces, but the line was dead. "No!" I screamed, frustration beating in my temples.

Before I even knew what I was doing, I was outside my front door, limping as fast as I could toward the Timmens' house. Golden light had begun to break on the horizon, but everything looked gray to my eyes. The air was cold, and the ground was still wet from the rain. Stabbing pain ripped through my ankles with each step as if I were walking on sharp rocks. My knees had that sick feeling I associated with my worst flares, and it seemed as if my hip sockets were grinding the balls of my femurs into sharp glass fragments, but I didn't slow down. Not one whit. Not one tittle.

The house looked the same as it had the night before. The front door was still locked, but my fifteen years in law enforcement had taught me many, many lessons. One of those lessons was how to kick in a door without falling on my ass.

The first impact sent a shockwave of pain slamming up my leg, and I understood at once that kicking a door open was no longer an option for me. So I grabbed the door handle with my left hand, rocked my body weight back like I was trying to pull the door open, and then rocketed forward. I slammed my shoulder into the door as hard as I could as close to the door jamb as possible. Through the haze of agony in my arm and shoulder, I heard a dry cracking noise, like tinder being readied for a campfire. Still, the door didn't budge.

I set my jaw and repeated the process and failed again. The pain making me nauseated to the extent that, on top of everything else, I had to battle a case of dry heaves before I could try again. On the third hit, the door buckled inward, shards of wood flying from the door frame like shrapnel from a bomb. I staggered into the foyer, sliding a bit on the slick marble tile (which made no sense in the Northeast or anywhere else that's buried in snow and ice for half the year).

The pain in my legs, back, and left arm made me want to curl up in a ball and cry for mercy, but I had to know for certain that Jane and Siggy were not somewhere in the house. I had to know if Bobbie Timmens was as insane as she sounded—or maybe just as insane as I must have sounded when I talked about what had happened the night Hatton put me in the hospital. That thought made my stomach churn. I *knew* what Hatton was capable of. What if the other things Bobbie had ranted about were true?

Lurching like Frankenstein's monster, I dragged myself around the first floor. The place was a disaster: cabinet doors hung open, their contents on the ground; closets exposed and cleaned out; furniture up-ended like so many forgotten toys. The Two Bobbies had cleared out in a hurry.

I set my mouth in a grim but determined frown and pulled myself up the stairs. I had to rest every couple of steps, teeth gritted against the pain. The irony of how easily I'd climbed the steps in my own house yesterday ate away at the back of my mind; the pain was the price of my night of stress.

The upper story was even more of a disaster area than the ground floor. Loose clothing was strewn on the carpet, even in the hallway. In the master bedroom was a half-packed suitcase full of men's

jeans, T-shirts, and even a couple of ball caps—
Bobby's "at home" wardrobe. On top of a pile of
poorly folded T-shirts lay a pistol and several loose
magazines. It was a blackened semi-automatic—a
Heckler and Koch .40 caliber with a Picatinny rail
mounted to the frame beneath the barrel.

Without thinking, I scooped up the pistol and
shoved it in the back of my jeans. The magazines I
rammed into my front left pocket. I rifled through
the packed clothes, looking for anything interesting,
but all I found was the smell of dryer sheets.

The master bath looked as if a madman had
whirled through it, smashing everything that looked
fragile. Pieces of the broken mirror reflected the
morning sunlight in strange patterns on the ceiling
and walls. Perfume from broken crystal vials made
the place smell like a whorehouse.

There wasn't much of use on either of the two
above-ground floors, but that was as I expected. Most
sociopaths manage to keep up appearances for the
neighbors, after all. Still, I wondered how long the
Two Bobbies had been over the edge, right across the
street from me.

I wondered how many victims had been brought
to this house and butchered.

Our houses had been built in a similar fashion—
both had basements consisting of large, open spaces
with the house's physical plant tucked under the
stairs. That was where the similarities ended. My
basement smelled like any moist room that was kept
shut up and closed away: moldy and disused. The
Timmens' basement smelled more like a zoo. As I

rounded the corner at the bottom of the stairs, I saw why.

Looking around the basement of the Bobbies' house, all my questions about them were answered. The Two Bobbies had finished their basement—although not like any finished basement I'd ever seen. This basement was more like a medieval dungeon. Manacles hung from chains driven into the walls at shoulder height. Makeshift cells formed a small warren in the center of the floor. The most disturbing part, however, was the hundreds of pine-scented car air fresheners hanging from the floor joists. The sheer quantity of air fresheners could only mean one thing: the Timmens had kept decaying bodies here.

There was a sheetrock wall on the far end of the room with a door set in its center. I pulled Bobby's pistol out of my waistband and checked the magazine. It was loaded to capacity. I pulled the slide back a fraction and saw a round gleaming in the chamber. I felt the old confidence returning. Point shooting is like riding a bike—you never forget how to do it.

I flung the door open and took a step to the left of the opening, pointing the pistol at the darkened doorway. I was set for an ambush—ready for some screaming maniac to lurch out of the darkness at me, swinging a rusty knife like something in a horror movie. But the only thing that rushed out of the room was the foul stench of decomposition.

I heard a strange hissing noise from over my left shoulder, and I pivoted to that side, snapping the gun around and almost firing a shot. I didn't see the source of the noise until it hissed again: a small cream-colored box mounted in the left corner of the main space, up near the rafters. It was an industrial air freshener, one of those automatic jobs like you'd see at a hospital or nursing home. Instead of masking the stench from that little room, though, it just mixed with it to make a noxiously sweet nauseating smell— rotten meat dipped in French perfume.

I felt around inside the door and flicked on the lights. Old brown bloodstains were everywhere. Bones were stacked against the walls, and a barrel of decomposing flesh and discarded organs sat in the far corner. In the center of the small floor space lay the bodies of the Bobbies' Welsh Corgis amidst puddles of day old blood.

It was an abattoir like the one Hatton kept—not as elaborate, and not as well concealed, but a slaughterhouse nonetheless. I felt sure they had been slaughtering people and animals here for years. I wondered if they were a part of Hatton's circle at the time of the investigation or if they were somehow converted to the cult of human meat in the time since.

I looked at the two Corgi corpses. The two little dogs that had earned Bobbie the nickname "Crazy Dog Lady" were dead, but at least they didn't look like they'd been used as meat for dinner. She'd always treated those dogs like her children, and the fact that they would kill them for Hatton and Tutor spoke to the depth of their loyalty. Or lunacy.

I backed out of the room and slowly closed the door with relief sweeping through me. Jane and Sig weren't in there, and they were the only people I cared about at that moment.

I went back to examine the makeshift cells. They were about three feet deep and six or seven feet long. Each cell had its own small four-feet by four-feet gate. The ceiling of each cell was made from rusting sheet metal. Old blankets and burlap sacks lay on the floors.

I stopped in front of one of the cells, my heart breaking. Inside, a set of vampire teeth lay on a piece of thick cream-colored vellum paper spotted with red drops. I flung the gate open so hard its hinges bent. I got down on my hands and knees and crawled into that little space, wincing every time I put my weight down.

I shoved Sig's teeth into my pocket. I put the pistol on the ground beside me and scrabbled at the piece of vellum until I could peel it off the floor.

The red spots were too bright to be dried blood— they were the color of maraschino cherries. I sniffed them, and a grim smile surfaced on my face. Those spots were drops of the cherry syrup that made Sig's vampire teeth look bloody. I could imagine Siggy getting tired of keeping the teeth in his mouth but not wanting to put them on the skeezy floor. Finding something to set them on was just something he would do. I let the paper drop.

As I turned to crawl back out of the cell, something about the paper caught my eye. It had fallen with the spotted side down. On the back was a message. It was written in a script that resembled Peter Jackson's vision of Tolkien's elvish, but I could make out the letters of the English alphabet. It said, "Chase me, Hank. I can show you so much."

I thought of the character Roland Deschain in Stephen King's *Dark Tower* series. Specifically, I thought of the opening line of the series: "The man in black fled across the desert, and the gunslinger followed." Then I thought about how the series ended and a cold sort of dread settled over me like mist.

I looked down at my hand, now a ball of shrieking pain. I had squeezed it into a shaking fist so tight my knuckles were white. Hatton's note was crushed inside that fist, crumpled into a ball. I wondered what was in store for me. I wondered if I was destined to follow my own man in black for the rest of eternity, never being able to savor the victory, winning every time, but losing everything in the process.

I opened my hand, letting the crumpled ball of vellum fall to the dirty floor. I no longer cared about questions of eternity. There wasn't anything to consider. I'd made my decision when I asked Jane to marry me.

I hoped Hatton was a man of his word because I intended to follow him forever if that's what it took to find Jane and Siggy. And if he wasn't, it was my sincere intention to give him a true test of his supposed godhood.

I left the Timmens' house for the last time. I left the front door swinging in the harsh November wind and strode across the circle—no longer allowing myself the luxury of limping. As I walked, I looked around, seeing all the Halloween decorations in the golden light of dawn. They all seemed defeated and dead and gray. They were insignificant, wretched things really, devoid of substance, devoid of meaning—like so much of the produce of a culture in which everything of unique significance was bleached into sempiternal inconsequence in the name of profit margins. Everything seemed different—achromatic, tattered and bedraggled, as if the part of me that saw beauty in sunrises and nature had been dimmed by what I'd found in the Timmens' basement. Maybe it was because I'd decided to follow Jane and Sig to wherever they were, even if that place was the land of the dead.

There was nothing I wouldn't do for Jane or Sig. *Nothing.* Without them, nothing really mattered.

Standing in my kitchen, I scribbled a hasty note addressed to my old boss in the state police, Lieutenant Gruber. It read:

> Lt. Gruber,
>
> Don't worry about me. I'm sane and healthy. I didn't do anything to Jane or Sig. I'm going to save them.
>
> I'm going after Chris Hatton and Elizabeth Tutor. They convinced my neighbors, Robert and Roberta Timmens, to kidnap Jane and Sig. I know this because Bobbie Timmens called me early this morning—you should be able to pull the number from my LUDs. Locate her cell if you can. She told me

she was in that cave—the dump site for Hatton's victims.

I know this sounds crazy, and I know I shouldn't be going there alone, but if what she says is true, I really have no choice. I do believe her, just like I believe what I said about Hatton after the safe house fiasco. I know you don't believe my version of that night, but it is what it is. Not everything in this world can be explained or codified.

I hope you never read this—I hope I destroy this note later this morning when I come back home with my family. I don't have much conviction in that hope, however. I think the two most likely possibilities are that either I disappear like Jane and Siggy have, or you will find our bodies deep in the cave at the dump site.

I don't know if you read Stephen King or not, so I don't know if you will understand this. In one series of his books, there is this thing, this Dark Tower, that stands in the center of the multiverse and acts as the lynchpin for reality. I doubt that it really exists (but who's to say? It's no more fanciful than any of

*the world's religions to me), but
I do know that Jane and Sig are
the lynchpins of my universe. I'm
going to get them back or die
trying. You have kids, so I know
you understand that part.*

*I don't think I can justify what
I'm going to do if they are dead.
I know it sounds insane to go
chasing after four psychotic fucks
by myself, but it isn't. Not really,
given what I know Hatton can
do and given the atrocities we
all know Hatton is capable of. I
can't prove to you that I am
sane, but I promise you that I
am. I saw what I saw that night.
I hope you can believe me this
time.*

Yours, Hank

*P.S. Bobbie Timmens said
Hatton's real name is Luka.
That's all she said—no last
name. Maybe it will help. I don't
think it's a common name in the
States.*

I packed in a rush, stuffing an old hiking backpack with a few changes of clothes and some basic foodstuffs. I filled two canteens with water. Then I tucked Bobby's Heckler and Koch pistol and its magazines into the outside pocket and added my backup weapon—a Kimber Tactical Ultra II in .45 ACP—and one hundred and fifty rounds of ammunition. I planned on stopping on the way to Honeoye Lake to buy more ammunition and a cleaning kit for the HK.

I stood in front of the kitchen cabinet we'd converted into my medicine cabinet, staring at the cornucopia of drugs I consumed to treat my RA on a daily basis. I took antihistamines, blood-pressure medicine, anti-inflammatory drugs, chemotherapy drugs, biologically derived drugs, pain meds, and several minerals and vitamins. It was a ludicrous number of pills. Some were supposed to work together to suppress my immune system, and some were just supposed to stop the others from killing me.

I didn't want to carry them all so I separated them into groups of what I had to take with me, what I should take with me, and what I thought I could leave behind. Only a few medications did much to alleviate my symptoms—a chemotherapy drug called methotrexate, pain medicine (which I hated to take), and prednisone. Of these, the methotrexate was most critical. It was like a magic potion. The problem with it was that it either inflamed my liver or irritated my kidneys, and it required regular blood tests to determine if the dosage needed to be manipulated to keep it from killing me.

Methotrexate was a "black box" drug— strictest label warning the FDA used, the one reserved for drugs that could kill you, break something irreplaceable (like a kidney or two), cause birth defects, or burn the lungs right out of your body. I took it as a subcutaneous injection once a week. I'd have to take syringes and alcohol swabs in addition to the vials. I only had five syringes left. Then again, that was enough to last more than a month.

What would happen when I ran out of methotrexate was a problem for later. There was no way I could get more for another month because insurance companies ruled the world. Hopefully, I could get Jane and Sig back before that.

I tried to think of everything I would need to survive in the wilderness. Like most modern men, I really had no idea of what was important and what was a mere luxury, but I did the best I could. I was armed, of course, and took my cell phone, a flashlight, some batteries, a few cans of Sterno, clothes for all seasons, gloves, extra socks, and anything else that looked remotely useful.

When I finally arrived at the cave several hours later, that backpack felt like it weighed eighty pounds. Pushing it in front of me, I crawled into the tiny foyer-like space where the most recent victims of the Butchers had been found. It had lost the smell of forensic testing and had gone back to smelling like an animal den, but the trestles to support the earth making up the roof were still there.

With my flashlight, I followed the marks that my partner, Jax, had spray-painted on the walls when we explored the labyrinth-like cave. We'd left marks at intersections and branches, going as deep into the earth as he and I had ever been. When I reached the last mark, at a four-way intersection of tunnels, I was at a loss of how to move forward. I peered down the dark tunnel leading to my left but couldn't see anything. The tunnel across from me was also as dark as a tomb, but I thought I could see a faint glimmer down the tunnel leading to my right.

It was then that it dawned on me: I hadn't brought any paint to mark my passage into the maze of natural caves and carved tunnels that Hatton and Tutor had adopted for their abattoir. At the same time, the idea that this was some elaborate hoax to get me lost deep in this cave flashed through my mind.

I shrugged. I'd either find the end of that cave or I'd be lost until someone found me—or, I supposed, until Hatton, Tutor, or one of the Timmens murdered me. I walked toward the light glimmering far down the tunnel. When I finally reached it, I saw that it was a glow stick, like you give kids on Halloween—one that had almost consumed its chemical charge. It was lying in the middle of a three-way intersection. I peered around until I saw another glimmer and then walked toward it.

I went on that way, stumbling through the inky darkness of that underground warren, straining my eyes to see half-dead glow sticks, for I don't know how long. My thighs were burning when I finally came to the end. My stomach was in my throat, and my gun was locked and loaded in my hand as I approached the little room at the end of the tunnel.

The chamber was roughly circular and thirty yards or so in diameter. Across from the entrance was a bubbling body of water—a natural spring—and on its stony banks lay an abandoned cell phone. Other than that, there wasn't a single thing in the chamber.

No doorway. No bodies. No psychotic neighbors, no raving lunatic vampire-wolfman thing.

I let the pack slide to the ground with a jingle and a thump. I felt deflated. Lost. I was where Bobbie Timmens had wanted to lead me. Why else would her cell be lying here next to the spring?

I walked over to look more closely at the cell phone. I hoped she'd left a message on it, but if she had, the phone's dead battery robbed me of any insight. Despair oozed from my glands and pores like a vile sweat.

My legs were shaking and burning with fatigue. I doubted I could walk all the way back to the entrance of the cave. I leaned against the chamber wall and left myself sink to the ground with a rattle and a bump. I closed my eyes and turned off the flashlight.

When I opened my eyes, I saw it. The walls of the chamber were lit with a strange, dim fluidic pattern—too dim to see with the flashlight turned on. The spring glowed with a silvery, multicolored light.

I crawled to the edge of the pool and looked down. About three feet below the surface was a submerged tunnel. I glanced at the pack and then pulled it over. I set my phone, the flashlight, and my pistol on top of the backpack and, leaving it on dry land, rolled into the water to investigate.

The water was frigid. I gasped in the silence of the cave, the sound echoing away into the darkness. Then I took a deep breath and dove underwater. The submerged passage was ovoid with loose sand covering the floor. It opened into another chamber a short distance ahead; the light was coming from that chamber. The tunnel was wide enough for me, but I'd have to push the pack ahead of me.

I resurfaced and stuffed everything inside the pack, putting the pistols, ammunition, my electronic doodads, and my drugs in the waterproof pocket in the front. I pulled the pack into the water with me. I was starting to shiver. I had to make this swim in a hurry or hypothermia would pay a call.

I went under and pushed the pack ahead of me into the submerged tunnel. Halfway through, I realized it was longer than it looked. Maybe it was some trick of the water, or maybe it just seemed longer because of the temperature and the unwieldy weight of the pack. At the same time, it felt like something was pulling me forward—like some weird kind of magnetism that worked on crippled flesh instead of iron.

By the time I reached the lit chamber, my lungs burned like I'd breathed in fire. I shot up to the surface and gasped, slinging the pack onto the floor of the small, irregularly shaped room. I rolled over the edge of the pool, eyes closed and tried to breathe in slow, steady pulls.

The tugging sensation I had felt in the tunnel was much stronger in that second room. I opened my eyes and looked around. The light was coming from one of the strangest things I'd ever seen—and that's counting Hatton's metamorphosis at the safehouse. It looked like an oval standing mirror except there was no frame or legs. It just hung there in midair, shimmering with soft, silvery light. Taking a longer, closer look, what I had taken to be a mirror-like silver was, in fact, thousands of rainbow colors, swirling and intertwining about each other, reflecting various frequencies of light. It was mesmerizing; it made me want to get closer and take a better look.

The rainbow-filled oval was about seven feet tall and three and a half feet wide at its widest point. It was big enough to walk through without stooping or slouching. It looked like a movie special effect for a science-fiction epic. The more I looked at it, the more it drew me forward.

I fought my way to my feet, feeling the fatigue in every fiber of my being. I had to get closer to the oval, whatever it was. I took two steps forward before I remembered my pack. I took two steps back to retrieve it, and those two steps felt like I was walking against an outgoing tide. I bent with a groan and grabbed the pack, slinging it on my back through sheer force of will. I stepped closer to the shimmer and could see my own reflection in its rainbow-colored surface. Standing that close, the pull coming off those gleaming colors was beyond my capacity to resist.

"Jane, I'm coming," I croaked. I didn't want to think anymore; I didn't want to resist. I did what it wanted me to do—no, what it *demanded* of me.

I stepped into the shimmer, feeling terrific heat and terrible cold wash over me as I touched its surface. The faint sensation of being pulled swelled into something that felt more powerful than gravity, and I lurched forward. I was submerged like I had been in the frigid water—and then I was out and into thin air, far above the ground and falling.

FIVE

For a split second, I was in midair, arms pinwheeling as if that could somehow stop me from falling. I sprawled on my face on a wide sheet of ice. With a terrible cracking sound, the ice shifted beneath me. The wind was howling and hurling snow around me in enraged eddies and sulky swirls. The temperature was arctic and biting, stiffening my water-soaked clothes.

The ice continued its relentless popping and cracking as my weight settled onto it. White lines shot away from me like lightning bolts trapped in the ice. The water beneath the gelid surface was black, making the lake look like it was covered in black marble shot through with white veins. I lifted my head, and the ice made a sound like a gunshot.

Ahead of me, a barren rock island jutted toward the sky like the dorsal fin of a gargantuan, hunting shark. Sharp, ragged chunks of ice surrounded the little island like fangs, cutting me off with nature's savage efficiency from the only land I could see. Not that I had any interest in being trapped on a barren island in the middle of an icy lake during a monstrous blizzard.

My pack was on my back, and if I were going to survive this without drowning in the freezing water below me, then I would have to roll toward shore because if I stood, I would plunge through the cracking ice. I tried to wiggle out of the shoulder straps of the pack and the ice crackled and snapped with every little move I made. My hands hurt like someone had dislocated all the joints of my fingers and then lit them on fire. Another gift from my personal monster.

I snaked my right arm through the shoulder strap of the pack—grunting at the pain that moving that way caused. I didn't want to lose it—never mind that the pack had dry, warm clothes and food, both of which were necessary for my immediate survival, it held all my medicine and all my weapons. I tried to sinuate my left arm through the strap, but my wrist locked as I tried to force my hand through. Intense burning pain shot up my arm, and I started trying to yank my hand out of the strap without conscious thought. The symphony of *pops* from the ice below me sent rimy fear shivering through my mind.

I made myself stop moving and lay very still, waiting for the ice to decide if I was going for a swim or not. I endured the searing paroxysm of agony that had sunk its fangs into my wrist. Thick new cracks shot away from me like bullets and a foot or so away from me, creating a chilling sight—a jagged "step" in the ice about an inch high. That meant the ice I was on was tilting and separating from the rest of the sheet, and if I allowed that to happen while I lay there, I was sunk.

I pulled my arm out of the strap, groaning with relief, and without giving myself time to think about it, I rolled to the left, making a sound on the ice like a flat tire thumping on pavement every time the pack came around and slapped into the ice. The sheet of ice was banging and snapping in accompaniment, but I didn't dare stop. Over it all, the wind shrieked and screeched, blowing snow and tiny shards of ice across the lake.

Powered by my fear, I rolled all the way to the shore and into the snow drifted up there. I was dizzy from all that spinning, and my hips and shoulders felt like so much broken glass, but I had solid ground beneath me.

With a twisted lip, I thought back to how much better I'd seemed back home after the new meds. I *was* better than I had been, but if nothing else, my little romp on the ice underscored how far away from "normal" I still was.

The blizzard was building in strength and fury, and the temperature was dropping at an alarming rate. The only plus side to how cold it was getting was that it would soon be too cold to snow. If only the wind would stop at the same time.

I started to shiver, teeth chattering like a typewriter. I needed a fire, dry clothes, and a coat, and I needed to get out of the blizzard before I froze to death. I had my coat (what man in New England would leave the house in early November without one?), but it was stuffed into the pack, and I didn't want to put it on over wet clothes anyway.

I forced myself to my feet and looked around. The storm was blowing enough snow around me that getting a glimpse of anything more than ten or twenty feet in any direction was impossible, and what I could see was disheartening. There was no shelter from the wind in my immediate vicinity—no rocks, no trees, no buildings. The cold was like a wet blanket around my head, smothering the air around me, forcing me to breathe harder and deeper than normal just to get the same amount of oxygen.

The outcropping of rock, that I was already calling Shark Fin Island in my head, and the silvery shimmering oval hanging in the air were both hidden by the whiteout. I stood there, searching the air above the patch of cracked ice, enraptured by swirling snow and the absence of silvery-rainbow light.

With a start, I shook myself and made myself turn away. Standing there in a raging blizzard and staring into the white out in hopes of seeing a magical door was not going to accomplish anything.

Walking around in an unknown place in the middle of a blizzard was dangerous, but if I stayed there on the shore of that frozen lake, I'd end up creating an ice sculpture from my frozen corpse. I had to get to shelter, or build one, and even a copse of woods would help. I couldn't afford to go stumbling around in circles, however. Without a visual landmark, I wasn't sure how I could keep from doing just that.

I dug my cellphone and its built-in compass out of the waterproof pocket of the backpack. I started walking away from the lake, due north according to the phone. I couldn't remember (or never had known) if the phone relied on global positioning satellites to determine cardinal directions, but for now, it didn't really matter. I needed something that pointed in the same direction every time.

Within minutes, forcing my way through the snow and the harsh, frozen wind became impossible. My body sang with pain and cold. I had gone as far as I was going to be able to and there was nothing to help shelter me. I couldn't afford to push myself to exhaustion; I needed the energy to build a shelter, and I needed what little body warmth I still had to warm the shelter up. I had to get a quinzhee built before I turned into a flesh-colored popsicle.

I let the pack drop from my shoulders and started kicking snow into a pile, wincing with each impact of my foot. Darts of pain shrieked up my spine. I kept kicking and pushing snow to the pile, ignoring the agony of it, and using my body weight to pack the mound of snow as tight as I could get it. Each time I stepped up to stomp fresh snow into the mound I was building, I wanted to scream with pain or throw up, or maybe both at the same time. My hips were like hot coals buried in my groin, and my knees…my god, my knees felt like lumps of cancerous, eviscerated flesh grinding and grinding and grinding against a sharpened rasp.

I kept drifting away and suddenly waking up to find myself standing next to the mound, and just staring at it, or just standing next to a pile of fresh snow, staring at the wall of blown snow swirling around me. Each time I did, I wondered how long I'd been standing there freezing to death and fear would snap through me like a whip.

Somehow, I kept working at it until I had a mound four feet high and about eight feet in diameter. I didn't have the time to allow it to sinter, and that was a risk because it might collapse around me once I got inside, but compared to me staying out in the ever-decreasing temperatures and wind, it was an acceptable risk. I dropped to my knees on the lee side of the mound, thankful for any break from the biting wind. I began scooping snow out of a short tunnel. The tips of my fingers turned a bright shade of cherry red—a color I'd come to associate with flares of the old R.A.-monster, except the red would have been in my knuckles. I was even colder than before. I dug out a small room, just big enough for me to crouch in and long enough for me to lay flat. By the time I'd finished the basic excavation, my hands were raw, and my knuckles felt like someone had been at them with sand paper and a chisel. The tips of my fingers felt like hard pellets of ice.

I was very cold, perhaps colder than I'd ever felt in my life, Norwegian genes or no. My heart was beating at a syncopated, furious rate. I was shivering with a violence that scared me, but even so, I had to build one more thing. I needed something to block the snow and wind from blowing through the open doorway and piling up inside the quinzhee.

I pushed more snow together in front of the door and made another small mound of packed snow. I dug out an L-shaped tunnel and ended up inside the quinzhee. My hands felt like they were frozen into claws, but my fingertips felt strangely warm.

With shaking hands, I managed to get a small can of Sterno out of the pack. I lit the jelly and held my hands over the flame—resisting the urge to put my fingers in the bluish flames. Even after years of coping with intense pain, it amazed me how extreme physical feelings made insane notions not only sound rational but desirable. As my fingertips began to warm up, they began to throb and sting.

I started fighting my frozen clothes off my body. Buttons that had been a problem for me since the R.A. bit into my fingers like they had teeth. It was even worse when it was cold, but fear and desperation were strong motivators. I pulled a spare set of clothes out of my pack and slipped into them. They were cold, but at least they were dry. At least they weren't sheathed in ice and melting snow.

I dug around in my pack until I found the inner shell for my coat that I so rarely used and then zipped it into the outer shell. I put the coat on and curled around the little can of Sterno trying to capture all the warmth it could give off. I stopped shivering with an agonizing slowness as the small space got warmer and warmer. When I slid the lid on top of the little can, smothering the flame, I was almost sweating, and the fuel was almost depleted. I let my eyes close and soaked up the warmth.

Outside, the wind continued to howl and scream.

When I woke, the wind had fallen silent, and my mouth felt like a family of gophers had lived in it while I slept. I hadn't meant to sleep, but the physical exhaustion and heat trapped in the little room built of packed snow had had their way with me. I'd been sleeping curled into a ball, arms crossed over my chest with my right fist on the floor, and the left tucked under my right arm. I tried to open my right hand, but my fingers were too stiff to move. Morning stiffness was a thing I was accustomed to—another gift of the disease I lived with—but I'd never experienced it to the point I couldn't move my fingers at all.

I lay there, staring at my hands, trying to open my hand and fighting panic—both by sheer force of will. If I'd been thinking straight the previous night, I would have been wearing my gloves, instead of flopping around in the frigid wind and digging in the snow with bare fingers. I started blowing into my closed fists, alternating breaths between the right and the left. After ten minutes or so of that, I could loosen my fists and straighten my thumbs. It wasn't much, but it was a start, and the flood of terror in my system began to recede.

I pushed the lid off the can of Sterno and managed to work the lighter with both of my thumbs. I held my claws close to that blue flame and tried to take a physical inventory. I felt like hammered shit that had been run over by a freight train. My hips were twin points of burning agony every time I moved my legs. Moving my feet caused pain to shoot through my ankles and up my shins to my knees. My knees…well, they were on a different continent of pain, maybe a different planet. After a few more minutes of "Sterno-therapy," I could force my fingers into an almost straight position.

It has been said that there should be more than one word to express the concept of love. The same was true for pain. It was silly to think one single four letter word could adequately express the myriad kinds of pain I had felt since I'd been sick.

I'd been lucky—lucky enough not to fall through the ice into the lake, lucky not to have been overcome by confusion and disorientation, lucky the quinzhee hadn't collapsed on my head.

I pulled on my boots, fighting waves of nauseating pain in my knuckles to tie the laces. I pulled on my gloves, wincing as my swollen finger joints rubbed against the lining. I had always loved winter, but there's nothing like having a personal monster to cure you of everything you love.

With one last breath of warmth, I kicked my way through the snow blocking the entrance of the tunnel and then turned back to get my pack. I crawled outside on my hands and knees, gritting my teeth against the fresh assault of pain and tottered my way to an upright position.

The snow around the quinzhee was waist deep. If the smooth white plane that stretched in every direction was all as deep as it was near the quinzhee, walking was going to be even more painful than I'd planned on. The forest was no more than a quarter of a mile away, but with the snow as deep as it was, it would feel like miles instead of a quarter of a mile.

Shark Fin Island was visible behind me—the snow cover on the lake making the illusion of a circling shark even more realistic. The temperature was brutal and disheartening. Not as cold as it had been the night before, but cold enough to kill me if I wasn't careful.

The quinzhee sat there taunting me with its warmness, and I longed for it in a way that seemed perverted and disgusting. It could be kept warm for a long time, and the idea of crawling back inside and waiting another day was very tempting. I looked back and forth between the cold woods and the warm quinzhee several times, but wherever they were, Jane and Sig *weren't* inside the quinzhee, so I turned toward the woods and started slogging through the snow. I needed food, shelter, and a way to find my family.

It took me most of the morning to cross the three hundred or so yards to the forest. The trees still had green leaves on them, but they were shriveling and turning brown and black from the cold. Snow was caked on the tops of the black branches and plastered on their west-facing side. It was beautiful in a strange sort of way. I found myself staring at the shriveling green leaves more than once, wondering what kind of storm could flash freeze an entire forest with no warning.

I walked—or at least I shuffled and limped— all through the afternoon, refusing to let myself stop and stare at the strange beauty. At least the trees had blocked some of the snowfall, and it was easier going inside the forest. I kept to a northerly path, using the phone for a compass, because it was as good a direction as any, and because it was easier travelling.

As the afternoon stretched on, light started reflecting from the trunks of the trees and shadows stretched out to my right. I came across what would have been a pleasant babbling brook except for the fact that it was frozen solid. Ripples still showed on the surface of the ice. I'd never heard of any freeze happening so fast that ripples were frozen into the ice and again found myself wondering about the previous night's storm with the kind of awe reserved for things like hurricanes and earthquakes.

The brook ran northwest, and I turned to follow its bank. If I followed it far enough, the brook would lead to a river, and a river would lead me back to civilization. The bank was treacherous—slick with snow and ice and steep, and I had to pick my way along it carefully.

After trudging along for what seemed like an entire geological age, the brook led me to a small wooden bridge. A snow-covered path stretched away from either side of it.

The bridge had been handcrafted and was well-maintained. The carved hand rails depicted elaborate scenes, and I brushed the loose snow off for a better look at them. It was like something out of Scandinavian history—trolls, Viking warriors, dragons, and ships. Lots of ships.

The sun dipped toward the horizon in the east as I was admiring the carvings, and I was surprised to see a flickering light coming from up the trail. Maybe the brook had led me back to civilization without the help of his big brother river.

I lumbered across the snow-covered footbridge and followed the buried path on the other side. It curved toward north, and as I followed the curve, more lights flickered ahead.

A gas lamp perched on top of a metal pole like a weird bird. Scrolled metal supported four glass panes that protected the gas flame from the wind. Civilization, of sorts, at least.

Ahead, the buried path became a tended, cleared path stretching away into the woods. Chest-high drifts on each side of it, and more gas lamps lit the way.

I floundered forward on legs that felt light but uncoordinated and ungainly. I longed to sit and rest, but if I did, my chances of getting up again were slim and none. The cleared path dipped into a valley up ahead, and that coupled with the growing darkness meant another drop in temperature. Barely distinguishable in the gloom, smoke swam from the snow-covered roof of a log cabin nestled inside the valley's protection.

The cold was drilling into my hands and cheeks. Despite the protection of the trees, the wind had picked up and was hurling frozen bits of ice into my face. I trudged down into the valley, close to exhaustion. I had done more in the past two days than I had in the past seven years, and my body screamed for rest. I sighed with relief as I came abreast of the cabin, its roof peeking above the tall snow berm on my right.

"Help me!" The cry was just audible over the wind. It came from ahead of me.

Dark was coming on at a rapid pace. The temperature was about to plummet if last night was any predictor of the weather in this snow-bound place. The smoking chimney of the little cabin promised warmth, rest, and probably food. I longed to be warm, and more to the point, my aching joints demanded warmth, and soon.

"Help me! Please!"

I couldn't turn my back on a call for help. There was something hardwired into my soul that demanded better of me. "Here!" I called. "I'm here by the cabin. Where are you?"

"Oh, thank you, sir!" The voice was male and was watery with weakness.

"Keep talking. I'll follow your voice."

"I'm trapped by this gods-forsaken tree fall. Up the path around the bend."

With a last look at the cabin, I trudged on past it. The path curved to my left and around the bend was a mess of evergreen limbs, roots, and tree trunks up against the right-side bank.

"Is this you?" I asked.

"Yes! Here!"

Some of the branches began to rattle, and I set to work trying to clear the loose stuff out of the way. "You've made quite a mess here, mister. How'd you manage to bring a tree down on this side of the berm?"

"It flipped over."

There was something about the situation that was tickling my Cop Radar. No alarm bells, yet, but a definite tickle. "What are you doing out here, old timer?"

"Old, is it?" The man chuckled. "I'm going home. I finished clearing the path as far as I could, and now it's time for supper."

As I cleared the evergreen branches, an old man was revealed. He had flowing white hair and a long, but well-kept, white beard. He was wrapped in clothing made from cured animal skin. "There you are," I said.

"Yes, here I am. And there you are."

I grinned at him. "Now that we've established we are both where we are; maybe you can tell me what I need to shift to get you free."

The man grunted and slapped a thick trunk that lay at an oblique angle to his torso. "This bastard here," he muttered.

The trunk was thick. "You don't sound like you are in pain."

"No," he said. "The damn thing is just pinning my legs. The snow, is soft and comfortable, albeit a little chilly."

My Cop Radar twanged again. I scanned the woods around us, but nothing was moving. The forest had fallen silent.

I shook my head at the trunk. "Not sure I can move this, old timer. I'm not as strong as I once was."

"It doesn't need to move much," he said. "I can slide out if you can move it even a few inches."

"I'll try," I said. I bent over and wrapped my arms around the tree trunk. "Count of three," I grunted. I set my feet on the frozen path.

"Yes," said the man.

"One...two...three!" I grunted with effort and pulled as hard as I could. The weight of the tree trunk was immense, and a yell tore itself from my chest. Just when I thought I would have to give up, the tree shifted a little...and then a little more.

"Okay!" said the man as he rolled to the side.

I let the tree sag back to the ground with a loud thump. The muscles across my back were on fire, and the pain from my legs made me want to vomit.

"Thanks, friend," said the old man.

I nodded but stood there with my hands on my knees and a grimace on my face.

"Nasty curse, that," he said.

"Rheumatoid arthritis. It sucks."

The man shook his head and got to his feet. There was something in the easy way that he moved that set off alarm bells. He was short and skinny—maybe frail is a better word—but something about him felt like a threat. He dusted himself off, and I forced myself to stand up straight.

The pistols were tucked up nice and dry in the waterproof pocket of my pack. I hadn't wanted to risk them in the snow, but as the hinky feeling about the little old man grew, I wished I had one in my hand.

He cocked his head at me. "I'm no threat to you, Hank Jensen," he said in quiet tones.

"How do you know my name?"

He shrugged. "It's a talent of mine. Nothing to be worried about, however."

"You know my name, how about telling me yours?"

He treated me to a vulpine grin. "My parents called me Tyarfer-Burisonur."

It wasn't the whole truth, and for some reason, the evasion felt like a test. "And what do *you* call yourself?"

His grin cracked into a smile. "Smart."

"Smart or smart-assed?"

He laughed. It was a booming, friendly sound, and some of the tension eased across my shoulders.

"Might as well ask if a brook can stop to take a rest." He looked me up and down and held out his hand as if to shake. "Meuhlnir," he said.

I took his hand and was amazed at the strength of his grip. "Hank, but you seem to know that already. Just Meuhlnir? No last name?"

He winked and gestured toward the path behind me. "My cabin's just there. Let's continue this by the fire."

I looked up the path. "How far to the next village?"

"Far enough to kill you in this weather. Come," he said, putting his hand on my arm. "You need my help, now, as I needed yours minutes ago. Let me repay the favor."

Again, I looked up the path. Each hour I spent resting was another hour's distance between my family and me. "Have you seen any other travelers?"

He applied firm pressure to my arm, turning me toward his cabin. "No. You are the only walk-in to come through."

My shoulders slumped. I had been afraid of a trap back there in the cave, and maybe it had been after all.

"What's troubling you, Hank?"

For some reason, it felt like Meuhlnir already knew the answer to the question, and it irked me. "Don't you know?"

Meuhlnir nodded with a calm expression on his face. "Yes, but it's considered polite to use conversation."

I looked down at his smiling face. Something felt wrong about it, but I couldn't place what. "Who are you, Meuhlnir?"

He shrugged and swept a hand at the woods around us. "I am the keeper of this place. I am Meuhlnir."

"Are you supposed to be some kind of magician? A mind-reader or something? And where, exactly, is this place."

"This used to be called the Snyowrlant Province before the empire fell."

"What's it called now?"

He shrugged and showed me a wry smile. "Cold. Snyowrlant is a word from the *Gamla Toonkumowl* that translates to 'snow country.'"

"The game of what?"

His smile stayed on his face, but there had been a momentary twitch of impatience. "It's the language of my ancestors, the old tongue. *Gamla Toonkumowl*."

"Yeah? Winter sucks here in Snow Country."

Meuhlnir chuckled. "It does, indeed, but this is spring." He tugged on my arm, and reluctantly, I let him pull me back toward the cabin. "Too cold to stand around out here," he muttered.

"You have blizzards like the one that rolled through here last night in the spring?"

He laughed and shook his head. "That storm had nothing to do with the season. It was a *sterk task*."

"Starkblast? Like in the *Dark Tower* series by Stephen King?"

"I don't know of King Stephen or his dark tower, but I didn't say 'starkblast,' I said *sterk task*. It means 'strong slap' in the *Gamla Toonkumowl*. It's a special kind of storm."

"For being the language of your ancestors, it seems the *Gamla Toonkumowl* gets a lot of use."

He chuckled. "You don't know the half of it, Hank." He led me to a cut through the berm that I hadn't spotted on the way to him and motioned me through it.

"Okay, I give. What is a *sterk task*?"

Meuhlnir shrugged. "Well, you lived through one last night. It's a kind of super-blizzard. Cold enough to flash freeze moving water, fierce winds, yards of snow."

"Strange weather here in Snyowrlant, Meuhlnir."

"They aren't limited to Snyowrlant. *Sterk task*s appear all over the world. No one knows why, though there are more theories than stars in the sky." He shrugged and made a motion like he was tossing something to the side. "End of the day, it doesn't matter why. They happen. They are reality. Any fool can see that." He pointed ahead of us. "Welcome to my home."

Snow was plastered against the walls on the windward side of the cabin, covering it in white from the top of the drifted snow to its snow-covered roof. Long daggers of ice pointed at the ground from the eaves. Warm light shined through the leaded glass windows. Torches burned next to a pair of massive doors made from thick planks and studded with iron. Like the bridge, the doors showed scenes that would have made a Viking craftsman sick with jealousy.

Meuhlnir threw one of the doors open and invited me inside with a gesture. "Be welcome, Hank. Be at ease. Within these walls, you are under my protection, and in this land, that is saying a lot."

The cabin looked smaller from outside. I thought it must have been some trick of the poor light and large drifts of snow surrounding the place. The thick wooden front doors were set into walls built from dry-stacked stone, tan and brown in color. The ground floor walls were built from large logs that had been stripped of their bark, but the second-floor walls were plastered up to the steeply-pitched plank roof. The floor of the cabin was made of six-inch-wide wooden planks, that matched the ceiling in color and texture. I would have sworn it was a one-story affair when I was crawling over the berm, but across the room from the vestibule, were twin stair cases leading up to a semicircular balcony with several doors set in the far wall. The great room had a massive stone fireplace on one end, and a hallway leading to other parts of the cabin on the other.

"Why have you come to this *klith*, Hank?"

"This what?"

"*Klith*. This side. This place. Snyowrlant." He was busy unwrapping himself and getting the snow off his leggings so I couldn't see his face.

"I didn't have much choice," I said, stomping my feet in the tiny nook that held his front door to clear snow off my boots. "I was..." I was at a loss for how to tell him what had happened.

He favored me with a knowing smile. "You came through the *proo* and then..."

"*Proo*? That's the shimmery thing that dumped me out on the lake?"

Meuhlnir nodded. "Yes. It's the way between the other *klith* and here. Pretty, yes? Like a rainbow."

"Is there only the one then?"

"Oh no. There are potentially infinite numbers of them, I suppose. *Proo* means bridge in the *Gamla Toonkumowl*. The *proo* you travelled across was *Kyatlerproo*. In general, though, these things are called *Pilrust preer*. *Preer* is the plural of *proo*." He bent and began pulling at the laces of my boots. "Let's get you out of these and over to the fire."

"Are there other *preer* to... to my *klith*?"

Meuhlnir shrugged. "Yes, anything is possible, as it is possible to move *preer* and anchor them where you like. Like ten feet in the air over a frozen lake." He chuckled into his beard.

"So, it's not the normal place for Katterproo to end?"

"*Kyatlerproo*," said the old man. "No, I haven't seen that particular *proo* in a very long time. It popped into place two days ago. Maybe it spawned the *sterk task*."

"Why would it cause a storm like that?"

"Kick those off and come sit by the fire." Meuhlnir straightened, and I was again struck by how easily he moved—like he wasn't as old as he appeared. "*Preer* are things of great power, Hank. Unimaginable power, really. Think on it—they span vast distances of space. They can be made to ignore the constraints of time. Some think they may even breach the boundaries of the universe. I've certainly been to a few places where the natural laws of this universe don't seem to apply." He sank into a leather-bound chair and put his feet up on the hearth stones. He closed his eyes and smiled. "Ah... That's comfort. Come sit, Hank."

When I didn't move, he cracked open one eye and looked at me. "It's hard to believe things you've been taught aren't possible. Believe me, Hank, this is just the start of your awakening."

I shook my head, fighting the headache that was building behind my left eye. "This is...a different dimension? Planet?" I sighed and sank into the chair at last. "I don't understand any of this. How can I be here?"

Meuhlnir chuckled. "Those are all very good questions. Questions I don't know the answers for. You're here because you ran the rainbow."

"Ran the rainbow?"

"Crossing *Kyatlerproo*." Meuhlnir sighed and wiggled his toes. "You were going to tell me why you've come here."

"My family... My family was kidnapped. I was a cop, and I investigated a serial murder case seven years ago. I found a note written by the primary suspect, a guy named Chris Hatton. He said that if I followed him, he wouldn't hurt my family. There was a cave, and down at the bottom, there was the *Kyatlerproo*. The damn thing dumped me on the lake, but they must have come this way, too. You say no other travelers have been through this way. How am I supposed to find them? How can I follow Hatton if I have no idea where the fuck I am, or where he is?"

"There are ways," said Meuhlnir. "A *vefari* of sufficient power could help you find them."

"A *vefari*?" Irritation was burning in my mind, making my headache worse and worse.

Meuhlnir nodded. "Yes. A *vefari* of the *strenkir af krafti*—a weaver of the strings of power."

I glared at him and sighed. "Magic."

He favored me with a small, knowing smile. "My ancestors were a curious people. They plumbed the depths of the universe, stealing its secrets. One of those secrets is that there are strings of boundless power that underpin the universe. My people were given the power to manipulate those strings, to do things that would appear magical to the natives of your *klith*—"

"I don't have time for this," I said, lurching to my feet and ignoring the aches and shooting pains the abrupt motion caused. Frustration percolated in my veins.

"Hank," said Meuhlnir in placating tones. "I'm just trying to explain things—"

"My family has been taken from me, Meuhlnir. I don't have time for philosophical discussions. Or metaphysics, or whatever this is. I need help finding them. I don't need a history lesson about your ancestors or your religion." I took two jerking steps toward my boots and pack.

"Hank," said Meuhlnir. "Leave now, and you will surely perish. How can you help anyone if you are dead?"

"So, I just sit here and spend the evening chattering away? Safe and comfortable in your cabin? Are they safe? Are they comfortable?"

"For the moment, the answer to all of those questions is 'yes.' If you run off half-cocked and die in the snow, those answers will no doubt change."

"How do you *know* that?" I yelled. "How can you know these things? Are you a part of this?" I took a menacing step toward the frail looking old man, frustration and fury stampeding through me.

Meuhlnir stood and turned to face me. "Hank, I assure you that I am *not* part of this bad business. I would not participate in such nefarious affairs, except to put a stop to them. The question is simply whether I can help you or not. Whether I *should* help you."

I couldn't think of anything to say. I just stood and stared at the man.

"There are things on this *klith* that you need to be prepared for, Hank. This *klith* is vastly different from where you come from. *Life* is different here."

"I'll learn what I need to learn as I go," I snapped.

"You will fail if you attempt this alone." Meuhlnir's voice was flat and matter-of-fact. "This place is beyond you. Things you will face here will beggar your imagination. They will make you question your sanity."

I scoffed. "As if I'm not already doing that! Magic *preer*! Wizards! Giant fucking magical snow storms!"

"Yes," said Meuhlnir. "Those are just the tip of the dog's nose, Hank."

"Look, Meuhlnir, I don't have time to swap histories and learn about this place. I have a family to rescue! I have to—"

"Hank," he said. "I won't help you unless you deserve to be helped."

That stopped me cold. "What does that mean?"

"It means exactly what I said. You must convince me that you are worthy of my help."

"Well, I don't have time for all this. I've got to go." I stomped to my boots and started to shove my foot into one of them. "Thanks for letting me warm up."

"Oh, sit down, you stubborn fool." The little man's voice snapped with authority. "You are alone. You don't even know where you are. You will be lost within hours, and you have no provisions. You will die."

I stood there looking down at him with blood throbbing in my temples. "I have some food," I said.

"You *need* my help, Hank."

Frustration beat against the inside of my head. I wanted to be moving, but he was right. If I went at this alone, in this strange place, I'd fail.

"Things are different here, Hank," he said in a resigned tone. "There are far fewer people on this *klith*, and there is a rigid class structure. You exist outside that structure so it will be hard for you to find help from anyone, even if you are lucky enough to stumble through the wilderness to a village.

"If I help you, it will take planning. It will take provisioning. All of that will take time—not much, only a day or two, but there's nothing to be done tonight." He sank back into his chair. "I need to know what kind of man you are." He put his feet up on the field stone hearth and turned his face to the fire. "But it's your choice, you know. Leave now, or sit and tell me the tale of how you came to be here."

All of a sudden, I felt too tired to stand, much less slog through miles and miles of snow in the dark. The knowledge that I couldn't help my family without this little old man dragged like a millstone around my neck. With a sigh, I kicked my boot off and stomped to the chair and sat down, trying not to look like an impatient teenager.

I glanced at him askance, sure I'd find him watching me, but he was only staring into the flames. His face was passive—no sign of anger or even interest. "I'm sorry," I said. "I'm just so frustrated and scared—"

"It's nothing, Hank. I understand."

With a sigh, I put my feet back on the hearth next to his. It was like heaven—luxurious warmth from the fire and warm stones under my heels. I sighed and said, "I worked for the New York State Police—to be more specific, for the Bureau of Criminal Investigation. That's the detective branch. Part of the job was to assist local jurisdictions investigate major crimes.

"Seven years ago, two boys playing in the woods found the entrance to a small cave, and inside they'd seen a dead body. Their parents called the local sheriff's department, and when the deputies stuck *their* heads inside the little cave, they'd seen *six* bodies. That's when the sheriff put in a call to the Bureau of Criminal Investigation, and I was assigned to head up the case. That turned out to be my last case as a New York State Trooper."

"You were a *toemari?*"

"A what?"

"A judge. Someone who enforces the rules of law."

"Not a judge, no. I was a police officer. Someone who investigates crimes and builds a case for the prosecution of criminals in a court of law."

Meuhlnir stroked his beard. "That seems like a small distinction."

"No, it isn't. It wasn't up to me to judge anyone, just find out what they did and pass it on to the prosecutors. They took the case before the judge and the criminal was allowed to defend himself."

"But if you found out what they did, what defense is there?"

I shrugged. "I could be wrong."

"Strange system," grunted Meuhlnir. "Leave that for now. Tell me what happened in this investigation of yours."

"By the time I got called in, the media had already broken the story."

SIX

"Six gruesome bodies discovered in cave! Bristol Butcher strikes!" was the headline of the Democrat and Chronicle that morning.

I drove south from my home near Rochester, marveling at the speed with which everything had transitioned from winter to spring. Just a week before, two-and-a-half feet of accumulated snow coated the landscape and temperatures had been in the low single digits. It was already in the mid-fifties, and the only snow left was heaped in old drifts too stubborn to melt. Crusty, gray, and shriveled looking, those snowbanks looked like so many abandoned toys.

The cave was in a ravine between Honeoye Lake and Bristol Mountain and couldn't be reached by car. I pulled off the road and parked my cruiser next to the medical examiner's van. A large white tent, like you'd see at a backyard wedding reception, had been set up beyond the cars. Crime-scene tape ringed the tent.

I flashed my credentials to the deputy sheriff keeping the log and signed in the right spot on his clipboard.

"Morning, Hank."

I turned and saw Dr. Wilkes standing in the entrance of the tent. He was a short and heavyset man in his forties. His hair stood out in multiple directions like a rat and a gopher had staged a fight in it. "Hey there, Dr. Wilkes."

"Sheriff punted already?"

I shrugged. "I don't mind. I'd rather get involved earlier rather than later." I held out my hand, and the ME shook it. "Long night, Dr. Wilkes?"

He grunted. "You'll notice I didn't say *good* morning when I greeted you. What's worse than getting a late evening call for a postmortem?" He put his hand on his head and succeeded only in making his hair stand up even more.

"Getting a late evening call for six of them?"

He cocked his finger like a gun and shot me with it. "Right on the money, Trooper. I can think of nights I had more fun, I'll tell you that free of charge.

They start with the night I almost burned my house down cooking dinner..."

I laughed and shook my head. "That sounds like a story you should tell me over a beer sometime."

"Yep." He leaned against the front of the ME's van and crossed his arms. "It's pretty rare to get a call for more than three." Dr. Wilkes sighed and shook his head. "I believe this is my new all-time record high body count for a crime scene. Disasters don't count."

"Must be serious to get you out of that cozy office of yours."

Dr. Wilkes cocked his finger and shot me again.

I crooked my thumb toward the tent. "Anything useful in there?"

"Come on," said Dr. Wilkes. "It's easier to just show you." He turned and walked back inside the tent, and I ducked through the opening.

The first thing that hit me was the smell. It was an overwhelming odor—almost sweet and yet shockingly vile, kind of like the sweet, sick smell of compost, but about ten thousand times more intense. Active decay isn't the easiest thing in the world to stomach, and I was glad I hadn't eaten that big breakfast Jane had been cooking when I left.

The bodies were laid out on cheap, plastic-topped folding tables from the local box store—hardly the sterile, clinical feel of a morgue. I'd seen my fair share of bodies. I'd seen them in almost every possible form, skeletal, mummified, fresh enough that the blood still dripped. I'd seen people who had been beaten to death with hammers. I'd seen accident victims crushed between cars. Gunshots and stabbings, you name it, but these bodies were something else entirely.

"Six bodies in all," said Wilkes. "One of them is pretty fresh, as I'm sure you've noticed. The other five victims have decayed quite a bit—nothing more than skeletons at this point, but that is informative in and of itself. The five older remains are more than a couple of months old, taking into account the frigid temperatures of the past winter."

The most recent victim was in worse shape. Her hair was starting to come out, and her skin had cracked open and was starting to slough off in other places. Even so, that wasn't the terrible part. The wounds showing on her body were horrific. There were deep gouges wherever there were big muscle groups, and there were multiple ragged wounds. Her abdomen looked strange, sunken in. She had ragged tears in his arms and legs.

"Are those bite marks?" I asked.

Wilkes nodded with a sour frown.

"Awful," I muttered.

"The wounds are all awful. The perp didn't just bite and release like you sometimes see. No, this guy is more like an attack dog. He bit deep and then savagely tore away chunks of flesh."

I glanced at the other bodies and saw similar wounds in what flesh remained. I shook my head in disgust. "Bites go to the bone?"

Wilkes nodded. "I think it's safe to assume the tooth marks on the bones will support the M.O. Trophies were taken," he grunted.

"Genitals?"

"Surprisingly, no. Offal—the liver, the kidneys, the heart, the lungs, the stomach, the spleen, even the pancreas were taken from the recent victim. You can guess why."

I wished I couldn't, but it was all too clear. "Haggis, blood pudding, sausage."

Dr. Wilkes grimaced.

My stomach rolled. "Doc, is there anything else you need me to see?"

"No," he said. "Let's go back outside."

The air outside had never smelled so fresh, and I took a deep, steadying breath. "Who the *fuck* could do that to another human being?"

"You'd know better than I," said Wilkes. "I deal with the dead, you have to find the guys who made them so."

I took another deep breath. I knew we were supposed to be emotionally detached when dealing with murder victims, but it wasn't always possible.

SEVEN

"**A**s much as I loved being a cop, sometimes I wanted to be a shoe salesman. We—"

"These bodies...they were eaten from?" asked Meuhlnir.

"Yes, and they were just the start. There was a cave-in toward the rear of that small antechamber, and when we dug it out, we found more bodies. And more behind them."

"How many more bodies?" Meuhlnir was trying to sound casual, but there was a thread of tension in his manner.

"Remains littered the floor throughout the rest of the cave, which was huge. The final count was more than fourteen hundred sets of remains, which is really unbelievable for one person to have—"

"*Itla sem Yetur*," breathed the old man.

"What?"

The old man shook his head. "*Itla sem Yetur* means *the evil that eats* in the *Gamla Toonkumowl*."

"The evil that eats? Hatton was just a man. An evil, cannibalistic man, yes, but still..." Suddenly, the memory of what happened in the safe house flooded into my mind, unbidden, unwelcome. *Was he just a man?*

The old man turned his head toward me. His expression was carefully neutral, but his eyes danced with an intense interest. "Hatton."

"Yeah, Chris Hatton. He and his girlfriend, Elizabeth Tutor, were practicing cannibals. Everyone thought they were suffering from a *folie a deux*, but—"

"I don't know that phrase," said Meuhlnir.

"It's a shared delusion between two people. Even I thought that in the beginning. In fact, I believed that right up until I saw Hatton change."

Meuhlnir leaned toward me, his eyes burning. "What did you say?"

I shrugged. "No one believes me about this, but I saw it. He changed into a wolf thing right in front of me. I shot him, but it just made him mad. He batted me through half the house after he crushed my service pistol. He said he was a *wendigo*."

Meuhlnir was looking down and muttering something to himself. "*Wendigo?*"

"It's a cannibalism taboo myth of the native people of my land. I think it means 'the evil that devours.' Strange coincidence there, but I don't believe in coincidence."

Meuhlnir was staring into the fire, but one of his hands was curled into a fist.

"All this mean something to you?"

He tilted his head to the side. "There is a cult of sorts that call themselves the *Briethralak Oolfur*: the brotherhood of the wolf. They break the *Ayn Loug*—the One Law."

"I've never heard of any brotherhood. It was just Hatton and Tutor. What is the One Law?"

"It is forbidden to eat the flesh of men."

I shook my head again. "And you only need one law?"

"We yarls consider it the high law of our kind. All other laws are subservient to it. Breaking the law is a dark path that stains the soul of all those who follow it. It's a short cut, a cheat, and one that twists character. The practice was taught to my people by an evil people named the Svartalfar."

"But this Brotherhood is allowed to—"

"Here on this continent, they exist in hiding, never daring to show their true selves because they would be punished. Far to the north, across the Tempest Sea, however, they are allowed to follow their beliefs in the open." He waved it away. "Never mind for now, we'll come back to this later. Go on with your story."

After a moment of silence, he made a 'go on' kind of gesture with his hand.

"We had the bodies, and Dr. Wilkes was doing his postmortems. There wasn't much to go on until Hatton picked a fight with a couple of kids.

"Hatton and Tutor were in this big black Lincoln Continental they had, just out for an afternoon drive in the spring air."

EIGHT

Liz smiled at the breath of the warm spring air on her cheek. She had her hair pinned up and covered in her favorite silk scarf. It was a pink paisley pattern, and Luka said it was "hot" every time she wore it. They had the top of the Lincoln down, and the sun warmed her skin like a lover's caress.

She glanced at Luka and smiled at the dopey-happy expression on his face. Why shouldn't he be happy? They were gods in this place, and there was no one who could challenge their reign.

He stopped at a traffic light and turned to her. "It's a beautiful day, my Queen, but it's nothing compared to you."

She laughed. "My Champion," she said and reached across the expanse of the front seat to caress his cheek.

A small green car pulled up in the lane to her right. Inside sat two black men, laughing and looking at the Lincoln, smiling and pointing. They had their windows down and were playing that disgusting rap music.

Her lip curled as she turned toward them. She lifted a languid hand and waved it at the open window. "Turn that shit off," she called.

The man driving scoffed at her and then looked away.

"Hey!" yelled Liz. "I said to turn that disgusting shit off!"

The man looked back at her and turned up the volume until the bass was rattling the little car to pieces. He sneered at her.

When the light changed, Liz was pushed back in her seat as Luka floored the accelerator, and the Lincoln's big-block V8 roared to life. The back tires squealed, and the car leapt forward. As they swept away from the intersection, she lifted her hand and shot the bird at the driver of the green car.

Luka cranked the wheel to the left and slammed on the brakes, letting the big car slide to a stop blocking both lanes.

Liz glanced at him, and he gave her a little wink. "Dinner?" she asked with a small laugh.

"Meals on wheels," Luka said and sniggered.

The old green car screeched to a stop, and the driver sprang out of the car. "What the fuck you think your doin', man?" he yelled.

Still grinning, Luka looked over at him and flapped his hand, as if waving away an insect. "Sorry, buck, didn't notice you over there."

"Just let it go, Aten," said the other man in the green car.

"You could've killed someone with that dumbass stunt. Move that piece of shit out of the way." He hit the rear door of the Lincoln with the heel of his hand.

Anger snapped through Liz's veins. She turned in her seat until she could look at the black man. "Listen, boy, I know you think you are hard—"

"Don't you call me *boy* you old two-dollar whore!"

In the corner of her eye, Luka's body tensed like he'd been hit with a cattle prod.

"—but you are like tissue paper compared to my man." She paused and then laughed. "Did you call me a two-dollar whore? Aw, did I offend you, Little Black Sambo?"

Luka's hand moved toward his door handle. His face was rigid, eyes squinting, mouth a fierce slash across the bottom of his face.

"Get back in ya damn cah, ya fool," yelled an old man in the little car next to Aten's.

The black man was tall but nowhere near as tall as Luka. *Plenty of flesh on his bones, too*, she thought with a carnivorous smile.

He was just standing there, fists clenched and staring down at her. His lips were quivering a little bit.

Seeing the man's rage sent a little thrill of excitement shivering through her. "What? Nothing else to say? Well, fuck you, *boy*." She sneered and turned in her seat to look out the front window as if the man was of no consequence.

"No, you goddamn motherfuckin' back-alley crack whore, *fuck you*!" He leaned close to her, almost screaming in her ear. Little flecks of spittle flew with each syllable.

Liz ignored him. Luka would sort him out in due course.

When the man hawked and spat a big glob of snot into her hair, her rage-monster snapped its teeth. She jerked the scarf off and scrubbed at the side of her head. "Oh, you *goddamn nigger*!" she screamed. Rage bubbled through her bloodstream, and it felt glorious. Exultant.

Liz spun around on her knees in the seat. Her movements were brisk, concise—without wasted energy. She pointed up at the man's face. Her face crinkled in an expression that was half-snarl, half-smile. "*Pred—*"

"No, my Queen!" shouted Luka. "Not here."

"Is that supposed to scare me?" demanded the man.

Liz glanced sideways at Luka and squeezed her eyes into slits, irritated at the interruption. "I *want* to do this, Luka."

"My Queen, it would be unwise."

"You better listen to your man, you goddamn bitch," snapped Aten. "I'll slap the ugly right off you."

"That's it," said Luka in an almost conversational tone. His hand had finally reached the door handle, and he pulled the door open. His other hand hit his seat belt release.

The black man jumped into the back seat of the Lincoln and bounced his way across the car.

"Aten! No!" yelled the other man from the green car. A look of dismay danced across his face.

Liz sneered at the other man and shot him the bird.

Putting one foot on the top of the door, Aten jumped out of the car. He landed on the macadam like a cat and swung his fist in a great whistling arc.

Aten's fist collided with Luka's cheek bone with a dry *crack*. Luka unfolded from behind the driver's seat like a huge insect, showing no reaction to being sucker punched. He towered above the black man but looked sick, wasted in comparison to the other man's bulk.

Without changing expression, Luka kicked the man in the knee, the heel of his black cowboy boot making a sound like an axe striking wet wood. He shrugged his shoulder into the haymaker the black man was in the middle of throwing and managed to look bored while he did it.

As the punch bounced off Luka's bony shoulder, Liz couldn't help but titter. Watching Luka work was a special treat.

"That'll be enough of that, buck," said Luka. Lightning quick, his hand shot out and grabbed

Aten's ear, twisting it savagely until the man, already off balance from the kick to his knee, teetered into the side of the Lincoln.

"You better leave my brother alone, string-bean!" yelled the other man. He was sprinting around the front of the Lincoln, hands curled into fists.

Luka grinned like a maniac into Aten's face, showing his teeth. He put his hand on the black man's cheek and pushed him roughly to the ground. He turned toward the front of the car, eyes twinkling, grin stretching until it looked more like a predator showing threat than a man's smile.

The other man from the car rounded the front of the Lincoln and came at Luka with one hand cocked over his shoulder.

Luka laughed, stepped to the side, and swatted the man into the side of the Lincoln. He did a strange little jig, feet blurring too fast to see. He grabbed the man by the back of his neck and slammed his face into the wide black expanse of the Lincoln's fender. He cackled and winked at Liz.

"Instruct them, my Champion." The violent glee with which Luka was dealing with the two men appeased her. Despite her frustration at not being able to act in the way she most wanted to, she began to enjoy the show.

"Don't you bleed on my car, you little baboon," said Luka in a chatty, mocking voice. His foot blurred again, and there was another of those axe-on-wood sounds, and the other man was flat on his back, staring up at the sky. Luka lifted his foot and brought it down hard on the black man's chest, grinning at the dry-twig-snapping sounds of ribs breaking.

Aten struggled to his feet, and Luka turned to face him, a small grin playing around the corners of his mouth. "Ready for more?" he asked in a sing-song voice.

Aten raised his hands. "Come on and dance, motherfucker!"

Luka's laugh was bright, almost manic, but his movements were full of a lazy grace, looking for all the world like he *was* dancing as he stepped closer to Aten. "Oh, yes, buck. Let's dance." One hand arced out, and as Aten lifted his hand to block the blow, Luka cackled and slammed his other fist into the other side of his head.

It was like a butcher hitting a steer with a killing hammer. Liz cheered and laughed as Aten fell to his knees. "Told you that you weren't hard, boy."

Luka put his hands on his knees and leaned over the man. "Tell me, little cotton-picker. Do you drink?"

From his knees, Aten tried a right cross, but Luka batted it away, a little grin playing in the corner of his lips.

"Such spirit," cawed Luka.

"So slow," sang Liz. "So weak."

"What?" asked Aten. "What?"

"I asked you a question, nigger." The tension left Luka's muscles, and he straightened. His manner was casual and open, almost friendly. "Do you drink?"

"What did you say?" wheezed Aten.

Luka winked at Liz. "Do. You. Drink. It's an easy question."

Aten shook his head, trying to clear it. "Why do you—"

"Oh, for fuck's sake, boy. Are you retarded or something?" shrieked Liz. As the man turned to look at her, she laughed and gave him a jaunty little wave.

"I want to know if you drink alcohol. You know, because it ruins the taste."

"Taste?" The man looked up at Luka in confusion.

"Yes, buck. Alcohol ruins the taste of your liver. Yes or no?"

The black man's face went gray as he finally understood what Luka was asking. "Look, Mister, this—"

"Hear that, my Queen?" asked Luka in a laughing voice. "We've progressed from 'motherfucker' right on up to 'mister' already."

Liz chuckled. "Not so hard, are you, boy? I tried to tell you."

The black man looked back and forth between them, his mouth hanging open, blood trickling slowly down his chin. His eyes were open wide, his brow scrunched up in fear.

"Has all that bravado deserted you already, buck?" asked Luka. Suddenly, his hand lashed across the black man's face like a whip, sending Aten over on his back.

Luka stepped forward and squatted over Aten's chest.

"Look, that blonde bitch—"

Luka's finger pressed upwards under Aten's chin, closing his mouth with an audible *snap*. "Don't call her that again," he said in a cold, hard voice. "Maybe I'll eat you slowly, keeping you alive between meals. Maybe I'll keep you conscious while we dine." His tone was hateful, nasty.

Aten couldn't meet his gaze. "Mister, I…" His eyes went toward the other man's. "My brother don't have no part in this." His voice shook like a child's.

"Oh, no, buck. You don't get to make any rules here." Luka glanced at the other man and then back at Aten. "But don't worry. It won't happen now. Not out in public like this. No, that would not be healthy at all."

"What?" asked Aten.

"What? What? What?" sneered Liz. "Is he retarded, Luka?"

"Are you really that stupid?" asked Luka. "That's the fourth time you've asked that question. Aren't you listening to me?" He slapped the man on the cheek. "Wake up, little sambo. Pay attention."

Liz cackled and clapped her hands. Luka was a master at this.

"Let me spell it out for you, buck. I'm going to come for you later. You'll try to hide, but you can't hide from me. I'll come to where you are, and you will try to run. You can't escape me. No, don't even think it. I'll take you, and you'll try to fight me, but we both know you stand no chance."

"And if you *do* fight him," said Liz, "I'll come for your brother over there." She let some of the pent-up rage seep into her voice, making her sound cold and cruel. "I'm nowhere near as nice as my friend here."

"There you go, buck. Better not fight if you love your brother."

"What—"

"Oh, do shut up, dumbass," said Liz.

"I'm going to hurt you. After I've hurt you a little, I'll start eating you. Just a snack, really. Maybe my queen will have a few bites before dinner. Who can say?" Luka glanced at Liz and waggled his eyebrows, then glared down at Aten. "Then, I'm going to kill you, buck. I'll take your liver, your heart, maybe even your kidneys. For later.

"I'm going to put you in a dark, dank place and let the rest of you molder away to nothing. You won't get a burial. No one will speak over your grave. No one will find your corpse. I'll keep you forever. In. The. Dark." Luka patted Aten on the head and stood, beaming a sunny smile down at him.

Aten looked up, first at Liz, then at Luka.

He looked like a lost child, terror-filled eyes, quivering lips, the works. Liz loved every second of that forlorn glance.

"Just don't make the mistake of thinking you have much time to live," said Luka. "Because you don't, buck. You really don't."

"You can't mean all this, man," said Aten in a weak, fear-filled voice. "You are just trying to scare me."

"Oh, no," said Liz. "He means every word, boy. I cook a wicked liver and onions." She laughed. "And you are already scared, kitten."

"Can't be serious," the man muttered.

"Don't think that, buck. Never in life." Luka stepped away from Aten and opened the door of the Lincoln. "I'm a doer, boy. If I say I'm going to do something, I do it. You can take that to the bank and invest that shit."

"Look, it was just a stupid fight, man. Road rage—"

"Buck, no. Don't be lily-livered." Luka glanced at her with a silly grin on his face, and she cackled at his dumb joke. "You motherfucked me, buck. You sucker punched me." Luka glanced at the back seat. "You scuffed my beautiful Italian leather." He took a deep breath and looked down at the man, his expression turning hard. "Worse for you, buck, you motherfucked *her*. You called her bad names. You impugned her honor and made dispersions about her worth as a courtesan—"

"Plus, old," cackled Liz. "He called me old! That alone is worth a liver, isn't it?"

Luka winked at her and nodded. "Plus, you called her old, which is just rude, and you really have no idea, anyway." His grin turned feral as he turned back to stare into Aten's eyes. "But that's not the worst of it. No, not the worst by a long shot." Luka shook his head as if he couldn't fathom anything worse. "You *spit* on her."

Luka slammed the door and took two quick steps back to Aten. His booted foot arced back and then slammed into Aten's side. "She is a *queen*!" His boot thudded into Aten. "She is a queen, you *motherfucker*, and I will absolutely *not* have it!" His voice rose with each word, betraying the rage that lurked under his silly comedy. The raw, brutal malignancy of his hatred leeched into his expression.

Aten turned his face away and closed his eyes.

"It might have been just a fight to you, buck, but it wasn't for me. Honestly, you should have known better."

"You can't threaten to… You've got to be—"

"Oh, no, sambo. I'm as serious as death." Luka straightened and turned slowly, his eyes marking each person watching. "I'd prove it to you right now, but there's plenty of time." He looked down at Aten. "I'll see you soon, and that's a solemn promise."

"Mister, my brother don't have no part in this. This is my fault—"

"Don't worry," said Luka, glancing toward the other man. "I kind of like your brother. He reminds me of one of my own."

A horn blew down the line of cars that had stacked up behind them. Luka stood up tall and glared at the cars. After a protracted moment of silence, he folded himself back behind the wheel of the Lincoln and started the car.

"Bye, boys," said Liz in a sing-song voice. "Have a good afternoon!" The expression on Aten's face made her cackle long and loud as the Lincoln roared away, bumping up over the curb and then back down into the street.

NINE

"I built a case against those two based on that street fight. Both men they fought that day ended up in the hospital. The two men were named Aten and Marcus Kennedy. In the middle of the night, Aten disappeared from the hospital. No one saw anything, of course, and the next morning, Aten's body turned up inside the cave. He'd been tortured and then eviscerated.

"Somehow, Hatton had gotten by several officers and troopers who were tasked with keeping the dump-site secure. He did that while carrying

Kennedy's body. No one saw a thing. No one suspected a thing. It was like magic."

I shook my head. "My boss, Lieutenant Gruber, was furious. He started an internal investigation and demanded that the Sheriff's office do the same thing." I glanced at Meuhlnir. "I tell you, though, I believe those officers when they say no one got past them."

He smiled and nodded. "It sounds perfectly sane on this side of the *proo*, Hank. It would be a simple matter, in truth."

"The only upside was that they found a passage in the rear of the cave. There had been a cave in, and it looked intentional to the engineers."

"And what was on the other side of the cave in?"

"More bodies. A lot more," I said. "The cave complex was huge, but the first chamber was small and dank. I had to crawl on my hands and knees to get inside…"

TEN

I got down on my knees and peered into the cave. It was everything I'd expected it to be—dank, earthy and smelling of stale mold and decayed flesh. At least someone had already strung up some lights. "No time like the present," I muttered and squeezed my shoulders inside the cave. There were downsides to being a powerlifter, and small cave entrances were right at the top of the list.

I could see the subtle depressions where the first bodies found had lain. Each depression was marked with a little flag, numbered one to six.

I felt like a bull wedged into the branding chute, and a part of my mind wanted to get out of there as fast as possible. I don't mind tight spaces, but something about that cave freaked me out. There was something about the place—something that felt evil.

I ran my hand through my buzz cut, expecting to feel spiders crawling around. I hated spiders almost as much as I hated small, dank caves.

"Did you notice where the slide in the back of the cave was?" asked Jax, squeezing into the cave behind me.

"Yeah. That's where Aten Kennedy's body was dumped."

"I'd make a joke about lucky number seven, but…"

"Yeah," I said. The day that had felt so warm a short time before now felt cold and bleak. Funny how learning the extent to which a mind can be twisted does that.

I glanced at Jax and motioned for him to go through the portal that the slide had hidden. I followed on his heels. The technicians had set up two more of the short-legged trestles in the tunnel at the back of that first chamber. Lights were being strung up and coming on in the space behind the short passage.

The air smelled sharp and spicy. It was almost a pleasant odor, but I knew what we would find in the rest of the cave. Mummified skeletal remains. Or worse.

The second chamber was much larger than the first. It was tall enough to stand in, for one thing, but only just, and we both got to our feet while ducking our heads. The chamber was roughly rectilinear, maybe sixty yards by forty. There was an obtrusive, inky blackness at the far end of the chamber.

Human remains in various stages of advanced decay lined both walls of the chamber and extended into that murky darkness on the remote end. Two aisles led deeper into the cave, and each was lined with remains on both sides.

Jax whistled. "How many are here?" he muttered.

"To put it technically, a metric shit ton," quipped one of the forensics guys.

I counted the visible remains. There were seventeen per row, so thirty-four visible victims, per aisle. Sixty-eight more victims to add to the first seven. I shook my head. "This one's been busy."

"How far back do you think this cave stretches?" murmured Jax.

"There is a passage at the end of this chamber. We haven't gone back there, so your guess is as good as mine," said the forensics technician.

"One way to find out," I said, turning on my flashlight.

"Do you think that's safe?" The technician was peering into the darkness.

"Not really," I said. "Don't try this at home, kids."

The man nodded at me, more than a little uncertain. "Be careful," he said and then shivered. "It feels weird in here tonight."

I patted the butt of my service weapon. "We'll be fine." I watched the technician fiddle for a moment. "I thought you guys didn't get jumpy at crime scenes."

"We don't," he said. "I don't. But, still…" He shrugged.

Jax flipped on his flashlight, too. "No time like the present, Hank." He started forward, his steps resolute and steadfast.

We walked toward that black hole in the back of the cave, our flashlights sending fruitless beams of light in cones ahead of us. After we'd walked for ten minutes, we could see the floor of the cave begin to slope downwards.

Jax stopped. "This is…"

"Cockeyed? Insane? Preposterous?" I said in a low voice.

"Yeah, all of those and a few four lettered cousins. This guy has to be the most prolific serial killer ever. I mean how many did that Russian guy get?"

"The Red Ripper? Chikatilo?"

"Yeah, that guy that killed people on the trains," said Jax. He ran his flashlight over the row of bodies lining his side of the cave.

"Mid-fifties, I think. But the South Americans have him by a huge margin. I think the most prolific killer was from Columbia. There's a guy there that has over 300 victims, though he only admitted to 147 of them."

"I'm willing to bet the body count in here is higher."

I scrubbed my face with my right hand. "I want to disagree with you, but…" I stared into the murky blackness of the passage in front of us and wondered what kind of world I'd brought Sig into. "He's already at seventy-five victims, so even if the rest of the place is empty, he's toward the top of the list." I drew in a long breath and let it whistle out between my teeth. "Ready for this?"

"Absotootly," said Jax with a bravado that rang false.

I nodded and started walking. My flashlight beam bounced ahead of us, lighting the aisle in the middle of the passage. Jax played his flashlight across the left side of the cave, briefly throwing light on the line of skeletons on that side. Water trickled down the rough stone walls.

I'd like to say it didn't give me the creeps, but that would be a lie. Something about the meticulous placement of the bodies, the clean center aisle, gave me a serious case of the jitters. Somehow, this part of the cave felt colder than the previous chamber. "You don't suppose this guy comes back to see all his trophies, do you?"

Jax shrugged, and in the dim light, it was something I sensed more than saw. "I'm sure he does. There must be a reason for this aisle."

I ran my flashlight over the row of skeletons on the right side of the path. "Have you noticed anything different on any of these remains?"

Jax played his light on the bodies to his left. "No. I see what looks like bite marks in some of the bigger bones, but nothing that looks like an edged weapon." He pursed his lips. "It's kind of disquieting to think that someone can bludgeon over a hundred people without leaving a single witness."

"I agree. Beating someone to death makes noise— a lot of noise." I said.

"Then he's got a kill room somewhere."

I nodded. "This is much too…tidy to be the actual scene of these murders—as creepy as that thought is. The murders themselves are disorganized…like he's in a frenzy."

We continued walking.

"I don't understand this," I said.

Jax grunted. "It's too weird. Why keep all these bodies? If he just wanted to hide the bodies from sight, burial would have been a better option. Hell, dumping them out in the middle of Lake Ontario would've been better."

"This is not about hiding these remains. This is a trophy room. It has to be."

"A very large trophy room," said Jax. "He comes back here and walks through these chambers. He gets off on this."

"These corpses remind him of the kills. He can relive the murders here." I scratched my head. "Even so, this seems…different. This doesn't feel like it's *just* a trophy room."

"Couldn't we clear out and set up surveillance here? Maybe catch him coming back for a peek?"

I shook my head. "Too late for that. He's not coming back here."

"How can you be sure?"

"He's already been back to dump Kennedy's body. He knows this place is blown. That was his message in dumping Kennedy in the front chamber."

"How can you be sure, boss?"

"Call it instinct. I don't know how or why, but I'm sure of it."

We had walked three hundred yards into the passage. Up ahead, a fork in the cave structure loomed out of the darkness. "Can you see that branch ahead?"

"Unfortunately, I can."

"This part of the cave could turn into a maze. We should have some kind of fluorescent marks or lights to blaze our trail."

Jax snapped his fingers. "The DayGlo paint troopers use to mark-up accident scenes."

"That would work. Good thinking, Jax."

"I'll go get some from one of the troopers standing post."

I nodded. "I'll wait here. Maybe I'll take a closer look at some of these bodies." The truth of it was that I just wanted to stand there and see if I could somehow crawl into the mind of the killer. The cold precision of the cave seemed at odds with the brutality and frenzy shown by the bodies. Maybe the man from the car did the killing, and the woman did the arranging.

Despite what I'd told Jax, I didn't think the reason for the aisle was just to facilitate looking at trophies. That seemed too trite of an explanation for the sheer volume of victims. But why else keep them? Serial killers didn't do things like this without a reason.

"If I were a serial killer, what would be worth this kind of risk? Especially with such an unsecured place," I muttered. "There must be something I'm not seeing."

All these *complete* bodies laid out on display didn't really make sense. Serial killers might take trophies, but they didn't tend to keep the whole body—they buried or dumped or burned them.

"There must be a reason." I'd gotten over feeling self-conscious about talking to myself. It was just part of my process. "Wilkes said there were chunks of flesh—bites—missing from the victims. I wonder if Wilkes can figure out whether the bites were pre- or postmortem."

Bites of flesh. The thought swirling around my head was lurid. *Are you eating them? Is this your buffet? Do you come back here to feed? Are you like an alligator? You prefer carrion to fresh meat?*

The almost peaceful silence amid all those corpses was ended by the sound of something scraping on stone in the left fork. I felt ten years old again, scared of the dark. A hinky feeling of being watched by a predator of some kind started screaming in the back of my mind. "Would you come back here to see who's looking at your food?" I murmured.

The scraping sound came again, sounding closer this time. I pulled my Glock out of my holster. I held the pistol near my right thigh, pointing at the floor of the cave with my trigger finger resting along the side of the gun. "Are you watching me right now? If you are, come on out and let's have a friendly little chat."

I stood still, listening for that telltale sound again, taking shallow little gulps of breath. I was still standing there listening when I heard Jax come up behind me. He stopped a little behind and to my left. I glanced at him and saw he also had his pistol out and was staring into the darkness ahead of us.

"What is it?" he breathed.

I waved him to silence. We stood that way for what seemed like an hour but was probably only a minute or two. That hinky feeling was gone. I let my breath out and holstered my side arm, waving at Jax to do the same. "I thought I heard something in the left fork."

Jax shot me a perplexed look. "What could be in there? We control the entrance to the cave."

"Maybe there is more than one way into this cave." I shrugged and laughed a little. "Or maybe Zombies?"

"*World War Z*, huh?"

"Okay, maybe it was my imagination." My smile was sheepish, but something deep inside my mind was shouting that I hadn't imagined anything.

"Just as well," said Jax, "you are much too big to be played by Brad Pitt in the movie version. Lou Ferrigno, or maybe Arnold." He pronounced the last name "Ahhhnahhld," as it should be.

"Jackass," I said, smiling. "Did you remember the paint or what?"

Jax pulled a rattle can of bright orange paint out of his windbreaker's left pocket. "There were these two young nuns tasked to paint a room in the convent, but the Mother Superior told them not to get a drop on their habits. The two nuns lock the door, see, and strip. They start painting. There's a knock at the door, and they ask who's there. A man said, "Blind man." The nuns look at each other and shrug, then let him in. The man takes a long look and says 'Nice tits. Where do you want these blinds?'"

I chuckled, feeling the tension drain out of me. "I bet the nuns at your parochial school loved that one."

Jax shrugged. "Not a single one was younger than ninety. Worse yet, none of them had nice tits."

Still smiling and shaking my head, I waved my hand toward the fork in the cave. "Which fork?"

"Eeny, meeny, miny, moe," said Jax. "The left one, of course."

I took the spray can and stepped gingerly around the remains closest to the left-hand fork. I painted an arrow pointing toward the entrance. "We'll do it like that. Each turn we take, we'll mark like that. The side of the cave with the mark indicates which direction we took."

"Okay."

We started walking down the left fork, seeing more remains followed by more of the same. The body count was starting to seem infinite.

"It's going to take forever to identify them all," said Jax. "Aren't you glad you are not an ME?"

"In more ways than one," I said.

We walked in silence for another hundred yards or so and then came to an intersection of the tunnel we were in and a perpendicular tunnel. As we approached the intersection, Jax shone his flashlight on both walls on our side of the four-way. His light illuminated a roughly hewn wall sconce. The sconce held an unlit torch. The primitive torch was covered in thick white cobwebs, and the thought of being down there in the dark with spiders made my skin crawl, of course.

"Why would anyone use a torch like that in here?" Jax asked. "Why walk around with a smoky torch in a place like this?"

I shrugged and tried to keep my tone light. "Maybe his flashlight was out of batteries?"

"Either that or…"

"Or what, Jax?"

He shook his head slowly. "Either that or these bodies have been here longer than we think."

I played my light across the remains near us. "Come on, Jax. Maybe the torch has been here for a while, but these remains could be in this state in as little as two months from the time of their deaths."

"Yeah, maybe," he said. "But that doesn't *feel* right to me. Does it to you?"

I didn't want to answer that question, so I walked into the middle of the intersection and pointed my light down the left branch. The rough rock walls of the cave gave way to crudely worked stone about thirty yards from where I stood as if someone had cut a tunnel from the rock using nothing but a pick ax. "Look at this, Jax"

He came to my side and followed the flashlight beam with his eyes. "No way."

I gestured at the tunnel as if to say: 'there it is for all to see.'

"This is too weird for my beard," muttered Jax.

"Yeah, well, you don't have a beard."

"I would if I could." Jax took a deep breath. "What in the hell is this, Hank? I mean someone cut this side tunnel. Just to store more bodies? Why not just find another cave? Or hell, just *stack* them."

"I wish I had any idea why serials do what they do," I said. I shook my head and blew breath out my puffed cheeks. "But this can't be the work of one man, can it? I mean this would take serious effort."

"Years and years of work." Jax nodded. "All of this is too much to be one person. If it was one man, this took a long time and that just doesn't make sense for a serial killer to cut a new tunnel. There's more cave ahead."

"The scale is just too big. I thought that maybe this cave served to cure the killer's meat, but these caves go on and on. There's plenty of space for more bodies, right? There must be some other purpose for this labyrinth,"

Jax gave me a strange look. "What kind of purpose could there possibly be beyond those two?"

"Maybe he connected multiple caves? That could account for more than one entrance, right?" I sighed again. "The simple fact is that the cave is here and it's up to us to catch the guy using it—whatever the twisted reason is. Let's go look at the worked part of this mausoleum." I marked the left wall, starting the arrow in the new corridor and painting it right around the corner so that it ended in the tunnel that led back to the surface.

"How much deeper do you think this can go?"

I shook my head. "I hate to keep saying this, but I have no idea. Maybe radar or sonar could map these tunnels?"

Jax was silent for a few moments, and I let him think. He looked me straight in the eye and said, "This has to be twenty years of victims. Or more."

I sighed and brushed imaginary spiders out of my hair. "Just going by the count we know for sure, seventy-five, I'd guess we've seen at least that many on our little walk, right?"

"More," said Jax. "Maybe three times as much."

"Okay, so going with two hundred bodies, and assuming this guy kills regularly, that would be a victim every month. I can't imagine it's gone on for even ten years, let alone twenty. Not at a victim a month. Someone would have noticed a pattern like that, right?"

"And that only accounts for the bodies we've already seen. I have a terrible feeling this is just the tip of the iceberg." Jax waved his hand toward the darkness in front of us.

"I hate to even think it, but I do believe you are right on that score. Just think of the passages we've seen but not explored. Then think of what might be left in the rest of the cave."

"I don't like this, Hank."

"Heh. Me neither."

We went on, always sticking to the left-hand branch and painting our little arrows on the walls. After a while the cadavers seemed to fade from our notice—there were just too many of them to process. We walked through natural corridors and caverns, and man-made corridors and rooms walled in worked stone. We saw plenty of sconces, but the torch we discovered at the first four-way intersection was the only one we saw. The different areas of the cave all had one thing in common, though. No matter if the walls were natural, rough cut, or lined with worked stone, the center of the floor was always worn smooth as if thousands of footsteps had polished them.

When we finally gave up and made our way back up into the crisp air at the cave entrance, I estimated that the body count had to be over six hundred. More than a little dejected, we walked back toward our cruisers parked up on Gulick Road. My mind sluggish and torpid—too numb to think. Part of that was fatigue, but most of it was a deep desire to avoid thinking about the sheer number of murder victims.

"Hank, I..." Jax's voice trailed away, and he made a helpless gesture with his hands.

"We have to get back into the minutiae. Stop yourself from thinking about the..." I made a very similar gesture to the one Jax had just made. "The enormity of this..."

"This nightmare," Jax finished.

"That's as good a description as any, I suppose."

We walked the rest of the way to our cars in silence, each lost in his thoughts. I was walking with my head down, my thumbs hooked into the front pockets of my dirt smeared jeans.

Jax stopped and gasped. "What in the hell?"

I glanced at him. His face was a canonical picture of shock. He was breathing fast as he turned to look at me. His eyes were open wide—as wide as I'd ever seen anyone's eyes get. He lifted his arm and made another helpless little gesture up ahead of us.

I looked toward the cars. On the side of Jax's car was a bright, DayGlo orange arrow, pointing straight down at the ground. My mind was trying to reject the reality of what that arrow meant, trying to construct a scenario where that arrow was some kind of joke played on us by another trooper or the crime scene guys.

All of that was nonsense, though, and I knew it. The arrow meant that the killer had been in the cave with us. He had seen the arrows we painted on his walls, and he wanted us to know it. He wanted to say hello. He was reckless, perhaps wanting to be caught.

"That sound you heard..." said Jax in a small, quiet voice.

I nodded.

"If I hadn't come back when I did—"

"No use playing what if; you did come back. We better get some forensics technicians out here to dust your car."

Jax nodded, but neither of us moved. "Of course, there won't be any prints. He would have made sure of that."

I nodded and ran my hand over my hair. "We have to at least tell Gruber."

"Should I leave the car where it is?"

"Yeah, you know Gruber will want a full forensic workup of the car, so let's do that." I pointed to my car, but neither one of us moved toward my cruiser for a long time.

EL'EVEN

"**I**f I understand the implications of your story," said Meuhlnir, "the person responsible for all those bodies was in the grotto with you?"

"Yes. Hatton let it slip later."

Meuhlnir shook his head. "This Hatton sounds quite brazen."

I nodded. "You don't know the half of it. Alone, he was a terror, but when he was with or under the influence of Tutor, things got really bad."

Meuhlnir sniffed but nodded. "This folie a deux?"

I sighed, long and loud. "She was like gasoline to his flame. She... I don't know, maybe he was trying to impress her with how ferocious and bloodthirsty he could be. Maybe he just couldn't stand for her to be upset."

Meuhlnir turned at looked me in the face; his eyes narrowed, and his lips pursed several times before he spoke. "Tell me of this."

I cleared my throat. "Could I have some water?"

Meuhlnir sprang to his feet like a man who was much younger than he looked and walked out of the room. He returned with two mugs and a steaming pitcher. "This is much better for you than water!" He poured me a mug of the translucent amber liquid and pressed it into my hands.

It smelled of spices and nature. The warmth of the stoneware mug felt delicious in my hands. I took a sip and was pleased with the crisp, dry taste of spring honey. "What is this made from? It smells like honey."

Meuhlnir smiled. "It is made from water, yeast, honey and a secret blend of spices. My wife, Sif, makes the best mead in the Snyowrlant."

"It's good," I said. "Very good. But I probably shouldn't have this. The medications I take put me at risk for liver damage."

Meuhlnir scoffed. "Don't worry about such things. Sif is a healer."

It was home brewed, but didn't smell like a high alcohol content. I shrugged and gave in to the aroma and wonderful taste lingering on my tongue.

"Now," said Meuhlnir, "tell me about the woman."

"Like I said, because of the fight in the street, we knew the make and model of their car. DMV records gave us their names and address, but other than the battery from the street fight, we couldn't charge Hatton with anything, and we had nothing we could charge Tutor with. So, we went to see Tutor. The idea was to get her to tell us something we could use to get a search warrant, which we hoped would give us some evidence that would tie them to the murder of Aten Kennedy for a start."

"It didn't work out that way, I take it?" asked Meuhlnir.

"No, it didn't. Jax and I got in the car and drove."

TWELVE

After talking to Gruber and getting things started on Jax's cruiser, we piled into mine and headed toward the address the DMV had for Elizabeth Tutor.

Neither of us had much to say, and when his phone buzzed at him, Jax jumped a bit. He grunted at the screen and clicked away like a teenager. His phone buzzed at him in rapid succession, and he just stared at it for a moment before sliding the phone into his breast pocket.

"Text from the missus?" I asked.

"Yeah."

Jax was tight-lipped about his personal life, and normally I wouldn't press him, but something in his demeanor told me he wanted to be pressed in this instance. "Okay. Is she doing okay?"

"You could say that, boss." His tone was bright, and when I glanced over at him, his face was blazing with happiness.

"Well, don't just sit there, man. Spill."

Jax chuckled. "We are finally pregnant. She just got home from the doctor, and everything looks good."

I knew they had been trying for a while, and I knew the only other success had ended in a miscarriage. "That's great news!"

"She still has to take it real easy, given the... Well, you know."

I nodded. "It's your job to make that easy for her."

"I was just telling her to quit her job."

I looked at him sideways and arched an eyebrow at him. "You told her to do that, did you?"

He grinned and glanced at me with a sheepish expression. "Yep. She was just correcting my misconceptions about our relationship."

I laughed. "Yeah, the sooner you get with the program, the better it will be for you. Happy wife, happy life. Just memorize that."

"She's still going to quit that job. I just have to figure out how to make it her idea."

"Now you're catching on. By the way, if you tell Jane I said any of this, I will have to kill you. It will have to be quick, though, because she will be coming for me with an axe or something."

He sat there, grinning, with a kind of shell-shocked expression on his face.

"Congratulations to both of you. Oh, and you'd better make sure your wife hears about them this time."

"Ten-four, boss. I'm so happy I could split down the middle." His sunny smile clouded over a tad bit. "At the same time, I'm a little scared."

"Understandable," I said. "Kids change everything."

"So people tell me. We've been trying for a while now, though, and I don't want Aud to go through what she had to last time." His smile disappeared altogether. "I don't want to go through that either," he murmured and stared at his hands in his lap.

"I can't even imagine," I said. "But no more of that thinking. Positive thoughts from here on, Jaxon."

He nodded without looking up.

"It *is* scary to try to bring a child into the world. There is so much hope and anticipation."

Jax nodded. "Yeah, we are trying not to get our hopes up, just in case."

"That's probably smart, but at the same time, you both should try to enjoy this. Jane and I had a lot of fun—there was so much material to tease her about. And vice versa.

"After Sig was born, and they both were still in the hospital, I went shopping for bottles and diapers and stuff. I told Jane we were all set, that I'd taken care of it.

"Who knew you needed more than twelve diapers and six big bottles." I laughed. "Who even knew there was such a thing as a small bottle or a medium bottle. They never have those in the movies."

Jax chuckled.

"I thought I was over-buying to make sure we had enough. Six," I said with a laugh. "Can you even imagine the look Jane gave me?"

Jax looked up, and his smile was back, which was what I wanted after all.

"Anyway, I ended up back at the store every day for the next week, buying more bottles. It didn't help that the store only put four or five bottles out at a time."

"Yeah, I'm glad you told me that story. I've got to leave myself a note."

"Boy howdy."

"Boy howdy?" he laughed. "Where do you get this stuff."

I arched an eyebrow at him and put a lofty lilt in my voice. "I grew up in a diversified environment, Mr. Local-yokel."

He smirked in my direction. "You 'might could' say that. You grew up in Redneckville, and you know it."

"Pshhh!" I said. "You wouldn't know a redneck if the sun burned him right in front of you. Anyway, quit distracting me with your orneriness." We were driving north on County Road 37—which was long and straight and boring. "Keep an eye out for two barns built close together in an L-shape on the left. The house we want is across the street."

"You mean like those two barns coming up?"

I squinted and could make out a blob of red but nothing more. "Damn whipper-snapper," I said. "Quit lording your youthful eyesight over me."

"Someone has to keep your ego in check."

"That's exactly what Jane says."

Jax grinned. "Well, great minds and all that."

We approached a sea-foam-green house sitting across the road from the two barns. A pristine white picket fence surrounded a lot with old-growth yellow birch trees mixed with red maples. There were two breaks in the white picket fence, each servicing one leg of a crescent shaped driveway. I pulled the cruiser into the drive and turned off the engine. The yard was well-maintained with nice flower beds up near the house and more trees out back.

"How should we handle this?"

I shook my head. "We don't know anything. Polite and friendly."

Jax nodded and opened his door. I got out and looked at the house itself. It was a two-story colonial with a full veranda on the front side. The paint looked recent. The sea-foam-green was set off nicely by black shutters and white trim. The front door was painted black and had a brass handle and knocker.

I came around the car and headed up the walk toward the door.

Jax came up short, a strange expression crossing his face. "I've got a weird feeling, boss."

I stopped and turned toward him. "What kind of feeling," I asked in low tones.

"I dunno. Like we are being watched, maybe."

I nodded and turned back toward the door. "Probably are."

"Like we are being watched by a bear or something," Jax murmured. "Just be careful."

That's another "great minds" sentiment, I thought and nodded. "That's how I felt in the cave back there."

As I climbed the four steps to the veranda, the front door slammed open. A skinny blonde woman came out and pointed at us. "What do you want?" she demanded. She was wearing tight fitting jeans and a gray bolero jacket over a black T-shirt. Her cheeks glowed with high color, and her faded denim eyes were snapping with anger.

"Hello, I'm Hank Jensen with the State Pol—"

Her face wrinkled up like a little kid's right before a temper tantrum. "I didn't ask for your names, moron, I asked what you want."

"So much for polite and friendly," Jax muttered beside me.

"As I was saying," I said. "I'm Senior Investigator Jensen with the State Police. This is my partner, Investigator Ritter. We have a few questions for Elizabeth Tutor." I held out one of my cards. "That you?"

She looked at my card like it was some kind of bug and then waved her hand as if dismissing an errant waiter. Her face maintained the look of pique, but curiosity made a brief appearance before resentment took over again. I had a feeling annoyance was her native expression. "What do you want with her?"

"We are tracking down owners of black 1966 Lincoln Continental convertibles. She is listed with the DMV as having an active registration for one."

Her grimace got stronger as if pique was not enough for this situation and so she had decided on vexation. "And?" Finally, she snatched the card out of my still outstretched hand. She put an unlit cigarette in the corner of her mouth and then crossed her arms under her breasts. It was almost flirty, except for everything else in her demeanor. It was like she couldn't help the flirt.

"I'm afraid the rest of the discussion is only for Ms. Tutor."

"Get off! Get off my steps, you little man," she screeched at me like a cat. Her face was screwed up in a hateful expression.

She'd gone from zero to irate in about a second and a half. I backed down off the steps and took several steps back from them to appease her if possible. "I really only need to speak with Ms. Tutor."

She came off the veranda and down the steps in a blink and raised her finger to point it in my face. I thought for a moment she was going to hit me. Her eyes were brilliant with hatred.

"Just stop it." she snapped. "You know you are speaking to her. I'm not stupid, you know." Her unlit cigarette bounced in the corner of her mouth. "What do you want to ask me? Be quick." She snapped her fingers at me.

No one had ever snapped at me in a situation like this. Everything about her behavior was off somehow. *Wrong.* "We think you may have witnessed an accident a few days ago."

"Impossible," she snapped. "I would know if I had."

She was quite tall, taller than I had thought when she was up on the veranda. She wasn't as tall as me, but I thought she was taller than Jax, who was only two and a half inches shorter. She was very skinny and had an unhealthy air about her. She had wide shoulders, wider than was fashionable for a woman, even one as tall as she. Her eyes were sunken into their sockets as if she were starving.

"Ms. Tutor, do you still own the car in question?"

She sneered at me. "What do your records tell you, cop?"

I shrugged. "Records are only as good as the people keeping them. In this case, they show you do own the car, but also that you are the original owner, even though you don't look more than thirty years old."

"There you have it," she said. Her tone of voice became smooth and confident. "If I were the original owner, I would be forty-two years old if I bought the car the day I was born. Explain that."

"People make mistakes. People also give bad information on purpose from time to time." I knew our best chance was to play nice and lead her where we wanted the conversation to go, but there was something about her, something subliminal, maybe, that made my hackles come up. That little voice I relied on to keep me out of trouble was screaming for me to get gone.

If only I had listened.

She nodded her head with thinly veiled sarcasm. "And I suppose you mean that to be me."

"You said it, not us," muttered Jax. "Is it freaky Friday or what?"

Her eyes snapped over my shoulder and sent daggers of disdain in Jax's direction. "Shut up, buck," she said. "I can only stand to speak with one little man at a time." Her gaze shifted back to me. "To answer your stupid question, no, I don't have the car anymore. It was destroyed in an accident a few years ago."

"Did you report it?" I asked.

"Of course! Of course, you annoying little shit! To the local idiots. Go talk to them!" Spittle flew from her lips as she spoke, but the cigarette only jerked in the corner of her mouth.

"To the Ontario County Sherriff's Department?"

"Yes! Yes, isn't that what I just said? Local. Idiots."

I shook my head. "It seems strange that it would still be registered in your name after being destroyed, even if it happened in the recent past."

She took a short step closer. "I said a *few* years ago. Don't you listen? Can't you even listen, you idiot?" Spittle flew from her lips, but the unlit cigarette seemed to defy the laws of physics and stayed right in the corner of her mouth.

I found myself staring at that cigarette, fascinated by its bobbing and weaving with the flow of her words. "But you're keeping it insured and registered? Even after a few years? That doesn't make sense to me. Can you help me out there?"

She took another short step forward. "Are you calling me a liar?" Her tone of voice changed from hectoring to an icy calm, and I found myself straining to hear her. Somehow, this change in her demeanor was scarier than the wild woman act.

"I'm asking you why you would pay insurance and registration for a car you no longer own. I'm asking you how you maintained the inspection sticker with no car. I'm not asking you if you think we are stupid—that much is obvious. I am asking you if you think anyone will believe this tripe."

"It's true." She seemed almost bored with the conversation, and her eyes began to drift around the yard, looking at the flowers, the cruiser, the trees. "I don't care what you think."

"Ms. Tudor, do you own a pink paisley head scarf?" I asked.

She stared at me for a long, quiet moment and then narrowed her eyes. "I thought you wanted to know about some accident?"

It was my turn to let the silence stretch out—what Jane and Sig called the "Cop Silent Treatment."

She sneered again. "Maybe the question isn't how stupid I think you are, but how stupid you think I am."

"The question still stands, ma'am."

"Do I look like the sort of trollop who would wear pink paisley?" She rolled her eyes.

I sighed. I was coming very close to the end of my patience and the only thing keeping it in check at that moment was the idea that losing my patience was what the woman wanted me to do. "Ms. Tutor, we can clear all this up if you can prove to my satisfaction that you no longer own that car."

"And just how would I do that? How can I prove a negative? What would prove it to you?" Her voice was no longer calm and quiet. It was quickly inching its way back to jeering.

I hooked my thumb over my shoulder. "Consenting to a search of those two barns would be a step in the right direction."

"A step in the right direction," she scoffed. "You cops. Next, you'll be telling me you just want to do a cavity search. That it would be a step in the right direction." Her voice had gone cold and dead again.

Her lability made me want to be far, far away from her. "No, ma'am. No cavity search required. May we have a look?"

Anger exploded across her face. "No! You may not! I want you off my property unless you have a search warrant. No, I want you off my property *even if you do.*" She wasn't quite screaming in my face. Jax came up on the balls of his feet next to me—getting ready to take her down, if necessary.

"If we had one, Ms. Tutor, I would have served you by now. Of that, you can be certain." I tried to make my voice as calm as I could, trying to bring the whole conversation down a notch or two if possible.

"Get off my property this instant. I've wasted too much time on this nonsense as it is." Her voice was calm, but her face was writhing with emotion.

"I hope you realize that I'll just go get a warrant." My voice had gone cold and crisp, and at my side, Jax almost thrummed with tension.

She waved it away as if beneath her notice and spit out of the corner of her mouth that was not strangling a cigarette.

"One last question, Ms. Tutor. Do you know a tall, thin man? Your boyfriend, maybe?"

She snatched the cigarette from the corner of her mouth and balled it up. She threw it as hard as she could toward my cruiser. She looked just like a four-year-old throwing a fit. "Get out of here! I said you should go, and I *want you gone*. GET OUT! GET OUT! GET OUT!" she raved.

"We will go, but we will be back," I said. "That is a promise."

She glared at me and started clenching her hands into fists and then relaxing them. Clench. Relax. Clench. The tendons and ligaments in her hands creaked with each movement.

She snapped up a hand and pointed at me—the tip of her finger wavering in my face. She opened her mouth to say something but then quirked her head to the side and looked at me through slitted eyes for a moment. "Your blood is too thick to just throw away. Be glad. *Thyowst!*" she said with venom. "*Thyowst ath ayleevu!*"

The words hit me like someone had sucker punched me in the stomach and had stolen my air. Jax kept me on my feet, his hands steadying me. I had no idea what the strange collection of sounds was supposed to mean, but whatever it was, it was affecting me somehow.

"That's enough, you crazy bitch," said Jax.

She tilted her head at him, a funny little half-smile on her face. "A baby!" She laughed with evil-spirited delight and then her face turned grim as her eyes narrowed. "*Your* blood is thin, thrall. *Tuyta fyrur thig*! *Owthuur en thoo sihrd kvolp thitt*! You will *never* see that child!"

"I don't believe in your voodoo hoodoo," Jax snapped, "so you can just stow it."

She laughed brightly. "You will believe it soon enough. You will. *Ehk bulva ther.*" She sounded satisfied and upbeat. "I curse you both," she said it like it was an afterthought as if she had already said what needed to be said. She flipped her hair and turned away from us, her manner letting us know we were no longer part of her world at all.

We got back in the car. I still felt hinky, and I'm pretty sure Jax did, too. I also felt nauseated. I started the cruiser and got us the hell out of there. The bad feeling didn't leave either of us, however.

The only positive thing to come out of that encounter was a surety that she was the woman we were looking for. There was no basis for that feeling—people lie to the police all the time, sometimes just because the truth would embarrass them—but the feeling was strong.

"She seems pleasant," I said.

"What was all that mumbo jumbo about?"

"I think she was saying we are not on her Christmas card list this year."

"Whatever it was," said Jax, "it gave me the creeps. I mean, 'I curse you both?' Really?"

"Maybe in her delusion, she's a witch. Maybe in her insane little world, blabetty yadda yaddy *is* a curse."

"Yeah, but in our reality, she's just a bitch."

We both chuckled at that, and the hinky feeling evaporated like morning mist.

Jax cleared his throat. "But how did she know about the baby?"

I shrugged. "You're the right age. Lucky guess?"

"Well, whatever. It's not like she can really curse us, right?" He shrugged. "I wish we had a search warrant. I sure would like to get a look in those barns."

"I'd like to go over that property with a corpse dog, as long as we're wishing wishes."

"I bet it would alert on every square inch of her property. That was one creepy woman."

I grunted. "No doubt. I wonder where her long, tall, and ugly male friend was."

"I'd give odds that he was there, watching us the whole time."

"That hinky feeling you got when we first arrived?"

"Yeah. The barns," said Jax. "I could have sworn we were being watched, but it felt different from the woman somehow. I bet both the man and the car were in the barns. Did you see how she reacted when you asked to search them?"

I nodded. "Is there any way you could buy that Aten Kennedy ran into those two in the street fight and then just happened to meet a serial killer later that night?"

"No way at all, boss."

I gave him a weary nod. "That's all this case needs. A *pair* of psychos instead of just one. We probably need to step up our vigilance a couple of notches."

"Agreed. I don't think you should ever go back there alone."

"Yes," I said. I was modeling scenarios, trying to find one that ended with us getting a search warrant.

"—do you think?" asked Jax.

"I'm sorry, what?"

"I asked if it was time to organize some surveillance on her property. You know, looking for the car and the guy."

"That's a great idea. Can you call Gruber and see what resources we can get?"

"Sure," said Jax.

"Maybe some guys from Troop E who would like some overtime in plain clothes."

"Like Ben?"

I shrugged. "If he wants it, it's fine by me. Ben was always solid as an investigator; he just stopped believing after that Sanchez case fiasco. None of which was his fault, by the way."

"I've never heard it any other way," said Jax. "Ben's good people."

"Amen to that."

I heard Jax start his call to the lieutenant and let my mind wander back to the various scenarios that might lead to a search warrant. The easiest one would be to find someone who knew she still had the car, but she really didn't come across as the type to have a lot of friends. Then again, people tended to react in an atypical manner when speaking with a law enforcement officer. I'd have to ask the surveillance teams to keep a watch for visitors who were treated to the crazy hoodoo priestess routine.

The next best way I could come up with was to tie Tutor to one of the other victims—with or without her giant friend. That could be a hard sell, depending on how closely she could be tied to the victim. We could also try to goad her into a response while under surveillance and then arrest her to get inside. Chances of that seemed small, however. She seemed wily on an instinctive level, despite being a total and complete wackadoodle. Another way would be to determine that someone else owned the property, and get the owner's consent for a search whether Tutor liked it or not. That didn't seem very likely, though. She didn't act like a typical renter when we spoke to her. She seemed...I don't know...somehow autarchical about the property. No, the more I thought about her mien during our encounter I seriously doubted we could get her on that last one.

Jax put his phone away. "Gruber's on it. He said to tell you that you have *laissez faire* on this one. He will rubber stamp whatever we need. Has he done that before?"

"Yeah. It's a measure of how...I don't know...desperate he feels about a case. It's not a good sign."

Jax pulled on his lower lip. It was a habit he had tried to break for a few years now without success. He always said it ruined his poker face. "He also said that they've counted another whack of bodies. And that there's no end in sight."

"Tell me how much a whack is again?"

Jax grinned. "Well, it's less than a metric ass load. Gruber said, 'upwards of several hundred,' whatever that means."

"It means our killer just passed the known victim count for the Columbian Beast."

To that, Jax only shook his head. "And more to come, I bet," he muttered.

THIRTEEN

"**A**re you certain those sounds are what she used?"

"It was all gobblety-gook to me, Meuhlnir. Why?"

He sighed. "It sounds like *Gamla Toonkumowl* to me. Is '*thyowst ath ayleevu*' what she said to you?"

I shrugged. "Sounds about right. What does it mean?"

"Suffer forever. To your friend, she said: '*dauda fyrur thig*' and '*owthur en thoo sihrd kvolp thitt*,' right?"

"Sure," I said with another shrug.

"Those phrases mean: 'death for you' and 'before you see your whelp.'"

"She was a treat."

"The last phrase was probably *'ehk bulva ther'* which just means 'I curse you' and it's clear she meant the both of you. Did your partner die?"

I nodded, not trusting myself to speak.

"Before his child was born?"

"Yeah. No one saw the child born. His wife took her own life the night after Jax died."

Meuhlnir looked away, shaking his head. "So much to pay for," he muttered.

"That interview was the biggest mistake I've ever made." I took a large gulp of the mead. "That one meeting with Tutor led to so much death. It led to their escape."

"Go on with the story, Hank."

I wriggled deeper into the chair, luxuriating in the warm comfort of a seat by the fire. "I spoke with Hatton for the first time that night."

FOURTEEN

I fumbled with my ringing cell phone, trying to keep one eye on the traffic while hitting the accept button instead of cancel. "Jensen," I said.

"Hello, Detective Jensen. My name is Chris Hatton."

I had been thinking pleasant, expectant thoughts about an evening at home with Jane and Sig, but those thoughts disappeared as soon as I heard his name. "Mr. Hatton?"

"Oh, I don't stick on formality, Detective. It's just Chris." His voice was a pleasant baritone and had a slight trace of an accent that I couldn't quite place. His accent had a lilting quality to it that sounded out of place in American English. He reminded me of one of those high-priced Scandinavian actors, like Peter Stormare or Stellan Skarsgård.

"Okay. What can I do for you, Chris? You know I've been looking for you, right?"

"Indeed, and I hope you don't mind me calling. I got your name from my on-again, off-again girlfriend. You met her earlier today, so I've no doubt you understand the on-again, off-again part."

"Are you calling for Ms. Tutor?"

"No, not really. I hate these damn cell phones, though. I'd like to meet you somewhere and talk face-to-face."

I hesitated, pretty sure that I was talking to the person who'd lurked in the darkness of the cave, watching me. Something about the guy was just off.

"I'm not dangerous," he said. "I have some information about Liz that might be helpful in eliminating her from your investigation."

"What do you think I'm investigating her for? What kind of information?"

He cleared his throat. "It's... Well, the nature of the information is private. It's medical. I don't want to discuss it on the phone. Couldn't we meet somewhere? A diner? A coffee bar?"

"I'll be honest with you, Mr. Hatton—"

"Chris, please."

"—I'm on my way home. We could meet tomorrow at the Trooper substation in Penfield. Would that be convenient?" There was something about the conversation that had my Cop Radar pinging away in the background. It was all too coincidental. The timing of the call seemed…too good to be true.

The line was silent for a moment, and then it crackled as if Hatton was moving the phone around. "If this doesn't interest you, that's fine. You'll find everything out in due course. I thought I'd save you a bit of leg work is all."

"Tomorrow—"

"No. Tomorrow is out of the question." There was a note of finality in his voice.

"Okay, okay," I said, suppressing a sigh. "As luck would have it, I'm about two minutes away from Jay's Diner in Henrietta. Would that work for you?"

"What a coincidence. I'm just down the road from there."

I'll bet it's a coincidence, I thought.

"I can meet you there in five or ten minutes if it suits."

Again, I found myself listening to the sing-song lilt of his buried accent and trying to place it. "That's fine. I'm in plain clothes, but have short-cropped hair—"

"It will be easier for you to recognize me. I'm six foot nine, so I'll probably be the tallest man there."

I thought about the street fight, Cop Radar being drowned out by alarm bells.

"I know what you are thinking, Detective. Liz told me about your visit, and I know this is about that inane little argument with those two boys. I have a feeling the version you got from them has been…embellished."

I could hear him breathing easily on the other end of the call, even as my own breathing accelerated. "There are a few questions I would like to ask you about all that. Given that everything is out in the open, I'd like to suggest, again, that we meet at the Trooper substation. It's in the same building as the library on Baird Road if you are familiar with the Penfield area."

The line hummed as Hatton hesitated. When he spoke next, his voice was cold and distant—angry. "That does not suit. I would not be comfortable there, and I would feel I had to bring representation. No, that just continues to escalate this very minor incident further out of proportion."

"Minor incident? You put those two men in the hospital, Mr. Hatton."

"It's Chris, Detective. Just Chris. Let's just meet at the diner, as planned, where I will be most comfortable."

I shook my head. "I can assure you that if you did nothing illegal, the substation will be just as comfortable as any diner."

"I said no," he snapped. "And I didn't put anyone in the hospital. Why, I never even got out of the car. We just exchanged philosophies about driving etiquette. Nothing more." He sighed into the phone's microphone, sounding like he was in a wind storm. "Now, do you want to hear the tale or should I just drive on?"

I grunted. The way he spoke was so strange, beyond the accent. There was something that felt put-on about his diction, his careful word choice. "If you only knew how often I've heard things like that—"

"Yes, yes. I know you hear a constant stream of lies in your profession, but I'm willing to bet you've developed a pretty sophisticated instinct for recognizing untruth. Am I lying to you now or not?"

"It doesn't work over the phone," I said in clipped tones.

"I understand that, Detective, that's why I suggested we meet in person," he said as if speaking to a recalcitrant child. "Meet or not?"

I let the silence spin out between us. I thought about all the promises I'd made to Jane to be careful—extra careful—on this case. The whole conversation was hinky, but Jay's was a public place, and I was armed, after all. Coupled with my strength and size, I felt confident that if it came to a fight, I'd be in control. It's one thing to outclass a couple of young men in a street fight, but it's quite another to face a trained police officer who was a powerlifter on the side.

"Please remember, Henry—"

"Hank," I said. *What the hell, in for a penny and all that.*

"Please remember, Hank, I called you. I didn't have to do this. I am coming forward to help you eliminate us and to explain Liz's outlandish behavior."

I pulled into the parking lot of the diner and sighed. "Yeah. I'm there now."

"Fine, fine," said Hatton. "Five or ten minutes."

"That will be—" I stopped talking when I realized he'd hung up on me.

I went inside and sat in the last booth against the wall. I had a clear view of the entrance and the door to the kitchen at the same time.

He was right, he was easy to recognize. When he ducked through the front door, I knew it had to be him. He was wearing black jeans, black cowboy boots, and a black T-shirt with what looked like Norse runes splashed playfully across the front in dark gray screen print.

He looked taller than six nine, but then again, he was incredibly thin. He looked like he was in his last few weeks of life, with one foot already in the void. At the same time, his frame was wide and large, what my mother used to call "big-boned." His bones looked like they were pressed against his skin from the inside without the benefit of fat or tissue to soften the look. His skin had an ashy, unhealthy look, and his eyes were sunken into their orbits.

He scanned the room slowly, and when his eyes met mine, a flicker of recognition danced in his eyes. He walked gracefully across the diner with a small smile playing across his lips. He moved like a predatory cat or wolf, all grace and power. His eyes were fierce and sharp, but at the same time, friendly.

I didn't stand as he approached. I had the Glock in my lap under the table and had my right hand resting on it.

He slid into the booth with a soft grunt. His eyes danced with humor. "Booths are not a tall person's friend. But then you probably know that." He held his hand across the table.

I stared at his hand for a moment and then shook it. I could shoot with either hand, after all. My hand looked childlike in his grip.

Again, he flashed a disarming smile at me and then lowered his hand to the table.

I put my hand back on top of the Glock, my eyes scanning across his gaunt frame.

"I just finished a round of chemotherapy," he said. "It can be brutal."

"I hope it was successful."

He nodded. "It was, but I didn't ask you to meet me to lament about my health. I know you'd rather be at home with your family."

"Yes," I said. "How long have you known Ms. Tutor?"

He chuckled at the question. "Oh, it feels like eons some days. Other days, it feels like I just met her. She's… Well, I can't describe what she is to me. I'm not sure I know."

"Do we ever?"

Again, he chuckled. "No, I suppose not." He glanced over his shoulder at the rank of newspaper machines and the headlines screaming about the Bristol Butcher. "This isn't really about those boys, is it? This is about that mess."

"I'm here to listen to *you* explain things, not the other way around."

He grinned and nodded. "Very well, Hank." He sucked a deep breath in through his nose, his nostrils flaring like a dog searching for a scent, and then let the breath out in a rush. "Liz has changed over the years. I'm not sure I could still call her sane, whatever that means." His eyes had wandered around the room as he spoke, but by the last word, they were again locked on mine.

I made that rolling, go-on gesture with the fingers of my left hand.

His eyes roved across my upper body, and he seemed to find my tense posture amusing. "She has these… I don't know what to call them. Fits, I guess. She grows angry at nothing. She becomes acerbic—almost vicious. Her mood goes foul, and once it does, it stays that way for days or even weeks on end. Nothing I do—nothing anyone does—seems to be able to bring her out of these moods.

"I'm afraid she gets quite paranoid, and she views any visitor as a threat." He shrugged and looked down at the table. "Many of her friends have tried, but she refuses to be helped." His voice was mournful, resigned.

"Doctors? Has she been evaluated?"

"Oh, no," he said, looking aghast. "Doctors are all out to get her, you see. They want to force her to drink 'root juice' that will sap her will and make her into their puppet." The tall man sighed and shook his head, sadness all but dripping from his eyes. "She has told me this many times over the past few years. I am at a loss for what to do, to be honest."

"There are ways to force the issue," I said. "We can commit—"

"Hank, you've met her. Do you think a forced commitment will be of any use?" he snapped. "At any rate, she's not dangerous. She is averse to human contact of any kind. The root juice can be applied to the skin, you see.

"The most she ever does is pretend to curse people."

"But her quality of life would be better if she were treated."

"Absolutely not. A forced commitment would just make matters worse, especially for me."

The picture he was painting was clear and believable. I'd seen similar things in the past. But still...

"What did you need to know from her? She was in such a state by the time I arrived... Well, I couldn't get much sense from her."

I thought about her screaming that gibberish at us earlier in the day. "Unfortunately, it seemed the more we asked questions, the longer we stayed, the worse she got. By the end, she was jabbering nonsense words at us. The curse."

He made a noise that sounded like half-grunt and half-laugh. "Yes. She was furiously washing her driveway when I arrived. With a mop and bleach. She kept saying something about getting the dust of your shoes off her property."

"Like in the book of Matthew," I said.

His face froze for a moment, and the muscles across his chest and shoulders tensed. Then seemed to relax. "Oh. The Bible, right?"

I nodded.

He laughed and made a strange, pushing down gesture with his hands. "I'm not a religious man."

I was not a religious man, either, but his reaction struck me as extremely strange. Anyone growing up in the modern world couldn't help gaining some peripheral knowledge of the major religions. I believed that any American would recognize any of the first few books of the New Testament as something from the Bible without having to think about it. "There is a passage in the book of Matthew that says something about shaking the dust of your shoes off when you leave somewhere that doesn't welcome you. But to be honest, it should have been my partner and I doing the shaking off of dust. She made it quite clear we were not welcome."

He made that grunting-laugh sound again. "It does sound like something you and your partner should have done after your visit with Liz. Don't take it to heart, though, sometimes she treats even me that way. You don't want to know how many times I've been cursed." He shrugged. "It's just part of her new reality, I guess."

He looked around the diner again, like he was looking for someone. "Where's that partner of yours?" he asked with a wink.

"I didn't feel the need to call him."

He glanced at where my right hand lay on top of the pistol as if he could see through the table top. "Evidently." His voice was sardonic, but he made a placating gesture with his left hand. "You needn't worry in any case. You are safe with me tonight."

I tilted my head to the side and looked at him for a drawn-out moment. It was a strange turn of a phrase, and it wasn't very reassuring. "Back to Ms.

Tutor. We were there to ask her if she still owned the 1965 Lincoln Continental that is registered in her name."

Hatton made a little disparaging noise. "That was dishonest of you, Hank. We both know it is a 1966. Black with white leather interior. I love that car." He folded his hands together on the table in front of us. "I am here to be honest, Hank. You don't need to test me like that."

I shrugged.

Hatton sighed with a little grin dancing on his face as if he realized I was never going to stop testing him until I ruled him out or saw him convicted of murder. "At any rate, she is still the registered owner of the car in question, but in truth, it is my car. I leave it in her name because I want her to have it when I pass." He looked at me with a frank, earnest expression. "I am not a well man, as I think you can see. I am not well enough to put two young men in the hospital in some street fight. The idea is simply ludicrous."

"Not even if the men in question called Ms. Tutor a bitch and a whore?"

He shrugged with what seemed like a practiced nonchalance, but there was something in his eye that sent chills down my spine. "You've met her, Hank. She can be a royal bitch when she's in one of her moods. And on that day, she was in one doozy of a mood. She cussed that young man—the driver, I mean—up one side, down the other, and then back and forth a few times. She said some ugly things to him. Racially insensitive things, to be honest, and I was growing as cross with her as the young men were. I've been dealing with problems her mouth creates for years now. That argument was just another in a long line of arguments she starts and expects me to finish for her." He sighed with an exaggerated bitterness that struck me as false.

"Let's talk about how you 'finished' that particular argument."

He smirked as if to say he knew every trick about interrogations I did. "I must say that my temper got the best of me. I wasn't feeling at all well, and that tends to make me into a bear. I was angry mostly due to my irritation with Liz, but also in part because of how the boy reacted. He spat on her." He looked at me in disbelief. "He *spat* on her."

"Go on," I said in a quiet voice.

"Well, we had a few words, it must be said. The boy challenged me to get out and fight with him, which was ridiculous, and not just because I'm so sick; we were waiting at a red light in the middle of traffic. His brother seemed to get quite cross with him and got out on his side of their little shitbox car and began to yell and curse at the one who had challenged me to brawl.

"Before we knew what was happening, the first one seemed to snap, and he leapt across the hood of his car and started punching his brother. Needless to say, we were completely confounded by such behavior, and I drove away as soon as it was safe to do so."

"You never so much as touched either man?" I didn't believe Hatton for a second—if I put the surviving brother and Hatton side by side, it couldn't be any clearer who was credible and who wasn't.

"No, I assure you, I did not. As I said, I didn't even get out of the car, and the boy never came to my side at all. The closest he got was when he spat on Liz.

"Oh, I've just remembered something. There was a witness—some old Yankee in a tiny little Chevy from the late seventies or early eighties. I misremember the name of the model, but it doesn't matter because I've got something better—his license plate number. You can find the old Yankee who saw it all, and he will reinforce everything I've said tonight."

"Why would you write down his license plate number?"

"I believed those two boys were going to do just what they did—concoct some story making Liz and me to blame for their actions. Probably some attempt to extort money from us."

That was bullshit, but it would be easy enough to check out. With a small shrug, I dug my leather-bound pad out of my back pocket. "What's the number?"

"I wrote it down on an old receipt. I seem to have left it in the Lincoln, but luckily, I drove the car tonight." He leaned back in the booth, head held away from me at an extreme angle. Again, he tilted his head and squinted his eyes at me. "Say! You could see the car if you came out with me."

I looked up at the dirty ceiling tiles, considering. He might just want to get me out away from people, but then again, why come here at all if his intention was malignant? Why not just waylay me on the road? He had to know we thought Tutor was suspect, and he had to know that bad behavior on his part during our meeting would only make our suspicions stronger.

"It's perfectly safe," he said. "I can even stay inside if you like." He glanced at my hand, still under the table, still holding my pistol, and grinned. "Besides, you are the one with a weapon, are you not?"

I inclined my head.

"As you should be, Trooper." He winked and looked smug.

We sat looking at each other with yet another silence ticking away between us. He pulled a set of keys out of his pocket and slid them across the table to my left hand. "Have a look," he said. "I'll sit right here. Promise."

I took the keys with my left hand and slid my pistol into the holster on my belt. "I think I will." I gave him my most intimidating cop look. "You stay here while I do."

"Knock yourself out," said Hatton with a small grin.

The air outside was brisk, and darkness had fallen while we spoke. I got the long-barreled flashlight out of my car. His Lincoln was parked in the back of the lot, behind the open kitchen door. Light spilled out through the doorway and cast long shadows through the lot.

The black canvas convertible top was up, and I pointed the flashlight through the driver's side window. I recognized two things immediately, the car was unlocked, which I thought was strange for such a valuable car, and the interior was immaculate as if it had been recently detailed.

I opened the driver's side rear door and played my light across the white leather back seat. I didn't expect to find anything so simple as a greasy shoe print that was Aten Kennedy's size, but I thought maybe there would be a scuff in the leather—anything to disprove Hatton's version of the tale. I walked around the car, looking for dents or scars in the surface that might indicate Hatton had smashed someone's head against the car.

Of course, there was nothing visible, and I doubted daylight would expose anything earth shattering either. If things had gone the way Marcus had said, and the car was marked up, Hatton would not have come to me.

I slid into the car on the passenger side. It felt cavernous inside the car, and looking across to the driver's side, it seemed like you would need an intercom to have a conversation if the top was down. The fold-up arm rest was down, creating a separation in the huge bench seat.

I opened the glove box, looking for the receipt Hatton had mentioned, but it was empty—not even an insurance card was inside. I made a disgusted noise and slapped the glove box closed.

"I lied about the receipt," said Hatton.

With my heart pounding, I peered through the windshield, into the shadows cloaking the farthest extent of the parking lot where it sounded like the voice had come from. I couldn't see a thing.

"Why would you lie about something like that?"

I heard the scrape of a leather sole on asphalt, now sounding like it came from behind the car to the left. "If I'm honest, and I almost always am, I was hoping to get to speak to you without all that hubbub inside the diner." His voice sounded like Jax.

I got out of the car and pointed my flashlight at where I thought that scraping sound had come from, but there was nothing there—not even a scuff mark. "And what do you have to say that you couldn't say inside?" I should have felt uneasy to be out here alone with a man who was still the best suspect I had, but I didn't. I felt irritated and a little hostile—another two nails in my coffin as far as my wife was concerned.

"This case... This 'Bristol Butcher' thing. Neither Liz nor I have any part in it, but I know you think we do. I'd like to be left out of the rest of the investigation." This time, his voice seemed to come from the darkness in front of the car, but a bit to the left. It no longer sounded like Jax.

"For that to happen, I have to clear you of any involvement. You need to be honest with me about everything. No more silly little games to get me into the parking lot alone, as if I'm your prom date or something."

He chuckled. It was more like a suppressed cackle than a quiet laugh. "Point taken. The thing is, I don't want to explain anything else or have you poking any further into my life or Liz's. I hope you can understand that. I'm not in the mood for this, and Liz is above such things. I think it would be best for you to simply move on to finding the real killer."

I held my hands up, palms pointed at the starry sky and shrugged like a kid in the principal's office. "As I said, I have to rule you out. I just can't take your word for it and move on. If you were the victim of a crime, you'd pitch a fit if I did that on your investigation."

"Come now, Detective. You ignore possibilities all the time."

The voice sounded like it was right behind me—like he'd spoken in my ear. I whirled around, my hand going to my pistol, but the lot behind me was empty all the way to the kitchen door.

Hatton chuckled from somewhere off in the darkness.

My irritation at being startled grew into a certified annoyance at this arrogant fool. "I follow the best evidence I have. Right now, that evidence points to you and your friend Liz. Your dumb little parlor tricks are not helping you, either."

Hatton stepped forward out of the shadows ten feet from where I was standing. He looked at me with a raw intensity that was unsettling. "You think I'm being rude, do you?" His hands were in his pockets.

I sighed and shook my head in exasperation. "You don't think this farce is rude?"

He laughed, long and loud. It was a very unsettling noise—like fingernails grating across sandpaper, or two cats fighting outside your window at night. "No, you misunderstand me. Of course, it is rude to drag you out here to listen to a pack of lies. At the same time, you think I'm a serial killer capable of prolific acts of violence, yet what concerns you is my rudeness."

"And that is funny?" I asked, my face growing hot in my rising anger at this pedantic giant of a man.

"No, no. You think I'm a serial killer; that is what amuses me. What kind of *evidence* can you possibly have that points to a man as sick as I am? A man so sick from the chemo drugs that he weighs approximately the same as a ten-year-old girl." A smile was on his lips, but his eyes seemed anything but amused.

"We found DNA on Aten Kennedy. I believe it's your DNA." I was lying, of course, something that sometimes helps spur an investigation along, but that isn't what I was doing. I just wanted to crush his smug tone of voice. "We know all about you. The cave. The car." I waved my hand at his Lincoln.

Again, he laughed, his loud, abrasive cackles ringing across the parking lot. "You are *funny*, Hank. I didn't expect that." He smiled to himself and nodded his head. "Surprising," he muttered.

His manner grew grave. "You don't have DNA. You didn't even know my name until I called you. You don't know anything about me. If you did, you wouldn't have taken this meeting." His voice sounded vicious as he uttered the last sentence.

"Is that a threat?"

"I don't threaten," he snapped. "I'm not a talker. I *do*, Hank. I do."

I thought I heard real emotion in his voice for the first time. "I know more about you than you think, and I'm learning more and more as we continue to chat."

He looked at me with a strange expression on his face, his head tilted a little to the side. Maybe it was eagerness and greed, or maybe it was simple lust. His eyes glinted with humor. "I'll bite," he said with a malicious little smile playing across his lips, and the skin on his nose all wrinkled up like the skin across the snout of a snarling dog. He paused, letting the moment draw out. When I didn't react, his smile faded, and he went on. "What do you know about me? What are you learning?"

"You can make light of this if you like, but it's true." I tried not to sound a bit unnerved by his strange behavior.

Hatton spread his arms with his palms up. "Enlighten me, please. One is never too old to learn." His eyes twinkled with what looked like genuine amusement. "You're a tough guy, aren't you?"

"Whoever is using the cave the papers talk about is a cannibal."

Hatton's pleasant expression faded. "Do go on."

"Hit a nerve, did I?"

Hatton waved his hand at me as if he were tossing something into the weeds. He looked annoyed, his smile fading altogether. He seemed irritated with the turn of the conversation, but not enough to outweigh his curiosity.

"What the papers don't say is that the cave was used by multiple killers. There are too many bodies for one man to be responsible. The timeline is unbelievable."

"Oh really?" The tension melted out of Hatton's bearing. Until it was absent, I hadn't realized that he'd been wound up tight, ready to spring. His annoying, smug smile surfaced again on his face but again didn't extend all the way to his eyes. "I was right before. You know nothing."

Something inside me wanted to wipe that smile off his face again. "I do know one thing for certain." I took a small amount of pleasure in seeing his arrogant expression falter again.

"I'll bite," he said again. This time, his smile turned nasty.

"I know I'll be on you like the hair on your back. I'll be in your life up to my eyeballs until I either get enough to arrest and convict you, or I can rule you out and be done with you forever."

He sneered at me, and *that* expression did reach his eyes. "I had such high hopes for this meeting, too." His voice was laced with sarcasm. "And tell me, Hank, if I were the man you want, why would I not just leave the area now before you get enough so-called evidence to convict me?"

"Because that would be an admission of guilt. Once I had that knowledge, I would be on you like a tick on a dog. I would follow you and catch you." I looked at him with an intensity equal to his. "And plus, it would be an admission that I'm right. You can't admit that. Your ego won't let you."

"So, you are going to follow the killer wherever he may lead? Are you prepared for what that might require?" His tone of voice was nasty, all pretense of politeness gone.

"I can assure you, I will do what I say," I said, feeling full of bluster and as obvious as a lying twelve-year-old.

"You would leave your job? Your pretty little wife? Your child? Your possessions? Everything that defines your petty life?" He scoffed. "I don't think so."

I just stared at him, wondering what had possessed me to meet with this man in the first place.

A smug little smile bloomed on his face. "I didn't think so."

"Let me tell you something, Hatton."

He made a prissy little gesture, which I took as permission to go on.

"My petty life, as you call it, is defined by investigating smug assholes like you. People who, like you, think they are too smart to get caught. I've made it my business to be the guy that can and does finish the chases that no one else can. You and people like you are my area of expertise.

"I've chased down serial killers before. If you are a killer, you go ahead and run. Every time you look over your shoulder, it's my face you will see. I'll have handcuffs and an order of extradition in my coat pocket. Or stay here and pretend I don't know anything. It will all amount to the same thing."

Hatton's expression grew somber. "I appreciate your honesty, Hank, and feel I should reciprocate." He closed the rear door on the driver's side and slid behind the wheel. "You are making a grave error in your reasoning."

I walked around to the driver's side of the car, standing next to the rear door on that side. "Educate me," I said. It wasn't lost on me that he'd flipped back to the polite persona. I was willing to bet that when Hatton moved, it would be from a place of cold reasoning, rather than anger or rage.

He pulled something out of his pocket, and I tensed, my hand moving to the butt of my pistol. He chuckled. "I told you, Hank. You are perfectly safe from me tonight," he said. He held up another set of car keys and jingled them. He then slipped one of them into the ignition, and I relaxed. "You assume all so-called serial killers think alike. More to the point, you assume they all run to a place where you can, with a letter from your lieutenant, be in a position of authority. What happens when someone runs to a place where there is no extradition? What happens when you follow someone to a place where they are the authority, and you are the one who will be hunted?"

I grunted. "I suppose the same thing that will happen when I follow someone to Lilliput."

Hatton looked at me without recognition.

"Jonathan Swift. *Gulliver's Travels*, just another fictional place from someone's imagination."

Hatton laughed. "I like you, Hank. You remind me of someone I had a lot of fun palling around with many years ago. His name was Jon Black. Jon Calvin Black."

I shrugged. The name seemed familiar for some reason, but for the life of me, I couldn't place it.

Hatton shook his head, looking sad. "You people have no sense of family. No sense of the past." He perked up and put his hands on the steering wheel.

"But perhaps, in the future, we will be friends, too," he said and then started the car. He turned and looked at me like a mongoose looking at a snake. "There is just one more thing I want to tell you."

"I'm still here; I'm still listening." I wasn't really listening though. I was playing the conversation back in my mind, trying to find something he said that would give me grounds to slap the cuffs on him and put him in a cell—even if it was only for one night. But he had said nothing actionable; he had only made implications and innuendoes.

He ducked his chin to his shoulder and then nodded like a coquettish school girl. He put the car into drive, his foot on the brake splashing red light across the parking lot. "I was with you that night in my abattoir. Your instincts for the hunt are quite invigorating."

As the words rang in my ears, I seemed to be trapped in a world defined by slow motion, but he'd made a mistake. Finally, I had him. My hand was still on the butt of my pistol, and I was trying to draw it, but it seemed like I was mired in an invisible viscous fluid. It was like one of those dreams where you can't get away, can't move fast enough to avoid the Bad Thing, except this was real, and the Bad Thing was about to get away.

Hatton was leering at me over his shoulder as the car started to pull away from me at idle. "Chase me!" he yelled. He took his foot off the brake and gunned the engine. The big Lincoln roared toward the back of the parking lot, tires shrieking, both front doors slammed shut by its momentum. "Catch me if you can, Hank!"

My gun was free of the holster at last and was rising into firing position. My other hand snapped forward to support my shooting hand. "Stop!" I yelled. "Hatton, stop!"

I could hear him cackling over the roaring engine. The car slewed around in a large, sloppy half circle until it was facing me—and the only exit of the parking lot. I could see Hatton's eyes glinting through the windscreen. A huge predatory grin was plastered on his face.

My pistol was halfway between my hip and the place I was most comfortable shooting from. I was a point-shooter, relying on muscle memory to put the bullets where I wanted them instead of using the gun's sights to aim. I was good at it. I didn't need time to aim, so I was fast on the trigger.

The car roared at me, head lights still off, and its tires shrieking like demons.

As I was about to pull the trigger, Hatton waved and swerved the big car off line, pointing the nose so he would miss me by a car length. Despite the relief that washed through me, I was angry and disappointed, because as Hatton probably knew, with the direct threat to my life alleviated, I couldn't risk a shot at the car with an unknown backdrop like the shadowy rear parking lot and whatever lay beyond the weeds and shadows.

"Stop, Hatton! You are under arrest!" I yelled, knowing it was senseless but unable to just stand there and watch him drive away.

He waved again, extending his arm out the window and flapping his hand around and then blipped the Lincoln's horn. He roared by, and time seemed to catch up to me. I spun on the balls of my feet and sprinted after the car.

The car roared through the front parking lot, tires screaming as he slid from the lot out onto West Henrietta Road. I ran toward the street and then changed my mind and cut toward my cruiser, ignoring the sickening pain that shot through my knees as I did so. I put my gun away and ripped the door open. I jumped in and cranked the engine, snapping on the siren and lights. As soon as it caught, I slammed the car into a sliding J-turn, sliding until the front of the car pointed at the road. I raced south on West Henrietta, straining my eyes to catch a glimpse of that big black Lincoln's tail lights.

I had lost him, though, and took my foot off the gas. I turned off the emergency lights and siren and radioed in to put out an APB I spent an hour canvassing the streets of Henrietta, but Hatton had gotten away clean.

As I sat in my car, more than a little dejected, I tried to comfort myself with the knowledge that Ben Carson was watching Tutor's house and had no doubt heard the APB. He'd be on the lookout for Hatton, and with any luck, would nab the bastard before morning. I couldn't think of a better man than Ben to be sitting out there on the side of the road in an unmarked car, waiting to snap cuffs on Hatton's bony wrists.

FIFTEEN

"At the time, it didn't dawn on me that he was being so specific about the people I loved. I thought he was just talking. How much I wish I'd realized he was talking about Jane and Sig. I would have pulled my pistol and shot him in the face, consequences be damned. That might have saved Ben Carson's life, but I doubt it. It didn't help when I finally did shoot him." I shrugged.

Meuhlnir was looking at me, one hand to his chin, stroking his beard. "All this talk—"

"Meuhlnir," I said. "I'm sitting here feeling like you know more than you are willing to tell me."

"They've done this before," he said in a quiet voice. "They've brought people from your *klith*, and from other *stathur*—places, or realities if you like— as well."

"Why? What do they want from me?"

Meuhlnir turned to face me, his expression grave. "Ultimately, to destroy you—either by getting you to become a disciple or by breaking you, mind and spirit."

"What happened to the others? Did they become disciples?"

Meuhlnir scowled into the fire.

"Are my neighbors his disciples now?"

Meuhlnir scoffed. "It's doubtful. Most likely they have become the Midnight Queen's courtiers. That Black Bitch collects and twists the hearts of the weak-willed like offal collects flies."

"Tutor is this Midnight Queen?"

"Without doubt," said Meuhlnir with a twist to his mouth. "She allows the *Briethralak Oolfur* to operate with impunity in the land of her exile. She *encourages* such depravity."

"And she is one of these…what did you call it… She's a *vefari*?" I asked.

Meuhlnir nodded, eyes downcast. "Yes. A very powerful one."

"You said 'in the land of her exile.' Where is that?"

Meuhlnir sighed. "Far, far to the north across the Tempest Sea. She was exiled to the island nation of Fankelsi when she was disposed of her empire."

"But she is one woman, how can—"

"Don't be foolish. The Midnight Queen is a woman of vast power and enormous will. She has been behind the rise and fall of nations, peoples, even empires."

"The woman I met was not very old."

Meuhlnir laughed and patted me on the arm. "Looks can be deceiving, Hank. At any rate, that is enough talk about these matters for now. You must be starved and exhausted beyond compare. Are you warm enough yet?"

I leaned back in the chair and nodded. My eyelids felt like they weighed about ten thousand pounds, and it was a struggle not to nod off.

"Are you in a great deal of pain?"

I started to nod, but then it struck me. I had a severe case of muscle aches, but for once, my joints seemed content to let me be. "No," I said, surprised. "I feel okay. Tired, but okay."

"Good," he said, tipping me a wink. He had a twinkle in his eye and wore a knowing smile as he stood up. "Let me invite you to dine in my hall."

"Food sounds great," I said. I didn't know if I could trust him, but what other options were there?

He started to walk away and then came back. He lifted my hand from my lap and put it on the wide arm of the overstuffed chair. "Here is more mead," he said slipping a warm mug into my hand. "In case you are thirsty."

I tried to nod, but lethargy overcame me. I didn't intend to fall asleep. I just wanted to rest a few minutes—quiet time with my eyes closed.

Meuhlnir woke me with a firm squeeze on the shoulder. "Time to eat, Hank," he said. "We've quite a feast laid out before us."

I opened my eyes wide and shook my head, trying to shake off the fatigue that had set on me like a pack of wolves. "How long was I out?"

"Not long," he said. "A few minutes."

I'd slept longer than that. I had that head-stuffed-with-cotton feeling I always got when I napped too long.

He watched me as I pushed myself to my feet. "Much pain?" he asked.

I opened my mouth to say what I always said—"I'm fine"—which was usually a lie. "I still feel fine," I said, surprised. "I'm not even stiff."

Meuhlnir broke into a sunny smile, his wrinkled and cracked face scrunching up with good cheer. "Good. I am pleased."

He led me toward the hall opposite the fireplace. "The great hall is just through here," he said.

We walked in a companionable silence. I was trying to remember the last time I'd felt so normal, and not having much success.

At the end of the short hallway, was a room that looked more like it should be in some Viking long house than the quaint little woodsy cabin. Thick wooden pillars lined the sides of the hall, the space between them obscured with thick blue curtains with a gold brocade pattern. There was a long fire pit down the center of the rectangular room and a fire blazing in it. To each side of the fire pit stood two long tables with benches on either side. The benches were padded with thick animal skins. Opposite the entrance was a dais on which stood a third table, much shorter than the other two but made of the same dark wood. Two straight backed wooden chairs—more like thrones, really—sat between the wall and the table, so that people seated at that table would look out and down at anyone seated at the long tables. The roaring fire lit most of the room, but the light was supplemented by candles burning in large chandeliers made from antlers. Three such chandeliers hung from the rafters over each of the long tables.

Meuhlnir beamed at me as he held out a hand toward the raised dais. "You are an honored guest in my home, Hank. Please sit at my table."

I nodded, not sure what else to do, walked to the table, and pulled back one of the heavy chairs.

"You won't see much of this anymore," said Meuhlnir with a melancholy tone, his left hand sweeping toward the large hall. "Few follow the old ways these days."

"It's majestic," I said.

He grunted. "You should see it when it is full. Women serving full tables; men shouting and laughing; the mead flowing like water." He shook his head. "No matter," he said and clapped his hands.

Two women came into the room from behind one of the curtains on the left. The first carried a large stoneware pitcher balanced on her hip, and two matching mugs in her other hand. The second carried an oblong platter with a large, roasted fowl arrayed in its center. They put the food and drink in the middle of the table in front of us and left the room the same way they came in.

"In the old days, we would have butchered a lamb or an elk, and roasted the meat in the fire below," said Meuhlnir. "Of course, we would have had to feed many more men with huge appetites."

"If it's any consolation, I feel like I could eat an entire elk by myself."

"Good," said Meuhlnir with a chuckle. "Although, I don't think you know the size that elk can grow to on this *klith*. Here, they can be two or two-and-half strides at the shoulder—as tall as you!"

"I don't think you know the size of my hunger," I said with a smile.

Meuhlnir laughed again and took a long pull from his stone mug. The two women were back, each with a platter. One of the platters had bread, honey, and slices of salted fish. The other platter was full of steaming pork. This time the women stood there, looking at Meuhlnir.

"Hank Jensen, meet my two wives. The one on the left is Sif, and the one on the right is Yowrnsaxa."

"Nice to meet you," I said.

They nodded back to me, and Yowrnsaxa tipped me a wink.

He turned a critical eye on the feast before us and grunted. Both women curtsied, and one of them said something that sounded a touch disrespectful in a sing-song tongue. Meuhlnir smiled at them both and then waved them away.

"Rituals," murmured Meuhlnir. He nodded in the direction the women had come from and disappeared back to. "Those two still appreciate the old ways. Then again, they remember a time when the old ways were not old." He reached out and pulled a leg off the roasted fowl. "They are wonderful wives."

It was larger than most of the turkeys I'd seen back home and smelled somewhat gamey. I grabbed the other leg and ripped it off. The meat was succulent and juicy. It tasted a little like a turkey, but was obviously some kind of game bird. "It's delicious," I said. "What kind of bird?"

"Mmm," he said, wiping his mouth on his sleeve. "These are rare these days, but a flock still migrates to the lake you landed on. They are Svart Mollies."

"They are Tasty Mollies, if you ask me," I said.

Meuhlnir chuckled. "Yowrnsaxa and Sif will be pleased to hear that. Try the fish—also from the lake." He grabbed a slice of the salted fish and shoved it whole into his mouth.

We ate in silence for a while. The food was excellent—one of the best meals of my life, and not just because I was practically starving. Somehow, we drained that large pitcher of mead, but I didn't feel the least bit drunk.

After the initial eating frenzy subsided, Meuhlnir glanced at me out of the corner of his eye. "To be honest, I did underestimate the size of your hunger," he said with a teasing smile.

"Most people do," I said. "I have Viking blood, after all."

He laughed and slapped me on the shoulder.

I flinched, expecting the pain to come rolling in. It was a common gesture, but almost any touch to my shoulders and upper back usually brought on a fit of agony. This time, however, it never came. Maybe I was drunker than I felt.

Meuhlnir was looking at me wearing a small smile at the edges of his mouth. "You won't feel those aches and pains while you are in my house," he said as if he could read my mind.

"It's okay," I said. "I'm used to them by now."

"You misunderstood. I mean that you won't feel the Dark Bitch's curse under my roof. I won't allow it."

I put down my mug without taking the drink I had intended to take and turned in my chair so that I faced him.

"What's more," he said, his old, rheumy eyes fierce, "It is possible that I can teach you how to block her curse for a limited time as well."

I didn't know quite what to think but figured I might as well give it a shot. After all, I tried everything the doctors wanted me to try, and none of that worked very well. "There won't be a high bar for success given the things I tried back home."

He nodded. "This *klith* was once like yours. My ancestors believed in science to the exclusion of everything else. They were arrogant and superior, rejecting anything not measurable by their technology. They didn't see the contradiction in that. Their folly almost destroyed this world," he said. "They wanted to know everything. It wasn't enough to see that something worked, they had to know why."

I shrugged. "I'm a simple man. If it works, I'm in."

Meuhlnir laughed. "Even so, your science tells you that you are sick, no? But they can't tell you why you are sick or how to get better?"

I nodded.

He nodded back. "I have told you why you are 'sick.' You've been cursed, and you won't get better until that curse is broken or lifted."

I shrugged again. "There's an expression we use back home. It goes like this: put your money where your mouth is."

"I'm afraid I don't know that one." Meuhlnir scratched his bearded chin.

"Okay, how's this one: the proof is in the pudding."

Meuhlnir looked perplexed. "Why would you store something in pudding? Unless that word doesn't mean what it used to? A kind of sausage?"

I shook my head and chuckled. "Not sausage anymore, it's a sweet dessert. But its use is figurative anyway. I think it came from an older expression. Something like: the proof of the pudding is in the eating of it."

Meuhlnir eyes lit up. He laughed and slapped me on the shoulder again. "We say something similar: Actions, not words, are a testament to any man's mettle."

"Yeah, that's it. To tell you the truth, though, I'm sort of confused by this Queen What's-her-name. Speaking of which, what is her name, anyway?"

Meuhlnir sobered and bunched his eyebrows. "People here don't say her name much. Quite a superstition has grown up around the Dark Queen.

"She was once named Suel. Her empire, which spanned this entire continent and part of the one to the north of the equator, was called Suelhaym—Suel's home."

"I assume, since you said 'once,' that her name has changed?"

Meuhlnir nodded. "Names here can be dangerous. A powerful *vefari* knows when you use their name. Or can know if they want to."

"I see." I looked down at the top of the table. "So," I said, "you know when someone speaks your name?"

"Oh yes. Even when people on your *klith* use it incorrectly."

I looked up, surprised. "People back home use your name? I don't think I've heard it before."

"Yes," he said, looking away. "There was a time in the past when it was considered great sport to...influence the developing peoples on your *klith*. Some of us came to be known by your ancestors." He glanced at me and then looked away again. "It is something most of us came to regret."

"So, you came to my *klith* and influenced 'developing people?' And somehow, because of that, people in my world still use your name?"

"Incorrectly," he said.

"What 'developing people' exist in my world?" I demanded.

"Truly, this is a topic for a different time."

He seemed embarrassed, but it didn't stop me from pressing him. "Meuhlnir...I don't think I've ever heard it."

"They say 'ma-jol-ner.' As I said, it is used incorrectly."

"Mjolnir? Thor's hammer? Are you trying to tell me your people influenced the Vikings?"

He waved his hand out at the feasting hall. He wouldn't meet my eye. "I did not copy the architecture of the Vikings for my feasting hall. They copied ours, just as they adopted our language and changed it to suit themselves."

"But that was over a thousand years ago."

He nodded, still looking at his lap. "A bit longer than that, actually. We thought it was great fun, and who can say if it was detrimental to your world."

"You said 'we.'"

He looked up at me and searched my face. "Yes," he murmured, "my brothers and I, Suel, others." He shrugged.

I shook my head. "You must be quite old, indeed."

"One of the few benefits of our technocratic past."

His skin sagged under his jaw. His hair was white and thin. His fingers were gnarled and had thick joints. "Just how old are you?"

"A man's age isn't as important on this *klith* as it is on yours."

"Meuhlnir, why is your name the same as the name of Thor's hammer?"

He chuckled, and some of the tension drained out of the room. "I did say most people used my name incorrectly."

"I thought you meant they mispronounced it."

"That too," he said with a grin splitting his face.

"How did your name come to be associated with Thor's hammer?"

"The short version is that my brother often called me '*pror*'—which means brother—when we spoke. The natives misheard what he was saying and came to think of me as Tor. I often carried my warhammer into battle—it has my name inscribed on the head of the hammer. Well, my brother also often explained the blackened craters left by the result of my fondness for lightning as the work of Meuhlnir, which the Vikings took to be the name of my warhammer because of the inscription."

"Are you telling me that you are Thor? The God of Thunder? That you cast lightning bolts?"

Meuhlnir grinned. "That is how the Vikings thought of me. I used to call down lightning at the slightest provocation." He chuckled. "My wives will say I still do, truth be told."

I scoffed. "More magic?" I shook my head. "This is all getting a little bit…"

"I will show you later. Until then, can you withhold judgement?"

"And is your brother also a god in the old Norse pantheon?"

Meuhlnir sobered and pursed his lips. "Yes, all three of them, though only one still lives."

"Which one?" I asked, wracking my brain for the names of Thor's brothers. "Baldur?"

Meuhlnir shook his head. "No, not Paltr." His face filled with an old sadness. "Paltr no longer lives."

"Oh, I'm sorry," I said, ducking my head. "Um, Vidar then?"

"No," said Meuhlnir. "Veethar is not my brother, though he is a friend of mine and we often visited Mithgarthr together." He scratched his beard. "They thought we were brothers? I suppose we did look alike, though I am the prettier of the two."

"Mithgarthr? Midgard? Is that what you mean?"

"I said it correctly," he said with a hint of reproach.

"I read about Norwegian mythology as a teenager, but I can't remember the names of Thor's other brothers."

"It is no matter," he said. "It is evident that this mythology is based on our visits to your *klith*. The Dark Queen often visited, as did Vowli..." Meuhlnir shook his head as if it hurt. "I haven't thought of that evil bastard in years. He was one of my brother's first disciples after... or vice versa..."

"So, it's not Vowli."

"Vowli is not a brother. We knew him at court—"

It hit me then, and I shoved the chair away from the table and stood up. "Loki?" Anger and rage seemed to flow through my veins without the need of blood. My fists were clenched tightly, for once not causing me pain.

"Luka," whispered Meuhlnir. "You said his name in your tale."

"I don't care how it's pronounced! Are you telling me you are Chris Hatton's brother?"

"Yes," he breathed, head down. "My brother's name is Luka. We haven't spoken in many, many long years." He hadn't moved. He sat there looking at the table while I towered over him, shaking with rage.

"Did you have something to do with—"

"No! Hank, I told you, I came to regret… I took a different path from my brother."

"And Luka is a…"

"*Oolfur*. Yes. He was known as Loki and eventually as Fenrir the Wolf to the Vikings. My brother founded *Briethralak Oolfur*—the brotherhood of the wolf—on this *klith* and with the Vikings on your *klith*. His actions were…" Meuhlnir grimaced. "The Midnight Queen, Vowli, and my brother broke the *Ayn Loug* to gain vast amounts of power—power over life itself. This was their downfall. I am sworn…"

I suddenly felt very tired, too tired to stand. I sank back into the chair feeling a thousand years old. "Sworn to what?"

Meuhlnir turned to face me. "Hank, there are things I should tell you—things that can't be rushed like this. I needed to decide—"

"What?" I sneered. "You needed to determine if I was trustworthy? You needed to decide if you should continue to lie to me?"

"I never lied to you, Hank," said Meuhlnir. "Maybe, I…" His face fell, and he couldn't meet my gaze. "Hank, I… I couldn't risk helping you get to him if…"

"If what?" I snapped.

"If you were *itla sem yetur*. That is part of the reason for this feast. To see if you would eat."

That hit me like a bucket of cold water and washed most of my anger at his deceit away. "I see," I said with a sudden calmness. "What have you sworn to do?" I felt wrung out, exhausted. I felt more fatigued than I have ever felt, illness be damned.

Meuhlnir looked me in the eye for a long moment and then nodded curtly. "I swore to redeem my brother if possible."

"And that is all of it?"

"All of what?" he asked in a flat voice.

"All that you were keeping from me? Everything?"

He looked at me for a long moment. "Fair enough. I believe you've been open and honest in what you've shared with me. The least I can do is the same. There's one more thing."

As I stared at him, his features began to move—like his skin was melting. His boney shoulders swelled with muscle. His thin white hair thickened and reddened to a bright rust color. His hands stretched and grew. When it was all over, the slight, bent old man was gone, and I was sitting next to a muscular, middle-aged man with red hair and a red beard.

"This is how I truly appear," he said. "I was younger when my brother and I visited the early Vikings." He held up one thick hand and pointed at a ring of yellow gold with a large turquoise stone set in it. "I worked a glamor on this ring many years ago—a kind of defense, really. A test for the many supplicants who come to my door."

"A test?" I asked.

"Yes. It helps me decide who can be trusted."

I shook my head.

"I have many supplicants. I need to know who has a good heart and who has…otherwise. I—" He cleared his throat. "I once taught someone I regret having taught. The Black Bitch herself." He shook his head. "This glamor helps. It is hard to intimidate people as a little old man, but as I truly am, I find many people try to tell me what I want to hear. People find it easier to drop their guard and act as they really are around a little old man."

"Am I a supplicant then?"

He shook his head. "I had to know your heart before I decided whether to help you or send you on your way."

"So, my people need to be tested, but your people feel justified in manipulating mine?"

"I've said most of us came to regret that."

"You and your brother? All those others? The Midnight Queen?"

Meuhlnir looked away. "I said most of us," he said.

I shrugged. "If the queen was so evil, why was she exiled? Why wasn't she killed?"

Meuhlnir's gaze strayed to the fire. "Even then," he whispered, "she was powerful. She must have been breaking the *Ayn Loug* long before we knew about it. It took many of us to even banish her. And to make it stick. It was a powerful shunning. It had to be, or she would just break our spell and do as she wished."

Meuhlnir shuddered and hugged himself. "I was sick for months after that *vefnathur strenki*—that weaving of the strings of power. The failed war to depose her killed so many. It was perhaps the deadliest war since the *Geumlu*—the old ones—broke the world. She made us pay a heavy price, and in the end, we decided the price would be too high to continue to fight." He turned toward me with a stricken look in his eyes. "Can you understand?"

"She and your brother remained free to come to my side, and hundreds of people have died that I have personal knowledge of. That was the result of your decision, so I'd say the price was high either way." His shoulders fell, and his eyes left my face. "But, yes, Meuhlnir, I think I do understand."

He looked back up at me and put his hand on my shoulder. "I think you are starting to."

"Do you understand my side of this?" I asked, holding his eyes with mine.

Meuhlnir nodded, slow and deliberate. "Yes," he breathed. "You are here for them—for your wife and boy."

I nodded.

"But are you also here for vengeance?"

This time, it was me that couldn't meet his eye. "I...I really don't know. I don't want to be."

Meuhlnir looked at me in silence for a long time. In the fire, bits of sap trapped inside one of the burning logs popped and snapped. "Vengeance against Luka? Against my brother?"

I couldn't read his expression—his face seemed flat and still, as frozen as the lake I'd so recently gone face first onto. "He—"

"He killed your friends. The ones you told me about."

"More than that. He killed innocent people. He killed people whose only crime was playing cards with the queen. He's kidnapped my wife and son and inflicted who knows what terrors on them." I shook my head. "Can you tell me he shouldn't pay for what he's done?"

Meuhlnir chewed the inside of his cheek. He pursed his lips and tilted his head to the side. "Are you the one who decides?" he countered.

I shrugged and shook my head. "I don't know, Meuhlnir. I just don't know."

"But you do know what you want to do."

I shook my head. "I really don't. I am conflicted as hell. I've spent my life as a law enforcement officer—I tracked down criminals and helped put them in prison. But even then, my job wasn't to punish them, I only found out who they were and documented their crimes. A judge and jury decided if they were guilty or not, and a judge passed down the punishment.

"Do I have the right to play judge and jury? I can't say. I just know that he can't be allowed to get away with it."

Meuhlnir stared into my eyes. The atmosphere in the great hall started to feel rather ominous. The hairs on my arms and the back of my neck felt like they were standing on end. There was a kind of pressure building that I could feel in my chest. Abruptly, Meuhlnir looked away. "It's late," he grunted. As quickly as it had come, the malefic pressure and grim atmosphere disappeared.

He stood and clapped me on the shoulder. "You are a good man, Hank Jensen, and you are welcome in my house."

I stood, and only then did I realize how big of a man Meuhlnir was. He wasn't as tall as Luka, and he had more flesh on his bones, but there was a resemblance.

One corner of his mouth twitched upwards into half a grin. "Yes. Everyone always said how much we looked alike."

I nodded. "The kinship is still there, but your brother…"

"Yes," whispered the big, red-headed man. "Breaking the *Ayn Loug* takes its toll."

I looked at my feet, feeling somehow guilty.

"Come, let me tell you a story of how things were before the fall." He led me out of the great hall, and back to that cozy room in the front of the house.

We sat in the comfortable chairs in a companionable silence for a while.

"Oh, I forgot," he said, getting up. "I'll be right back."

When he came back, he was holding what looked like an overgrown rock hammer in one fist. The hammer's head was forged as one single piece and looked brutal. The handle was about eighteen inches long and sculpted so that it looked like the neck and head of a dragon, the haft cross-hatched in the shape of dragonscales to provide grip. At the bottom of the haft, the head of the dragon leered, mouth open as if it were ready to breathe fire. The head of the hammer was maybe three inches tall, ten inches from the tip of the spike to the other end of the head and maybe two and a half inches thick. It had a sharp spike sticking up about two inches from the top of the hammer's head, like an extension of the haft. Inset in gold on both sides of the head was a set of runes.

"My name, written in the *Gamla Toonkumowl*," said Meuhlnir.

"Ah, the reason for confusion on my *klith*."

"Indeed," he said. "Here."

He handed the hammer to me. Because of how it looked, I'd expected it to be heavy, in spite of the way Meuhlnir tossed it around, but it wasn't. It was light, weighing less than five pounds. "It's light," I said with a grin. "It's nothing like what I expected, I have to say.

"In fiction and movies, warhammers are always great big lumps of metal that look like they weigh a hundred pounds. And your myth says this is so heavy only you can wield it."

Meuhlnir smiled. "Warhammers aren't much good in battle if they are so heavy you can't swing it more than two or three times. Same thing with swords and axes."

I traced the engraving on the haft, following its sinuous curves with my finger. "It may sound strange, but it's beautiful."

"It was made for me in my youth—commissioned by the Dragon Queen herself as a reward for valor. Before she...fell. She was a good woman, once."

I thought of the crazy woman standing on her porch with that cigarette bouncing in the corner of her mouth and shook my head. "If you say so."

"In the beginning, she was a fair ruler. In the days that she still went by the name Suel and named her empire Suelhaym."

I shook my head again.

"Oh, I know," he said. "It's hard to imagine such big swings in character when your life span is so short, but when you live a long life, things can change. Even if just out of boredom." He got a faraway look in his eyes and sank back into the chair.

"She was beautiful, then. I think we all loved her. Well, everyone did really. But we of the *Vuthuhr Trohtninkar*—the Queen's Guard, that is—we saw her every day. We heard the music in her laughter; we saw the strength of her bones. She was grand." Meuhlnir turned his gaze toward the fire and slumped his shoulders. "How different things might have been if only…"

"It sounds as if you miss those days."

"What's that?" he asked, shaking himself out of his reverie. "Oh." He frowned at the hammer and took it back gently, standing it on the hearth, head down. "I told you she gave me that for valor."

I nodded.

"She was loved by her people, and in general, it was an easy thing to be a *Vuthuhr Trohtninkar*, but there are always…"

"Crazies," I said.

"Just so. There are always crazies who are not content. On this occasion, it was a very rich man who didn't think he should pay taxes to the crown. He was a merchant, you see, and traded goods far and wide, spending much of the year out of the empire.

"He became quite bitter and decided to take Suel to task.

SIXTEEN

Meuhlnir had guard duty through the night, but he didn't mind. It was easy enough, and despite the feeling of nausea he got from staying up all night and trying to sleep through the next day, it had its rewards. Queen Suel was up most of the night, and bored. She often spoke to her *Vuthuhr Trohtninkar* or asked them to play a game of *tafl*.

She had a light way about her. Even though she was the queen of a large empire, she acted as if every man was her equal. No one ever felt that they were beneath her station—even when they were. She was kind, and soft, and easy to spend all night looking at.

That evening, after all the courtiers had gone to their chambers for the night, and all the *Trohtninkar Tumuhr* were in their lace covered beds, dreaming of meeting a prince from some far-flung province, Queen Suel sought him out.

"There you are, you great oaf of a man," she said with a crooked smile.

"Where else?" Meuhlnir asked arching an eyebrow. "I'm the only one worthy of standing in one place in this hallway all night."

"So brave," she laughed. "Are you protecting me from the shadows?"

Meuhlnir put on his war-face and growled at the shadowy corner at the end of the hall. "Stay behind me, my Queen," he said. "I shall kill the bastard with lightning."

Her laugh was like the tinkling of glass bells. She slapped him on the shoulder like a playful kitten. "Why isn't your brother as funny as you?" she asked.

"He's not as good looking, either," Meuhlnir said. "Everyone knows this." He wiggled his eyebrows at her.

"Nor is he as modest." She smiled up at him, but he could see the worry written in her face.

"More stupidity from the court?" he asked.

"Ah," she sighed, "seems like that's all there is these days."

"Shall I change my rotation? I could growl and mutter at your signal. I have quite a fierce glare, too."

She smiled, but it was brief. "I bet his Highness, the Grand Lord of Merchants, Rikur, would cower before you."

"Taxes, again?" asked Meuhlnir.

She waved her hand. "What else?" she asked. "He is fine using our materials to create his goods, our labor to craft them, our horses to transport them, but feels put upon to pay taxes on the income he derives from all that." She looked pensive for a moment and then tried to shrug it off. "Walk?"

"I am yours to command, my Queen."

They walked to the gardens in a comfortable silence, but Meuhlnir could feel the strain his queen was under. He hated that people mistreated her. She was such a fair ruler—taxes were low! That anyone would begrudge paying them spoke to greed more than any fault of the queen's.

The night was cool, but not cold, just a relief from the heat of the summer. Even so, the air in the gardens was warm and smelled of the sea. Tropical plants and flowers lined the paths through the queen's gardens—a cornucopia of color and shapes and sizes.

"I love it here," she whispered.

"I do too," he said.

"Am I a good ruler, Meuhlnir?"

He scoffed. "You might as well ask if the sun shines and the sea feels wet."

She chuckled. "May I take that as a yes, then?"

"Might as well ask if I'm prettier than little Luka."

That got a laugh from her—a full throated laugh. "I'm going to tell him you said that."

Meuhlnir chuckled. "Do. He should learn to accept his failures with equanimity and grace."

She laughed harder, a tear trickling from the corner of her eye. "Ah, Meuhlnir, my friend, what would I do without you?"

"Be bored?" Meuhlnir shrugged and affected apathy, but he was pleased.

"Indeed, sir. If I asked you to, would you beat Rikur with a stick?"

"Hmm," said Meuhlnir. "Would said stick have a sharp and pointy end?"

The queen put on a pensive expression and scratched her chin. "Is there such a thing as a stick that is not pointy?"

"Ah, my Queen, I am but a lowly warrior. I can't follow these deep philosophical discussions."

"Always want to have the last word, don't you?"

"Might as well ask if Takmar's Horse Plains smell of horse shit."

"Meuhlnir!" she laughed. "Such language in front of a lady!"

"Oh, my," he said. He turned to face a palm with wide green fronds and bowed at the waist. "I apologize, Lady Palmfrond! I didn't see you there!"

"Cad!" said the queen, pretending to slap him. "Misogynist!" Another pretend slap swished by his nose accompanied by the glass tinkle sound of her laughter. "Bounder!" Another swish, this time with the opposite hand. "Cur!" She play-slapped him on the chest. "Friend," she said, suddenly serious.

"Loyally so, and forever, my Queen," he said.

"How is it you always know just the thing that will make me feel better?"

"Might as well ask why the Forest of Kvia is in Kvia," he said, affecting arrogant disdain.

"Is this *another* veiled geography lesson?" she asked pretending at petulance.

"Might as well ask if the Darks of Kruyn—"

"Are dark!" she shouted, her face full of glee.

"Well, if you want to be obvious, I suppose that works…"

She sighed. "Oh, Meuhlnir, do I have to go through the cad synonym list again so soon?"

"Might as well ask if Suelhaym is where you live, Queen Suel," he said.

She made a funny face and shook her head. "What a silly name for an empire," she said. "What kind of person would have so much hubris that she would name her empire after herself?"

"One never knows," said Meuhlnir. "Perhaps a great, beautiful ruler, well worth the title of queen?"

"Might as well ask if Fankelsi smells of swamp gas."

Meuhlnir sighed and shook his head. "And I had such high hopes after the Darks of Kruyn incident."

"Yeah, it doesn't quite work, does it?"

"Might as well ask if the sun is cold and snowy."

"Oh, you! You think you are so smart."

"And pretty," he said, pretending to have hurt feelings.

"Oh yes, pretty."

"Well, for a start. There's also strong, brave, good looking, smart, awesome, brilliant… Feel free to stop me at any time."

She smiled at him. "No, no. I want to see how long you can keep going."

"Oh. Uh… Well, did I say smart already?"

"You did," she said.

"Pretty?"

"Yep."

He scratched his beard and pretended to tick things off on his fingers. "Ah!" he said. "Pretty!"

She pretended to swoon. "I am overcome with your wit. Or was it your smell?"

"Might as well ask if the Sea Dragon Islands are surrounded by water."

"I feel so much better," she said with a laugh. "Rikur can just rot."

Meuhlnir looked at the ground and let his shoulders slump. "I was so looking forward to finding the right stick with a pointy end for the beating."

She laughed, her voice booming across the garden, a real belly laugh.

Meuhlnir started to laugh with her, but something flashed in the corner of his eye. He tensed and spun in that direction, one hand going to the hammer in his belt, and one pushing the queen behind him, turning her laugh into a squawk.

"What is it," she whispered.

"To me!" he bellowed. "Queen's gardens! Protect the queen!" His voice echoed through the still night air.

"Too late, clown," grated a voice from behind him.

Meuhlnir whirled and stepped between the queen and the darkness beyond. "Face me, then, coward." He slid the hammer from his belt and began to focus his mind to *vefa strenki*.

"Might as well ask if Meuhlnir is a great oaf."

An arrow shot out of the darkness and Meuhlnir deflected it with his hammer. He held up his left hand, palm up. "*Ehlteenk!*" he boomed. *Lightning!* Thunder peeled in the sky above, and a bolt of white hot lightning lanced from the cloudless sky and struck the earth near the garden wall. Soil flew through the air.

During the brief flash of light, Meuhlnir spotted the assassin. The man wore a long, hooded cloak of dark gray over loose-fitting black cotton clothing and was squatting behind a bush to their right. "*Ehlteenk!*" screamed Meuhlnir, pointing at the assassin. Thunder shook the ground, and another bolt of lightning flew toward the earth. The bolt struck the assassin and dropped him like a steer at a slaughter house. Languid smoke wafted from the man's head.

"Meuhlnir!" the queen shrieked.

He spun toward her and saw another assassin behind him.

The assassin had a bow fully drawn, moonlight glinting on the poisoned point of his arrow. The bow twanged, and the queen shrieked in terror.

There was only one thing Meuhlnir could do, and he did it without thinking about it. He leapt forward, roaring a mighty battle cry. He smashed into the queen, sending her sprawling in the dirt. He tried to fend the arrow off as he had the first, but he was too slow. The arrow slammed into his shoulder, spinning him in a half-circle.

He heard the bow twang a second time. "To me! Assassins in the queen's garden! To me!" he cried. The second arrow hit him high in the chest, on his left side, and he could feel the sting of the poison biting into his blood.

"*Ehlteenk*!" he tried to scream, but all of a sudden, he had no air to scream with.

The assassin smiled a nasty, hateful smile. "Goodbye, clown," he said. "You have failed your queen!" He nocked another arrow and aimed at the queen.

Meuhlnir felt weak, and his vision was going black. He tried to call down another bolt, but it was impossible; his mind was too scattered. He took a weak step forward and lifted his arm.

"Fool," said the assassin, pulling the bow string to full draw, still aiming at the queen.

Meuhlnir threw his hammer with all his remaining strength and all his weight behind it; his own momentum flung him forward to his hands and knees. The hammer whistled as it spun through the air.

The assassin saw the hammer coming, his eyes growing large and round, and he tried to dodge it, releasing the arrow as he did so. The arrow sailed off over the garden wall into the night.

The hammer smashed into the assassin, striking him just below the chin. Blood erupted from the man's throat, his wind pipe pulped by the head of the hammer. The assassin scratched at his throat as if trying to pull away a noose.

Meuhlnir grinned at him and shook his head. "I've killed you, coward," he whispered. "I've killed you both, and *saved* my queen." He collapsed at the same time as the assassin, both men falling forward into the dirt.

"To me!" shrieked the queen. "To me! Bring my healers!"

Meuhlnir tried to tell her not to worry, but he couldn't draw enough breath.

She knelt at his side and took his hand in hers. "Hold on, brave Meuhlnir. Do not die, my friend." She had tears in her eyes. "I command it."

Meuhlnir wanted to tell her not to cry, but the effort seemed beyond him. Fire raced through his veins as the poison ate its way toward his heart.

"Where are they?" she cried. She looked into his face, and he saw her fear. "TO ME!" She screamed so hard her voice broke and cracked.

He could hear booted feet pounding toward them. *Too late,* he thought. They were too slow. He tried to tell the queen how much he loved her, but there were no words, and there was no time.

She was looking into his eyes. "Stay!" she implored, dashing tears from her eyes. "No, my truest friend, don't go. I want you to stay."

He wanted to obey. He tried to obey, but he could feel himself falling away from his life as if he were falling down a deep, black well. Her face seemed to look down at him from the top of the well, sorrow writ large on her features.

"I won't allow this," he heard her say. "*Tvelyast*!" she screamed, and power crackled in the air around her. *Stay!*

His fall down the well slowed. He saw her eyes widen in shock. To his knowledge, it was the first time she had ever attempted to *vefa strenki.*

"*Anta*!" the queen cried with enough force to make her voice crack and go silent on the last syllable. *Breathe!* Again, the power crackled around her.

Meuhlnir felt the hair on his arms buzzing with the potency of the queen's magical command. His blood stirred, and he gasped a painful breath. He started to rise up the tunnel toward the light, toward his life and his queen.

"*Lifa ow nee*!" she shrieked, her voice sounded broken and ruptured. *Live again!*

The very air around them seemed to pop and glow with the thaumaturgical power she had spawned in her desperation. She was using *strenkir af krafti* to pull him out of the jaws of death, wielding power to change the skein of fate.

He felt stronger, no longer falling away from his life, but rooted to it by her will.

"You will not die today," croaked the queen. She seemed to be in shock over what she had done and the success she had achieved. Her voice was cracked, weak and wrecked, but firm.

Finally, the *Vuthuhr Trohtninkar* stood in a ring around them, and he could hear the healer calling as she ran, demanding to know if the queen was injured.

Meuhlnir looked into the queen's eyes and opened his mouth to thank her for saving him. He couldn't draw enough breath to make the words, so he mouthed them instead.

She smiled at him, dashing tears from her eyes. She nodded and put a hand to her throat, grimacing in pain.

The healer ran up and started ordering everyone around, as she was wont to do. She took the queen by the arm and was trying to pull her away. The queen pointed at Meuhlnir.

"My Queen, come away so I can treat your wounds in safety," said the healer, searching every shadow with wide eyes.

Queen Suel pointed again at Meuhlnir and tried to speak, but only a froggish croak came out. The healer continued pulling at her arm, the healer's eyes were wide and kept stealing away to the bodies of the dead assassins.

Suel slapped the healer hard enough to make her stumble.

It was the first time Meuhlnir had ever seen the queen act in anger toward one of her subjects, and the casual brutality of it shocked him. It shocked the healer as well, and she finally bent to treat Meuhlnir's wounds, tears filling her eyes above the bright red hand print that burned on her face.

The queen looked on with a strange expression on her face. She looked to be caught between remorse and a perverse contentment in the result of her violence. If Meuhlnir hadn't known her so well, he might have wondered if she enjoyed slapping her healer the way she did.

"He will be okay, my Queen," the healer said in a teary voice. "The poison burned itself out it seems. All that's left is to deal with the bleeding."

SEVENTEEN

"She began to chant in the *Gamla Toonkumowl* to close the wounds made by the two arrows. The queen stood by and watched until the healing was finished.

"It was a full week before she could speak aloud again, and when she could, her voice was different. The musical quality of her laugh was gone— sacrificed in her desperation to save me." Meuhlnir gazed at the fire, his eyes misty. "I often wonder if that blow she dealt the healer because of me was the start of her fall."

He sighed and shook himself. "At any rate, two weeks later, the queen honored me before the court and presented me with this hammer. I've had it ever since. A reminder, you see."

"Of your friendship," I said.

"Yes, and the gods know I've needed that reminder in the years since. But more than that." He cleared his throat, and the noise of it was harsh, angry. "You see this hammer reminds me that people can change. What was once pure and good may be so again, given the right motivation."

"I see," I whispered.

He looked at me and grunted.

I shrugged my shoulders and stretched my neck from side to side, enjoying the absence of pain. "What happened to the rich guy?"

"Rikur?" Meuhlnir smiled.

"Sharp, pointy stick?" I asked.

"Might as well ask if snow is cold," said Meuhlnir with a brutal smile. "His treachery was repaid, I can assure you of that."

I nodded. "Vengeance," I whispered.

"Justice," said Meuhlnir into his beard.

"So, you understand my position as well."

Meuhlnir looked at me with irritation on his face.

We sat for a moment, watching the flames consume the dry wood in the fireplace. "What were those words?" I asked.

"Words?" Meuhlnir looked at me with confusion.

"Yeah, while you were telling the story, you said some words in what sounded like this *Gamla*

Toonkumowl. You know, when you called down lightning, and when the queen was healing you."

"Oh, those. We use the *Gamla Toonkumowl* to describe what we want to happen. It's the same as the curse the queen put on you."

"Magic words?" I asked, arching my eyebrows, and trying to hide a smile.

Meuhlnir shrugged. "I don't know how to explain that to you. When the *Geumlu* shattered the universe, there was a war. A war that my ancestors won. One of the reasons my ancestors won was the power made accessible to them. The *strenkir af krafti*—the strings of power. We use their language to access them."

"You said the queen had never used that power before that night. Can anyone do it? Access this power business?"

"Well, the queen is a natural *vefari*, a natural adept. The things she can do with her power are...beyond what one would expect. Think of it, her very first attempt to work the power that spins the universe was to fight death not only to a draw but to submission. I've no doubt that without her intervention I would have died before the healer arrived. No, that's not quite it. I believe I was already mostly dead. I think she may have brought me back from the threshold of eternity."

"So, can anyone do it, then?"

Meuhlnir turned in his chair and looked at me, a stern frown on his face. "So, you are a supplicant after all?"

I held up my hands between us, palms toward him. "Hey, just asking."

"Might as well ask if Vikings like fish." He laughed, the frown melting away. "You traversed a *proo* unaided."

I shook my head. "I just lifted my feet and stepped through it. Not hard at all."

He chuckled. "That's what Suel told me when I asked her how she had been able to save me. 'I just shouted what I wanted you to do and you did it,' she said. 'Not hard at all.'

"I will tell you what I told her: What is not hard for someone with a natural talent for archery takes a master archer years of practice. What is easy for a musical savant takes years of dedication for someone merely talented at music."

I scrunched up my face. "With all due respect to you, your beard, and that big hammer of yours, I've never been able to make anything happen by wishful thinking. And believe me, over the past seven years, I've done a lot of wishing."

"Hank, with all due respect to you, your puny little goatee, and," he said as he looked me up and down, "your willingness to run around in the wild without a suitable weapon, you didn't know you could. Even so, becoming a *vefari* requires…the right genetics *and* the right training."

"Voodoo hoodoo," I muttered, thinking of Jax.

"What was that?" he asked.

"Nothing. Just something my partner used to say."

Meuhlnir flapped his hand like a little kid. "Sounds as good a phrase as any."

"There were always people on my *klith* who claimed they could do magic."

He nodded. "Yes, but they were charlatans, weren't they?"

I shrugged and then nodded. "Yeah, I guess."

"What was it you said earlier?" Meuhlnir's forehead wrinkled as he struggled to recall. His face suddenly cleared and a boyish smile sprang to his lips. "Crazies! That's it, right?"

I laughed at his obvious delight. "Yeah, crazies."

"And the authorities, the men of science and the priests of your religions? Did they believe magic existed?"

"Sort of, I guess. Not the scientists, but the priests—except they called it miracles and said it only worked if you had enough faith."

Meuhlnir nodded. "And did you ever meet anyone with enough faith?"

I shook my head. "I see your point, I think. On the other hand, except for that magical mirror I stepped through—which could easily be explained as a self-delusion on my part—what is there to convince me that this hocus-pocus is any more real than miracles?"

Meuhlnir nodded with a small smile on his face. "Don't believe in fairies?"

I chuckled. "Well, I've never seen one."

Meuhlnir nodded. "Fair enough," he said. "Come with me." He stood up and walked to the front door.

I followed him out into the frigid cold, shivering and wishing I hadn't asked that last question.

Meuhlnir pointed behind me in the direction of the cabin. I turned and stared at it, feeling slow and stupid. It hadn't been a trick of memory after all. The cabin looked to be about forty feet long and thirty or forty feet deep—square, and small. There was also no way a second floor could have fit beneath the low roof.

"Thoughts," he asked.

"Smaller on the outside," I muttered.

"Maybe bigger on the inside," he said.

"Don't get all Doctor Who on me now."

He arched an eyebrow. "A man of science?"

I laughed. "Sort of. It's too long to explain out here in the cold, and probably not very important."

"Ah," he said. He looked to his left, deeper into the woods. "*Ehlteenk*," he muttered. The air shook with thunder, and a bolt of purplish lightning slammed into the ground about fifty yards into the woods. "Happy?"

I looked at the steaming hole in the snow out there in the woods, then back at him. "*Ehlteenk* is what you said?" I asked.

He nodded. "It means 'lightning.'"

"You do enjoy lightning, don't you," I laughed.

"Might as well ask if Thor likes hammers," he said. "But I think you are turning blue." He put out his hand and turned me toward the door and gave me a little shove.

Back inside, I noticed that the door outside was a single panel, but inside, there was a twin standing beside it. "Okay," I said. "How do you do the cabin trick?"

Meuhlnir laughed and hefted his hammer from the hearth. "Glamor, do you think?"

"Could be," I said, "but I'm far from an expert." A wave of exhaustion swept over me, and I leaned against the wall of the entry.

"Enough for tonight?" He stretched and yawned.

"Yeah, I think I'm done in."

He nodded and pointed up the left set of stairs to the second floor that didn't exist from the outside and then led me upstairs to my room.

EIGHTEEN

I woke to the smell of cooking sausages and the sound of two women haranguing Meuhlnir in a language that sounded somewhat like the *Gamla Toonkumowl*. I stretched beneath the heap of thick furs that had served as my bedclothes. The fire had burned down to mere embers, but the room still had that pleasant smoky smell that permeates the air around a burning fireplace.

I threw the furs back, expecting a bolt of pain through my shoulders and was surprised, but pleased, when it didn't come. Then I remembered what Meuhlnir had said—that I won't feel 'those' pains while in his house. A nice benefit and he wasn't even charging me room and board. Better than any doctor I'd been to on my side of the silvery mirror, the *proo*. I stood and stretched, luxuriating in the first pain-free morning I'd had in seven years.

On the other side of the door, the talking slowed down, and Meuhlnir said something stern. Yowrnsaxa and Sif were silent a moment, and then all three burst into laughter. I was glad of that. I didn't want to be the source of discord amongst them.

I pulled on my boots and went downstairs. I found Meuhlnir sitting in the same plush chair he'd favored the night before. A tin plate with the remains of what looked to be an extensive breakfast rested on the arm of the chair next to his knee. There was a blazing fire in the fireplace, and the heat felt grand. Of Yowrnsaxa and Sif, there was no sign.

"Sit," he said. "Your breakfast will be here in a moment."

"Trouble with the ladies this morning?" I asked. "I hope not because of me."

Meuhlnir waved his hand in my direction. "Cooking dispute." He grinned at me with a sly look in his eyes.

"Okay," I said and grinned back at him.

Yowrnsaxa or Sif, I didn't know which, came in with another tin plate. She patted my shoulder and then stuck her tongue out at Meuhlnir.

"Oh, you're in trouble now, Hank. I think Sif likes you."

The woman made a shushing noise at Meuhlnir and treated me to a pleasant smile. She said something in that sing-song of hers.

"Sorry," I said, shaking my head. "I don't understand you."

She just went on smiling and looking at me as if she was waiting for something. I shrugged at Meuhlnir for help, but he was looking at me with the same expression as his wife as if he were waiting for me to realize something.

"What?" I asked.

"Well, it's simple, really. We are waiting for you to understand that you do know what Sif said to you."

I shook my head. "Long wait I guess. I don't speak that language."

"Really?" asked Meuhlnir, attempting to hide a smile. Sif didn't even try to hide hers.

"What?" I asked, starting to feel like the butt of some joke I didn't understand.

Sif shrugged. "Enjoy…" and two other words I didn't understand.

"Thank you," I said. "She speaks some English?"

Meuhlnir couldn't hide the wide smile that cracked on his face. Sif laughed aloud. "No, Hank. Sif doesn't have any of your English. Neither do I."

I scoffed and took a bite of the thick porridge-like stuff heaped on the plate. It was good—lots of honey and milk that didn't taste like any cow's milk I'd ever had. "I did just wake up, but I'm actually awake and aware. If you don't speak English, exactly how have we been talking to one another? I don't speak any language from this *klith*. How could I? I don't speak any other language than English."

Meuhlnir shrugged. "I've never even heard English spoken. You are speaking the language of Suelhaym, which is basically the modern derivation of the *Gamla Toonkumowl*."

"How is that possible? Two days ago, I would have said this place couldn't even exist."

"It's just something that happens in the *preer*. Some legacy of the technology that created them, I guess. When you travel a *proo*, you speak the language of the *klith* where the *proo* terminates."

I shook my head and took a bite of the buttered bread. "If that's true, then why don't I understand Sif?"

Sif patted my shoulder and gave me an indulgent smile.

"Because she talks like a mush-mouth," said Meuhlnir. Sif swatted at him, and as he ducked, he smiled and shrugged. "When you arrived here, you didn't find it strange at all that I spoke English so well?"

"Silly of me, but I never even thought of it."

Meuhlnir rolled his eyes toward the ceiling. "Yes, with your extensive experience traveling the *preer*, I expect all this would be old hat."

Sif made a disapproving sound and smacked Meuhlnir on the top of his head with a little more fire behind it than before.

I chuckled at that. "I guess I don't need a translation for that."

"Might as well ask if acorns fall from oak trees," he muttered. "In any case, the longer you are here, the easier it will be to understand everyone. Now that you know you can, that is."

"If you say so," I said.

"I do," said Sif. "Now stop talking and eat."

I smiled at her and started shoveling in the food. "Will it be like this with everyone?" I asked between mouthfuls.

"No," said Sif.

"As with everything else, it's a new skill for your brain to adapt to. The more you are here, the more you talk to us, and the more people you are exposed to, the easier it will get. In a short time, you will be as fluent as any speaker of his non-native tongue. Unless we keep you locked away here in the middle of the wilderness with only myself and two old women to talk to." He flashed a grin at Sif as she prepared to hit him again. He held up his hands in surrender, chuckling. As Sif turned and left the room, Meuhlnir tipped me a wink. "Got to do something to keep those two in their proper place."

He said it just loud enough for Sif to hear, and in response, she blew a raspberry. "Keep it up, goose liver," she said. "Maybe you can go from two wives to zero before lunch."

"Ah, marital bliss," said Meuhlnir. He winked at me. "I try to irritate them as any good husband knows he should."

I grinned. "Might as well ask if snow should fall down from the sky or up from the ground."

Meuhlnir tilted his head forward and glanced my way from under his bushy brows. "Need to work on that, but at least the attempt shows promise." He clapped me on the back. "Now, if you are done eating like a pig at the trough, we have things that need doing."

"Oh?" I asked, standing and grabbing my plate. I turned toward the hall to the back of the cabin.

"No, no, Hank. If you know what's good for you, you'll just leave your dishes lie."

I shrugged my shoulders. "I want to do my part."

"Your part is to be the guest. My wives will not like you 'doing your part' as you put it."

"On my side, being a guest means you try to help out and minimize your impact on the day to day of the household. Not so here?"

Meuhlnir shook his head. "No. Here, you are granted the guest-right when someone invites you to stay. That means anything you desire that is in the host's ability to provide is given to you. You do no work unless specifically asked. For example, a host might ask his guest to go hunting or to put wood on the fire while the host is otherwise occupied. But dishes? Oh, no. Yowrnsaxa and Sif would never hear of it."

I shrugged. "Okay, I guess. When in Rome, right?"

"I've never been to Rome, so I wouldn't know."

"I've been thinking about the story you told me last night. About Suel."

Meuhlnir arched his eyebrows at me. "Yes?"

"I think you should hear what she's become."

He looked at me with thunder threatening on his forehead. "I'm not sure I want to."

"You should," I insisted. "You need to know."

"I know she's not that girl anymore. Too much has happened. We fought a war against her, after all. We banished her."

"Even so, I'm willing to bet it's worse than you thought. Listen, Meuhlnir, and decide for yourself how much she has changed."

He shrugged. "Wait a moment, then." He turned and walked down the hallway. He came back in a few minutes with Sif and Yowrnsaxa in tow. "They should hear this, as well. They knew her at least as well as I did."

I nodded. "We set a man on her house like I told you last night. A man named Ben Carson. He was a good friend of mine. She must have sniffed him out, or seen him or something."

NINETEEN

Swathed in shadows, Liz stood at the edge of the trees and watched the man who was supposed to be watching her. He was sitting in a car parked across the road down at the base of the hill, looking up at her house without guile or subtlety. Every few minutes he took a sip out of a stainless-steel coffee mug and then looked down at his phone.

The night was chilly, as spring nights in this forsaken land often were. Even so, the man had the front windows of the car down, and every once in a while, he whistled tunelessly like he was trying to keep himself awake.

Despite the chill in the air, Liz was flushed and hot. Anger burned in her blood like alcohol. *How dare they?* she thought. There was no doubt that the man watching her house had been sent by the detective who'd come by earlier. *The special one, the cursed one*, she thought with a small smile playing on her lips.

Luka would be home soon, and when he arrived, the little man at the base of the hill was going to learn respect.

The man opened the car door and got out. He walked to the front of the car and leaned against the grill. He was heavy. *Fat*. But even so, he carried himself in a way she recognized. A certain set of the shoulders, a dancer's grace. He moved like a warrior.

The Lincoln roared up and skidded in the gravel next to the barn across the road. The doors to the barn opened, and then the rumble of the Lincoln's engine fell silent.

So, she thought, *the talk went as planned.* Something unclenched deep inside her—some tenseness she didn't want to admit had been there. She was relieved Luka was back and unharmed, and why shouldn't she be?

The cop at the foot of the hill was staring up at the barn.

With a small, feral grin, Liz sprinted down the hill. Luka had seen her standing in the shadows, she was sure of it. He would know what she wanted. What she *required*. He always did.

When she was opposite the car, she squatted behind one of the trees in the row that had been planted to combat blowing snow. She peered around the trunk and saw the cop with his back to her, looking out at the fields on his side of the road and whistling like a kid wishing away monsters in the dark.

"What are you doing here?" asked Luka in a gruff, angry sounding voice.

Liz smiled as the cop jumped. Luka squatted in the field on the other side of the road, but she doubted the cop could see much of anything except his phone screen.

"I asked you a question, little man. Did Hank Jensen send you here?"

"Trooper Carson, State Police," said the cop. "I'm here on official business. Step out of the shadows and show yourself."

Luka laughed in that mocking way he had. Usually, that laugh made people furious, but Carson stayed cool and calm.

"What are you doing here?" snapped Luka. "Spying?"

"I'm not going to ask you a second time, sir. Come out and let me see some ID."

Luka laughed again and rose to his full height. He took a graceful, almost dancing step toward the man.

Liz felt a little trill of excitement in her stomach. Sometimes, the way Luka moved when he was stalking someone excited her in ways no other man ever had.

"What will you do if I refuse, little man?"

"Partner, that 'little man' shit won't work with me," said Carson.

Luka rocketed forward, closing the twelve-yard gap in eight large steps and knocked the cop's phone spinning into the road. He towered over the fat man, leaning forward, glaring down at him with menace. "You *are* a snooping little spy, aren't you?"

The cop retreated down the length of his car and Luka followed on his heels, a mocking grin on his face. When they reached the end of the car, the cop set his feet and put a hand on Luka's chest.

"Back off," he said.

Luka looked over at her, picking her out of the shadows with ease, and winked, sending another excited trill bouncing around her tummy. He liked showing off for her, and she liked that he wanted to.

"I don't think so," said Luka. "I want to tell you something. Something secret. It's a special word I know."

"Don't say I didn't warn you, partner," said Carson. He stepped forward and grabbed at Luka's wrist.

"*Oolfur*," said Luka, his grin stretching, widening until it appeared his face was splitting in half.

Liz saw the change begin and the trill of excitement became a shiver. "*Byarnteer*," she breathed. Bear to Luka's wolf. The perfect pairing for a hunt.

The cop tried to draw Luka off balance by jerking him forward, but he might as well have been trying to pull a branch out of a tree trunk.

Liz's breathing deepened, making a chuffing sound deep in her chest. Her heartbeat pounded in her ears like tympani, racing with *prayteenkin*—the change. Her skin felt like it was stretching until it would certainly split. Her bones ached until she wanted to cry out in pain.

Luka was smiling down at the cop like a wolf grinning at a cornered rabbit. The cop stepped to the side and tried some fancy martial arts move, levering himself against Luka's side and trying to wrench his arm around. Luka straightened his arm and lifted the man off the ground.

The cop kicked his leg over Luka's head and snapped it down across her lover's neck.

Liz tried to laugh through the pain of her change, but she sounded more like a big animal rooting in the dirt than a woman laughing.

Luka laughed aloud, his voice deep and gravelly with his own *prateenk*. "Are you done playing around, Trooper?" he growled.

"Stop resisting," said the cop.

Luka glanced across at her with an amused, incredulous expression twitching on his face. He was growing taller and wider by the second, as was she.

Carson let go of Luka's arm and jumped toward the back of the car.

Luka's T-shirt stretched tight across his chest, and the button of his jeans pinged off into the darkness.

"Don't think so, little man." Luka's voice was almost unintelligible. His throat sounded like it was packed with dirt. He took a giant step forward and batted the cop to the ground.

Liz's mouth watered when panic blossomed in the cop's face. Her shirt ripped up the back, and she flung it away with an irritation that bordered on distemper. She wanted to roar, but she fought that instinct. She wanted to see the little cop's face when she appeared out of the darkness and ripped out his neck.

The cop went for his gun, but Luka caught his wrist in one of his large, clawed hands. Carson began to scream as Luka began to squeeze. Luka took the gun from him with his other hand and threw it high into the night.

Luka stood up straight, dragging the man into the air by his wrist. With a snarl, he swatted the car, and it slid into the ditch at an angle. The cop hung there in the air, feet kicking to no effect, while Luka peeled the remains of his black T-shirt off and dropped it on the road.

"What the fuck are you?" Carson breathed.

Luka looked at him and grinned his lupine, mocking grin. He growled in Carson's face and slowly squeezed until the man's wrist popped. Then he dropped him to the ground.

The cop lay there, looking up, face blank. Carson lurched to his feet, looking dazed and lost. His head came to Luka's waist.

Luka stooped over him and shook his head like a dog. He made a croaking noise and then shook his head again. "Run," he croaked.

The shiver of excitement in her belly became a torrent. Luka knew what she liked. He always knew how to excite her.

"W–what?" squawked the fat little man.

"Run!" roared Luka with saliva dripping from his fangs in long, ropy streamers.

The cop turned and started to run up the road toward their house.

With a snarling bark, Luka sprinted behind him. He grabbed the cop's leg in his mouth and shook him hard, Carson's limbs flopping around like a rag doll. Then Luka twisted to the side and flung the man clear across the road, where Carson skidded face first into the field.

When the man staggered upright, he turned and looked at Luka like a lost child. His hand scrabbled at his empty holster as if he no longer knew his gun was gone. A useless instinct, in any case.

Luka roared, saliva dripping from his jaws. He was magnificent, standing fifteen feet tall, his upper body covered with a thin, tawny fur. His muscles rippled under his skin as he moved. His jaws were elongated like the muzzle of a wolf. Claws sprang from the ends of his fingers and toes. His most striking feature, however, was his eyes. They'd turned a chartreuse color and had stretched to an almond shape. He looked vicious.

Carson turned and sprinted away in a direction that seemed to have been chosen by panic.

Fighting to contain her glee, Liz sank to all fours and galloped toward him on an intercept course. Her clawed paws tore huge chunks out of the rich soil of the field as she thundered toward the man.

He must have heard her, or sensed her coming, because he looked right at her. His eyes went wide and fresh panic spasmed across his face. A cry of terror escaped his lips, and he tried to run faster.

She imagined what a shock it must be for these thralls to see her coming. In her current form, she stood fourteen feet on her hind legs, and her bulk was massive, her snout and fangs were like those of a bear.

Liz roared with triumph. Her roar echoed across the field and came back to her, and the shivers of excitement in her stomach became tremors of desire. Air chuffed out of her in great gusts as she poured on the speed.

When she hit him, she was galloping flat out, and the noise of the collision elicited another triumphant roar. Luka danced around them and howled at the night sky. The cop lay in the field like a broken doll, and Liz had no doubt that parts of him *were* broken. She'd never been weighed in this form, but she was sure it was at least half a ton, and she'd hit him *hard*.

She stood on her hind legs and glared down at the man. He wasn't dead, she could hear his heart pounding, but he was pretending he was. She shook her head and grunted at Luka.

Quick as the lightning his bastard of a brother was so fond of, Luka darted in and grabbed the man's ankle. He picked the cop up upside-down and shook him again, before flinging him back to the dirt.

Liz dropped her front paws down on the man's arm and released a satisfied growl at the sound of his bones breaking. She squatted down and put her muzzle right in the man's face and roared as loud as she could.

He cringed away from her, but there was only so far he could go with her weight pinning him to ground. "What the fuck are you?"

Luka made the strange chuffing growl sound that was the laughter of the *oolfur*.

Liz twisted her massive head to look at Luka over her shoulder. There was something in the joy on his wolfish face that made her long to be human again, and without delay, but when she turned back to the cop, a different kind of lust filled her mind.

She could smell his terror, and it filled her with a savage joy. She leaned over him again, putting her long snout within inches of his face and snapped her jaws shut. She shifted her weight, grinding her claws into the cop's arm. When he threw his head back to scream, Liz darted forward and took a massive bite out of his trapezius muscle. Luka yipped behind her, and she gave a barking grunt in reply. Liz swatted Carson's face in a playful manner—if she hit him with serious intent, she'd break his neck, and the fun would be over—and raked her claws across his cheek. The cop's blood mixed with the loose top soil, making a thick mud that splattered every which way as Liz moved her bulk around, nipping Carson here and there

The cop looked up at her, blinking. "What the fuck are you two?" he wheezed. "Werewolves? But you look more like a bear… *Wendigo?*"

She smiled, and the irony that bears used the expression only as a threat was not lost on her. She stood tall and backed away from Carson, waving Luka away as she did so. She grunted and jerked her chin toward the sky. Carson watched her but didn't move. Again, she grunted and jerked her chin toward the sky. Luka growled with savage menace.

"Y-you want me to get up?"

Liz grunted and jerked her chin.

The fat cop shook his head but struggled to his feet. He stood before them, his eyes wide with awe and fear. "Can you change like this whenever you want?"

Liz slammed down to all fours and roared. Even on all fours, her eyes were at the same level as Carson's. She took a step forward—a step that was as full of threat and the promise of pain as she could make it.

Carson's face was slack as he turned and fled, his mind lost to terror.

Beside her, Luka laughed. They let the cop run for a few minutes, putting distance between them. Luka stretched his jaws open wide and pawed at the earth. Liz yowled and bolted across the field at Carson, footfalls again sounding like thunder. Luka howled at her side, modulating his pace to match hers.

It had been a long, long time since they'd hunted together as beasts. Too long.

They closed on the running man with ease and then slowed to stay behind him. Every once in a while, Luka sprinted away to one side or the other and snapped his jaws at Carson, herding him where they wanted him to go.

Carson's chest was heaving, and he was making a whistling sound with each breath. Blood soaked his clothes and dripped from him like sweat.

As they crossed back over the road, Liz advanced with a burst of speed and swatted Carson to the ground with a mighty blow. The man hit the macadam and slid, like a kid on ice, face first into the back tire of his cruiser.

With a howl, Luka darted forward and clamped his fangs on Carson's thigh, pinning him to the ground.

Liz walked forward at a slow pace, enjoying the anticipation of the kill. The man was screaming something over and over, but she couldn't understand what he was saying. She raked her claws down Carson's side, digging deep, delighted by the splatter of blood across the road's surface. Luka shook his head back and forth like a dog worrying a chew toy. Carson's flesh tore and popped under their onslaught. Liz sank her teeth into Carson's upper arm and ground her jaws together, pulverizing the bone. Carson screamed, but his voice had broken, and what came out of his mouth sounded more like radio static than human speech.

Liz rolled him onto his back and butted his face with her snout, but when he continued the pathetic noise, she opened her mouth and closed her fangs on the man's face. She pulled back, ripping skin from his cheeks and leaving long gouges across his forehead.

Luka growled and with a mighty heave, ripped a chunk out of the cop's thigh muscle. He danced several paces away and began to eat his prize. He sounded more like a pack of wolves than a single creature. Liz grunted and took her own bite out of Carson's flesh.

When they were finished with him, it was hard to tell by what remained of Ben Carson, if he was human.

"*Mathur,*" Liz grated and began to shrink and change.

Luka voiced a mournful howl and then uttered the same word.

When they were finished changing back, they shoved what was left of Ben Carson into the driver's seat of his cruiser and turned their backs on him.

"That was fun," said Liz.

"Yes, my Queen. We should do that more often."

Liz smiled and took his hand in both of hers. "Where would I be without you, my Champion?" With a gleam in her eye, she led him across the road and up the hill toward home.

As they came through the row of trees that surrounded the house, someone gave a small scream.

They were both naked and covered in blood and gore.

A woman stood in the front yard—Virginia Gunsel. Her mouth hung open, forming a perfect O of astonishment. Behind her, in the drive, were two cars, Virginia's little Toyota, and the racy luxury sedan of Marianne Markey.

Liz had forgotten it was Bridge night. She glanced at Luka, and he sprinted toward the car. She raised her hand to point at Virginia. "*Predna*," she said.

Emerald green flame exploded across Virginia Gunsel's face and torso. The woman shrieked and beat at the flames with her big purse, but the movement only spread the flames. She danced and screeched until she could no longer breathe.

Glass shattered, and Luka jerked Marianne Markey out of the car through the driver's side window. With a savage twist, he broke her neck and then looked at Liz with a small smile on his lips.

He was magnificent, and a desperate lust for him blossomed through Liz like an early spring. She smiled back at him, but the smile turned into a rictus of horror as another set of headlights washed across the yard and the carnage they had just wrought.

"Luka!" she shouted, pointing at the car.

He turned and ran toward it, but it was too late. Tires screeching, the car tore off down the road. It was their fourth. It was Melanie Layne's car.

TWENTY

"The driver of the car was the fourth member of the Bridge game that night. Her name was Melanie Layne. She was a tough bird, I'll tell you that. She took one look at what was going on in that yard and decided." Hank snapped his fingers. "In an instant, she had the car going down the road. When she was sure she was safe, she called the police and reported what she'd seen."

"The killings of the two other women," said Sif.

"Yes. By the time the cops responded, the house and barns were on fire, and the bodies were gone, but they found Ben Carson down the hill, just like Liz wanted them to."

Yowrnsaxa reached over and squeezed my hand. "I'm sorry about your friend."

"Thanks," I said.

"How do you know…" started Yowrnsaxa.

"How do I know about the beast parts? Forensic evidence. Blood splatter analysis. Huge, animal-like footprints." I waved my hand in the air. "At the time, I didn't know what it all meant. Not until after I saw Luka do the trick in person. No, at the time we just had a lot of confusing shit no one could explain. We thought Luka and Liz—the Dark Queen, that is—had tortured and murdered him and then set him back in the car. We thought they might have worn some kind of boot to make the tracks. As far as I know, that's still the official story."

Meuhlnir was looking at the ground between his feet. He didn't move for a long moment and then shook his head. "She has fallen so far. Luka, too," he said in mournful tones.

"Yes," said Sif. "It's hard to reconcile the memories of the queen and Luka with that story."

"This other, the last one, she got away?"

"She did that night," I said. "Ultimately, however, they got her. We had her in a safe house—"

"No," said Meuhlnir. "No more for now."

Sif put her hand on Meuhlnir's cheek. "It's not your burden, husband."

"Yes, it is," he snapped. "It's all of ours."

Sif looked down and sighed. "But what's to be done?"

Meuhlnir shook his head. "Something. I don't know what, yet, but I do know Hank and I need to go up to the lake. To see what's become of the *proo* he traveled." Meuhlnir shrugged into a huge coat made of black bear fur. "Going to be cold, so bundle up."

I put on my coat, fingering the modern materials in its construction. It might be warmer than what Meuhlnir was wearing, but there was no question as to who looked cooler. I mean, a big white guy with light brown hair wearing a coat with a green, gray, and white pattern, or a giant of a man with red hair wearing a bulky bear skin full length coat? No contest.

Meuhlnir pushed through the door and beckoned me out. He led the way back to the path in silence, head down, hands loose at his sides.

"So…" I said to break the silence, "you didn't go to Rome? I figured you for Jupiter and Zeus with the whole lightning fetish."

"Hmm," said Meuhlnir with a shrug. "They say imitation is the purest form of respect. Anyway, I never said I didn't visit Greece," he said with a sly little smile so I couldn't tell if it was just a joke or a hint.

It was cold outside, a brisk wind blowing from the south. Even so, the sky was bright and blue, as if no cloud would dare set foot in its domain—as if no *sterk task* had covered it from horizon to horizon just a day or two before.

"What's the plan, boss?" I asked.

"I keep a *proo* tethered near the lake. I want to see if it's still there or whether my brother moved it, too. He always did like to prank me. Damn inconvenient prank, if he did."

"I'll say," I said. "Meuhlnir…"

He glanced over his shoulder at me. "Spit it out, Hank."

I shrugged and looked away into the woods. "It's just that I have to find my family. I can't spend time on anything else."

"Yes, I know. That's part of why I want to know where my *proo* went."

"Another trip through time and space?"

Meuhlnir grunted. "The *proo* I keep at the lake leads to a juncture of many different *preer* at Trankastrantir—northeast of here. It was very convenient for traveling, believe me."

"As long as no one moves the other side around on you and tries to drop you in a freezing lake."

Meuhlnir nodded. "Could be he wanted to dunk you in the water, but meant no real danger to befall you. Luka was always fond of practical jokes."

"Good intentions of evil men, eh?"

Meuhlnir grunted. "I suppose you could view it that way, but I've known my brother a lot longer than you have. A lot longer than you've been alive."

"How will you know he hasn't moved the other end of your old *proo*? As another joke."

Meuhlnir shrugged and continued trudging down the path.

"You said your *proo* leads to a junction of others?

"In a way, yes. Veethar has designed a vault made of stone. Each stone in the walls is imbued with a rune. Each rune is tied to a *proo*. Invoke the rune and the proper *proo* is summoned forth."

"That does sound convenient." I took a deep breath of the cold, crisp air. "Sounds complicated, though. How does Veethar maintain the place?"

He fell back to walk beside me. "Veethar and I learned the secret of that when we were young men. Young, *traveling* men. We learned it in one of the strangest *stathur* I've ever visited."

I looked him over in the day light. People from home would have guessed he and I were of an age. He didn't look a day past fifty. "Young men? You don't look much older than me. Still keeping your age a secret? Is how you look now how you really look?"

He looked at me sharply, but saw my grin and chuckled. "Might as well ask if dragons like jewels. But I guess I deserve your suspicions after last night."

"Dragons?" My right hip popped—a kind of warning shot—and mild pain flared down my leg.

He laughed at the expression on my face and smiled a secretive and cryptic smile. "Want to meet one?"

"I'm not sure I do," I said. "I guess it depends on what they really are." I rubbed my hands together without thinking about it, trying to massage the blossoming pain in my knuckles back to sleep. No matter how many times it had failed to work in the previous seven years, something in my mind insisted that if I rubbed them enough, my hands wouldn't hurt anymore.

"Wise words, Hank. But, in any event, we don't see them much anymore. Most have gone north—closer to Fankelsi and the Dragon Queen." Meuhlnir looked at me sideways, watching me rub my hands. "The pain comes back?"

"I'm okay," I said. The thing about Norwegians—at least all of them that I knew—was that they'd rather admit they were monkeys than that they were suffering. "This Dragon Queen, that's Suel?"

"The curse will return as we travel farther from my little cabin in the woods," he said. "Yes, Suel was called the Dragon Queen in better times."

I shrugged it off. "So, these dragons you've got, they are evil then?" I asked. A sharp twinge ran from my left shoulder up my neck, and I winced.

"Some, yes. You want absolutes? Nothing in life is so black and white, Hank. The Dark Queen may do evil, but is she really evil?"

"I think you want the philosophy professor named Hank Jensen. I'm just a cop from New York."

"Being a cop means you don't think about the greater nature of things?" He shook his head. "As far as being 'just a cop'…you are selling yourself too cheaply."

"I've seen a lot of evil in my day," I said. "I can't really grasp how evil deeds come from good men."

"Can any one person be only evil or good? Aren't we all just a mishmash of both states at any given moment of any day?"

"Can we ever really know what goes on inside a man?" I countered. "Aren't the actions of a man the only measure of his character we have?" My knees were getting that sick, I'm-about-to-make-you-wish-for-a-chainsaw feeling that I'd come to know so well.

"Hmm," said Meuhlnir. "Actions, not words, are a testament to any man's mettle, eh? Well argued. But even so, are any man's actions limited only to one of the two categories? Aren't there actions that are only partly good and partly evil? Or neither one?"

We walked in silence for a while, our movement punctuated by the crunching of snow under our boots. "I don't know the answer to that," I said. I'd developed an obvious limp—my right foot had begun to feel like I'd stepped on a sixteen-penny nail and it was stuck right through the ball of my foot.

"What about the man that does something good but doesn't do it for the sake of the work, or because it is right, but because he derives some benefit from it?" Meuhlnir was walking with his hands clasped in the small of his back, head bowed.

"You mean like someone who donates food to charity because he gets points he can use to get something for free?"

"I think that's it exactly," said Meuhlnir. "Is that a good or an evil act?"

"I guess that depends on whether being selfish is evil or neither one."

"Ah, you see it. If a man's actions can be defined ambiguously, or can't be defined as good or evil at all, then is the man good or evil?"

"I think," I said, "that a man can be judged by the sum of his actions. Maybe evil men do random acts of good, but if they commit more evil acts, how can you call them anything but evil? What about a killer of children who helps little old ladies cross the street? Isn't random murder of a child more impactful than helping an old lady for thirty seconds."

"Good questions," muttered Meuhlnir. "And ones I don't know the answers to, but given that I don't, am I fit to be the judge of that man?"

I held up my hands in exasperation. "Someone has to be, or society becomes chaos."

We listened to the sound of our boots packing snow beneath our feet once again.

Meuhlnir looked at me with an assessing gleam in his eye. "Shall we rest a moment? Would that help?"

I shook my head. "Walking is better than standing, and if I sit here in the cold, I'll just get stiff, and you'll have to carry me."

He nodded and put his hand on my shoulder in sympathy. "Does a judge on your *klith* have to be more open minded than most? More willing to give the benefit of the doubt?"

I shrugged, the synthetic materials of my coat making an annoying, abrasive noise in my ear. "I don't know. In our system, a man has to be proven guilty beyond the shadow of a doubt, but once he is, he can be judged with a clean conscience."

"I think that even so, a good man might be improperly judged in that system. People are people, after all. People see what they want to see, no?" asked Meuhlnir.

I chuckled sourly. "Yeah, sometimes they see innocence where only guilt exists."

Meuhlnir waved his hand. "The price of protecting the innocent, no?"

""I guess that might be right," I said. "I get the feeling, though, that this conversation is less about the general case and more about the specific cases of Luka and the Black Queen."

Meuhlnir put his chin on his chest. "It may be," he said. "It may be."

"Do you think, then, that family members should be the only judges?"

The redheaded man tugged his beard and grimaced. "Who better?" he grumped.

I scoffed and looked at the uncrunched snow in front of my feet. "Almost anyone? Don't you think family members would be biased?"

Meuhlnir shook his head. "Who would know a man better than his own brother?"

"Let me tell you about the last time I saw your brother. You need to know this."

Meuhlnir sighed and waved his hand for me to tell him.

"When I first got sick, when the curse first started in earnest, it was horrible. I'd just been dealing with the forensic evidence from Ben's murder, and we found Melanie Layne and got her report from the previous night. Because of the nature of the murders and what she reported seeing happen to the other two women, we put Ms. Layne into protective custody.

"My illness—my curse, whatever—was taking its toll by then. I'd been to the doctor, and I was heading back toward the safe house that afternoon. A retired trooper named Richie Duvall had the house across the street, and he picked up a few shifts here and there keeping watch from his front porch. Anyway, when I got to the safe house that afternoon, something felt off about the place. Wrong."

TWENTY- ONE

I got out of my cruiser and stood very still, hand on the butt of my gun, eyes bouncing from one lengthening shadow to the next. The house sat as quiet as a tomb. It was too quiet—like everyone inside was already dead.

The ground floor windows were dark, empty, and dead. Something was wrong. I glanced across the street, looking for Richie Duvall, but there were no lights on at his place. No movement.

I went inside, trying to be quiet. A slimy, coppery smell pervaded the air. It was a familiar smell. Blood. I could hear it dripping, dripping. I pulled my Glock out of its holster and held it ready. I stepped into the little mud room and froze, straining my ears to hear in the silence, my eyes to see into the gloom of the interior.

I slid into the cold darkness of the house and opened the door to the laundry room. A dark shape lay on the linoleum floor—Melanie Layne.

I switched on the lights, and soft yellow light washed over her, unconscious and handcuffed to the rusty radiator. There was a small trickle of blood at the corner of her mouth. Her eyes were pinched closed, but her breathing was regular. I got her uncuffed and scooped her up, cradling her like a newlywed. I backed out to the gravel drive.

The air outside was cool and sweet, not like the air inside. The air inside the safe house smelled like an animal's den—a meat eater's den.

"That our witness, Jensen?"

I jumped, almost dropping Mrs. Layne, her shoulder-length gray hair dancing in the breeze. Richie Duvall stood at my elbow, peering at Mrs. Layne's face.

"She okay?" he asked.

"Jesus Christ, Richie. Give a guy a heart attack," I whispered.

"Gotta die sometime," he said.

Richie held his Colt 1911 at his side.

"Can you stand watch out here? I can't leave her alone, and I have to go back inside and find Jax."

He sighed. "Wait for backup, man. You know better."

"You would do that?" I asked, my voice incredulous. "You would stand around while your partner was in trouble?"

"Hell, no."

"I'm going in," I said.

"'Course y'are. Watch your six and be careful. Sing out if you need me."

"Stay with her," I said, putting Ms. Layne down on the gravel.

Adrenaline hit as I climbed the steps to the house, and my senses kicked into overdrive; the smells of a New England spring evening were almost overwhelming, and the sound of bees buzzing in the woods a couple of acres away. With one last glance at Richie, I stepped back into the foul-smelling house. I had my gun out again, holding it ready in front of me.

The utility room light was off again, and my eyes tracked to the dark room beyond. I heard the subtle scrape of an athletic shoe on a wooden floor, and I snapped into the 'move and shoot' stance that I had drilled to exhaustion. I glared into the laundry room, eyes straining to sift the shadows.

As I stepped inside, all sound ceased. It was like being thrust deep underwater, where the only sound was that of my own pulse beating in my ears. I slid forward on the balls of my feet, muscles as tight as high-tension power lines, nerves crackling. I tried to move like a wolf stalking a rabbit, smooth and quiet.

Something clicked on the other side of the room, the lights flared, and I was blinded for a moment.

Bloody tracks of athletic shoes trailed across the blue and gray linoleum. Two troopers were dead on the floor. They had been…tortured. Bitten. Blood was everywhere.

As I stared at the two dark doorways across from me, the pain in my neck and shoulders ratcheted up until it was as intense as any pain I'd ever felt. I tried to roll my shoulders, but that only made me want to scream.

"Don't be timid, Hank. Come the hell in." It sounded like Jax, but there was a strange quality to the voice—like it came from a throat more used to growling and snarling than speaking.

The sound came from the doorway to the right, and, after a brief hesitation at the door, I stepped into the darkness. I couldn't see anything but inky blackness—my night vision was gone. It was like being blindfolded.

"You know how good I am with this pistol," I said. "Give up now, Hatton."

"I would expect nothing less than perfection out of you with your preferred weapon." The voice belonged to Lieutenant Gruber.

A chair across the room creaked, and I hit the lights. I wish I hadn't. There was a mutilated body on the table that looked broken, ripped, twisted…savaged.

Hatton snickered. He sat in one of the dining room chairs, arms out on the backs of two others. He looked pleased with himself.

I fired my pistol without thinking about it.

The bullet struck Hatton in the right shoulder and went right through him to paint the wall behind him with blood. He didn't stop smiling. Yes, the impact jerked him around a little, but Hatton didn't even flinch.

It wasn't an effective shot, certainly not a killing shot, but getting shot *hurts*, and humans react to it. They scream, they clutch the wound, they fall down. The man across from the ruin of my partner's body didn't do any of those things.

He laughed.

I didn't know how to react to that. It was like my brain was numb.

Not my hands, though. No, they did as I'd trained them to do.

The next bullet hit him right above the solar plexus, center of mass. He took another round at the base of his neck, and either shot should have killed him. He didn't die, though.

He was still laughing. I couldn't understand how he could even be breathing, much less laughing like a hyena.

The Glock wavered in my hand like I was a rookie on his first trip to the firing range.

"Ah, Hank," said Hatton, while wiping at the tears on his cheeks. "This is why I like you so much." His throat was full of blood, and as he spoke, it trickled out of his mouth. "You act. You don't talk about it, you don't beg or question how things are the way they are. You just act—you just do it. Where I come from, that is the mark of a good man to have on your side of things."

My mouth opened, but I had no words. I just stared at him, feeling slow and stupid, both arms drifting down to my sides like balloons with slow leaks. He pointed a blood-speckled index finger at me a mimicked taking a shot. The blood that had been pouring out of him a moment before slowed to a trickle, as I watched. I shook my head to clear it. "That's...impossible"

"Nothing is impossible, Hank." His voice already sounded better, strong and full, but he didn't look better. Still gaunt, still ashen. As I watched, the bullet wounds closed. I stared at him, struck mute or stupid or both. "You can't kill me. No matter how many times you fire," he said. He held up his hands, palms toward me. "Not that I want you to go on trying. It hurts, you know."

My gaze drifted back to the body on the table, and what I saw tore the air from my lungs. Jax lay there, his face bloody and torn, flesh ripped, bones broken. "You killed Jax."

Hatton winked at me and grinned. "Yes. He was delicious. Not as tasty as your friend the other night. Would you believe he fought me at first? Not that he stood any kind of a chance. I was already changing, and Liz was just across the road." He was gloating, goading me.

I was surprised to find my pistol pointed at the spot between Hatton's eyes. I *wanted* to pull the trigger, to put him down. Or at least wipe the smug grin off his face. I wanted to shoot Hatton in the face like I've never wanted anything else.

His hands went up. "I surrender, Hank."

Every particle of my being wanted me to pull the trigger. I'm not sure I'd ever wanted to shoot someone before that night, but to my shame, I did want to shoot Hatton in the face, and then to shoot him again and again and again until the pistol ran dry. Then I wanted to eject the magazine, slam in one of my spares, and shoot him until that was also empty. It was a powerful temptation, and my hands trembled with the intensity of it. But it would be murder, and I couldn't stoop that low.

"I surrender, Hank," Hatton said again, looking down at the gun shaking in my hands.

Feeling disgusted, I reached for my cuffs and tossed them over Jax's cooling corpse to the fiend who had been sitting there feasting on my friend. "Put those on. Don't make me shoot again, Hatton. I…I don't think I could stop."

Hatton nodded. "I understand, Hank. Though, you disappoint me." His voice had changed. It was deeper, torn and abused. "The queen said you wouldn't have the guts."

I pointed at his other hand with my Glock. "Other hand. Now."

He smiled and closed the chromed bracelet on his other wrist. "No problem, Hank. I'm not resisting. I surrender." He looked down at the table and sighed. "I do want you to know that if it were up to me, I would not have killed your partner. You two were so cute together. Like an old married couple."

I gestured with the gun at the gruesome display on the table before me. "It *was* up to you." The volume of my voice swelled as I came to the end of the sentence. The tip of the gun was again pointing at Hatton's face, as if by magic. My hands were almost convulsing with agitation, and I could feel the muscles and tendons of my trigger finger creaking with the strain of not pulling that trigger.

"No. No, it wasn't up to me. She ordered it, you see. She decided his fate that first day you went to the house and confronted her. She cursed him."

The image of Tutor screaming gibberish at us, her cigarette bouncing in the corner of her mouth flashed through my mind. "If she cursed Jax, then she cursed me."

"I warned you she had a vicious tongue." Hatton shrugged, a small smile playing on his lips. "She commanded me to kill your partner tonight. She told me to remind you of her... What was the phrase?" He brought his handcuffed hands to his chin and scratched it. "Hoodoo voodoo?"

Something dark and terrible warred with an icy fear as it built inside me. "What in the hell are you two? What brand of crazy?"

He laughed. "We are anything but insane, Hank. We are *gods*. Don't you understand that yet?"

Whatever was building inside me popped like a balloon, and I couldn't help it—I laughed. It was a harsh sound, anything but amused. I couldn't process what he was saying with anything approaching rationality. Jax had been murdered for a delusion of grandeur.

"I know how it sounds," he said.

"We've been here since before white men appeared on their wooden ships. I was here at a time when only the native tribes ran in these woods and fished in these streams. They thought we were gods for a long time—hardly the first time those labels were ascribed to us. Then they began to see our way of life as a curse. *Wendigo*, they called us, as they tried to drive us from their lands. My, but we had fun slaughtering them." His voice had taken on a wistful quality. "Before that, I was other places—in this world and in others."

"All this," I said, "all this for some vampire delusion." A melancholy exhaustion seemed to seep into me from the very air.

He laughed. "Vampire? There is no such thing as vampires."

I shook my head.

"Listen, Hank. You can be one of us. I want to—" Hatton snapped his mouth shut and seemed to perk up, like a dog hearing something in the distance. Then, he looked me in the eye with what appeared to be sadness and regret. "I wish we had more time, Hank. I want you to understand. All the power I have—you could have it, too."

His left deltoid twitched. It looked like a rat moving under his skin. He was…growing. His shoulders widened as I watched.

Dread took my mind in an iron grip. Once again, I was surprised to find my gun pointing at his face.

"No, Hank," he said. His voice sounded several registers deeper than it had a moment ago. "No more bullets." It sounded as if his mouth were filled with pebbles and dirt.

I pulled the trigger twice.

Hatton sat there like a statue, glaring at me. Blood ran down his face and neck, from bullet holes in his cheeks and forehead. His left eye was gone. "I told you not to do that." His voice took on a basso quality that made me want to turn and run. It was like his voice had been piped through a vocal synthesizer. "Why don't you ever listen?"

The darkness building inside me exploded, erasing coherent thought. The gun bucked again and again. When the slide locked back, my hands hurt like they'd been crushed under some heavy weight.

He roared like some kind of cornered predator. A bear or a lion, something like that. A loud, ringing kind of popping noise resounded in the small room, and my handcuffs fell off of cockamamie wrists larger than they had been when he'd cuffed himself.

The chair groaned and creaked beneath him right before it broke. He hopped to the table top, shoving Jax's remains to the floor with disdain.

He reached out with slow deliberation, his arm stretching, growing a length that belied belief, and took the Glock in one hand. He squeezed, muscles and tendons popping out on his forearms. The composite body of the pistol cracked like ice, and he tossed it to the floor in disgust.

"I should kill you for that," he howled. "I would if she hadn't forbidden it! She wants you to suffer, and suffer you shall!"

It seemed my feet had taken lessons from my hands and arms—I was backing away on autopilot, staring into his too-large face, watching his blood drip from his lips like drool. Sores were breaking out across his face and chest. Pus dripped to mingle with the congealed blood on the floor. The air was full of the reek of putrefying flesh. Bile burned the back of my throat.

He crouched on the table and glared at me, picking chips of his cheek bone from his face and neck. "Stupid," he growled. "Waste." The table cracked and popped beneath him, and he took a giant step forward, off the table to overshadow me by at least a couple of feet.

He was getting bigger, but it was like he was stretching rather than bulking up. If anything, he looked even skinnier than when he was normal sized, his bones seemed to be trying to escape from his skin.

He was getting taller by the second. He started making a weird grunting noise.

"She…was…right…to…curse…you." He struggled to speak as if he had to force the words out through a throat that didn't want to cooperate. "Teach…you…something."

For the first time that evening, it struck me that I was a dead man, standing there watching Hatton turn into I don't know what.

Hatton's chin began making weird, animal-like jerks to one side or the other. In time with those jerks, he made a strange sound—something that sounded like he was trying to up-chuck while humming a tune. His eyes were riveted on mine. "Not…insane." He leaned forward and put his face in front of mine. He growled with menace.

"What in the hell are you?" I asked in a still, small voice, wondering why I wasn't running away. It was like I was in one of those dreams that you just can't seem to escape no matter how much you wanted to.

He made a strange barking noise that seemed like a laugh. "*Ooooo…Oolf…hye…thidn.*" It was the last thing he said. He was staring at me like he'd like to take a bite, even as he continued to stretch and grow.

His display of…well, whatever it was, it terrified me. All I could think of was the night at Jay's Diner when Hatton kept repeating: "I'll bite." He had to hunch against the nine-foot ceiling. His face began to look like a plastic mask stretched over a wolf's skull. He smelled like an animal.

In the distance, I heard the sirens. I could tell by the look in his eyes that there was still a human intelligence inside and that he knew I could hear them.

I balled my hands into fists and tried to stay loose in the face of the distending, purulent monstrosity. I had a sinking certainty that my time to die had arrived, and I wanted to die well.

Run, you fool! Just get the hell out of here before he finishes...becoming whatever he's becoming, yelled a querulous voice, deep inside me. I wondered if there really was any such thing as 'dying well'—or if it was only dying. Either way, I didn't want to see the monster that lived at the end of Hatton's twisted metamorphosis.

Hatton bared his fangs at me and made a harsh, chuffing sound.

It dawned on me that he was waiting for something. I shook my head, squinting up at him and trying to figure out what he wanted.

He made the harsh sound again and then growled. I have heard a lot of dogs growl over the years, but none of them made me want to cower in fear. Hatton's growl did.

"What do you want?" I asked, sounding like a child.

He snapped his teeth in my face and, as slow as glacial ice, brought his hand up to his head and twirled his claw-like finger in a circle. Then he growled with even more menace than before.

"No," I said, and the sound of my voice brought the vision of a puppy rolling over on his back to my mind. "I don't think you are insane anymore. Maybe I'm the one who's insane."

He jerked his head back and snapped his teeth twice.

I steeled myself for the bite I felt certain was coming. Instead, stars and light exploded from the left side of my head, and I was airborne. I smashed through the plaster and lathe wall, still airborne and moving fast. I slammed through another wall and only came to a stop when I hit the cast iron tub in the bathroom, and everything went dark and hazy.

I lay there for who knows how long, dazed. I heard two shots from outside the house and then both the roar of a large animal and the shriek of a very scared man. I thought of Richie standing up to the monstrosity that Hatton had changed into and groaned. I struggled to my feet, dizzy, nauseated, and felt sticky blood all down the left side of my face. My muscles threatened to betray me as the room spun and tilted around me, and my feet seemed to want to tap dance. They just flapped around by themselves while I tried to stay upright and start moving.

Outside, it sounded like there was a pack of wolves in a feeding frenzy—growls and barks filled the air, and beneath that, the shrieking wail of approaching sirens.

I made myself move, holding my hands out to my sides, pressing my hands against the walls to keep myself upright. I stumbled down the hall and into the kitchen. I slipped in the blood of the two troopers and fell hard, bruising my hip.

I didn't think I could get up—not again, so I crawled through the laundry, through the tiny mudroom, and down the three steps to the gravel; I fought for consciousness the entire time, my head hanging in front of me, my eyes closed against the spinning and nausea. When I felt the bite of the gravel on my palms, I no longer heard the wolf-pack noises—only the sirens caterwauling as they approached.

I forced my eyes open and fought the urge to vomit as I turned my head this way and that. The broken, torn body of Richie Duvall lay in the middle of the driveway. The shattered remains of his gun lay by his side in a tidy pile.

I moved away from the house, away from Richie and the remains of his Colt, shambling along on my hands and knees. I tried to push myself to my feet, but the effort was too much, and I faded out again. When I came to again, I was lying on my side, facing the farm land behind the house. As if on cue, Hatton burst out of the darkness to my side, Melanie Layne's limp form thrown over his shoulder.

"No," I muttered. "You leave…her alone."

He looked at me with such arrogance and menace that it felt like he stared at me a long time, but it couldn't have been more than a few seconds. I remember thinking that I could feel his malice much better in this monstrous form than when he appeared as a man. He looked like a giant crossed with some kind of demonic wolf. His gaze drilled into mine, accompanied by a low growl, like a dog that feels challenged.

The sirens sounded very close, and I wanted to keep him there until the special operations team arrived. I hoped that enough guns firing in unison would be able to make him drop Melanie Layne and run.

There was another roar from behind me, something that sent icy terror racing down my spine. I turned and looked over my shoulder. A huge figure stood in the grass at the end of the drive, like a bear crossed with a woman.

Tutor, but not Tutor. She was very tall, maybe twice my height or more. Her upper body was wrapped in shaggy brown fur, and her skull and face were twisted—deformed. She met my eye and made a low noise, deep in her throat. She pointed at me with a clawed finger, as if marking me.

Hatton made that strange, barking laugh noise and stepped over me, and snapped his fangs as he did. He looked toward the fields and took a couple of steps and then looked at me and roared. It was a challenge, I thought.

Side by side, Hatton and Tutor ran off through the fields behind the house. The last I saw of Melanie Layne was her unconscious body bouncing on Hatton's shoulder.

There were cottonwood trees, bent and twisted— each one a unique and twisted sculpture of asymmetry—planted as a shelter-belt along the side of the drive. My gaze locked on the cottonwood spores dancing in the light breeze, and I was mesmerized by how beautiful they looked.

TWENTY-
TWO⊙

"I still dream about that night," I said. "Nightmares. I don't think it will ever leave me."

"It has been my experience that all things fade in time."

"I hope you are right." I shrugged. "Well, Meuhlnir? Do you still think you know your brother?"

Meuhlnir put his chin down on his chest and pursed his lips. "It may be that you bring up a valid point."

"I don't have all the answers here. I only know your brother as a sadistic and indiscriminate murderer. Someone who seems to thrive on the terror and debasement of others, regardless of who those others are."

Meuhlnir was silent, chin tucked against his chest, his eyes on the brilliant white snow in front of him. "Yes," he muttered, "and yet, I only know him as a fallen, lost soul."

"Maybe the truth of it is somewhere in between."

"It may be."

"Tell me, Meuhlnir, what was it Luka said when I asked him what he was."

"*Oolfhyethidn*. Wolf-warrior. He uses that word as a name sometimes."

I chuckled, and it tasted sour, bitter. "I should've figured that out myself."

We came out of the woods then. The distance from the *proo* to the lake via the path was much shorter than the route through the woods I'd taken. The pale winter snow sparkled on the ice covering the lake. My quinzhee was still standing not far from the shore of the lake, but part of the roof had fallen in.

"Your shelter?" asked Meuhlnir, walking over to it.

"Yes," I said. "I didn't have the time to make it right, but I survived, so I guess it was good enough."

Meuhlnir chuckled and stuck his head in through the hole in the roof. "Ingenious," he said. "A house of snow."

"On my *klith*, some people live in brutal winter climates who used to live in houses made from snow and nothing else."

"A hardy people then. I assume they live close to the poles?"

I nodded. "Yeah, close to the northern pole. Were there no Laplanders in Scandinavia when you visited the Vikings?"

Meuhlnir scratched his beard. "I don't recall meeting anyone who said he was a Laplander, but there could have been. People don't often label themselves in the same way that others do, especially when separated by the gulf of time."

"I think they called themselves the Sami. I think the Laplander reference comes from a word that means the edge of the world or something. They lived above the arctic circle in Scandinavia. They also had igloos and quinzhee for houses in the cold months."

Meuhlnir shrugged. "We spent most of our time on the coasts where it was warmer." He held up a hand to shade his eyes and then waved the hand before us like a tour guide. "I don't see the *proo* you traveled."

"Just as well, I don't have any use for it until I find Jane and Sig."

Meuhlnir looked at me from the corner of his eye. "I'm sure we can rescue them," he said.

"Any sign of your *proo*?"

Meuhlnir peered around at the island, muttering under his breath. "None. If he has co-opted my *proo*, my brother and I will have words, I can tell you that." From the sound of his voice, I didn't expect that the words would be very polite. Meuhlnir made a disgusted noise in the back of his throat, squinting at the area around the lake. "Well, no use standing around grumbling," he said. "If it's gone, it's gone, and there's nothing to be done about it."

"Can you use another *proo* to get to Veethar?"

Meuhlnir sighed. "If I had one handy. No, this development means we will be riding for days."

"Riding?" I asked.

"Horses." Meuhlnir grimaced. "People should be more mindful of the work other people have put into something." His voice rumbled like a pissed-off bear.

"And old men should be more mindful of standing around in the cold and snow," boomed a voice from the edge of the woods.

A tall man sat on the biggest horse I'd ever seen in my life—it must have stood seven-and-half feet at the shoulder. The horse was a dark bay, and the man had long, flowing red hair and a mid-length beard of the same color. He wore twin axes shoved through his wide leather belt.

"And youngsters should be mindful of old men carrying hammers," said Meuhlnir with a hint of mildness in his tone.

The rider walked the horse toward them, his eyes roving over the quinzhee. "Nice hut," he said, "if you like cold walls."

"It served its purpose," I said.

The rider's eyes shifted toward me. They were a piercing blue, bordering on pale gray. His face was impassive as he rode toward us. "Did it, now?" he asked. "How did you let yourself be caught out in a *sterk task*?"

I sighed. "I guess I should get used to that question, eh? I arrived in the middle of it and not by plan."

The tall rider's eyes roved over me from head to toe and then shifted toward Meuhlnir. "*Kanka-ee*, then?"

"Might as well ask if young men are brash and rude," said Meuhlnir. "He's my guest, and you will afford him the guest-right the same as if he was yours."

"As you will, Father," said the rider who had now reached us. He slid off the magnificent reddish-brown horse and patted it affectionately on the neck. Then he turned toward me and arched his eyebrow, and I couldn't repress a smile. "Something?" he asked.

"Nothing," I said, still smiling. "It's just that your expression was so much like one Meuhlnir has shown me about nine hundred times since I met him last night."

"Ah, yes. The quizzical look, I know it well." He smiled, but the smile faded. "I didn't know I did it." He shot Meuhlnir a reproachful look. "My name is Mothi."

I couldn't help, but I chuckled.

"Something?" he said again, a strange expression on his face. "Not many men laugh at me."

"Not at you, Mothi," I said. "At the strangeness of all of this. What is a Ganka...whatever?"

"*Kanka-ee*. It means walk-in in the *Gamla Toonkumowl*," said Meuhlnir. "Hank, this is my son, Mothi. Mothi, this is Hank Jensen. He's Norse by descent. His trip has been..." Meuhlnir shrugged.

"It's been eye-opening," I said. "Meeting men out of myth and legend. Meeting 'gods' and all that."

Mothi's face wrinkled. "I see. Not all of us believe that those visits were—"

"I told him," snapped Meuhlnir. "What brings you from Krimsnes?"

Mothi waved both arms out wide. "The *sterk task*, of course. I've come to see that you, mother and Mother Yowrnsaxa are okay."

"And this great lout?" Meuhlnir patted the horse on the muzzle with obvious affection. "How is little Skaytprimir?"

Mothi smiled. "Still snorting when he runs."

Meuhlnir gave the horse a final pat. "Come to the house, Mothi. We've things to discuss and do."

"I thought as much, for all your 'why are you here' nonsense. A son knows." He grinned.

"A son knows nothing," said Meuhlnir with a poor attempt at hiding a smile.

"A son knows nothing will please his father more than the son pretending his father is always right."

"Might as well ask if there are any intelligent young men."

Mothi let loose a great booming laugh. "Here we go. Now, I know I'm home if I 'might as well ask.'"

Meuhlnir shrugged. "One does what one can."

Meuhlnir led us through the woods to the cabin, and as soon as we arrived, Mothi shoved the reins of Skaytprimir to his father and barged through the door. "Mother Sif, Mother Yowrnsaxa, I've come to rescue you from Father!" he boomed. His cry was answered with squeals of delight and laughter.

"Mothering noises," grunted Meuhlnir. "No matter how big they get, no matter how old, they will always be a little boy to their mothers. Nothing to be done about it."

"Nope," I said. "Might as well ask mothers to fly."

"Hmph," grunted Meuhlnir. "Like any other skill, practice is required." He tied Skaytprimir to a convenient bush near the door. "Now, don't go pulling up all the plants and trees this time, you great lout of a snorting fool," he said, petting the horse's forehead and tugging at his forelock with obvious affection.

"Mothi will have to go get a few more steeds. You don't mind if I ask Mothi to come with us, do you?"

"Come with us?" I asked in surprise. "You've decided to help me?"

"How could I not? You don't know our ways. You don't even know how to get out of these woods."

"That is very generous of you, Meuhlnir. If you are sure?"

Meuhlnir looked me in the eye, his gaze unwavering. "I am sure."

"To be honest, I am relieved. It seems like a lot to ask. Not to mention—"

"My brother Luka," finished Meuhlnir.

"And what has that great idiot of an uncle done now?" asked Mothi from the doorway. He waved a big hand in our direction. "Are you two not smart enough to come in out of the cold?"

Meuhlnir made a face and patted the horse. "Skaytprimir was distraught at your abrupt disappearance. He cried."

Mothi looked at the horse with mock severity. "I've spoken to him about his manipulative nature."

"He's perfect as he is," said Sif, peering over Mothi's shoulder and shoving at him to make way. She gave the horse a great hug. Yowrnsaxa came up beside her and patted the horse on the muzzle. It was as if the horse were part of the family.

I hadn't even thought about the language barrier since breakfast and found that it was much easier that way after all. I'd understood Mothi easily enough, and now Sif's speech was clear as well.

"Mothi," said Meuhlnir. "I—"

Mothi looked pleased. "I know. Horses, right?"

"Might as well ask if the sky lords itself over Father's Spine Mountains."

Mothi sucked in a breath. "I'd hate to be Luka when Father catches up to him," he said with a conspiratorial wink at me.

It was an awkward moment. No one quite knew what to say, or where to look. Meuhlnir broke the silence by clearing his throat. "We will speak more of your uncle on our journey. Leave it for now."

Mothi looked back and forth between his father's face and mine. "Okay," he said with a severe expression. With two running steps and a great leap, he was astride the big horse. He reined the horse around, and they raced off, the horse snorting with every other step. "I'll be back tomorrow," shouted Mothi over his shoulder.

Yowrnsaxa chuckled. "That horse still snorts," she said, and they all laughed.

TWENTY-
THREE

The next morning, Mothi was sitting on the hearth when I came downstairs. None of the others seemed to be around, so I sat in one of the chairs.

"Good ride?" I asked him.

He grunted. "I like to ride, but I think we'll all have our fill of it soon." A serious expression stole over his face. "Father told me what Luka is doing to you and your family. I don't know what to say, other than I'm sorry."

I lifted my hands from the arms of the chair in a shrug. "Luka is quite separate from the rest of you in my mind."

Mothi shook his head. "Nothing has been as it should be for many, many years. Luka follows a dark path, far from the one any would have guessed at in his youth. That Black Bitch is to blame."

"That's what I understand. She hasn't endeared herself to me, either."

"The curse...the pain is bad?"

I sighed. "Not in your father's house, but everywhere else..." I shrugged and gazed into the fire. "I'll be okay."

Mothi tilted his head and looked at me for a long moment. "You look like you have a great deal of strength, even so."

I shook my head. "Not so much anymore. Before this damn disease, I used to train hard, but since..."

Mothi grunted. "Father will get you sorted. He is a *vefari* of the highest order."

I nodded. "He has told me he likes lightning..."

Mothi laughed. "That old man and his lightning. I don't know which he likes better, smiting the ground or making the sky shout."

"Might as well ask whether a horse snorts because it is running fast or if it is running fast because it snorts." Meuhlnir walked into the room from the hallway that led to the feasting hall.

"You leave him alone," growled Mothi with pretend fierceness. "He is sensitive to your scorn."

"Hmph," grunted Meuhlnir. "Sensitive to my corn more likely. That snorting lout got you there and back in good time."

Mothi snorted. "I guess snorting has its uses, then?"

Meuhlnir chuckled. "Your mouth always was smarter than your head."

Mothi snorted again and stood next to his father. "Smarter than you, old man. And taller."

Meuhlnir waved that away. "But I am prettier. All the women say so."

"Bah. You are an eyesore to the female population. A blemish on the skin of mankind. A blight to the non-blind members of the fairer sex. A monstrosity of—"

"Oh yes, bring the blind into it. As if they can judge my looks."

Mothi laughed. "They can sure judge your smell."

Meuhlnir looked around in mock surprise. "But I've just bathed!"

"You two idiots still bantering?" called Yowrnsaxa from the top of the stairs. "Always, it's the same. Mothi comes to visit, and no one else can talk for the next three or four days due to your nonsense." She was holding a pack and had a shield slung across her back.

Meuhlnir's face tightened, and he gave Mothi an imploring look.

"Oh, no," said Mothi. "You're not dragging me into this. You three have to figure it out for yourselves." He patted me on the shoulder. "You probably want to be somewhere else. Unless, that is, you like hearing women swear and an old man wheedle and beg."

"I don't swear!" said Sif.

"And I don't beg," said Meuhlnir.

Yowrnsaxa rolled her eyes. "As if anyone would believe that."

Mothi pulled me up by the arm without much effort. No small feat, given that I must have weighed close to three hundred pounds. "Come on, Hank, I'll introduce you to the best horse before Father has a chance to claim him."

"That's not fair," said Meuhlnir with a pout.

Mothi shrugged. "Guest-right," he said with a wide grin.

As I followed Mothi through the front door, I heard Yowrnsaxa come down the stairs, her gear jingling. "And don't you think for a minute that you are going off on some big adventure and leaving Sif and me here to stew and darn your socks. It's as if you think you have enough common sense to travel without someone along to tell you what to do and when to do it."

"I am the man of this house," said Meuhlnir. "I am the one leading this expedition—"

"Oh ho! You are the man of the house, are you?" asked Sif with an edge in her voice. "Don't you mean you are the slug-about of the house?"

I glanced at Mothi and saw that he had his head down, but a grin stretched across his face. "He always makes the same mistakes with them," he whispered. "But don't worry, all is well."

"You are in charge, are you?" asked Yowrnsaxa. "You decide what your weak little wives will do, eh? It's as if you think you have the mental capacity to run things around here."

"Ladies, please. You are taking this all wrong. It's not that I don't value your opinions—"

"So now our opinions matter? Good," said Sif. "I am of the opinion that I am coming with you. If I don't, who will protect you from the dark? What is your opinion Yowrnsaxa?"

"I'm of the same mind," said Yowrnsaxa. "And besides, while you are holding his hand and keeping him from being scared of the dark, I can hold his other hand and sing him a lullaby."

"Well, it's settled then. Let's go pick our horses."

"Wait a minute! You two cannot simply decide—" said Meuhlnir.

"I hope Mothi brought Kutltohper. She is my favorite these days," said Sif.

Footsteps approached the doorway behind us. Mothi nudged my arm. "This is Slaypnir," he said in a loud voice. "He's very fast and very smart. He's the best around new riders, but he has quite the sense of humor." He pointed at a magnificent looking blue roan with huge hooves that were covered by shaggy white hair. It was a large horse, obviously from stock that was bred for war. At the withers, the horse stood taller than me.

"A horse with a sense of humor?" I asked.

"Slaypnir means trickster in the *Gamla Toonkumowl*," said Mothi.

"What does Skaytprimir mean?"

Mothi chuckled. "He who snorts while he runs."

"Ah, now I get all those jokes about snorting."

"Indeed," said Mothi.

Behind us, two sets of boots started crunching into the snow. "Oh, look, Sif, there's Kutltohper!" said Yowrnsaxa, pointing at the palomino mare standing next to Slaypnir. Kutltohper's mane was mostly white, but a bright blonde tuft hung forward on her forehead. "She is so pretty."

"Prettier than both of you," grumped Meuhlnir.

"Of course, Mother Yowrnsaxa. I brought Falhoefnir, as well," said Mothi.

"Now, wait just a minute!" said Meuhlnir standing in the doorway. His voice was hard and angry. "I've not given you two permission to join us. I don't think we could carry enough food to keep you two fat and happy."

I looked at Slaypnir and put my hand out to be sniffed, suddenly feeling like I had as a child the first time my parents argued in front of me.

"Did you know, Hank, that in our culture, a woman may divorce her husband just by telling him so?" said Sif, coming over to pat Slaypnir's flank.

"Indeed," said Yowrnsaxa from behind me. "Maybe we'd be better married to a man from your *klith*."

I wasn't sure what to say, but I felt a blush creeping up my face.

Mothi saved me. "Now, Mothers, we all know—except for Hank, maybe—that you are flyting with father and that, indeed, you have won, though he doesn't seem to know that. All this talk of divorce is about as real as a two-headed bear. You three are as bad as you claim Father and I are, Mother Yowrnsaxa."

"That reminds me of a story—" started Meuhlnir.

"Now, Father," he said, talking over him, "you know, I know, and they certainly know, that both of my mothers will be coming along. The only question is how uncomfortable the first day's ride will be—how long my mothers will insist on telling me things to pass on to you when you are standing right there. That, and how long it will take you to realize they've beaten you again."

"Mothi, tell your father to get his things," said Sif, as if they'd planned the timing.

Mothi rolled his eyes but grinned at me. "You see?"

"What is flyting?" I asked.

"A traditional exchange of insults—most of the time, all in fun, though it can be serious," said Sif.

"Deadly," said Yowrnsaxa with a nod.

"Should a man ever marry and have children? Might as well ask if trees can walk," muttered

Meuhlnir as he turned back inside the cabin and grabbed his pack.

"Mothi, tell your father not to mutter. We have company," said Yowrnsaxa.

Meuhlnir laughed, and like the key log in a log jam, his laugh let all the tension out of the argument. The atmosphere seemed to be about two hundred pounds lighter. "I can never beat these two at flyting," said Meuhlnir with a wink in my direction.

"Now, that you've given Slaypnir to Hank, what horse is left for my old rump?" asked Meuhlnir, looking at the pack of horses with a critical eye.

"I can ride another," I said.

"Don't be silly, Hank," said Sif. "Meuhlnir is just feeling cranky and difficult this morning."

"Mothi, tell Mother Sif that I am still her husband, and I have a back to both hands." Though his voice seemed hard, Meuhlnir had a huge grin on his face.

Mothi just rolled his eyes. "As if you could take her," he said.

"If Yowrnsaxa didn't help, I could," said Meuhlnir.

"No, you couldn't," said Yowrnsaxa. "Everyone knows this except you. And anyway, what makes you think I wouldn't join in and give your old rump a proper kicking?"

It all had the feeling of well-rehearsed burlesque.

"Sif could do that on her own," said Meuhlnir, "but two are better than one, I think."

"Anyway," said Mothi, a trifle too loud. "You can have your pick from these four horses here, Father."

He pointed to four horses that where standing in a small knot. "Lyettfeti, Keesl, Klader, or Sinir."

"I suppose your Mother Yowrnsaxa is insisting she ride Falhoefnir?" asked Meuhlnir, looking at a pretty black and white mare with shaggy white hair covering her hooves, like Slaypnir's.

"As if you would ever ride a mare," muttered Yowrnsaxa. She walked over to Falhoefnir and patted her withers. "She likes me better anyway."

Meuhlnir scoffed. "I see I will not have any choices on this trip," he grumped. "I suppose I will ride Sinir here." He put his pack behind the saddle of a black stallion. "I see that you again left Ploetughoefi, denying me the pleasure of riding a horse with a little vim."

Mothi rolled his eyes. "Are you losing your mind, old man? You told me to loan old Bloody-hoof to Veethar over a year ago."

"And? You couldn't bring him anyway?"

Mothi grinned and shook his head. "What is wrong with you?"

"Might as well ask what makes music good."

"Oh, so everything?" grunted Sif and they all laughed.

"Don't take any of this seriously, Hank," said Yowrnsaxa when she saw I wasn't laughing.

"I'm not," I said past the lump in my throat. "This reminds me of my family." The two women looked at me with sympathy, while father and son looked anywhere else but at me. If you can be sure of any one talent I am gifted with, it is the talent for killing the mood.

"Well," said Meuhlnir. "Time waits for no man." He lashed his pack on behind Sinir's saddle and swung himself up.

"Watching you mount a horse is like…" said Mothi.

"Watching a dancer?"

"A dancer falling down," laughed Sif.

"More like watching a Tverkr walk on ice," said Yowrnsaxa.

"Ah! You think I'm graceful under pressure then. Why not just say so?" asked Meuhlnir with a wink in my direction.

The others mounted, and I climbed on to Slaypnir's back. He tossed his head and snorted as if to remind me who was in charge out of the two of us.

"This is a picture to remember," said Meuhlnir. "The intrepid adventurers sit their horses in preparation to set out. It's—"

"Husband, do you ever shut that noise maker?" asked Sif.

Meuhlnir scoffed. "Might as well ask if The Dragon's Spine Mountains are made of wood." He gave Sinir a few gentle kicks with his heel and started off down the trail, whistling an aimless little tune.

"Might as well ask the sun not to rise," said Yowrnsaxa.

The rest of us followed Meuhlnir, trying not to laugh too loud. Conversation was hard on the trail through the woods—the horses didn't seem to want to walk too close to the snow laden branches of the trees overhanging the trail—so we rode in silence for most of the morning. The *clop-clop* of the horse's hooves was soothing somehow, but my curse and sitting in a saddle for extended periods of time were not exactly compatible.

The farther we got from the house, the more intense the pain in my hips, back, and shoulders got, and when we stopped for a bite to eat and a bit of warmth by a small fire, I had difficulty dismounting.

Sif took one look at me and clucked her tongue like a mother hen. "Mothi, get my bag," she said.

"Sif, it's a curse the Dark Bitch—" said Meuhlnir.

"I've told you not to call her that in my presence," Sif said with acid in her voice. "You forget Yowrnsaxa and I were *Trohtninkar Tumuhr.*"

He held up his hands in surrender. "You are right, my dear, and I apologize, though she is no longer worthy of the respect you pay her."

She gave him quite a look—one that promised there would be some fierce conversation on the subject later—and flapped her hand at Mothi. "My bag?"

"Sif, dear one," said Meuhlnir, "this man has been cursed by the Dark Queen. I'm not sure if the contents of your bag, or your gift, no matter how potent it is, will be of use."

"I will try, and then we will know, won't we," she snapped.

"Of course, dear one."

Mothi handed his mother a tanned leather bag that looked like a bucket bag Jane had owned on our *klith*. Sif rummaged around inside for a moment, muttering under her breath. "There it is," she said. She pulled a small wooden container out of the bag and pulled its lid off. A noxious odor filled the small clearing.

"Uff," said Mothi.

"Quiet, you," said Sif. She looked at me with a critical eye. "Where is the worst spot?"

"Hips and back, I guess," I said. "What is that?"

"Don't worry about what this is. Pull up your shirt and drop your britches."

I looked at her in surprise. "Uh…"

"For goodness sake, man. I'm married to that lout over there and have been surrounded by male children my entire life. Do you think you have parts I've never seen before? I haven't been *Trohtninkar Tumuhr* for centuries. Now, off with the clothes or I'll have Yowrnsaxa to help."

I looked at Meuhlnir, and he shrugged and turned his back to me.

I loosened my belt and let my trousers and underwear fall to my ankles. Sif was rubbing her hands over the fire, warming them. I pulled off my shirt, and the cold enveloped me. "What is Troutingins Tumer, anyway?"

"*Trohtninkar Tumuhr*," she said, turning to face me. She smeared some of the noxious-smelling gel on her hands and started to rub it into my hips, starting right next to my groin and moving outwards. "It means Queen's Ladies. *Trohtninkar Tumuhr* were companions to Queen Suel. Companions and *skyuldur vidnukonur*—shield maidens. We were the last line of defense if those great louts in the *Vuthuhr Trohtninkar* failed to do their jobs."

"On my side, a queen or princess would be surrounded by women who were kept chaste as companions to the royal woman."

"Ah, maids of honor," said Yowrnsaxa. "Some cultures here had that."

"Waste of a woman," grunted Sif.

My skin was beginning to burn where she had applied the cream, but it was a good kind of burn. Warmth seemed to be seeping into my hips, and the pain seemed much diminished. "What is that stuff? You could make a fortune selling that as a patent medicine on my *klith*."

Sif cocked an eyebrow at me. "Anyone who would sell medicine for money is contemptible. A healer is called to heal, not to make money." She had switched to the small of my back and was rubbing in the cream like my skin was her mortal enemy.

"Well, it works, whatever it is."

Sif grunted. "There are two coincidental pathways in the body related to pain. One is for real pain, and one is for things that irritate—like burns of the sun or a rash that itches. This works by overloading that second channel. The channels share a common path to the brain, the pain is partially blocked due to the overload."

"Genius," I said.

"Sif really is talented," said Meuhlnir.

"Shut your mouth, lout," said Sif. "I'm not done being irritated with you yet."

"Yes, dear," said Meuhlnir with a modesty no one in the clearing believed.

"And that won't work, either," snapped Sif.

Yowrnsaxa chuckled and punched Meuhlnir in the shoulder. "Oh, you've done it now, you great idiot."

"Clothe yourself, Hank, I'm done. We can repeat this again after we stop for the night."

Yowrnsaxa handed out small wooden bowls filled with a thick stew that I hadn't even smelled her cooking—which, given the odor of the gel smeared all over me, wasn't really a surprise. The stew was incredible, and to this day, I have no idea how she made such great stew in such a short amount of time over a campfire.

After we ate, I stood and stretched and was amazed at how much better the pain and stiffness was. I swung up into Slaypnir's saddle as if I'd been doing it for years, easy peasy.

Sif smiled at me and patted her bag.

"Again, my mother is right, and my father is wrong. Shall I pretend to be surprised?" asked Mothi with a big grin plastered on his face.

Meuhlnir didn't even grumble as he sat Sinir. "This time, I'm glad to be wrong," he said.

"Shut it," grunted Sif. "You are still in trouble."

Yowrnsaxa giggled. "You've really stepped in it, O' God of Thunder."

"Indeed," said Meuhlnir. "It's one of my gifts."

"Indeed, it is," said Yowrnsaxa.

Mothi grunted. "This is why I don't marry," he said to me with a wink.

"Don't start with me," said Sif. "You aren't so big I can't clout you between the eyes."

Mothi laughed and spurred his horse into a brisk trot. "You'd have to catch me first."

We rode until the sun dipped below the tops of the trees, and then Meuhlnir called a halt. The gel had made most the ride enjoyable, despite the cold and being cramped in one position most of the time, but it had started to fade about an hour before we stopped. I got down from Slaypnir and patted him on the neck, every joint stiff and sore. He whinnied and nuzzled me. He stood looking at me with his big eyes, ears cocked forward as if he understood that the pain was back and was concerned for me.

I caught Sif looking at me from the saddle of Kutltohper. She patted her medicine bag and raised an eyebrow.

"Not yet," I said. I didn't know if her gel would be like everything else, but seven years of disappointment as medicines lost efficacy after a few short months had made me cautious about using things up. It may sound silly, but I thought that I had to conserve what worked and only use it when I could no longer stand the pain. I sometimes went six months before refilling a pain prescription—in part, because I hated the way pain meds made me feel, but mostly because I was always doing what Jane called the 'Calculous of When.' The Calculous of When amounted to deciding when I felt bad enough to warrant a pain pill.

I stood there rubbing at the small of my back, watching night fall over the tops of the trees that surrounded us. Mothi gathered a stack of firewood and worked at getting a fire going. Yowrnsaxa walked back and forth between a large cook pot and one of the pack animals, ferrying ingredients for whatever culinary magic she had in store for us that evening. Yowrnsaxa was an excellent cook from what I could see, but the last thing I wanted at that point was to eat a hot meal. Meuhlnir worked with the horses, whispering to each one as he rubbed them down.

"He makes a big fuss and plays at being hard as iron, but all anyone has to do is watch him with his animals to know what is in his heart," said Sif from beside me.

"I hardly know him, but I believe he is a good man."

"He is," she said.

"It's hard to reconcile the fact that he and Luka are from the same stock."

Sif cocked her head and looked at me from under arched eyebrows. "Have you never met two brothers as different as they?"

I shrugged and looked away. "Of course, I have met criminals whose siblings were anything but criminal, but Luka..."

She nodded her head. "Luka goes beyond what you've seen."

I nodded.

"The great lout tell you we live longer than most?"

"Yeah, but he avoids telling me how old he is."

Sif chuckled. "He has gotten a bit vain over the years. Would it surprise you to know that I gave birth to Mothi over three centuries ago?"

I looked at her askance to see if she was joking, but she looked back at me with no hint of humor in her expression. "He wasn't my first child, either."

"But…Mothi looks younger than I do. I'm only forty-seven."

She shook her head. "A mere child," she mused. "You have a book on your side, don't you, that tells a mythical story of the creation of the universe?"

"Several," I said with a grin.

"This one talks about there being one god, though it confusingly describes that one god as made up of three distinct gods."

I nodded. "The Bible says something like that."

"And in this Bible, aren't there people who live a thousand years?"

"Well, there is mention of people living that long, but scholars seem to think it is either figurative, mistranslated or a different method of time keeping."

She waved her hand as if to dismiss those ideas. "Would it surprise you to know that the people in that book—at least those long-lived people—were visitors from my *klith*?"

I shook my head, trying to keep the anger I felt at the repetitive interference in the development of my world from splashing across my face.

She shrugged. "It was a different time. The ability to move the *preer* was new, and like any novel thing, everyone wanted a chance to play with them. At any rate, the *Geumlu* put little machines into the air that put other little machines into our blood that kill disease and abate the impact of aging on our bodies."

"Telling secrets, wife?" asked Meuhlnir from where he was brushing down one of the horses.

"He deserves the truth," she said with a shrug.

Meuhlnir grunted but didn't turn from his task.

"So, you can see that if brothers on your own side can change drastically from one another in such a short time, that brothers on this *klith*, brothers who live so much longer, can drift even farther apart?"

I nodded, looking at Meuhlnir's back. "The real question is if they can draw close again after drifting so far."

"Indeed," said Sif. "What's he told you about the Dark Queen?"

"Not much, really," I said. "He told me the story of her being attacked in the queen's gardens and how he saved her from the two assassins. He told me she didn't start life as she is now."

"Indeed not," said Sif. "She was an excellent ruler in the beginning. A good woman, who cared more for others than she did for herself. I knew that back then, even as she hit me. She cared so much for Meuhlnir that she couldn't stand seeing him brought to the brink of death."

My eyebrows shot up. "You were the healer she struck?"

Sif smiled. "He doesn't like to tell people that part for some reason. But yes, I was the healer who came to the gardens that night. I ministered to Meuhlnir after the queen's *vefnathur strenki.*"

"Wow," I said, not really knowing how to respond.

She chuckled and nodded. "Wow, indeed." She sobered. "Things were... I don't know, different somehow after that night. *She* was different after that."

"Meuhlnir said he wondered if her striking you was the start of her fall from grace."

"I know he thinks that, but I don't. Many things started her down the path she is on. Striking me might have dented her armor, so to speak, but there were many blows to that armor that caused it to fail. You understand?"

"Yes," I said. "People don't change by leaps and bounds, but by small, infinitesimal degrees, in my experience."

"Indeed," said Sif. "Now, let me administer more of this cream."

"I'm okay," I said. "Really."

"Hardly," she scoffed. "You think I can't see through male stubbornness and bravado? After living five centuries with that great lout yonder?"

"I heard that, woman," grunted Meuhlnir.

"And indeed, you were meant to. Now tell your friend here to stop being a typical man and let me minister to his pain."

Meuhlnir straightened from picking at something in Kutltohper's hoof. "Best do as she says, Hank," he said, tipping me a wink. "It's that or be harried until you do, and of the two options, let me testify that the first is much easier on the ego."

That was how I ended up standing next to a blazing fire with my pants down while a thick soup bubbled and popped beside me. "We will help you get rid of this curse," she promised. "Between Meuhlnir's skills as a *vefari*, my healing knowledge, and Yowrnsaxa's gifts, we will overcome the Dark Queen's curse."

"Well, this miracle cream helps a lot in the meantime."

Sif waved that away. "Merely treating the symptom, not the cause."

I chuckled. "That's all anyone has been able to do for me thus far. Relief, at this point, is good enough for me."

She nodded, expression sour. "Maybe so, but it is not good enough for me. We will help you be rid of this, Hank."

"Just so," said Yowrnsaxa.

"Well, thanks, but don't worry if there's nothing you can do."

"Of course there's something we can do," said Meuhlnir, walking over from the horses and looking into the cook pot. "We cannot allow you to suffer in this way."

I looked at their earnest faces, one by one, knowing that they meant what they said, but not knowing—

not really knowing—if they could deliver. When I got to Mothi, he cracked a big smile.

"Don't look at me," he said. "I'm just the muscle."

"With his biggest muscle right between his eyes," said Meuhlnir.

"Oh, don't you two start," said Yowrnsaxa with mock severity, pushing a bowl of soup into my hand. "Eat this, Hank."

Mothi had pulled up a couple of fallen trees so that we wouldn't have to sit in the snow, and I sank down on a comfortable-looking bend in the larger of the two. My appetite had awoken during the conversation with Sif, and I wolfed the soup down as fast as I could spoon it into my mouth. Sif elbowed Yowrnsaxa and pointed at me with her spoon, a large grin splitting her face.

"There's more," said Yowrnsaxa between chuckles. "Mothi can eat, but I'll not let him eat you into starvation."

"Good," I said. "I mean, it's good." I wanted to expand on the compliment, but there was more delicious soup in my bowl waiting to be eaten.

"Well, I'm glad you enjoy my trail cooking. We're going to be eating a lot of it, I fear."

Meuhlnir grunted.

Yowrnsaxa smiled at her husband.

"So," I said between spoons of delicious soup, "who will tell me more about the Dark Queen or Luka?"

Meuhlnir smiled and sighed. "I remember the time when Luka and I were boys and—"

"Oh, you great buffoon! He doesn't want to hear you reminisce about your youth. He wants to know what made them the way they are," said Sif.

"Then you tell him something," said Meuhlnir with a shrug.

"Yeah," I said. "Tell me about being one of the Dark Queen's ladies."

Sif cocked her head to the side and stared off into the darkness of the woods. "She was always flirting with the *Vuthuhr Trohtninkar* especially with that great lout across the fire. Not that any of them objected, as she was quite beautiful when she was young."

"I don't know that it was flirting," said Meuhlnir. "There was a lot of teasing and banter, that's for sure, but flirting?"

Yowrnsaxa burst out in a loud belly-laugh. "It's amazing that men and women ever marry," she said with tears running down her cheeks.

"Whatever do you mean?" asked Meuhlnir with a frown.

"Don't know if it was flirting? Men never do. They just play along and wait for a woman to hit them on the head with a sign that says, 'Kiss me, you fool.' Of *course* she was flirting with you and your lot. She wanted male companionship. She wanted…I don't know…intimacy."

"No," said Meuhlnir. "It was—"

"Yes," said Sif. "She told us many times. She wanted to be in love with someone, and where was she going to meet anyone?" She scoffed. "The court?

All those decrepit old men?" She made a dismissive gesture. "Not a chance. But she *was* surrounded by the bravest men in the empire. Tall, strong men with big, burly chests and great long beards."

Meuhlnir shook his head but kept his tongue.

"At any rate, she was always flirting with one of a select few *Vuthuhr Trohtninkar*—Meuhlnir, Luka, Veethar, Vowli, Paltr, Pratyi, and Huthr were the main ones she was interested in. That was back when they all got along."

Meuhlnir grunted with a sour expression on his face. "Before Huthr was tricked into killing Paltr and Vowli murdered Huthr."

"Yes," said Sif. "Before all that. Suel seemed to enjoy getting them all twisted up with innuendo. She toyed with them, even as she wanted one of them. It wasn't one of the finer points of her character."

Meuhlnir bristled and opened his mouth to speak, but Yowrnsaxa put her hand on his, and he looked at her and then closed his mouth.

"I remember a time when she invited Vowli and Luka to her reception chambers. The conversation that occurred was…dark. It started when she asked them if she should bother listening to the karls—the merchants and land owners."

TWENTY-
FOUR

"All these petitioners," said Queen Suel. "The headaches they cause me are almost constant."

"Ignore them, my Queen," said Vowli. He stood before her with a confident manner and a brash smile on his lips. "What are they to you?"

Sif scoffed without meaning to.

"Something to add, Sif?" said Suel.

Though the queen's voice was silky-smooth, it was laced with angry undertones. Internally, Sif cringed. That tone of voice was a strong indication that the queen was in one of her moods. "No, your Majesty. Forgive me."

The queen looked at her with stony eyes and a hard smile. "When I want to hear from you, girl, I will ask your opinion."

It used to be that Queen Suel valued the opinions of her *Trohtninkar Tumuhr*, and not only allowed but *encouraged* them to speak freely. It was becoming apparent, however, that she now viewed their opinions as interruptions at best.

"Yes, your Majesty," said Sif.

Suel continued to stare at her for a protracted moment, while Vowli and Luka tried to hide their amusement. "Is that a note of disapproval in your voice, *skyuldur vidnukona*? Are you my peer now? Are you my judge?"

"No, your Grace! I wouldn't think of it."

"You would do well to keep your cow's mouth shut in my presence today, *skyuldur vidnukona*," snapped Suel. "Go stand next to the wall. I can't stand the sight of you." The queen's voice was cold and distant, almost hateful.

Sif bowed low and took her place next to Yowrnsaxa along the side wall of the chamber. Yowrnsaxa gave her hand a quick squeeze as soon as the queen turned away.

The queen looked back at Vowli and treated him to a sweet smile. "My apologies, Vowli. Please, continue."

"As I was saying, your Majesty, what are these people to you? They are your subjects and must obey your will."

The queen shrugged. "That's true enough, but don't I have certain responsibilities toward the people I rule?"

"I don't see why," said Vowli.

"It is as Vowli says, your Grace," said Luka. "These people are lucky to have you as a ruler. This land is known for the quality of life you give your people. They should learn to appreciate you, instead of heaping new demands on you every week."

The queen pursed her lips and then laughed her new, gravelly laugh. "But what happens to the quality of life if I begin to ignore their grievances?"

Vowli shrugged. "To my mind, the quality of life of the karls and thralls are less important than the yarls, who in turn, are less important than yourself, your Grace."

"But surely it is the role of yarls to better the quality of life for our subjects. Isn't that why Isi set us above the lower castes?"

Luka grinned and shook his head. "Who can say why we were set above the others? Maybe because we are better than they are. Maybe our lives matter more than theirs."

Suel laughed again. "That seems like a decadent philosophy, my dear Luka. Possibly an immoral one."

Vowli shrugged and dazzled her with a smile. "As with all things, your Grace, morality is never black and white. It is, after all, a construct of mere men, and is bent this way and that to serve the wants of those who scream about it the loudest."

Suel looked at him and raised an eyebrow. "So then, what truly guides the actions of us all?"

"Our basest desires, dressed up as virtue. Aren't the sagas full of tales that illustrate this point?"

"I don't recall any sagas that could be said to support your hypothesis, Vowli." Suel cocked her head to the side. "Unless you mean that there are no selfless actions? Everyone has a hidden motivation for every act?"

Luka laughed. "Sometimes not so hidden."

Vowli clapped his friend on the back. "It's true. I have never seen anyone act in a way that can't be explained by wish gratification. Even the most selfless of acts."

"Interesting," said Suel. "So, you argue that there is no altruism, that everyone does what he does because he gets some reward from it? What about my actions these past years? What were my rewards?"

Vowli grinned with insolence and spread his arms wide. "This is quite a palace, my Queen. You've servants and courtiers to do your bidding and meet your every desire."

Suel's eyes narrowed, and her brows twitched together. "Your argument seems to judge me in a dark light, Vowli."

"Not at all, your Majesty. You, above all, deserve to be pampered. You are the best of us."

"Then I should make decisions based on what I want rather than what is best for all?"

"Your Grace," said Luka, "we are but *Vuthuhr Trohtninkar*. These questions are not for us to decide."

"We do your bidding, your Majesty," said Vowli with a smile.

"So, after all this, you hide behind your positions?"

Luka looked grave. "Who am I to advise Your Grace? I am not king." He smiled slyly. "Not yet."

Suel rolled her eyes and pretended to be offended, but everyone knew she was pleased. "So bold," she purred. "I think I like that."

She turned and looked at Sif. "*Skyuldur vidnukona*, make sure I have time in my schedule to speak to these two fine examples of manhood often."

Sif bowed but kept her 'cow's mouth' shut.

TWENTY-FIVE

"**I** believe that conversation with Vowli and Luka was the start of Suel's fall. It is what set her on this dark path," said Sif.

Yowrnsaxa nodded. "Indeed. It was as if she were looking for permission to give in to her baser desires, and their philosophy was that permission. She spoke with them many times after that, both alone and as a pair, and spent less and less time with Pratyi, Paltr, Veethar, and even Meuhlnir."

Meuhlnir nodded, his expression sad. "We all thought that we'd offended her somehow."

"We all thought she'd narrowed the field to Luka and Vowli," said Yowrnsaxa.

"And later, Huthr," whispered Sif.

Meuhlnir's eyes blazed at the name. He stood and stalked off into the woods.

Yowrnsaxa stirred to go after him.

"Let him be," whispered Sif.

Yowrnsaxa looked off into the woods but sank down again. "I wish I could help him."

"We all do, Mother Yowrnsaxa, but there are some things a man must do for himself," said Mothi, his eyes on the fire.

Sif glanced my way. "Huthr was another of Meuhlnir's brothers. Paltr, Huthr, and Luka."

Yowrnsaxa nodded. "They were all so close. Luka's treachery cut deep."

"Talking about philosophy was all it took to lead the Dark Queen astray?" I couldn't keep the distaste from my voice.

"Oh, no. Much happened that contributed to her fall."

"Indeed," said Sif. "Though none of us knew it, there was a great darkness growing in Suel—both in the queen herself, and her land. Some of the nobility had grown—"

"Jealous," said Yowrnsaxa. "Jealous of the queen's reputation, riches, the loyalty she inspired in the populace. They thought she had usurped their role with the peasantry."

Sif nodded. "More than a few were misled down a dark path filled with hatred and envy."

"The war," said Meuhlnir from the darkness ringing the camp.

"Oh, aye," said Sif. "The civil war completed what everything else had begun and cemented Suel to her own terrible path.

"She committed such atrocities against the people she once loved."

Yowrnsaxa sniffed back tears. "She did. She enjoyed it, too."

"Thus is the nature of darkness in the soul," said Mothi. "History has taught us this again and again."

"Misery loves company," whispered Sif.

"And all this…darkness infected Luka?" I asked.

My four companions were quiet for a long moment.

"Oh, he was a willing enough conspirator," said Meuhlnir, stepping back into the light of the fire. "She could be—"

"Persuasive," said Yowrnsaxa. "She was almost hypnotic in her intensity toward the end of her reign. It was almost as if she could persuade a certain kind of man to do anything."

"Luka and Vowli were…I don't know. It was as if they competed with one another to see who could commit the blackest act in her name." Meuhlnir gazed into the fire, misery etched on his face. "Paltr and I were—" His voice broke.

"The two of them were growing ever more disillusioned with Suel's reign," said Sif. "As were most of us."

"When Paltr told the Dark Queen he was leaving the *Vuthuhr Trohtninkar*, she…" Meuhlnir shook his head and dropped his eyes to the dirt in front of him.

"She pretended to accept it," whispered Yowrnsaxa. "But she didn't."

"No," said Meuhlnir in a broken voice. "She did not."

"Let's leave this for now," said Sif. "Plenty of time to finish that dark story."

"Yes," I said. "I think I get the gist in any case."

Meuhlnir looked up and held my gaze. "There's more to it then you've heard, Hank. But Sif is right. We, or she or Yowrnsaxa, can tell the rest to you later."

"That's fine," I said.

Mothi looked up at the position of the moon. "It's late anyway," he said. "We should try to get some sleep. It will be a hard ride tomorrow."

"Aye," grunted Meuhlnir. The two women stirred themselves to action and laid out bedrolls for all of us around the fire. Mothi and I were positioned on one side of the fire, and the three of them huddled close together on the other side.

Despite camping in the snow in the middle of a great frozen forest of fir trees, the small camp felt cozy and warm. I snuggled down into my bedroll, fully dressed still, but was comfortable nonetheless. I thought I might lie awake for a while, fighting the aches and pains of my condition. As usual. Instead, I dropped off as soon as I closed my eyes.

I was awakened sometime later by the strong feeling that something was wrong. The forest had gone silent—not just the silence of winter, but still like there was a predator close by. I lay there with my back to the remains of the fire, heart beating fast, straining my ears to hear in the stillness, straining my eyes to see in the gloom.

I had just about given up when the flickering light of the fire flashed on something in the dark shadows of the forest. I sat up and called, "Who's there?"

Mothi sat up. "What is it?" he asked in a sleep-fuzzed voice.

They came at us then, pouring from the forest. A confusion of forms running at us with an eerie wailing keen splitting the night.

Mothi leapt to his feet, kicking the bedroll away. He screamed "*Strikuhr risa!*" and seemed to grow as he ran, looming taller and bulkier, muscles bunching and twisting beneath his skin. "Father! Harriers!" He grabbed an axe in each hand and charged at two moving shadows at the edge of the clearing. As he ran, he muttered, "*Hooth ow yowrni,*" and a watery blue light coalesced around him like a tight-fitting suit of mail.

Across the fire, Meuhlnir, Sif, and Yowrnsaxa were awake and arming themselves. I pulled my pack toward me, still sitting on the ground with my legs tucked into the bedroll. I dug into the pack and felt for the grip of my Kimber .45 and my spare magazines.

"Do you know who you are troubling?" I heard Meuhlnir ask in a ringing voice that boomed through the forest like thunder. "No common group of travelers, this. Named Men and Named Women rest here!"

"About to be named corpses, then," hissed a reedy voice from the darkness.

"Come then, meet your death," said Sif in a voice so hard and brutal I would not have recognized her if I had not seen her speak. She and Yowrnsaxa stood on either side of Meuhlnir, large round shields on their left arms. Sif carried an axe in her other hand, and Yowrnsaxa had a short, but vicious looking sword. Meuhlnir easy, his hammer held in a loose fist by his side.

I was stiff from the cold, the previous days' exertions, and due to the gifts of my illness. I knelt on the ground next to my bedroll and racked the slide of the Kimber 1911 pistol. The gloom hid the harriers from me.

"Oh, we will come," said the reedy voice again. "But we won't be the ones meeting death on this cold night."

Yowrnsaxa shrugged and then her laugh boomed into the night. "Weak men talk," she said. "*Cowards* talk."

"Come," taunted Sif, her voice almost seductive. "Don't keep a lady waiting."

Something stirred in the darkness off to my left, a twig snapped, and snow crunched. "*Ehlteenk*!" yelled Meuhlnir. Thunder boomed and rolled through the woods. A blinding bright blue fork of lighting arced from the sky, through the trees and into the peaked metal helmet of a man standing in the woods. The night lit up like it was daylight for a brief second, just long enough to get a glimpse of the many men ringing our camp. Just long enough to see the man struck by Meuhlnir's bolt of lightning crumple to the ground. Just long enough to see a man with a bow taking aim at Mothi's back.

As soon as the bolt faded, I was blind, night vision shattered by the lightning, but my instincts and training took over. The Kimber snapped up in my hands, and it bucked twice, filling the silent night with a different kind of thunder and shattering the dark night with flashes of yellow-white light.

I knew I'd hit the man, even before I heard his bowstring thrum, even before I heard him crash over on his back. The forest was suddenly silent again. No one moved for the briefest of moments, and then one of the horses screamed, and the fighting resumed.

"*Au noht*," said Yowrnsaxa.

I felt a kind of pressure wrapping around my head, as soft as feathers and as cold as the snow I knelt in. My eyes began to sting, and suddenly I could see again.

Mothi snarled and swung his hands together at shoulder height, bearded axe blades glinting in the low light from the fire as he chopped into the neck of one of the men closest to me. Mothi seemed have grown a foot or so, and he got proportionally bulkier as well as taller. He was no small man before, but now he seemed to hulk over the remaining foe before him. He whirled to face the man closest to him. "I am Mothi," he hissed, "and if you stand before me, you die next." Fear bloomed on the man's face as he backed away, his eyes darting around as if looking for help.

A man lurking in the woods across the fire from me caught my attention. He was holding a dagger in each hand and was staring at Sif with hot hatred. She didn't see him—she was looking at a large man in front of her. As the man with the daggers snuck closer to her, Sif took a step toward the woods and beckoned with her shield.

The Kimber bucked in my hand again, and the man with the daggers buckled and fell to his knees. The retorts of the .45 rolled through the forest again, its muzzle flashes blindingly bright. Again, everyone froze for a breathless moment until the echo of the two gunshots died, and then the violence erupted again.

"*Ehlteenk*!" yelled Meuhlnir.

Thunder split the night again and a bright blue bolt arced from the heavens to melt one of the attackers into the snow. Yowrnsaxa screamed and leapt on a man close to her, the sword in her hand a whirling blur of sharp edges. Her opponent dodged and countered, but either her shield or her sword seemed to jerk into the path of his attacks. Fear glinted in his eye as her sword continued its mad dance. Meuhlnir took two big strides to Yowrnsaxa's side, and his hammer crushed the skull of the man.

"Fools," said the reedy-voiced man. "Don't fight them one by one!" He grabbed a man from each side and pushed them forward—at me. They stumbled a step or two and then saw I didn't have an axe or a sword in my hand. They glanced at each other and sprinted at me. The one on the left leered at me and laughed as if he were crazy. The one on the right ran silently, his face grim and set.

The Kimber roared twice, and the leering man on the left took two stuttering steps before he fell, blood misting the night air. As he hit the ground, he flopped to his side, his empty face staring at me in a rigid mask of death, two bullet holes in his chest. The grim man on the right leapt to the side and hunched over, trying to hide behind his painted wooden shield.

The .45 caliber pistol in my hand boomed, and the slide locked back. The bottom portion of his painted shield exploded in a shower of splinters, but I couldn't tell if I'd hit only the shield or the man behind it, too. I ejected the magazine and rammed a full one in its place. I thumbed the slide release as I brought the pistol to bear.

The pistol barked and coughed, its muzzle spitting daggers of flame three times. Three slugs almost half an inch wide slammed into the grim man, one in the shield arm, one in his jaw just below the left corner of his mouth, and one in the middle of the throat. For the third time, there was a stricken lull in the fighting.

The man facing Mothi threw down his sword as he turned and ran. Mothi spun in a circle, flinging blood from his bearded axes, looking for someone to fight. His face wore a savage, victorious smile.

The man fighting Sif was very large, but she barged into him with her shield and staggered him back a step. It seemed to enrage him, and he screamed at her. Her axe streaked low under her shield and chopped into his thigh—a vicious wound. He screamed in a high-pitched voice but grabbed the edges of her shield and flung her into a tree. She staggered, and the man snarled.

I brought the Kimber up to fire, but Mothi streaked by me, fouling the shot. He was screaming as he ran, and his scream was loud enough that the man glanced over his shoulder in fear. Sif shook her head to clear her mind, and her knee rocketed up into the big man's groin. He doubled over as Mothi reached them. Mothi hit him between the shoulder blades with an axe while Sif hit him in the face with the spiked back side of hers. The resulting mess was not pretty, and the man lay in a twitching mass as he died.

Dead attackers lay all around us, some with gaping bullet holes torn through their flesh and some with gaping wounds from melee weapons. The harriers no longer seemed very eager to fight, and even the reedy-voiced man was quiet. They gripped their weapons and looked around, all nerves and fear.

In a few short moments, their numbers had been cut by two thirds, and not one of us was injured.

"What's the matter, cowards?" snapped Sif. "Not interested in a fight of even numbers?"

"Shut up," said the reedy-voiced man.

The Kimber barked twice in my hand, two bullets slammed into his chest, and he had nothing more to say in his delicate, feeble voice.

Mothi looked at me with a strange expression on his face and then grinned. "I didn't like him, either," he said.

I was as surprised as he was, I hadn't even given it a thought. I'd just shot a man for talking too much.

"Who sent you?" barked Meuhlnir. "I'll have the name." There was a strange feeling of mounting pressure in the air, and menace seemed to drip from his voice.

Yowrnsaxa sliced the air with her sword and grinned at the man nearest to her. "Speak fools. This is Meuhlnir, He of the Thunder, and he gets grumpy when awakened by harriers."

Mothi pointed at Yowrnsaxa. "And she is Yowrnsaxa, Mistress of the Dancing Steel. This is Sif, Harvester of Blood. I am Mothi Strongheart." He turned and pointed at me. "And this fearsome man is called Aylootr, trouble him at your peril." His mouth crooked in a smile.

The four remaining men looked at each other with fear and uncertainty in their eyes.

"Come now!" snapped Meuhlnir. "I grow impatient." The air around him started to crackle and pop with electricity.

One of the harriers twitched his hand. He was holding a spear, but before he could bring it to bear, lightning slammed into him and drove him to the ground. Only a steaming lump of twitching, dead flesh remained.

As if a switch was thrown, the brief respite from violence was ended.

Sif snarled and bashed a man in the chin with the rim of her shield. His head snapped back, and her axe slammed into his throat, cutting his head from his body. Meuhlnir's hammer crushed the face of another man, and he fell like a bag of rocks dropped from a height.

Mothi grinned at the last man. He was a young man and scared out of his skin. "You should speak now," said Mothi.

"It was Vowli!" he said, his voice high and strained. "It was Vowli who sent us. He said you were bandits and had it coming. He said—"

Yowrnsaxa took two quick steps forward, and it looked like she punched him in the stomach, but when she pulled her hand back, her blade was sheathed with blood. "Do shut up now, coward," she said.

The man looked down at his bleeding stomach and then looked up and met my eye. "What is it?" he whispered.

"What?" I asked him, but he pitched forward on his face, dead. I looked at Mothi. "What?" I asked him.

Mothi just pointed at the Kimber in my hand. He seemed to be shrinking back to his normal size almost as if he was a balloon with a slow leak. "That's an unusual kind of magic," he said.

I shook my head. "Not magic," I muttered. "It's a machine. A tool." They were all looking at me. I shrugged. "It's a chemical reaction. The gunpowder explodes, expelling the bullet due to the pressure in the chamber." I ejected the magazine and then racked the slide, ejecting the round in the chamber. I held it up before them. "The chamber of the gun is strong enough to contain the explosion, leaving the barrel as the only way to expel the pressure, but the bullet is in the way, so it shoots out in front of the explosion."

They looked at me for a long moment, not speaking or moving.

"It's not magic," I said again.

Mothi laughed and looked around at the bodies. He grinned at Meuhlnir. "Looks like you aren't the only one fond of loud noises. And I don't mean your farts."

Meuhlnir snorted and arched an eyebrow at Mothi. "Aylootr?"

Mothi shrugged. "Seems to fit. And you know as well as I do that there is power in a name."

"What does Aylootr mean?" I asked.

"The ever booming," said Mothi with a laugh.

Sif let her shield slide from her arm. She looked around the campsite with disgust. "I don't want to sleep here again," she said.

Meuhlnir looked to the east where a glimmer of gold light was visible. "The day is upon us anyway. Might as well pack up and go."

I got to my feet, fighting stiffness and pain, and bent to start packing my things. The quick battle replayed in my mind's eye again and again. The words in the *Gamla Toonkumowl* seemed to be mist in my memory, I couldn't seem to pin them down. I straightened, stopping in the hunched position that was so familiar to me now, waiting for the sharp, burning ache in the small of my back to subside so I could stand straight.

Sif appeared at my elbow, her magic cream already open. "You know what to do," she said. "Where is it the worst?"

"The pain isn't so bad this morning, but I am as stiff as Meuhlnir's beard."

"That bad, is it?" She laughed as she pulled up my jacket and shirt, shoving the small container into my hands and digging out a dollop with her fingers. The warm burning sensation that I was already starting to associate with relief spread slowly across the small of my back. Her fingers worked my trousers down to my knees and spread more of the delightful warmth around my hips and knees. She turned me around and began working the cream into the joints of my hand.

"What did Mothi say at the start of the fight?" I asked.

"Harriers," she said.

"No, not that. The *Gamla Toonkumowl*."

Her eyes rose slowly to meet mine. "Ah. He said '*Hooth ow yowrni*' which roughly translates to 'skin of iron.' To protect himself. Armor," she said. "And he said '*Strikuhr risa*'—'strength of the giants.' He has always been jealous of his brother's natural strength."

"Also your son?" I asked.

"Yes, though Yowrnsaxa gave birth to him."

I wracked my brain, trying to remember the name of Thor and Járnsaxa's son. "Magni?" I asked.

She shrugged. "None other."

I shook my head, a small smile on my lips.

"Something?" she asked, taking the container of cream from me and waving her hand at my trousers.

I pulled them up and buttoned them. "It just amuses me at times to be standing amongst you. I pointed at Meuhlnir. "The god of thunder and battle." I pointed at Mothi. "The god of bravery." I waved at Yowrnsaxa. "The giantess, Yowrnsaxa."

"And me?" asked Sif.

They were all looking at me now. "Sif, goddess of the harvest," I said. It struck me as funny how closely Norse mythology matched the list of names Mothi had told the harriers. I chuckled a bit. "And Magni, god of strength. You all made quite an impression on my ancestors." They all seemed to find something interesting to look at in their packs or the woods around us.

"One of these nights," said Meuhlnir, "you should tell us of these myths."

"I wish I knew them better," I said. "They were first written down long after the fact, after centuries of oral history had mutated what I assume to be tales of your visits to the early Norsemen. They were known as the Sagas."

Mothi grunted. "It might be interesting to see how these tales have grown."

I nodded my head. "Unfortunately, I don't know them by heart. There are many of them."

Mothi nodded and then shrugged. "It's no matter," he said and went to ready the horses. "Maybe we will tell you the tales of our visits that birthed them."

Yowrnsaxa walked over to me and slapped my arm. "That giantess crap better not be a reference to my dimensions," she said with a grin.

"Are you kidding?" I asked. "After I've seen you fight? And anyway, I enjoy your cooking."

She laughed and started to turn away, but then turned back. "Eyes of the night," she said.

"What?" I asked.

"*Au noht*, eyes of the night. To help us see."

I nodded. "I understand. One thing, though."

"Yes?" she asked.

"You had to fix our vision because of my gun?"

She nodded. "That and the lightning from the great lout, though we are more accustomed to that and close our eyes when he yells the key. Your weapon was unexpected." She shrugged at my expression and punched me in the bicep. "It is no matter."

She left me looking at the bodies lying in heaps all around us.

TWENTY-SIX

Over the next several days, we woke early in the cold mornings and rode long into the dusk of early evening, averaging sixty or seventy miles a day. The cold was bitter and harsh, and we were all exhausted at the end of each day's ride, but Meuhlnir had wanted to get as far from the scene of the battle as we could, as fast as we could.

On the fifth day, we were watering the horses in the icy water of a large river when Meuhlnir called a halt in the late afternoon, and the sun was low in the sky, but not yet close to the horizon.

"Might as well camp here," he said.

Mothi glanced at the river and shrugged. "It's pretty enough."

"What would you know of 'pretty,'" asked Sif with a grin.

"Not much surrounded, as I am, by you lot," said Mothi with a matching grin.

Meuhlnir came over to me and put his hand on my shoulder. "Too tired for a walk?" he asked.

I felt good, given the week of riding long and hard. "Not at all," I said. "That will give these three the time to come to grips with my dashing good looks."

Meuhlnir stifled a chuckle. "Might as well ask peacocks to see the beauty of a sunset." He took my arm and walked me toward the edge of the sparse wood running along the bank. He walked beside me, lost in thought.

The forest of fir trees had given way to black cottonwood, soaring toward the gray skies. It was somehow more pleasant to me—the cottonwoods seemed to be more properly trees than the Christmas tree shapes of the firs. There was some snow-covered underbrush, but for the most part, the walking was easy. The snow was shallow here, and more like dust than the heavy, wet snow around the cabin. My cramped legs relaxed into the rhythm of walking.

"I have come to a decision over the past few days. You should go back to the cabin," he said.

My jaw dropped open, but I couldn't find anything to say.

"I may have made a gross miscalculation," said Meuhlnir. "I may have put us all in more danger than is reasonable."

"I'm not sure about that," I said. "If anyone did, it was me, dropping in uninvited and embroiling all of you in my fight."

Meuhlnir shook his head. He stopped walking and turned to look me in the eye. "That's of no consequence at all. This is something we needed to do if Luka is ever to redeem himself. We've spoken of it often."

"Still, I came and now—"

"No, Hank. I won't hear of it. If anyone is to blame for us being out here, it is Luka. And the Black Bitch." His voice was hard and firm. "But this is something else. I never imagined that Vowli would involve himself in your fight, and I should have," he said. "I made a mistake, and the risk to you is much higher than I had calculated."

It hung in the air between us. He was more concerned with my safety than his own, that much was clear. "But the risk is the same for me," I said. "The risk to you and your family has risen from nothing to being attacked by harriers in the night."

Meuhlnir shook his head and waved his hand. "No, that's wrongful thinking," he said, "though it does you credit. No, we have been in danger for many centuries, and instead of facing that danger, we have all chosen to hide here in the woods and the snow. It's time that we faced this."

He stroked his beard, looking at me with bright eyes. "But my point is this, I'm not sure we can guarantee your safety on this trip. It might be better for me to travel on to meet with Veethar on my own while the rest of you return to our cabin, or to Mothi's estate."

"That doesn't make much sense to me, Meuhlnir. We are already six hard days' ride from your cabin. Splitting up and turning back now seems to be more dangerous than continuing on. Dividing our forces. Presenting two targets."

He took my arm and started walking again, head down, his free hand stroking his beard.

I let him lead me. "It's not that I don't appreciate you saying this, Meuhlnir, but back in that camp the first night, I killed my share of attackers. I've trained for years in the use of a pistol, and I can protect myself."

Meuhlnir nodded. "Indeed, you did, Aylootr," he said with a trace of humor in his tone. "Against men from your *klith*, I'd have no qualms at all. Although your tools themselves might…" He looked at the holstered Kimber .45 I wore on my belt, and a strange look slid over his face.

"What?" I asked. "Would you like to hold it?" It was something I was used to being asked, after all, I'd been asked that question by every school kid who'd seen me wearing my service pistol.

"Oh no," he said with an appalled look on his face. "No, I'd rather not."

I tilted my head to the side. His reaction confused me. It was…overkill.

He saw my expression and smiled a nervous smile. "Your tools themselves might be dangerous here. We gave up all that." He waved his hand toward the pistol. "We almost destroyed ourselves with things like that." He was silent a moment and then looked me in the eye. "*Ragnaruechkr*," he said in hushed tones.

"Oh, come on," I said. "Ragnarok? Really?"

Meuhlnir stopped and turned toward me. His face was grave, with the slightest trace of confusion and a touch of hurt. "No. Not *Ragnaruk*. *Ragnaruechkr*."

I shrugged. "What's the difference?"

"Ah," said Meuhlnir. "*Ragnaruechkr* actually happened—here, on this *klith*. *Ragnaruk* is just a tale we told the ancient peoples on your *klith*. It was based on the actual event, true enough, but your people would not have understood the truth."

"Ah, back to that," I said.

"In this case," said Meuhlnir, "the tale was told to try to help your *klith* avoid the fate of the *Geumlu*. It sounds like it has worked thus far."

"Maybe," I said, unwilling to grant that their interference was of any benefit. "We've been pretty close to blowing ourselves to hell several times."

"This is what's left of Osgarthr," he said, sweeping his hands out in arcs to his side. "Do you see a difference?"

"Tell me about *Ragnaruechkr*, then."

"I told you before that the *Geumlu* studied the universe and unlocked many of its secrets. Some of those secrets had beneficial applications, such as our longevity and the *preer*. Others... less so." He tucked his chin down toward his chest and took my arm again, pulling me into a slow stroll. "Some of the universe's secrets should not be known by men. The knowledge of them granted the *Geumlu* godlike powers before they were ready for the responsibility. It is said that before their quest for knowledge, the *Geumlu* were just men like any others, like those found on your *klith*, and that there was no *vefnathur strenki*, no *preer*, nothing like that.

"The *Geumlu* relied on machines for everything, for travel, for treatment of the sick, for growing food—even to think and plan for the future. There was one *Gamla* named Mim—a great scientist, it is said, and a powerful man. He plumbed the universe for its secrets and hoarded the knowledge for his own estate. He sought power over the other *Geumlu*. He wanted to rule Osgarthr to the last person. The knowledge he hoarded began to eat away at his mind from the moment he learned it.

"Mim empowered his sons and made them his generals. He gave them each a thinking machine that could analyze the terrain and composition of the enemy and create a strategy for victory. Each thinking machine was embedded inside a unique mechanical war engine. To one son, the one named Vani, Mim gave dominion over the air and a great mechanical bird named Uhrn. To the second son, named Isi, dominion over the land and a mighty engine of war that crawled over the ground like a worm, named Nithukkr. To the last son, named Jot, he gave the mighty ship Nagifar that could swim under the sea like a whale, and dominion over the sea and all things in it. These three war engines ran on a powerful force—a force derived from the *strenkir af Krafti*. The force was somehow separated from the universe and contained in a big, round container of lead and artificial stone. It was said they never needed maintenance or refueling but could run for centuries on a single charge of those great power sources.

"The sons of Mim conquered all the nations of the *Geumlu* and established Mim as absolute ruler of Osgarthr. He was not a beneficent ruler. No, quite the opposite, according to the legends that survive. Mim was ruled by his lusts and the growing sickness in his head. It wasn't long, a few decades perhaps before his mind turned on itself, and he took his own life—or maybe was murdered by one of his sons. Who knows?

"After Mim's death, the sons of Mim were at play across the face of the planet, and even beneath it. Each one vied for absolute power, and each one claimed to be the rightful heir to their father's throne.

"Each son of Mim had grown more powerful during their father's reign—each continued to mine the universe's secrets, and each developed their own sickness of the mind. During this time, each of the sons of Mim began to alter the very nature of some of the *Geumlu* living within their realms—their militaries, their favorite advisers, their friends, and their families. It is said that one could tell the Jotun by their length of limb, useful when swimming, and very pale skin. It is said that the Vanir could be told by the tilt of their eyes and the darkened, greyish pigment in their skin. The Isir are said to be as you see me, thick muscled for moving boulders and digging in the dirt and pale skin from avoiding the light of the sun. It is also said that only Isir were given the power to *vefa strenki* so that they would have an advantage over the followers of Vani and Jot.

"A mighty, planet-wide war ensued. Each of Mim's sons became bitter that their brothers would deny them of their rightful inheritance, and each attacked the other with vengeance and hatred in their hearts.

"The war devastated the face of the planet. The grand cloud cities, built by Vani, fell burning to the ground. The mighty fortresses of the mountains built by Isi were mined and burned until nothing remain. The vast floating platforms built by Jot were set alight from the air and bombarded by stones flung from the shore.

"The populace was decimated, and those who weren't killed outright soon began to starve as each of the sons of Mim sought to deprive the other's army of food by attacking the farms in each domain. Soon, the armies began to commandeer any food they could find, and the populace declined even farther. It came to pass that the only people left on the planet were part of the military complex ruled by one of the brothers. These military complexes were called the Vanir, the Isir, and the Jotun.

"Safe under the oceans, the Jotun released a fiery weapon on the surface. A ghastly fire burned through the atmosphere killing anyone not protected by special garments. The unprotected who didn't die immediately from the fire became sick and soon died. This brought Vani and Isi into accord, and together they destroyed Jotunhaym, the home of the Jotun, killing every Jotun who lived under the sea.

"It is said that with the last remaining power of Nagifar, Jot transformed himself and those of his inner circle, into sea dragons, and that they rule the seas even today.

"The peace and accord between Vani and Isi did not last long, though. Soon they were intent on killing each other again so that each could become the undisputed ruler of the planet. Unknown to Vani, Isi had spent the time during the accord learning about our bodies and plumbing yet more secrets from the shadows of the universe.

"When the fighting resumed, Isi unleashed a plague. Using some means unknown to us, he made the plague kill only the Vanir while ensuring the health of the Isir. Seeing the devastation wrought on his men, the Vani used the secret knowledge he had stolen from Jot during the sack of Jotunhaym and the last bits of power left in Uhrn to transform himself and his chosen few into dragons of the air, and they rule the air to this day. It is said that some of the Vanir survived the plague of Isi, but they were changed into the subhuman kobolds that live under the mountains.

"The devastation from the decades of war and the mighty weapons devised by each brother had rendered most of the planet useless. Crops would not grow. The air became thin and noxious. Clouds of the fire released by Jot still floated through the atmosphere, burning anything it touched, killing any of the stunted crops near to its path, and killing Isir as well.

"Seeing the devastation wrought on the land, Isi wished he still had his brothers to help him restore the planet. He traveled to the shore of the sea and asked the sea dragons for help, asking them to writhe their bodies in the water and create great waves to put out the clouds of floating fire. They refused and promised to stop him from using the seas as a food source.

"Having lost the knowledge of the sky chariots when his brother, Vani, transformed himself, Isi traveled far up into the mountains and asked the dragons of the air for help. They laughed at him and spit fire and ice.

"Isi despaired. His depression was black and deep, but one of his scientists, named Haymtatlr, built a horn attuned to the skein of fate that underlies the universe. He sucked in enough wind that it is said he stilled all the winds on the face of the planet and then blew that mighty wind through the horn he named *Kyatlarhodn*.

"Upon the blowing of the *Kyatlarhodn*, the skein of fate began to vibrate in a harmony that hadn't been heard since the universe was formed. This harmony created the first of the *preer* at a place called Pilrust.

"Seeing that the *proo* led to another *stathur*, another reality, one pristine and lush, Isi started planning to conquer that land and use its resources to revitalize Osgarthr. The Isir, however, had grown tired of war. Indeed, Haymtatlr had created *Kyatlarhodn* in hopes of finding a way to escape Isi's madness.

"The Isir tricked Isi into taking Nithukkr into a vast underground cavern. Once he was inside, they sealed the cavern's only entrance to the land above. Falling farther into despair, Isi used the power of Nithukkr to melt the stone around him. He transformed himself and the crew of the Nithukkr into the dragons of the stone that reside deep in the heart of the planet. They are sometimes seen spitting their vile fire from the tops of shattered mountains in retribution for the Isir's treachery.

"The Isir used *Kyatlarhodn* sparingly, and only to retrieve things that couldn't be produced on Osgarthr any longer. In the beginning, vast foraging expeditions were sent to the *stathur* of the universe and returned with food, plunder, and metals that they used to build a new society out of the old.

"After the society was established, the Isir held a grand conclave at the Urtar Well in which it was decided that we would no longer use the weapons produced by the sons of Mim in warfare. The resolutions of the Grand Conclave have held through generation upon generation."

I kept my eyes on the ground in front of me. "Surely most of that is just myth."

Meuhlnir shrugged. "Who can say? That the *Geumlu* garnered great power from plundering the secrets of the universe can't be questioned. That the Great War occurred and left the planet devastated is almost a surety. Of course, it might have been some natural disaster, but whatever the cause, the devastation was wide-spread, and the planet was decimated."

"But all that about dragons and the—"

"None of that matters, Hank. The details and the exact whats and wheres do nothing but distract from the moral of the story—that some knowledge it is better not to know, that certain kinds of knowledge have the power to sicken the mind. Indeed, that using the fruits of that knowledge might be dangerous in and of itself."

The silence stretched between us as I reviewed the story in my head. Meuhlnir and his family all thought that the creation myths of my *klith* were seeded by their actions, but this fantastical story was rife with creation mythology that he seemed unable to see.

"Meuhlnir, I have the greatest respect for you and your people, and I appreciate what you are doing for me. I don't mean to step on your beliefs in any way, but the people on my *klith* use technology every day. Indeed, there are probably very few people left on my *klith* who could survive without the many technologies we use without thinking. I can't say that any one of those people is rendered insane by using technology."

"But we are not on your *klith*, and there are dangers here that you know nothing about. And, how could you? There are things here that don't exist on your *klith*."

"Yes, but—"

"No, Hank. There are dangers here left over from the Great War. Some of your technologies may awaken things best left sleeping."

I scratched the stubble under my chin. "Are you saying you don't want me to use my pistol?"

Meuhlnir shook his head. "No, to do so would hopelessly handicap you on this *klith*. There isn't time to turn you into a *vefari* of any reliability, even if you have the greatest talent and capacity for it. And, truth be told, from how you described it, it sounds like simple alchemy."

"I guess you could say that. Fire is just a chemical reaction—oxidation of fuel with heat as a catalyst. The explosion of the gunpowder in the shells I carry is just the oxidation of a much more powerful fuel."

"I thought as much," said Meuhlnir. "But you may have other bits of technology with you. Those things are the danger."

"Almost anything I would have brought from my *klith* would require technology outside of itself to work. I mean the devices themselves just use a different kind of chemical reaction to produce the small electrical charges they need to operate, but other than showing pictures on the screen of my phone, or using the flashlight, they can't do much here." I spread my hands toward the sky. "No WiFi, no Internet, no satellites."

"I will have to take you at your word. I know nothing of these things. Perhaps Veethar will know more, he has spent more time on your *klith* during modern times than me."

"So, you are okay with the gun?"

"Yes," he said. "Given what you've told me. Even with your gun, you are in danger here. More danger than you might guess at. There are those... There are things here that your gun might not kill.

"Vowli is as dangerous a man as Luka. You've heard the beginnings of what has grown into a very dangerous philosophy. This practice of gaining power by eating human flesh grew directly from his words."

"Itla sem yetur," I said.

"Yes. And *Briethralak Uolfur.*"

"The Brotherhood of the Wolf," I breathed.

"Luka and his disciples, of which Vowli is said to be the first, though who is whose disciple seems open to debate, are all the result of continuing their dark philosophy to a ridiculous extreme. Vowli is dangerous."

"I understand," I said, "but so is your brother Luka. So is the Black Queen."

Meuhlnir nodded. "But Vowli is different, Hank. You've spoken to me of true evil, and though I argued against it, the entire time we spoke, Vowli kept coming to mind. He may be the exception to my arguments."

"Be that as it may, he is dangerous no matter where I am, no? Here or at your cabin?"

"Well, yes," said Meuhlnir. "But there are protections at the cabin. Defenses that no one can dispel without a lot of effort and power. You're safer there."

"I understand your concerns, Meuhlnir. I do. But the fact remains that I can't just go back and wait at your cabin."

"But you *can*, Hank. I can go to Veethar, and with his help, we can sort out the—"

"No," I said. "I can't just go back to your warm cabin and sit while you put yourself at risk for me. They are my family, Meuhlnir. I have to share the risks, or I couldn't stand it. I couldn't stand doing nothing but waiting."

Meuhlnir nodded in a grudging manner. "If our positions were reversed, I couldn't either."

"I appreciate you thinking of me and my safety, but I have to go on."

Meuhlnir looked at me sidelong. "It is agreed, then, but on one condition."

"What condition?"

"That you allow us to lead you where we must."

"That…seems fair," I said.

"Good." Meuhlnir patted my arm. "You will see many things, Hank. Things you may not be prepared to face. Things that your tools might be powerless against, things that will shake your mind to its very foundations."

I laughed. I couldn't help it. I lifted my free hand and waved it in a wide semicircle. "This… All this has already done that."

Meuhlnir shook his head. "No, Hank. This has merely scratched the surface." He favored me with an enigmatic smile. "How are your pains?"

"Sif's cream is wonderful," I said with enthusiasm.

Meuhlnir laughed and clapped me on the shoulder. We turned back toward the camp.

"Whatever the cause, the tribulations of Osgarthr's past have left you with a beautiful land."

Meuhlnir nodded. "It is beautiful in most places on this side of the planet, but even now, so many eons later, there are parts of this planet that are barren, blighted. Some places are still so poisonous that it is certain death to walk there."

"Is there any kind of timeline? Any guesses at how long ago your *Ragnaruechkr* happened?"

Meuhlnir scratched his head. "No, not really. Remember that we are long lived. Remember that a generation for us is probably more than ten of your life times. Because of those facts, written history is less important to us than oral history. Written records don't last as long as we live, and to rely on them would mean we would spend an inordinate amount of time recopying old records, until, eventually, all we could do from dawn to dusk is recopy historical records.

"My great-great-great grandfather remembered hearing, as a child, tales of the Grand Conclave from a very old man who claimed to have taken part in it. Perhaps twelve and a half thousand years?"

"And do you not suffer memory loss as you age?" I couldn't believe there was space for a thousand years of memories in my brain, and if there was, I couldn't believe I'd be able to access them all.

"Ah, the Gift of Isi keeps our bodies and our minds in perfect condition until the end."

I shrugged. "I have to admit, having perfect recall would be a gift to the people on my *klith* who can't seem to learn from history—even *with* written records."

Meuhlnir chuckled. "Being long lived also makes risking one's life in some foolish war less and less attractive. We generally don't go to war, but when we do, you can be sure it isn't over religion, property, resources, or something trivial such as that."

"Are there any non-trivial reasons for war?"

Meuhlnir shrugged and patted Sinir as we walked past the horses. "That's a very good question. The only war that has occurred in my lifetime had as its purpose the ousting of the Dark Bitch from power. It was waged to protect the general population from the depravity her reign had become." Meuhlnir sniffed. "You may be the cause of the next war, Hank," he said in quiet tones.

"I just want to get Jane and Siggy back," I said. "I don't want to start any wars."

He looked at me with an arched eyebrow. "No more vengeance on Luka?"

I shook my head and shrugged. "I don't know. Maybe not."

He nodded. "You may be the catalyst that motivates the better minded people of Osgarthr to finally band together and stop the Black Queen's evil from spreading."

We reached the campsite, and Meuhlnir walked me to one of the logs set up around the fire.

"I don't want to be responsible for a war," I said.

"Maybe I should rephrase. The actions of my brother may be the catalyst that motivates us to address the depravity of the Dark Queen, Luka, and Vowli. Ultimately, Hank, Luka, and the Black Bitch bear that responsibility. They stole your family and forced you to follow."

Yowrnsaxa looked up from her cookpot and said, "And what he did before. To you and your brothers. That's a part of all this."

Meuhlnir winced. "Indeed," he said and turned back toward the forest. "Tell Hank of the tale of that *Toemari*."

Sif came over, her container of that magical cream in her hand. This time, she didn't have to instruct me to disrobe. She started rubbing the cream into my hips and back. "*Toemari* Ryehtliti," she sighed.

"It was some time after the afternoon Sif spoke of," said Yowrnsaxa. "Queen Suel had become darker and darker of mood as time passed. She began spending a lot of time with Vowli and Luka—and she had started excluding some of the *Trohtninkar Tumuhr* from those meetings, Sif and I included. She began scheduling the shifts of the guards, giving the better-hearted of the bunch duties that kept them away from her and making more time for Vowli and Luka to attend her. It was a hard time for her former favorites."

"It was a hard time for all," said Sif.

Yowrnsaxa grunted. "Aye. She was easy to anger and slow to calm herself."

TWENTY-
SEVEN

*I*t was as if Queen Suel had been replaced by an
evil version of herself, thought Yowrnsaxa as
Suel screeched in rage.

"How *dare* you!" Suel shouted. "How *dare* you
stand before me and question my judgement!"

Toemari Ryehtliti cringed. "Your Majesty, I
humbly apologize! I didn't mean to imply there was
any question about your judgement. Everyone

knows your reputation for square dealing with the citizens of the empire."

Queen Suel didn't seem much mollified. She glared at Ryehtliti as if she could make him disappear by the sheer force of her dislike. "Then what?" she demanded.

Ryehtliti winced and took half a step backward. "Your Majesty, if you will allow me to explain in full—"

"What do you think I'm waiting for, you pompous windbag?"

Ryehtliti grimaced and took another step backward. "Perhaps this is a bad time for this discussion." His desperate gaze scampered around the room, looking for a friendly face, but everyone had learned in the past several months to keep their faces blank.

Yowrnsaxa felt sympathy for the man. He might not know it yet, but he was stuck with the dragon's tail in his teeth, and there was little doubt he'd have the claws in his face soon enough.

"Perhaps you'd best speak your peace before I grow annoyed," said Queen Suel in a quiet voice that seemed even more threatening than when she'd screamed at the man.

Yowrnsaxa hoped the *Toemari* would get to his point in a hurry. She pitied the courtiers who were tasked with this matter of the new tax. If they did their jobs at all, it almost guaranteed Suel's wrath. When she'd established the role of *Toemari*, she'd seemed to want them to be independent and to tell her the truth. Since she'd been spending so much time with Vowli and Luka, however, it seemed she wanted them as mere sycophants.

"Yes, your Majesty, of course." *Toemari* Ryehtliti seemed to pull himself together by force of will and drew himself to his full height. He even took half a step forward again. "The fact of the matter is that the people in my district are not happy, your Grace. From what they've told me, the tax is simply more than they can afford."

The room grew still. Suel sat on her throne and stared at Ryehtliti. Her face was still, but her eyes burned like the coals in a forge. Her attendants lining the walls of the chamber found elsewhere to cast their eyes.

Toemari Ryehtliti met Queen Suel's gaze with a directness and a calmness that did him credit. His air of confident competence was only marred by the sight of his Adam's apple bobbing up and down as he swallowed again and again.

"So, *Toemari* Ryehtliti, what you mean to tell me is that this tax is too high for those in your district?"

Ryehtliti nodded. "Yes, your Grace, but through no fault of your—"

"*Well, who else would be to blame, you little frog?*" Suel screamed at him. "Is it…" Her burning gaze swept the room and stopped on Yowrnsaxa's face. "Is it Yowrnsaxa's fault?"

"N-no, your Majesty. I'm—"

"Then is it fair Pratyi's fault?" Suel flung her hand up and pointed at Pratyi, standing at attention to the right of the main door.

"Your Majesty, please allow me—"

"Not his fault either then? Then who, *Toemari?* Who is at fault?"

"It's not a matter of fault, your—"

"Oh, do shut up!" Suel snapped.

Ryehtliti shut his mouth and swallowed hard.

"What am I to do? Shall I set a different tax rate for your district or should I lower it across the board?" Suel had a sweet smile on her face, but it didn't extend to her eyes.

"Your Grace, I'm sure you will find the right of it. I merely wished to let you know of my constituents' fears."

"Oh?" Suel's voice was controlled, and her smile grew larger, but it was anything but pleasant.

Now come the claws, thought Yowrnsaxa.

"So, you merely wish to inform me that my tax rate is unfair to your constituents? You come to complain but have nothing to add? No ideas? No suggestions?" Her voice dripped honey, but the coals in her eyes burned brighter and brighter.

Toemari Ryehtliti swallowed hard and looked down at his feet.

"Oh, no!" screeched Suel. "You *look* at me, you gutless little squirrel." Suel shot out of her throne and almost ran to where Ryehtliti stood. She stopped with her chin a mere inch from his chest, head tilted back, her burning eyes glaring up at him.

No matter how brave he was, *Toemari* Ryehtliti couldn't stop from raising his hands to push her away.

Pratyi and Syurd took several paces from their posts at the doors, hands drifting to their weapons, but Suel's hand shot up and waved them off.

She arched her eyebrows at him. "Something?" she asked, her voice sounding like metal screeching against stone. "Am I making you uncomfortable, *Toemari*?"

"Truth be told, my Queen, you are indeed."

"Oh. I am so sorry." Suel enunciated each word crisply, snapping her teeth together at the end of each word. "You *dare* to come here and criticize me and then want to complain that I am not happy with you?"

"Queen Suel, I must apologize. It seems I've overstepped. For that, I am truly and deeply sorry."

Her hand blurred out and slapped him across the face. "That won't do, Ryehtliti!" She screamed it into his face, spittle sparkling across his cheeks. "No false contrition! No missteps! Here in Suelhaym—*my* empire, remember—we take responsibility for what we say and do."

It was almost comical to see *Toemari* Ryehtliti trying to bow with her standing an inch away from him, but that was his first instinct, and he tried to show respect as best he could. "Your will, your Grace," he said.

Again, her hand blurred to his face, but this time it left behind four long cuts across his cheek where she had gouged at him with her nails. "What did I just say, *Toemari*? What did I *just* say? What did I just *say*?" Each question was punctuated by another gouging of his cheeks with her nails. "Are you stupid?" she screamed at the top of her voice.

Ryehtliti looked around in panic. It was clear he no longer knew what to do. There was nothing in the rules of courtly manners that dictate how one should respond to being scratched by one's queen.

Yowrnsaxa's heart went out to him. She longed to tell him that there was nothing he could do or say now. In fact, anything he did or said would just make the fit of rage worse. Yowrnsaxa had seen this in the queen several times in the past week—long, screaming diatribes over imagined slights, physical violence toward messengers and courtiers alike. It was…horrible.

"M-My Queen, I-I—"

"I-I-I-I," mocked Suel with a nasty twist to her lips. "Eye, did you say?" she asked, voice suddenly as sweet as sugar.

Yowrnsaxa's heart leapt, and she couldn't stop taking a step forward. She was not alone—several of the *Trohtninkar Tumuhr*, including Sif, had moved forward.

"If another person in this room moves, I will become most upset," said Suel with viciousness in her tone, twisting her head to glare over her shoulder.

Yowrnsaxa glanced at Sif, but what was there to be done? Suel was their queen, no matter how she chose to act.

Suel turned her face back toward *Toemari* Ryehtliti, with a strange expression lingering on her face. "Well, *Toemari?*"

He shook his head. "I—"

"Thank you for clearing that up," said Suel and she drove her thumb into Ryehtliti's left eye. Her face twisted, and she twisted her thumb, grinding her nail into his eye socket. *Toemari* Ryehtliti screamed in agony and tried to pull his head away. "No, you don't, coward," growled Suel as she stepped closer, her breasts rubbing against his chest in some sick kind of mockery of intimacy. She snapped the fingers of her left hand toward Pratyi and Syurd.

Pratyi shot a horrified look at Yowrnsaxa. Syurd was shaking his head and looking around the room like he wanted somewhere to hide.

"Oh, no, Syurd?" asked Suel with that false sweetness back in her voice. She shoved *Toemari* Ryehtliti to his knees, his hands covering his eye. She glared at Syurd and pointed her finger at him. "*Predna,*" she said, and power crackled in the room.

Syurd's screams reverberated around the small room. Emerald green flames licked his neck from inside his armor. He started to run—to where it wasn't clear. His hair went up with a small sound like a stiff wind blowing through a keyhole. He bounced off the wall next to the door, setting the wall hanging alight, as flames burst from his eye sockets. His voice broke and finally his screams stopped. His mouth was still open, and he was trying to scream, but the only thing coming out of his mouth was green flame.

He fell into a heap, his armor and weapons glowing white hot. The green fire snapped and popped as the fat of his body ignited and burned. His limbs twitched a few times, and then he was motionless.

The smell was overpowering, like a pig roasting over an open flame. It was a sickly-sweet smell that turned Yowrnsaxa's stomach.

The room was silent, and even Queen Suel herself looked shocked at what she had done. She stared at the remains of one of her loyal *Vuthuhr Trohtninkar*, her face slack.

Sif rushed forward, ripping a wall hanging down as she ran past it and covering Syurd's burning flesh with it. She beat on the wall hanging, trying to extinguish the green flames. When they were out, she ripped the wall hanging aside and felt for a pulse. She rose slowly, what everyone already knew written across her face in an angry smear. "He's dead," said Sif.

As Suel looked at her, the rage crept into the queen's expression. "Good," she snapped. "It is what I intended, after all. I am sick—*utterly sick*—of being questioned." Her eyes swept the room, any traces of regret or surprise washed clean from her expression. "From this time forward, I *will* be obeyed. *Instantly.*" She snapped her fingers.

As lazily as a cat, Queen Suel turned her head, sweeping the room with her gaze. When her eyes met Sif's, she stopped and stared. "I told you not to move, Sif. I am disappointed."

Sif scoffed and shook her head in disbelief.

"I am your queen!" Suel's voice cracked like a whip. "I will be obeyed, Sif, childhood playmate or not." She raised her arm and pointed at Sif. "*Kvul,*" she breathed.

Sif fell to the ground, writhing in agony. Her scream burst forth in a voice-shattering shriek.

Suel watched, without much interest, and then snapped her fingers.

As suddenly as Sif had fallen, she lay still, panting, tears streaming down her face. She looked stricken, but no one dared run to her to help—if there was any help for what Suel had done to her.

"I will be obeyed," Suel said in a quiet, vicious voice, her eyes glued to Sif's face. Without looking up, she raised her hand and snapped at Pratyi. "Now, hold him," she said.

Pratyi looked as if he were about to be sick, but he stepped forward and grabbed *Toemari* Ryehtliti by his chin while wrapping his other hand around the man's forehead.

Queen Suel turned back to Ryehtliti. "You thought I'd forgotten you? Hoped so, I bet." Suel tittered like a mad woman.

Toemari Ryehtliti looked her in the eye, his courage evident in his bearing. "What has happened to you, my Queen?" he asked in the tones of mourning.

Suel shrugged. "I've just finally gotten sick of being taken for granted." Her hand blurred forward, and despite the strength in Pratyi's arms, *Toemari* Ryehtliti's head rocked, and blood squirted from his left eye socket. A scream burst from his throat, but he bit it off—almost turning it into the sound of a dog's yelp.

"No more eye," Suel said. Then she laughed and waved Pratyi away. "Get out of my sight. All of you," she snapped.

Yowrnsaxa ran to Sif. "Can you stand?" she whispered, offering her hand.

Sif nodded and let Yowrnsaxa pull her to her feet. "What is happening here," she asked in a gruff, throaty voice.

"Insanity," whispered Yowrnsaxa with a fugitive glance at Suel.

"Evil," whispered Sif back.

Together, they turned toward *Toemari* Ryehtliti, but Pratyi helped him to his feet and supported his weight as they stepped toward the door. Sif and Yowrnsaxa turned toward the side door. Unable to help herself, Yowrnsaxa glanced over her shoulder at the queen.

Suel walked to her throne and sank into it as if she didn't have a care in the world. She watched them file out with eyes like a dead lizard's.

Later that evening, Suel called for her *Trohtninkar Tumuhr*. She had a grand tea set up in the queen's gardens, and all were cordially invited. Yowrnsaxa arrived late, and the tittering and laughing were in full swing. Queen Suel was in great spirits as if the events of the afternoon had never happened.

"Ah, Yowrnsaxa," said Suel. "Setting the standard for fashionable lateness, as usual."

Yowrnsaxa bowed. "My Queen."

"Where is Sif? You two are usually joined at hip and elbow."

Yowrnsaxa shook her head. "She is unable to attend this evening, your Grace. She is feeling quite ill and sends her regrets." The truth of it was that Sif was so angry she didn't think she could face the queen without incident.

"Hopefully, one of her healing sisters can see to the heart of the matter."

"Yes, your Majesty."

Queen Suel waved her hand, ever the gracious hostess, at the elaborate banquet table laid out between two burning braziers. Yowrnsaxa bowed her head and walked to the table. It seemed no expense had been spared on the evening's festivities. Exquisite dishes were crammed on the table—lutefisk, pickled herring, gravlax, toasted bread topped with turbot roe and vinegar dust, howkari, raw razor shells with parsley jelly, grilled cucumber stuffed with bacon, smoked svart molly, hangikyut, and kyutsoopa. There were pitchers of mead to drink.

Yowrnsaxa didn't have much of an appetite but took small portions of the gravlax, howkari, and the smoked svart molly. It was expected, and the queen was watching.

The queen threw a companionable arm across Yowrnsaxa's shoulders and looked at her dish. "Watching your figure again?" she tittered. Her breath smelled of aquavit, and she held a full drinking horn in her other hand.

"No, my Queen, I've not much of an appetite this evening is all."

"You seem sad," said Suel. "What is bothering you?"

Yowrnsaxa looked down at her plate of food and wished she hadn't taken the howkari as the smell of the cured shark meat was making her feel nauseated. "Maybe I feel a little under the weather, as well," she muttered.

"Shall I call for a healer?" asked Suel.

"No, your Grace, it's just…a minor bug."

Suel tittered. "Well, that stinking shark can't be helping."

"No, your Majesty, it isn't."

"Queen Suel? May I approach, your Majesty?" boomed Meuhlnir from one of the arched entrances to the garden.

Suel sighed and rolled her eyes at Yowrnsaxa. "Must you?" she called.

Meuhlnir was long in answering. "I would like…" he started and then his voice trailed away, sounding like a little boy with his feelings hurt.

"Oh, very well," snapped Suel. "You may approach, but if you think you are going to whisk one of my ladies into the shadows for some hanky-panky, you are grossly mistaken, sir."

For once, Meuhlnir didn't rise to her baiting. He approached, his head down, hands grasped behind his back.

"Oh, bother," said Suel. "What has happened that has brought the mighty Meuhlnir so low?" Her tone was bantering, but it had that peculiar ring that Yowrnsaxa had begun to think of as Suel's warning bell.

Meuhlnir stopped several feet away and bowed. "Thank you for seeing me, my Queen."

Suel twirled her fingers impatiently.

"I wanted to speak with you about the events of this afternoon, your Grace," said Meuhlnir.

Suel's face went blank. "Come to chide me, eh?" she asked in her sweet voice that was like a claxon of eminent danger.

Yowrnsaxa cringed.

"I wouldn't dream of it, my Queen. I am concerned is all."

The queen put her hand flat on her chest. "Concerned for little me?"

"Yes, your Grace. The events of this afternoon seem…" He again let his voice trail away to nothing with the same hurt tone.

"Yes?" asked Suel in a flat voice.

"It's just that it doesn't seem like you," muttered Meuhlnir, his eyes scanning the circle of *Trohtninkar Tumuhr* surrounding them.

"Oh? Didn't I do all that? Was it some imposter?"

Yowrnsaxa cringed and tried to catch Meuhlnir's eye, but he only had eyes for the queen. He seemed oblivious to the hidden threat in the queen's voice and posture.

"Your Majesty, is there something I can do for you?" Meuhlnir asked, his concern for the queen evident in his voice.

Queen Suel softened a little and looked him in the eye. "I assure you, friend Meuhlnir, that I am fit in mind and body and that the only thing that has been bothering me is a certain...how shall I put it? A certain lack of respect for the crown of late. In courtesans and in others."

Meuhlnir nodded. "I haven't noticed, your Grace, but I assure you I will vigilantly watch for such disrespect. No one will disrespect you in my presence."

Suel put her hand on his arm, but the expression on her face was distrusting.

"Please rely on me, your Majesty. Allow me to deal with anyone who annoys you."

The queen's eyes narrowed. She opened her mouth to speak, but just then Luka and Vowli strode into the gardens without so much as a by-your-leave.

Luka laughed and swatted Meuhlnir's shoulder. "Stick to guarding the queen, brother. Leave the politics to those who understand them."

Meuhlnir's face knotted in irritation. "Please, your Grace."

"I can handle my own problems, Meuhlnir," said the queen, her voice as cold as arctic wind. Her hand left his arm. She held her arms out to Vowli and Luka, putting one arm around each man's waist when they came to stand by her side. Her eyes were like the space between stars—cold and empty.

Yowrnsaxa took a step back and put her plate down on the table. She was not going to stand idly by and let Meuhlnir be hurt as Syurd had been. She didn't care what Suel did to her afterwards.

"Your Majesty, can I call for a healer to speak with you?" asked Meuhlnir in a formal tone of voice.

"Whatever for?" asked Suel in that dead voice she had been using so much.

"For whatever has caused you such stress, such discomfort, to drive you to actions like those of the afternoon."

The queen stared at him for a long moment, and the atmosphere seemed to crackle with tension. Yowrnsaxa took a step closer to Meuhlnir and saw the queen glance at her in irritation. "I've told you that I am fine. You persist. I've told you I can handle my own problems. You push on. What do I have to do, Meuhlnir?"

"Your Majesty, it's just that this all seems so unlike the benevolent queen we've all dedicated our lives to," said Meuhlnir. He straightened his shoulders and met her glare with a calm expression.

Yowrnsaxa cringed and prepared herself to come to Meuhlnir's aid if need be.

"Ah, here's the heart of it," muttered Suel. She dropped her arms from the waists of Luka and Vowli and took a step forward, almost as close to Meuhlnir as she had been to *Toemari* Ryehtliti earlier that day. "I am *sorry* to so disappoint you. I am *sorry* if I don't fit in to the pretty picture of Queen Suel that you have painted in your head, Meuhlnir. Things have changed. Get used to the new me," said the queen with venom in her voice.

Meuhlnir's shoulders slumped, and he seemed to deflate. "Oh, your Majesty, I'm sorry to cause you upset," he said.

Suel stared at him blankly.

Meuhlnir hung his head. "I don't mean to overstep."

Suel stood still for a moment, and two expressions flitted across her face in rapid succession. The first was irritation. The second was boredom. Then her face froze in that blank rictus she had adopted so often of late. "You *do*, in fact, overstep. You are not my lover. You are not my brother. You are not my father. You have no right to…to…"

"You have no right to interfere in the queen's business," said Vowli.

Suel nodded her head.

Meuhlnir sighed. "I don't mean to be interfering, your Majesty. It's just that I care about you, your Grace. I want you to be happy."

Suel sneered down at the hammer she had given him after the assassination attempt that had taken place in these very gardens. She flicked it with a finger and set it swinging. "Don't presume that because I once honored you for bravery that you may speak to me thus," she said, and her voice was so cold it could have flash-frozen the sea.

"I apologize, your Majesty," said Meuhlnir. "You used to value my advice." He had a sick look in his eyes, but it wasn't fearful. It was mournful.

"No. No more talking from you, Meuhlnir. You are always talking, talking, talking. You will now shut up and listen to me." The queen's eyes blazed like firebrands. "Do not presume that you know me. Do not presume to lecture me on how I behave. Do *not* presume that your opinions hold weight in my decisions. I am your Queen, and you *will* show me the respect the crown deserves."

Meuhlnir stood before her as a small child stands before a parent during a tongue lashing. Yowrnsaxa longed to go to his side and comfort him, but after everything that had happened that day, she knew better than to oppose the queen. Unless she grew violent again.

"Too long, I've let you be overly familiar. Too many times, I've overlooked your disrespectful actions toward me—pedantically lecturing me on manners, patronizingly 'teaching' me about *strenkir af krafti*, about becoming *vefari*. From now on, you *will* show the proper respect. You'd be wise to remember what happens to those who do not." With that, Queen Suel turned her back on him, her long blonde hair brushing across his chest as she spun.

Meuhlnir stood there, staring after her for a moment, and then dropped his eyes, looking at nothing, saying and doing nothing.

"She's done with you, brother. You should go back to your *actual* duties now."

Meuhlnir raised his head to look Luka in the eye. His face was full of pain. He spun on his heel and walked toward the archway that led toward the barracks.

"I should have given that hammer to you, Luka," said the queen with the pretense of confidential tones, but loud enough for everyone to hear. Then she laughed in a mean-spirited way that made Yowrnsaxa want to scratch her eyes out.

Meuhlnir stiffened as he heard the barb. Then his shoulders fell, and he walked on, a picture of dejection and loss. He looked as if she couldn't have hurt him more if she had gouged his eye out instead of giving him a tongue lashing.

As he walked through the arch, Suel turned to face Yowrnsaxa. The companionable demeanor she had worn when Yowrnsaxa first arrived was no longer evident. "It seems you are feeling unwell, Yowrnsaxa. Perhaps you should return to your quarters until you are feeling well enough that I can rely on you." Her voice was pure acid, and her expression was one Yowrnsaxa would expect to show only to someone she deeply hated. "Perhaps it would be best if you, Sif, and I spent some time apart. Perhaps the two of you should see what I'm up against and maybe that will assuage your doubts about my actions." Anger was creeping into Queen Suel's eyes.

Yowrnsaxa nodded. It was clear that she hadn't kept her intentions of coming to Meuhlnir's aid quite as disguised as she had thought. "Your Grace knows best," she said in a neutral voice.

"Indeed, I do," said Suel, tilting her head forward to glare at Yowrnsaxa from under her eyebrows, seeming to make even such an innocuous statement threatening. "You and Sif will report to the

Ministry—to Luka and Vowli—tomorrow." The queen laid a tender hand on each man's forearm. "Perhaps they can educate you about the perils Suelhaym now faces."

"Yes, your Majesty." Yowrnsaxa bowed and walked back to the quarters set aside for the *Trohtninkar Tumuhr*. She went straight to Sif's room and knocked on the door.

"Come," called Sif.

Yowrnsaxa told her what had happened at the late tea.

"Suel is right," said Sif with heat in her voice. "It is best that we spend some time apart. Or else I might regret my actions."

The next morning, they walked together to the low building that housed the Ministry of the Queen's Justice. There was a single door into the building and no windows. Inside, the lobby was dark—lit only by a single torch near the door, and a single candle burning on the desk in front of another door leading deeper into the building. A short, rat-faced man sat behind the desk. He leered at them with a small sneer twisting the corners of his mouth.

"May I help you two ladies?" he asked.

"We are *Trohtninkar Tumuhr*. We are here to see your masters." The man was a thrall and beneath their notice.

"Oh, yes," he slobbered. "I was told to expect you."

"*And?*" asked Yowrnsaxa without looking at him.

"If you will follow me," he said, getting up and opening the door behind him. He went through and took a torch from a sconce in the next room and turned to beckon them. "I won't bite," he said.

They followed him through a warren of dim hallways with dark offices off to the sides. He led them to a set of steep stairs and scampered down in front of them, lighting torches at each landing. "We keep it dark here to keep the prisoners from—"

"Lead, don't talk," snapped Sif.

"As you command, m'Lady," he said in a sullen voice.

Yowrnsaxa lost count of the landings but knew they must be deep underground. The walls began to sweat moisture. Finally, the thrall stopped at one of the landings and handed the torch to Sif.

"Through the door, down the hall, third door on the right," he snapped.

"You may go," said Yowrnsaxa.

The thrall trudged up the stairs grumbling under his breath.

The two women walked through the door into a foul-smelling rectangular room. Cells ran the length of the room on each side, shrouded in shadow. The odor of human waste was strong enough to make their eyes water.

They strode down the center of the room, trying to ignore the grunts of the prisoners in the cells as they saw Sif and Yowrnsaxa.

"So many," whispered Sif.

"Luka and Vowli have indeed been busy," said Yowrnsaxa.

"*Trohtninkar Tumuhr* here?" It was croaked from a cell on the right. The voice sounded like it issued from a throat that didn't get much use. Or much water for that matter. "Am I dreaming?"

"Indeed, not," said Sif. "What is your name, sir?"

"I am *Toemari* Adalsteinn."

"What?" asked Sif.

"Why are you imprisoned down here?" asked Yowrnsaxa at the same moment.

"I stand accused of treasonous speech against her Majesty, though what I said that was treasonous, I have no idea." Adalsteinn's voice was getting stronger by the word—as if the words were knocking rust from his voice box.

"Surely this must be a mistake, *Toemari*?" asked Sif.

Adalsteinn sighed. "You are asking the wrong man." He sounded defeated. "The right man lies beyond."

"No mistake," said Luka. He stood at the end of the room, smirking. "No one on this floor is here by mistake."

Adalsteinn scoffed. "That is a lie," he grumbled. It was as if he knew the seeds of his argument were going to fall on stony soil.

"Come, come, Adalsteinn. Be honest. You came here by way of the floors above, and on each floor, you were given the opportunity to prove your innocence. You chose not to—or maybe you could not."

Adalsteinn made no reply, but they could all hear him shuffling farther into the cell.

"Don't let these sad sacks tug your heart strings, ladies," said Luka. "No one here is innocent or here by mistake. That's what all those rooms above are for."

Sif cocked an eyebrow at Yowrnsaxa, and she shrugged in reply. "Why are we here, Luka?"

"As her Majesty explained last night, you two are here to hear the truth of what the queen has to face every day."

"And what is that?" asked Sif with some scorn.

"Treachery. Plots. Cheats." Luka turned and waved for them to follow as he walked down another hall lined with cells.

"Even a *Toemari*?"

"Oh, yes," said Luka. "The karl class is not immune to greed and treachery, and neither is the yarl class, though there are fewer yarls here than karls and far fewer karls than thralls."

"Because thralls have the most to be angry about or because they have the least protection?" asked Sif with a curled lip.

Luka just shrugged. "I don't know, and I don't care. All I care about is rooting out the undesirables that surround or threaten Queen Suel." He came to the third door on the right and held it open for them.

Yowrnsaxa walked through the door and gasped. The room was filled with the stench of blood, sweat, and urine. Of fear and pain, in other words. There was a tall, naked man strapped to a cross of thick timbers, positioned so that his back was to the door, and his face rubbed against the rough-cut timbers.

Sif stepped through the door behind Yowrnsaxa. "Surely this can't be what the queen wants," she muttered.

Vowli was leaning against the wall, picking at his fingernails with the tip of a very sharp looking knife. "Her Majesty wants us to root this faction of malcontents, criminals, and rebels from her empire. She has invested us with the power to see the job done."

"By any means?" asked Yowrnsaxa.

"By whatever means are required to get results," said Luka. "Take this man, here. He is a wealthy karl. He was promised to the youngest daughter of another prominent karl. He had it all—riches, acceptance, and respect in the caste above that of his birth, houses, servants, friends, and even power."

"But he chose to squander all that," said Vowli. "He squandered it in an asinine attempt to make a fool of the queen. When he was discovered, he ran and hid like a coward. He tried to foster rebellion to save himself. Right here in her majesty's home city."

"A coward, through and through," said Luka.

"What more can be expected from a karl?" asked Vowli. He pushed himself away from the wall, examining his fingernails as if they were the end-all of his existence. "It fell to us to capture him and to squash his budding treason."

"Now it is our task to see how deep his treachery ran," said Luka. He turned to face them. "It is your task to watch us work and observe the results." He started to turn back to the man strapped to the cross. "But feel free to jump right in and assist us if you feel so motivated."

Vowli stood very close to the man's exposed back. "Who else did you corrupt, traitor?" he whispered, his mouth behind the man's left ear, the dagger held loose at his side.

"N-no one," said the man, "I just ran because I panicked when I heard the Ministry was after me. I didn't try to foster rebellion. I just tried to hide. I didn't—" The flood of words turned into a shriek of pain as Vowli used the tip of the dagger to slash from the man's shoulder blade down to his waist, leaving a trail of blood behind.

"Not that tired story again, Peli," said Luka with a sigh. "It's true the ladies haven't heard it, but Vowli and I have."

"Many times," said Vowli with some menace, his lips brushing Peli's ear.

"We know that story is a fabrication," said Luka.

"A lie," echoed Vowli.

"And the ladies don't believe you anyway, so you might as well drop the act."

Vowli rested the tip of the dagger half an inch from the top of the first cut. "We've dealt with this story."

"And two floors above, you admitted the story was a lie," said Luka. "We don't want to hurt you, but you are making us do so."

Yowrnsaxa glanced at Sif, whose expression was thunderous with fury. Yowrnsaxa took her hand and squeezed it. Sif met her glance and shook her head, full of sadness.

"Don't you want to tell us the truth any more, Peli?" asked Vowli, applying a subtle pressure to the tip of the dagger.

"What I said before was not the truth," Peli gasped.

"Oh, come now," snapped Luka.

Vowli moved the knife downwards a few inches and Peli shrieked. "It was all lies! You said if I gave you names that you'd let me go." Peli's voice was without hope.

Luka sighed. "So, we must start again, Peli?"

"It would be easier for you to just tell us the truth," said Vowli.

"I *have* told you the truth! Many times! And each time, you hurt me."

"Yes, how unfair your life is, Peli," said Vowli as he dragged the blade of the dagger down toward Peli's waist. "Maybe this is a waste of time, Luka. Maybe I should just kill our friend Peli, here."

"Oh, I don't know," said Luka. "What do you think, Peli?"

Peli whimpered and shook his head.

There was a knock at the door, and they all jumped a little, even Peli jumped as much as his bindings would allow. Yowrnsaxa looked at Sif with raised eyebrows. Sif squeezed her hand again and tried to hide a little smile.

The door swung open so hard it banged against the wall and swung back. Paltr kicked the door a second time, knocking it out of his way and strode into the room. "What's doing, little brother?" he boomed.

Luka's eyes went wide. "What are you doing here?" he asked.

"Sif told me she was invited to the Ministry to see you work. I decided to come along and see for myself. Sorry I'm late." He slapped Luka's shoulder with sufficient force to make his little brother take a step forward.

Luka bristled, but Vowli put out his hand and clasped Luka's shoulder. "That's fine, Paltr," he said, "as long as you are here to watch rather than to interfere."

Paltr held up his hands, the picture of innocence.

Vowli grunted and rested the tip of his finger about an inch from the last long vertical cut in Peli's back. When the tip of his finger touched Peli's skin, a little screech burst out of the tortured man. "Now, Peli. I want you to think long and hard before you answer my question. Can you do that?"

Peli grunted, too scared to do much more than that.

"Good," said Vowli. "Good. Keep in mind that we have three distinguished guests in attendance, any one of which has the ear of the queen."

Paltr slid past Luka to stand next to Sif. He looked at her and raised his eyebrows.

She glanced up at him and shook her head.

"Are you listening to your friend Vowli, Peli?" asked Luka with a hint of peevishness in his voice.

"Y-yes, Luka."

"Good," whispered Vowli in his ear, making Peli twitch and shiver. "Are the charges against you true? Specifically, did you attempt to defraud the queen by misrepresenting your income to avoid paying your fair share of taxes?"

"Yes. Yes, I did that," said Peli. Sweat dripped from every part of his body.

"Good," said Vowli again. "Did you become aware that the Ministry of the Queen's Justice was investigating you?"

"Yeah," sighed Peli. "I got scared, then. Really scared."

"Good," crooned Vowli. "Now, be careful with this next answer, and please recall that you have already confessed to this crime."

"But I said I—"

Vowli twitched the tip of his finger downwards, and Peli screamed and then seemed surprised that there wasn't any pain. "Let's just call that a little warm up, Peli—just a practice cut, on my part, using my finger." Vowli shoved his finger in Peli's face, just a fraction of an inch from Peli's eye. "Now that we are all warmed up again after the exciting entrance of our friend Paltr, the next cut is for real. I am putting the tip of my dagger on your back now. I want you to listen to the whole question and think about your answer. Don't just shout something out before I'm finished speaking."

Peli tried to nod with his head tied to the cross.

"Did you, after learning you were being investigated, try to run?"

"Yes," whispered Peli. "I panicked."

"Did you go to the house of your betrothed and hide there?"

"I went there," said Peli.

"And you convinced your fiancée to hide you, correct?"

Tears streamed down Peli's cheeks. "You are going to cut me if I tell the truth."

Vowli made a cut about three inches long in Peli's back. "I'm growing tired of this, Peli. I'm about to let Luka question you."

Peli whimpered and sagged against his bindings.

"Answer him!" roared Luka in Peli's right ear, making the naked man jerk his head away as far as he could.

"No, Oesk knew nothing of any of this. She's innocent!"

Peli screamed as Vowli made the three-inch cut stretch all the way to his waist. Then Vowli stepped back and sighed. "We tried this the easy way, Peli. I want you to remember that we offered you an easier way than you've chosen."

Luka walked to a small table that was covered with stoneware jars. The table was masterfully positioned so that it was just visible to anyone tied to the cross. Luka let his hand drift lazily from one jar to the next while Peli sobbed.

"She is innocent," Peli sobbed.

Luka's hand snapped to the lid of a tall jar and knocked it aside. He grabbed a handful of salt from the container, whirled and stomped over to the cross. "We already have her, you know," he whispered in Peli's ear. He spread the salt across the long cuts in Peli's back, and the man gasped and tried to twist away. "She may be being questioned even as we speak. Of course, were you to confess, we might find ourselves with all the answers that are required."

"Y-you'd l-let her go?"

"Well, you know that isn't possible," said Luka. "But we might be able to send her on her way to exile without continuing the questioning."

Peli looked torn, but then a look of calm acceptance settled on his face, and he sagged against his bonds. "Yes," he said.

"Yes?" asked Luka. "Yes what?"

"I did it. I did whatever you said I did. I did it all."

"Ah, progress." Luka beamed at Sif for a moment and then put his mouth right next to Peli's ear. "Now, let's move on to names. You will tell us every person in whom you tried to sow seeds of rebellion."

Peli's eyes opened wide with fear.

"We already know who they are," said Vowli. "We just need confirmation."

"Just list the names, Peli," crooned Luka. "Then we are done."

Peli began to spew names as fast as he could think of them. They were other merchants, his competitors mostly. Luka looked at Vowli and gave him a small nod. Vowli turned and left the room. Luka let Peli ramble on until he started to slow down, either running out of competitors or running out of breath.

"Now, Peli," said Luka, "you know that list was a false one."

"N-no! I promise you—"

"It's okay, Peli. We all understand the temptation to implicate your competitors and business rivals. It's human nature," crooned Luka. "We can all understand trying that. Once. We won't be able to understand any further attempts at side-stepping the question, though, so please bear that in mind as you begin again." Luka slapped his hand down hard on Peli's right shoulder. "The names!"

Peli began a new list of names, starting with a few members of his own family, and including some prominent karls who had the misfortune of being one of his customers.

"Peli, Peli, Peli," muttered Luka. He waved his hand at the doorway.

Vowli entered the room, pushing a naked woman covered in all manner of filth before him. The woman had probably been quite pretty before her visit to the Ministry, but now she was in a wretched state. Her long blonde hair was a mass of rat tails and matted tangles. She had long, half-healed cuts across her breasts and an ugly burn on her cheek. Vowli steered her around the cross and pushed her down in front of it. She didn't resist, just fell to her knees where Vowli pushed her.

Peli saw her and began to cry, hopeless and broken. "Oesk," he cried. "I'm so sorry, Oesk."

The woman didn't even raise her head. She didn't speak.

"Oesk, Oesk!" cried Peli. He began to thrash against the leather straps that bound him. "What have these bastards done to you, Oesk?"

Again, the woman just sat where Vowli had pushed her down, not moving, not speaking, not responding at all.

"*I'll kill you!*" Peli screamed, thrashing even harder. The cross began to creak and moan as he threw his weight this way and that. "I'll kill both of you evil sons of—"

Vowli took a quick step forward and punched Peli in the side of the head. Peli slumped against the straps, stunned but still conscious.

Luka smiled at Vowli. "Masterfully done, my friend."

Vowli gave a small bow.

Luka bent and picked up a bucket of oily looking water. He moved so that no one would get splashed and then threw the bucket of water in Peli's face.

Peli started and then sputtered. His eyes opened, and he looked down at Oesk, his face the picture of regret. "Oh, Oesk, I'm so sorry," he said.

"Oh, don't start that again," snapped Vowli.

Luka stood behind Oesk, and Vowli moved behind Peli. Luka grabbed a fistful of Oesk's matted hair.

"Leave her alone," whispered Peli. "Please."

"You know what you have to do to protect her," said Vowli.

"But I can't," cried Peli. "I can't tell you the names you want to hear. I don't know them!"

Luka pulled Oesk to her feet by her hair. She didn't react even as strands of her hair were pulled out by the root.

"No, please," whimpered Peli. "Just tell me the names you want me to say, and I'll say them. I beg you!"

"That's not how this works," said Vowli.

"Tell us," grated Luka, "or I can promise you will not be happy."

Peli slumped against the cross and sobbed.

"Come on, now," said Vowli. "Just give us a list of names we can believe. It doesn't have to be the whole list. Just a start."

Peli cried in exhaustion. "Where should I start?" he asked.

Luka jerked Oesk's head this way and that by the hair, but it was like she was stuffed with sawdust for all the reaction it got.

"Oesk?" asked Peli.

"Good," crooned Vowli. "Now who else? Maybe someone in Oesk's household? Her father perhaps?"

"Yes!" said Peli. "Oesk's father. And her mother!"

"Good," said Vowli. "Keep going."

"Um," said Peli, his eyes darting around the small room. "Their cook, Chellrune."

"Good. Who else?"

"The groomsman, I've forgotten his name right now. He's tall and red-headed."

"Oh, Peli," sighed Vowli. "He was one of our investigators. Are you just telling us what you think we want to hear?"

Peli sagged against the cross again and sobbed.

"I'm afraid you've upset Luka," said Vowli. "You know that isn't a good thing."

Luka stared at Peli, his eyes boring into the sobbing man. Then he turned his head toward Oesk and pulled her face close to his.

"No," whispered Peli. "Punish me, not her."

Luka looked at him coldly. "The worst thing I can do to you is to make you watch me hurt her."

"Brother, I think—"

"Shut up!" snapped Luka. "You're not in charge here."

"But I really think that this man doesn't have the information you want. It's clear he's just trying to please you," said Yowrnsaxa,

Luka darted his face forward, and there was a snicking sound. Oesk screamed—the first reaction she'd made. Blood poured from her cheek.

Paltr shook his head as if he couldn't understand what had happened.

Luka spit a chunk of Oesk's face into Peli's face. Blood and saliva dripped from Luka's chin. His eyes were locked on Peli's. "How's your memory now?" he asked in a savage voice.

Vowli laughed.

To everyone's amazement, Paltr roared, took two giant steps forward and cuffed Luka across the face with what looked like all of his strength.

Luka staggered as if he'd been hit with a log and shoved Oesk away so that he could catch himself against the far wall.

Sif darted forward and wrapped the bleeding woman in her arms, turning so that Sif's body was between Oesk and her inquisitors.

The next blow from Paltr was a closed fist that drove Luka into the table full of jars, sending both the man and the table crashing to the floor.

"Stop!" said Vowli.

Paltr glanced at him, and his look was so venomous and filled with rage that Vowli took a step toward the door. Paltr loomed over his younger brother, rage baking the air around. He was clenching and releasing his fists as if he longed to have Luka's throat in his hands. "What have you done here?" he hissed.

Luka shook his head, flinging drops of blood across the room. Vile liquids and various powders spotted his clothes. He looked up at Paltr with hatred. "It's not your place!"

Paltr gave a guttural roar, and one of those big fists smashed into Luka's face. "You are a disgrace to this family!" he bellowed. "What have you become? A worm?"

Luka sprang to his feet, his face a rictus of hatred and rage. "Hit me again," he hissed.

"I should hit you until you bleed from the soles of your feet, you disgusting little—"

"Then do it, big man!" screamed Luka. "Shut up and hit me. Let's see what happens."

Vowli looked like he wanted to be anywhere but in that room.

Sif pushed Oesk into Yowrnsaxa's arms and pointed at Vowli. "You get Luka," she snapped.

Vowli looked at her without understanding.

"They will kill each other, you fool! None of us want that," said Yowrnsaxa.

Vowli looked at her and hissed, but he started moving toward Luka while Sif started to pull at Paltr's shoulders.

"Come away, Paltr," she crooned. "This isn't the place for this. You are so angry—"

Paltr looked at her with rage in his eyes and then snapped his gaze back to Luka.

"—and justifiably so, in my opinion, but nothing should be decided in such a rage. Come away, now," she said. Pulling at the big man's shoulders until her fingers turned white.

Vowli was standing behind Luka, one arm around his chest, and crooning in his ear. Luka still seethed with rage and had eyes for no one but his elder brother.

"This isn't finished, *brother*," said Luka. He let Vowli pull him toward the far corner of the room.

"Get out," snapped Vowli. "All of you. The queen will hear of this."

Paltr glanced at Vowli as if he were a bug and drew his dagger from his belt. He cut the leather straps holding Peli to the cross. "This man and his woman are under my protection," he said with a voice still choked and shaking with rage. "We are taking them with us."

"No, you aren't!" shouted Luka, thrashing in Vowli's embrace.

"Just go!" yelled Vowli. "Do you think I can hold him forever?"

Paltr swept Peli up as if his weight were nothing and motioned for Yowrnsaxa to go out first. He nodded toward the door, but Sif shook her head and pointed into the hall, pushing him gently.

They left the Ministry, the state and nakedness of Peli and Oesk drawing many looks, but the grimace on Paltr's face stopped anyone from questioning them. Sif kept up a constant stream of calming words as Paltr walked forward, his face frozen in rage, eyes blazing.

"Where can we take you, Peli?" asked Sif. "The only place any of us has is in the palace."

Peli's head lolled as he looked around in a daze. "There's a hunting cabin outside the west gate," he said. "No one knows about it."

Paltr grunted and walked toward the west gate and, later, through it.

The cabin wasn't much. Two rooms—a small one and a really small one—and only a small fireplace to heat both. They put Oesk and Peli in the smallest room and went outside.

"What do we do?" asked Yowrnsaxa.

"I can't go back there," said Sif. "She has lost her mind, and if I go back, I can't guarantee my actions."

Yowrnsaxa shook her head. "She hasn't released you, Sif."

"I don't care. Let her come for me." Sif's face looked as if it were carved from stone and then layered in ice.

"Are you sure that is wise?"

"Wise?" snapped Paltr. "What would have been wise is to never have pledged into that hateful bitch's service in the first place." He paced in front of the cabin with fast, brutal strides. "I'm going to *kill* him," he muttered.

"You should go back, both of you," said Sif. "I'll stay and protect these two. Heal what I can." She shrugged. "I can't go back, but the *Trohtninkar Tumuhr* and *Vuthuhr Trohtninkar* need to know what those three vipers are doing to the empire."

Yowrnsaxa nodded. "We have to do something."

"You bet your shields that we do. I'll bring you weapons and armor, Sif." Paltr turned to go.

Sif put her hand on his shoulder. "Thank you, Paltr, but before you go, I need you to promise me something."

He turned back to her, one eyebrow arched.

"Promise me to let things with Luka lie until it is time to move on them all."

"But—"

"If you don't," Sif went on, talking over him, "it will tip our hand to the queen, and if she learns what we intend before we've made enough converts, it will be terrible for everyone."

Paltr's mouth snapped closed, and he nodded once.

Before he could walk away, Sif stepped forward and kissed him. "Thank you," she whispered.

"It makes sense," he said shrugging. "*You* make sense."

"No, not only that," said Sif. "For everything you've done this morning."

"Oh," he muttered. "What else could I do?"

"That's why I kissed you. There is nothing else *you* could do. You are a good man, and whatever Luka has become doesn't change that."

He nodded and for the first time since Luka had bitten Oesk, his face softened a little, and some of the rage drained out of his eyes.

"Talk to Meuhlnir," Sif said. "He's a good man, too."

"Yes, he is," said Paltr. He shook his head. "We are going to need more good men." He took Yowrnsaxa's arm and then led her back toward the city.

TWENTY-
EIGHT

Yowrnsaxa stared off into the dark night. "Then Paltr took my arm and led us back into the city. It very much felt like a different city than the one I had woken up in."

"Indeed," said Sif. "It was a wretched time. Peli recovered in time, but Oesk never really did. Oh, she got so that she would at least look at a person if they called her name, but to my knowledge, she never spoke again. She was just broken by the depravity of what she experienced in the bowels of the Ministry."

"You were able to keep them hidden?" I asked.

"Yes," said Meuhlnir. "Things changed somewhat rapidly after that, and the political power of the Dark Queen, Luka, and Vowli began to fold in the face of opposition."

"People were no longer willing to turn a blind eye," said Yowrnsaxa, "once Peli and Oesk's story was made public."

"I'd think not." I cleared my throat and considered what remained of the cooking fire. "I've never met Vowli, but the Dark Queen, as you've described her in that story, sounds a lot more like the woman I knew as Elizabeth Tutor than your previous descriptions. I can see the beginnings of the Luka I knew on my *klith* in the behavior of the Luka in that story."

They were all quiet for a moment, each thinking their own thoughts and keeping them to themselves. Finally, Meuhlnir looked at each of his wives in turn, and it seemed like something passed between them. He cleared his throat and looked up at the darkening sky. "I think it's time to tell you about how I lost two brothers, was exiled and started a revolution in a single day." His voice was gruff. "Though, I also won the companionship of two of the greatest ladies of my time that same day."

Sif looked at him with compassion from her place next to me, and Yowrnsaxa put her hand on his knee.

"Luka was in a rage the next time I saw him," said Meuhlnir. "He wanted the Midnight Queen to punish Paltr, but she wouldn't even discuss it."

"At least not out in the open," said Sif.

"As you say, dear. She called the three of us together later that evening. I hadn't seen much of Luka for a while, and I was disturbed by how he looked when I saw him waiting outside the doors to the queen's reception chamber."

TWENTY-
NINE

When he saw his brother, Luka, standing outside the doors to the queen's reception chamber that night, Meuhlnir was disturbed by the drastic change in his appearance. "Brother, have you been ill?" he asked.

"No," snapped Luka. "Why do you ask?"

"You look so thin, so pale. You've lost a lot of weight since I saw you last. You are wasting away."

"Serving her Majesty has kept me very busy of late."

Meuhlnir's face clouded over like a fast-moving thunderstorm rolling in over a lake. "Yes," he said with some heat in his voice, "Paltr told me about his visit this morning."

Luka bristled. "Of course, he did! Now both of you can have a crack at lecturing me! Or do you want to jump straight to the beating part?"

"I don't think you're being very fair, Luka."

"Fair? *Fair*? Did he not tell you that he beat me like a child in front of everyone? Is that fair?"

Meuhlnir broke contact with his brother's blazing eyes, feeling somewhat guilty. "He mentioned that—"

"I shouldn't have allowed Sif to stop it until I'd beaten more sense into you, Luka," barked Paltr walking up the hall toward them. "What were you thinking? Do you imagine that our father would be proud of how you conducted yourself? Do you think Father would be proud of your role in the so-called Ministry of the Queen's Justice? Do you?" His voice grew louder and louder with each step and each question he shot at Luka until he was almost yelling his brother's face.

Luka sneered at him. "Do you think our father would be proud of *you*? Because I'm willing to bet he'd have words for you about how you treated me. And the fact that you did it in public!"

"Gentlemen," said Queen Suel, leaning in the doorway to her reception chamber. "Perhaps we should continue this discussion in private?" She arched an eyebrow and looked first at Paltr, then Meuhlnir, and finally Luka. Luka was the only one she smiled at.

"As you wish, your Grace," said Meuhlnir, putting a meaty hand on the shoulder of each of his brothers and pushing them toward the door. "Perhaps standing in the hall of the palace is not the best place for a family matter to be discussed."

"Perhaps not," said Suel in a crisp voice. She turned on her heel and led them all into the room. Yowrnsaxa stood next to the queen's throne, but there was no one else in the room. Suel sauntered toward her throne, frowning at a spot of blood on the marble floor. "Tell me what all this ruckus is about," she said, "and why I had to hear about this incident from someone other than the people directly involved."

Luka and Paltr glared at each other, and Meuhlnir sighed. "They have always been like this, your Majesty. At each other's throats for a few days and then inseparable until the next blow-up."

The queen arched an eyebrow at Luka. "Is it so? Still, I'd think we are all old enough to leave the trappings of childhood behind us."

Luka looked at his feet, and even Paltr's snarl softened with what looked like embarrassment.

"Of course, your Majesty," said Paltr in a soft voice.

Luka nodded without looking up.

"Now, would someone please tell me what brought this division between brothers to pass?" the queen asked.

When neither of the brothers looked inclined to speak, Yowrnsaxa stepped forward. "There was an interrogation, your Grace. It seemed to have gotten a bit out of hand, and Paltr put a stop to it."

"Using force?" asked the queen, turning her gaze to Paltr.

"Yes, my Queen," said Paltr. "I...I hit my brother—more than once, I think—and I regret that."

Luka looked at him sidelong without lifting his head. His expression was inscrutable. "We were trying to get to the truth in a tax evasion case that led to some treasonous talk, and perhaps more. The subject was...stubborn."

"Indeed?"

"Yes, your Majesty. Vowli and I had been working with him for some time, and we had already gotten a partial confession that implicated his fiancée and her family—a rich karl family. We were trying to assess their involvement and—"

"By biting a chunk out of her cheek?" asked Paltr with heat in his voice.

Luka bristled, anger splashing across his face. "You don't know what it takes to—"

"Boys! Boys, please," said Queen Suel. "Can we not discuss this without coming to blows yet again?"

"My apologies, your Grace," said Paltr, keeping his eyes away from Luka. "The events of the day are still quite fresh in my mind."

"And you don't approve of the Ministry's methods?" Suel asked in a neutral tone.

"No, your Grace, I do not. The methods are...without honor. Not to mention being inadequate to the task of getting at the truth."

Suel stared at him for a long moment, long enough that Meuhlnir grew concerned for Paltr's safety. For his part, Paltr returned the queen's gaze without moving.

"I see," she said in her accustomed flat voice. "Perhaps, then, it's best for you to stay away from the Ministry."

Meuhlnir couldn't believe his ears. He'd expected some kind of rebuke to Luka and maybe a bit of mild reproach for Paltr's temper, but this was... It turned his stomach to think that the queen approved of such actions.

"You see," Suel went on in a voice turned sweet, "there are troubles in the realm. People are being...deceitful. Dishonest. Two-faced. They are plotting things in the dark of closets, and I need the Ministry to get to the bottom of all these plots and accusations. I need answers promptly. Luka and Vowli are very good at getting me those answers."

"I...I see, your Majesty. As you command," said Paltr with a waver in his voice and blood burning in his cheeks.

Meuhlnir could understand his emotions. It's one thing to think the queen has grown savage and vicious, but quite another to be confronted by the depths of the darkness that had grown inside her.

"You used to trust your people, your Grace," he muttered.

Suel turned her head and fixed him with her cold, lizard-like eyes. "My people used to trust *me*," she said with a hint of heat in her tone. She stared at him hard and then shook her head. "But we are not here to discuss politics. We are here to mend a rift between three brothers that I've come to rely on."

Luka's gaze locked on the queen's and some hidden signal passed between them. "You are right, your Grace, as usual. I fear this is mostly my fault."

"You do?" Paltr sputtered.

Luka sighed and treated them all to a self-deprecating smile. "Yes," he said. "I should not have exposed Sif, Yowrnsaxa, or my brother to such an interrogation on the first day. I should have started with an introductory interview with another subject so they could appreciate the level of deception practiced by these…people."

Paltr looked at Meuhlnir with some confusion. He shrugged. "And I've already said I regret how I handled things. I certainly didn't give Luka a chance to explain."

"No, you did not," quipped Suel. "Instead of trusting your brother, you waded in like a karl from some storybook, saving the princess and all."

Paltr chuckled, but to Meuhlnir it sounded forced. "It does sound like that, doesn't it?" he asked.

Queen Suel nodded. "Meuhlnir?" she asked without looking at him.

"Your Majesty, if my brothers are satisfied, then I certainly am. For my part, all I wanted was peace between us brothers."

"It's good to keep in mind that you three are— excuse me, the three of you and poor Huthr, are all the family you have left since your father's passing."

"Yes, my Lady," said Meuhlnir.

"All better then?" Suel asked, her voice bright.

Paltr looked at Luka and held out his hand. Luka looked back for a moment before taking it.

"Good," she said. "Now, let's all do something fun. Let's go visiting." She stood up and clapped her hands. "Nothing better than taking a trip to help put things behind us, eh?" She looked at Meuhlnir with something approaching the mischievous twinkle he used to see so often. "I've got a surprise for you three."

"A surprise?" asked Meuhlnir.

"Why, yes, Meuhlnir, a surprise." Suel grinned and led them all out of the room and down the hall toward the chamber in which she had anchored a *proo*. Outside the door, she stopped and said, "The surprise is in multiple parts, the first of which is inside this door." She opened the door and walked through.

Meuhlnir was the last to walk through the door, and once inside, a smile blossomed on his lips like the first flower of spring. His brother Huthr stood leaning on his walking stick next to the queen's tamed *proo*. Vowli stood next to him, beaming a huge grin at them all.

"Huthr!" exclaimed Paltr. "What are you doing here?"

"That's the first part of my surprise," crooned Suel. "All of the brothers united."

Luka grinned like a cat and walked over to thump Huthr on the back. He leaned close and whispered something in Huthr's ear, which made Luka smile wider and made Huthr chuckle. The two brothers had always been close, and ever since Huthr had lost his sight, Luka had taken special pains to keep that closeness.

"Brothers," said Huthr, smiling in their general direction. "Her Grace sent Vowli to bring me here so we could all travel together."

Still grinning, Meuhlnir bowed his head to the queen. "Thank you, my Lady. This surprise is a most welcome one."

She wrinkled her nose at him and grinned back. "There are still more to come," she said.

If it weren't for the fact that the mirth on her face did not extend all the way to her eyes, Meuhlnir thought it would have been like the old times with Suel. He smiled back, doing his best to hide the discomfort he felt and the sad pangs of loss for the friendship they once had shared.

"Most gracious, my Queen," muttered Paltr. "I thank you."

"You are very welcome, my friends. Now, let's cross this *proo* and see the other surprise I've got in store for you." She grinned at Vowli, and he grinned back.

Their grins made Meuhlnir even more uncomfortable. There was something about them...something hidden, deceitful.

Yowrnsaxa stepped up beside him and took his big paw in her small hand. She gave it a firm squeeze and grinned at him, looking demure and coquettish. "You see? All is not lost," she whispered.

Suel glanced at their hands with a small curl of jealousy to her lip but plastered a smile on her face as if she was not going to let anything ruin the moment. She gestured to Vowli.

Vowli took one of Huthr's arms, and Luka stepped up on the other side and took the other. Luka leaned close and whispered in Huthr's ear again, and then they both laughed. Vowli grinned as if he was in on the joke, and then they guided Huthr to the *proo*. As they stepped into the *proo*, the air around them made a loud *pop*, and they were gone.

Paltr looked at Meuhlnir and Yowrnsaxa and gave them a knowing grin and then he, too, crossed over with a loud *bang*.

Suel smirked at them and went across, leaving the two alone.

Meuhlnir looked at Yowrnsaxa with raised eyebrows.

She blushed to the roots of her hair and smiled. "It seems the queen doesn't mind," she said.

"Nor do I," said Meuhlnir with a grin, hoping that Yowrnsaxa couldn't see the pain caused by what she had said.

She grinned and pulled him toward the *proo*, but before they could cross, she stood on tiptoe and kissed Meuhlnir on the cheek.

"This has been quite a day for surprises," Meuhlnir said. He squeezed her hand and then pulled her through the *proo* with him. They emerged with a pop in the cave that the *proo* was anchored in the realm that they had named Muspetlshaymr. There was a small crowd in the cave, their party from the palace, but also Veethar, Pratyi, Frikka, Kertr, and Freya—the latter three being *Trohtninkar Tumuhr*.

"Good. We are all here," said Suel smiling at everyone in turn. "I know recent times have been hard on all of us. Things have… Things have happened that not everyone may understand. I know it has been difficult." It was very quiet in the cave—even the sound of their breath seemed to be suppressed. "I want you all to know that I have a reason for every decision and for every action. I am not losing my mind." She looked pointedly at Yowrnsaxa and then turned her gaze to Frikka. "I am faced with an impossible situation and have had to do things that I do not like, as I am sure I have done things some of you don't like. Please, my friends, have faith in our friendship. Have faith in me."

"Always, my Queen," said Luka, beaming his mischievous smile at her.

Suel put her arm on Luka's shoulder. "Enough of this serious stuff," she said. "I wanted us all together, here in the land of fire, so that we can get away from the things happening at home and so we can renew our friendship. Our palace here has been made ready." Suel looked at Yowrnsaxa with a sad expression plastered on her features. "I only wish Sif were here," she said with a hitch in her voice. "Please, Yowrnsaxa, tell her how sorry I am. Tell her that if she can forgive me, I will be happy to welcome her back."

Yowrnsaxa let go of Meuhlnir's hand and bowed. "Yes, my Queen. I'll be sure to tell her."

"Good. Now, to the fun!" Suel clapped her hands twice and then walked toward the entrance to the cave. "Don't just stand there staring at my little sister, Pratyi, beautiful as she is. Play us a merry tune," she called over her shoulder.

Pratyi blushed as Freya looked up at him and smiled. He unslung his harp. "I'd ask you to take my arm, my Lady Freya, but I need them both."

She laughed and walked closer to him, putting her hand on his shoulder. "Maybe this will do," she said.

Beaming a smile fit to split the heavens, Pratyi start strumming a jaunty little tune and walked after Queen Suel, her little sister in tow. Vowli and Luka led Huthr toward the daylight, lost in some hushed conversation that seemed to be quite funny by their smiles and chuckles.

Paltr looked at Yowrnsaxa and Meuhlnir. His expression was muddled. Meuhlnir shrugged with a small smile twitching at the corners of his mouth. Veethar looked at them from under arched eyebrows.

Frikka sighed and grabbed Veethar by the arm. "Sometimes a woman gets tired of waiting, Veethar," she said. She pulled him toward the mouth of the cave, with the quiet man looking at her sidelong in astonishment.

Paltr laughed and offered his arm to Kertr. She nodded and put her hand on his forearm. The four of them left the cave in silence.

Muspetlshaymr was a dark, dreary land in any season. The sky was darkened by swirling clouds of ash and smoke, what plants that could live in a place with so much sulfur and ash in the air were dark-hued—often approaching black. The dim light of Muspetlshaymr's star was further muted by the atmosphere. Most of the illumination came from the streams and pools of burning lava.

Outside, Suel stood beaming at them all with the dim light dancing across her features. Behind her, picketed in a line, were eleven magnificent horses, coats sleek and manes braided. Each wore an elaborate saddle accented with gold and silver that gleamed and reflected fiery highlights from burning stone in the valley below. "The next surprise: horses befitting gods," she said with a laugh. "Thanks go to Veethar."

Veethar blushed and, as usual, said nothing.

"They are magnificent, Veethar," breathed Frikka, which made him blush an even deeper shade of red.

"Indeed," said Meuhlnir. "You've outdone yourself, my friend."

Veethar hung his head, but everyone could see the pleased smile cracking his otherwise austere expression. "It's nothing," he said.

"Hardly," said Paltr. "Luka, take Huthr over so he can see them, too, if you please."

Luka flashed a look of irritation at Paltr that was very familiar to Meuhlnir, but instead of snapping something snippy, Luka just inclined his head and led Huthr toward the horses, muttering in Huthr's ear all the while.

"Do you care to assign horses to riders, Veethar?" asked Queen Suel.

Veethar shook his head, still looking down at the ground and blushing. Frikka rolled her eyes at Queen Suel and shook her head with a look of amusement on her face.

Suel motioned everyone toward the horses with a wry grin. She stepped close to Frikka. "Maybe he needs a kiss to warm him up," she said in a lilting tone.

Frikka chuckled and put her hand under Veethar's chin, forcing his head up. She planted her lips on his and kissed him long and hard. At first, Veethar's eyes widened with surprise, but he soon melted into the kiss, and his eyes drifted shut.

Suel mounted with a twinkle in her eye and a wide grin on her face. "This looks to be an interesting trip," she said.

The mood of the gathering was light, which was surprising, given the circumstances that had led them to this trip. Even Paltr seemed to relax as he climbed into the saddle and prepared to ride to the palace the Isir had built in this place back at the beginning of time. They rode for an hour across the dreary countryside, following the path paved with volcanic stone that led to the palace.

"You know, it is said that Haymtatlr himself built this place, though I can't fathom why," said Freya.

"At the time, I think anywhere was better than our planet," muttered Vowli.

"Indeed," said Suel. "And, besides little sister, Muspetlshaymr isn't that bad. Yes, it's dark. And yes, you might be called to fight off the fire demons from time to time, but it does have a certain beauty all its own."

Freya's nose wrinkled at the smell. "If you say so, sister-mine."

"I mean, just look at the beautiful dark shades, each reflecting different shades of the lava's light." Suel waved her hand at the countryside around them.

"It does have a certain something, your Grace," said Vowli.

The path of basalt led them down into a valley with a stream of lava meandering across the valley's floor. Through the haze and the heat, they could see the black, basalt outer walls of the palace. The palace had been built as a fortress, which could be seen in the utilitarian lines of the architecture, to serve as a toe hold in the wars waged against the so-called demons who had originated in the realm. As they approached, the huge gates swung outward in welcome.

"I've had my servants here all afternoon," said Suel. "Preparing yet another surprise." Sitting high in her saddle, she rode into the courtyard.

The courtyard was festooned with banners and garlands of sweet smelling white flowers. Men and women from the palace staff in Suelhaym scurried around adjusting the position of the garlands, straightening the banners and carting food and supplies into the kitchen. The courtyard was a wide rectangle with a canal of lava that came in under one of the basalt walls and led away into the smithy. Though the canal gave off a pleasant heat, the magical barrier protecting the courtyard from its extreme temperatures shimmered in the gloomy light.

Veethar walked his horse toward the hitching rail outside the stables. The rail was made from a strange, greenish colored metal that stood free of corrosion, even after all the years the palace had stood. He slid down from his horse and looped the reins over the rail, motioning Frikka to bring her horse over. The other men in the party followed Veethar's lead, first tying their own mounts and then that of the woman they escorted.

Suel stood, looking at them with a blank expression and what could at best be called a dim smile on her lips. Once they were all on their own two feet and all the horses were secured, she turned and strode toward the twin doors to the great hall. The doors were made from the same greenish metal, and were four or five man-heights tall. Suel leaned against the doors, and they swung inward on silent hinges.

The great hall was very large, stretching away into the dark recesses of the palace. Only the end closest to the courtyard was lit, leaving the rest of the grand room swathed in darkness and shadows. Two tables were set out next to the cold fire pit—no fires were necessary for warmth in Muspetlshaymr, but the original builders hadn't yet convinced themselves of that fact when the hall was built.

"Oh, it's hot," said Suel and sighed in misery. "I always forget how hot this palace is." She fanned her face with her hands. Bright red splotches dotted her cheeks and neck.

"Perhaps a cool drink, your Majesty?" asked Paltr.

"That would be grand," she breathed. "For all of us, I think." She clapped her hands, and when no one appeared, a small crease wriggled across her forehead.

"No trouble, your Grace," said Yowrnsaxa. "I'll find someone and arrange some refreshments."

"Yes, do that please, my friend."

Yowrnsaxa nodded and then flashed a smile at Meuhlnir before she walked off down the corridor leading to the kitchen. He watched her go, musing about the possibilities.

Freya snickered and jerked her thumb at Meuhlnir. "It looks as if there is a palace romance in the budding, big sister," she said.

Suel grimaced at her for a moment and then forced a smile on her face. "We are all adults here," she said. "Even you, little sister, though sometimes I do wonder."

Freya smiled and looked at Pratyi askance.

"We should all get out of our heavy clothes and armor. We are safe within the palace," said Suel. She began stripping away her heavy traveling cloak. The men and *skyuldur vidnukonur* began to divest themselves of their armor and stacked their weapons against the wall.

"Perhaps we men could entertain you ladies with feats of skill and strength?" asked Luka with a strange twist to his lips.

Suel nodded and smiled. "I would not be opposed to sitting here and watching for a while."

The men spent the next little while clowning around, showing off and wrestling with one another. By the time Yowrnsaxa returned, there were grazes, scratches, bruises, and even a bloody nose to contend with. Through it all, Suel laughed and egged them on.

"And for the finale," said Luka, "Huthr has something to show all of us. But we need someone to assist us. Paltr?"

Paltr grinned at his twin brother, even though Huthr couldn't see him. "What's this, Huthr?"

"Assist me and find out," said Huthr with an enigmatic grin.

"I guess I must then," said Paltr with a chuckle. "Where will you have me?"

"My assistants Vowli and Luka will position you while I prepare my mind."

Luka took one arm and Vowli the other, and together they led Paltr to stand against the wall. They positioned him so that he was standing with most of his weight on his left leg, the right they pulled in front and pointed his toe. They spread his arms, bending the left arm at the elbow so that his hand pointed up. "There," said Luka, "hold that pose, brother."

"So, Huthr's trick is to make me look an idiot?" asked Paltr in good natured fun.

"If that were the goal, would I need do anything?" asked Huthr with a teasing smile. "And, now, for a feat of skill not before seen in this land of Muspetlshaymr, my equipment please, Luka."

Luka scampered to where Huthr stood and handed him a small hunting bow. His face was a mask of impishness. He bowed at the gathering and then moved to stand behind Huthr.

"Behold," said Huthr in melodramatic tones. "The blind archer awakes!"

"Uh," said Paltr with a trace of unease.

"Don't worry, brother," said Luka.

Huthr drew the bowstring back to his cheek, the tip of the arrow wandering about.

"*Syow*," muttered Suel. The air crackled with power.

Meuhlnir glanced at her from under arched eyebrows, but she shrugged and made a shushing motion.

The tip of Huthr's arrow stopped wandering and centered on the square area of the wall outlined by Paltr's left arm and head. "Ready, brother?" he called.

"No," said Paltr to the general amusement of the gathering.

Huthr let the arrow fly, and it snicked into the wall in the dead center of the square. The men and women in the room whooped. Huthr bowed and fished another arrow out of the quiver on the ground at his feet. "For my next trick—"

"Woah, woah, woah," said Paltr. "I'm as game as the next man to let my blind brother shoot arrows at me, but is one not enough?"

"Come, come, Paltr," chided Huthr. "Don't be squeamish. How often have you had the pleasure of being a target for my arrows?"

Paltr laughed and tried to shrug and hold the pose Luka and Vowli had put him in. "Shoot away, then, master archer."

Again, Huthr pulled the bowstring back, the tip of the arrow unerring pointed at the space outlined by Paltr's right arm and torso. "And here we go again," he said, marshalling his breath so as not to spoil the shot.

Luka muttered something just before Huthr let the arrow fly and Huthr looked stricken by fear.

"*Fidna mida*," said Suel. Again, the air crackled with potential energy.

Meuhlnir watched the arrow fly, at first heading straight at the blank spot on the wall, but then curving midflight. The arrow impaled Paltr by the neck, blood spurting in bright red rivulets across the wall he was pinned to.

Freya screamed and clamped her hand over her eyes.

"What?" yelled Meuhlnir, leaping to his feet. "What have you done!"

"What has happened?" yelled Huthr in a breaking voice. "Why did you dispel my vision?"

Paltr looked at them, one hand pressed to his throat, the other working at the arrow, trying to break off the shaft. His mouth worked like he was trying to speak; his eyes were riveted to Meuhlnir's. He managed to snap the arrow in two and slid down the wall, leaving a bloody trail.

Veethar sprang to his feet and moved toward Paltr.

Yowrnsaxa glared at Suel with cold hatred in her eyes.

"What?" asked Huthr. He sank to the floor, ironically matching Paltr's slide down the wall. "What have we done?"

"Why have you done this?" Meuhlnir screamed.

"I didn't know," said Huthr, unable to see that Meuhlnir was looking at Luka. "It was supposed to be a clever joke to make Paltr... What has happened to Paltr?" On his brother's name, Huthr's voice rose to a shriek of his own.

Vowli took two strides to Huthr's side. "You murderer!" he yelled. Vowli jerked a dagger from under his tunic and sank the blade into Huthr's chest up to the hilt.

"No!" screamed Meuhlnir.

Everyone was yelling at once; everyone was trying to do something, anything, to help one of the two twins. Meuhlnir swept Vowli away from Huthr with the back of his arm and sank to the ground next to his brother. "Have they killed you too, Huthr?" he asked in a broken voice.

Through it all, Suel sat, still as a statue, and smiled.

Yowrnsaxa ran to Paltr and checked him for breath. She shook her head, and Meuhlnir let out a shriek of pure anguish as he closed Huthr's eyelids.

"My brothers!" yelled Luka. He tried to force his way between Huthr and Meuhlnir, but Meuhlnir shoved him away with enough violence that Luka staggered into the wall.

"You did this," hissed Meuhlnir, pointing one blunt finger at Luka. His other hand was dancing around his belt, looking for the hammer that was lying against the wall.

"I didn't do anything, Meuhlnir!"

"Gentlemen, please," said Suel. "Let's not jump to any conclusions."

"Come now! It's clear what has happened here," said Veethar and his normally blue eyes turned yellow.

Suel turned to him. "You too, Veethar?" she asked with venom in her voice.

Meuhlnir sprang to his feet. "Was all this just to get us somewhere out of the public eye?" he demanded, glaring at Queen Suel.

"You'd be wise to modulate your tone," said Vowli with contempt. "Have you learned no lessons today?"

Meuhlnir screamed and grabbed Vowli by the face and neck. He pushed him hard into the stone wall of the great hall and began to squeeze Vowli's throat. Spittle flew from Meuhlnir's lips as he grunted and shifted his weight to bring more torque to bear. "I'll kill you for this," he hissed.

"Stop!" yelled Suel.

"He murdered my brother. You saw it!" said Meuhlnir without letting his grip on Vowli's throat weaken one jot.

Suel snapped her fingers at Pratyi and Veethar. "Restrain him," she said.

Pratyi and Veethar stared at one another, neither moving.

Luka screamed a high, wavering battle cry and charged at Meuhlnir, shoulder lowered to catch his eldest brother in the ribs. Luka did not yet have Meuhlnir's bulk but was known for his strength, if not his strength of will in battle.

Meuhlnir grunted as Luka slammed into his side, and Meuhlnir lost his grip on Vowli's throat. The two brothers went down in a heap, fists, and knees thumping each other. Vowli stood looking down at Meuhlnir with a hate-filled expression. He retrieved his dagger from Huthr's chest, rubbing his throat and muttering to himself.

"Oh, no you don't," said Frikka. She leapt in front of Vowli and kicked his long-bladed dagger spinning across the floor to thud into Paltr's boot.

Vowli grunted and back handed her with as much strength as he could muster. Frikka shrieked and went down in a heap.

Veethar's eyes went big, and a snarl danced on his lips as he launched himself across the room at Vowli.

"I'll not be part of this, sister," said Freya with a frown. She gathered her weapons and ran out of the hall and into the courtyard

"Bitch!" Suel hissed at her retreating back. She turned on her heel and stomped to the door that led to the courtyard, yelling for help. Groomsmen, porters, and smiths swarmed into the room, grabbing the queen's guests indiscriminately and holding them fast.

Suel strode in a little circle, with rage burning in her eyes, fury twisting her face. She glared at each of them in turn. "This was an unfortunate *accident*! Who can believe otherwise?"

Meuhlnir grimaced and spit on the floor. "This was no accident!"

"*I* say it was. Who are you to contradict me?" Suel asked with fire in her voice and something that looked like hatred in her eyes.

"I am Meuhlnir! I heard you call on the *strenkir af krafti*. 'Arrow find the target!' You are part of this!"

"Don't be an idiot! Paltr's neck was not your brother's target, was it?" Suel looked at his face for a long moment, seeing only enmity there. "Okay, then," she said with a shrug. "So be it. I can see there is no reasoning with you." She glanced at the men holding Luka and Vowli. "Oh, let them go, you stupid dogs!" she snapped.

"I knew it would be this way," muttered Vowli. His face was twisted in a triumphant, but malevolent smile.

"Oh yes, you are so *wise*, Vowli," hissed Suel. "So, wise to suggest that this was a way to solve our problems. No one will suspect, you said. They will see it as an accident, you said. *Fools* surround me!"

"Justice!" demanded Meuhlnir. "You were a part of this, you've just said so. I *demand* my justice!"

"Oh, shut up, you great fool." Suel put her hands on her temples as if she were trying to stop her head from exploding. "Now, I'll have to kill you or exile you. Why couldn't you be more like Luka?" Her glance darted around at the gathered men and women of the party. "Do I have to kill you all?"

Meuhlnir looked at Yowrnsaxa and shook his head with despair and infinite sadness on his face.

Veethar looked at Pratyi and nodded.

Pratyi began to sing a slow, dirge of a tune, and Suel looked at him with irritation.

"Not now, Pratyi," she hissed.

"*Frist*!" shouted Pratyi, his voice discordant and loud. The smiths, porters, and groomsmen all froze in place, making it easy for everyone to wriggle out of their grasp.

"What are you doing?" said Suel with hate and a touch of fear in her voice.

Veethar pointed at her and screamed "*Thun*!" His voice boomed around the room, each echo seeming louder than the last.

Suel grasped at her throat, her mouth working, cords standing out of her neck, but she couldn't make a sound. She turned to Luka with panic dancing in her eyes. Luka grabbed her arm and pushed her out the door into the courtyard.

Meuhlnir made a grab for Vowli, but he slithered out the door after Luka and the queen, slamming the door after him.

"Weapons," snapped Meuhlnir.

They hurried to dress in their armor, jerking straps into place and shrugging into heavy mail. They armed themselves, each grabbing his own weapon. With a roar, Meuhlnir kicked the two tall doors. The sound was not what they expected—more like the tinkle of bells than the impact of a heavy boot on a metal door. Meuhlnir led the charge outside.

The courtyard was filled with fire demons. They stood half again as tall as a man and had two arms and two legs, but there the similarities ended. Their skin was a swarthy greyish-black, and their eyes gleamed red in the gloom. Their fingers ended in vicious looking claws, and their mouths, filled with sharp black teeth, glowed as if fire burned in their chests. Two black horns sprang from their skulls and curled up to point at the sky. Some of them were mounted on sleek black horses with eight legs, red eyes, and fiery, glowing mouths.

Their horses were gone. "The stables," Meuhlnir shouted.

The front tier of fire demons roared and began to advance toward the six Isir. They brandished brutal looking weapons that looked like perversions of the weapons carried by the Isir. Some carried unpolished swords that ended in jagged shards of metal rather than smooth points. Others carried clumps of misshapen metal attached to the ends of arm-length measures of black wood.

"This could be a challenge," whispered Yowrnsaxa, standing at Meuhlnir's left side and protecting his flank with her shield.

"For such a small woman, you have a gift for overstatement."

Yowrnsaxa shrugged and grinned. "Yes, you are right, of course. Nothing more than a slight delay."

With a cacophony of savage, ear-splitting screams, the fire demons fell on the party of Isir.

"*Ehltur ehlteenkar!*" shouted Meuhlnir. A wreath of burning lightning encircled the attacking fire demons, and their blood-thirsty screams turned into shrieks of terror and pain. The circle of lightning began to shrink, herding the demons closer and closer to its center.

"The stables!" shouted Meuhlnir over the din of demon screams. They began to edge their way toward the stables as the circle of flickering blue fire collapsed with a loud pop. Fire demons shrieked and ran in panicked circles, alight with a cold, blue fire that arced between them like lightning. As the party reached the stable doors, the demons began to collapse to the ground, burnt out husks of foul-smelling black skin.

"Frikka and Veethar, saddles!" ordered Meuhlnir.

The balance of the horde of demons began to howl at the deaths of the others. A loud hissing noise began in the back ranks of the horde and built in volume. Fire demons were shoved aside as if they were nothing, and a gargantuan specimen came forward, hissing in anger, his eyes blazing with hatred. He pointed one clawed hand at Meuhlnir.

"Get ready," hissed Meuhlnir. He felt Yowrnsaxa setting herself at his left. Kertr stood next to Pratyi, shielding his left flank. Each of the shield maidens carried a large round shield and a wicked looking short sword that was designed to be used in savage sweeping cuts under and above the edge of the shields.

The big fire demon set his feet with deliberation, glaring at Meuhlnir all the while. With an obvious effort, the demon twitched its mouth into a gross caricature of a human mouth. "You die," he croaked.

"Not at your hand," said Yowrnsaxa with a grim smile.

The demon sucked in a great breath, letting his mouth relax into its normal, gruesome shape. He stomped forward, bent at the waist, and spit a great plume of fire at them. Yowrnsaxa stepped in front of Meuhlnir and ducked behind the shield. Meuhlnir stooped low and still felt the flames tickling the air around him. When the blast of fire was over, Yowrnsaxa's shield was a blackened, smoldering mess, but still solid enough to serve its purpose.

Meuhlnir stepped to his right and threw his hammer with all his might. It spun, head over haft, flying across the ten-foot gap between them, aimed at the large demon's throat. The demon grunted and turned his shoulder to take the blow. His shoulder hunched, and he yelped in pain. The hammer fell at his feet, but the demon's left arm hung loose at his side.

"*Aftur*," said Meuhlnir and the hammer leapt from the ground back into his hand.

The demon's eyes shrank to slits, and he glared at Meuhlnir with hatred. He stepped forward and slashed at Meuhlnir with his right hand. Yowrnsaxa stepped in front of the blow. The impact almost made her fumble the shield, and the top edge slammed into her chin with enough force to send blood splattering away.

The demon's talons raked across the shield at an angle from the lower left edge, across the blackened center, off the upper right edge, and across Yowrnsaxa's cheek, leaving three long gouges in the wood and three vicious looking gouges across her flesh. She screeched in pain.

Meuhlnir roared and came up on his toes, raising the hammer as high as he could, then he brought the hammer whistling downwards to crack into the demon's big skull. The demon shrieked and fell back, blood raining from the wound. He brought his one working hand to his head and pressed it against his forehead as if he were trying to keep his skull from flying apart. The demon reeled into the smaller demons behind him, turning his head this way and that and striking out as if he had lost the thread of the battle and no longer knew who was attacking him.

"*Ehlteenk*!" screamed Meuhlnir, pointing at the big demon with his hammer.

Thunder boomed across the dark sky, and a bright-blue bolt of lightning shrieked from the sky and into the top of the big demon's head. The demon convulsed, spitting fire over the demons closest to him and slashing about him with his one working hand. The rest of the fire demons went quiet for a breath and then began to shriek in fear and shuffle away from the big demon and the group of Isir standing at the stables.

Meuhlnir glanced at the blood on Yowrnsaxa's face and his mouth twisted. He flung his hammer at the big demon again, and once again the hammer turned end-over-end in perfect circles until it crashed into the big demon's forehead. The demon fell into a heap, his skull split and bloody brain-matter dripping down his face.

"*Aftur*," said Meuhlnir. His hammer leapt to his hand, and he flicked it absently, shaking the demon's brains from the head of the hammer.

"Mount!" called Frikka, pushing reins at him.

Meuhlnir swept Yowrnsaxa up and set her on one of Veethar's magnificent horses. "Can you see?" he asked her.

"It's nothing," said Yowrnsaxa, absently wiping blood from her cheek.

Meuhlnir handed her the reins and then pulled himself on the back of his own mount. With a glance around to be sure everyone was mounted, the former captain of Suel's *Vuthuhr Trohtninkar* screamed his defiance at the fire demons...and at Suel. He gave his horse his spurs, and the beast leapt forward.

He swung his hammer in short, vicious arcs on both his right and, reaching across the saddle, on his left. Fire demons fell away from him as if he were Death itself, trampling each other in their efforts to get free of him. Yowrnsaxa and Kertr had both stowed their shields on their backs and were hacking their way through the press of fire demons. Frikka had a spear in one hand, and an axe in the other. She held the reins in her teeth as she skewered fire demons on her right and split the heads of fire demons on her left. Pratyi was shrieking a song of battle at the top of his lungs and sweeping a double-bladed axe through the fire demons within his reach.

As he rode through the gates of the basalt palace, Meuhlnir risked a glance at the parapet to his right. Suel, Luka, and Vowli stood looking down on them as the party fled. Suel had a hand to her throat and was staring daggers of burning hatred at Pratyi. Vowli looked in disgust at the demons falling all over themselves to make way for the mounted Isir. Luka stared at Meuhlnir with such a look of hatred it almost felt like a physical blow. Then he was through the gate and kicking the horse for even greater speed.

They could hear Vowli screaming at the fire demons, but couldn't make out his words. They were perhaps thirty strides from the gate when they heard a thin shrieking wail that set their nerves on edge. Hooves thundered from behind them, and a group of mounted fire demons raced out of the gate and after them, the black, glossy hooves of their eight-legged steeds striking sparks off the basalt paved path. As they ran, the fire demon's mounts let off snorts of steam, and little balls of fire dripped from their mouths.

"Fight or flee?" called Frikka.

"We have to beat Suel back to our *klith*," yelled Pratyi, "if we are to have any chance to escape the palace."

"We flee," said Meuhlnir. "She can't be allowed to continue as she is." His voice was as cold as a grave, but his eyes burned with passion.

THIRTY

Meuhlnir cleared his throat, a painful sound. "We fled the palace as if it were on fire, raising the alarm as we went."

"Some followed, but many didn't believe us," said Yowrnsaxa with tears glimmering in her eyes.

"We escaped and met with Sif and her charges and then fled north."

"Over the next month, we made our way out of the province and hid in the land we are riding through now," said Sif. Her expression was aloof, but her voice was soft and filled with emotion. "It was the end."

"She pursued us, of course, but it almost felt as if she were just as happy for us to leave the province as she would have been to capture us. I'm sure Luka and Vowli did not share her sentiment."

I stared into the remains of the fire. "I'm sorry for your loss," I said, looking up. "For the loss all of you shared that day."

Meuhlnir nodded his head. "It…" He cleared his throat. "It was a terrible day."

"She had a new sigil after that day," said Yowrnsaxa.

Sif nodded. "A wolf's head, half-white and half-black."

"Muspelheim," I mused. "Land of the fire giants."

"Your mythology?" asked Sif with raised eyebrows.

I nodded. "I wonder… How many such places are there?"

"An infinite number, I'd imagine," said Meuhlnir.

"There are nine in Norse mythology: Vanaheim, home of the Vanir; Asgard, home of the Æsir; Alfheim, home of the light elves; Midgard, home of the humans; Jotunheim, home of the giants; Svartalfheim, home of the dark elves; Nidavellir, home of the dwarves; Muspelheim, home of the fire giants; and Niflheim, the world of fog and mist, and the home of the dead which was ruled by the goddess Hel."

Meuhlnir barked a harsh laugh. "You already know that the Vanir, Jotuns, and Isir all originated here on Osgarthr, though each in a separate realm so to speak. Other realms are inhabited by elves and ones that are inhabited by what we call dwarves. Muspetlshaymr is the realm of the fire demons. And there are other kinds of 'demons,' which is what we've come to call the other races that are too different from our own to build any kind of lasting peace."

I nodded my head and looked at the fire.

"Something is bothering you, Hank," said Mothi.

I nodded. "These stories you are telling me, I appreciate knowing what happened, but if the intent is to show me another side of Luka and the Dark Queen, well…" I shrugged.

"Yes, these aren't the most humanizing tales," said Yowrnsaxa. "But it's important to know how they ended up as they are, not just that they fell from grace." She caught me looking at her cheek and grinned. "We do heal, you know."

"No scars?" I asked.

"Sif healed me without scars, but even if she hadn't, scars fade over time. It has been a long time, after all. Three or four centuries."

"More," said Mothi with a grin. "You always think I'm still a young man."

Yowrnsaxa grinned. "Our little boy," she crooned.

Mothi grunted and shook his head.

"Well, you asked for it, my boy," said Meuhlnir with a chuckle. He swung his gaze to mine. "The next story will be about the good times, when Suel was…admirable. Maybe our first visit to your *klith*."

I nodded and opened my mouth to agree, but Meuhlnir sat up straight and held up a hand for silence.

"Weapons?" whispered Mothi.

Meuhlnir shook his head and made shushing motions with his hands.

Yowrnsaxa stood, a faraway look in her eyes. "Yes," she breathed. "I see them now."

I turned and looked in the direction she was facing, straining my eyes against the darkness. My hand went to the gun holstered on my right hip. Meuhlnir hissed at me and shook his head.

"There are more than last time," said Yowrnsaxa. "They are not men."

I looked at Mothi with raised eyebrows, but he was relaxing and sinking back into a semi-reclined position. "Not close," he whispered. "She's using the *syown*—she can sense things that are not present."

"She has visions?" I asked.

"They remind me of Muspetlshaymr."

"Fire demons?" asked Meuhlnir.

"I can't see them, but I don't think so. Their flavor is…wrong."

"But not men," grunted Sif.

"No, not men. They are spreading out behind us, but I think they know where we are." Yowrnsaxa's voice was raspy and harsh with tension and effort.

"Herding us?" asked Mothi.

"Maybe. They are—" Yowrnsaxa gasped and sank to a sitting position. It was more like a fall than a controlled descent.

"They've seen her," said Sif.

Meuhlnir leaned forward with an intense expression on his face. "*Skyuldur ochkur!*" he muttered, and a translucent dome shape shimmered around our campsite. It shimmered and danced like the reflection of light in a soap bubble.

Sif rushed to Yowrnsaxa's side and took the other woman by the shoulders.

"Some kind of attack?" I asked.

"No," breathed Meuhlnir, "at least not an overt one."

"One has something like the *syown.*—or maybe more, it's hard to see them with clarity. He... *It* looked into me." Yowrnsaxa shuddered.

Sif squeezed her shoulders. "Bad?" she asked with empathy.

Yowrnsaxa nodded. "It was so... I don't know how to describe the feeling of it looking into me. It was like nothing I've experienced. Its mind was so..."

"Alien?" I asked.

"Yes, I suppose that's it. I couldn't make much sense of its thoughts, or even what it was sensing at its location." Yowrnsaxa shuddered again.

"But you are unhurt?" asked Meuhlnir with concern etched on his face.

Yowrnsaxa tried to smile with confidence and failed. "Yes," she said in a shaky voice. "I'm fine. It was just so strange."

"A demon then," muttered Meuhlnir. "This changes things." He looked Sif in the eye and something flittered between them. Some thought or some understanding was communicated through the experience of being with one another for so long. He grunted and waved his hand. "*Kverfa.*" The dome of energy around the camp flickered and then disappeared with a *pop*.

"What does this change?" I asked.

"They shadow us instead of attacking. They let us sense them so that we are sure they are there in the darkness on our back trail," said Meuhlnir.

"In other words," said Mothi in jovial tones, "they are trying to herd us into an ambush. Fun, fun."

"You don't have to sound so happy at the prospect," snapped Yowrnsaxa. Then she covered her mouth with her hand. "I'm so sorry, Mothi," she said.

"It's nothing, Mother Yowrnsaxa. It must have been unnerving, indeed." Mothi shrugged and smiled at her.

"Indeed," she muttered. Her eyes were faraway once more but turned inward. "I should just go to bed." She turned her back to the fire and began rummaging through her pack.

"I'll help you, dear," said Meuhlnir, rising to his knees.

"No, no," she said. "Sif will help me."

"Of course," said Sif.

The women moved about, getting a bedroll ready, and I looked from Mothi to Meuhlnir.

"So, you've told me what they are doing," I said. "Now, tell me what this knowledge changes."

Meuhlnir looked uncomfortable as he slid back to sit on his rump. "I told you earlier that Vowli's involvement would make it hard for us to protect you."

"You did," I said with a small nod.

Father glanced at son and cleared his throat. "The fact that there are demons on our trail, and that they are so brazen, probably means that the Black Bitch has taken an active role in this." He waved his hand around the camp.

"Old man!" snapped Sif from the gloom outside the light of the fire.

"Sorry, dear one, but I can't help how this makes me feel," said Meuhlnir over his shoulder. "How *she* makes me feel."

"Even so, respect me if you can't respect her."

"Always, my love," he said.

"From my point of view, she has been involved since the beginning." I chuckled.

Meuhlnir scoffed but not unkindly. "Your curse? Given the Midnight Queen's abilities, that curse amounts to no more than brushing away an irritant. Swatting at a buzzing fly, if you will."

I shrugged.

"No, if she were intent on doing you harm, you'd have died on the spot, probably engulfed in emerald flames. This bit with the demons means she's beginning to take all this seriously. You included."

"Congratulations, you are no longer a bug," said Mothi. He grinned at me.

"Somehow I find that less than comforting."

Mothi shrugged and laughed. "It is no matter. Your fate was written long ago. There is no use fighting it."

"The skein of fate woven by the All-Father?" I asked with a smile.

"You wound me, Aylootr. Don't mock." Mothi smiled from ear to ear and chuckled. "Besides, the Nornir weave the skein of fate."

"So, what do we do?"

"First thing we must do is decide if we want her to know that we know what she is doing or if we want her to think we are slow and old," said Meuhlnir with a thoughtful expression on his face.

Mothi frowned. "If she is aware that we know of her involvement, then she may take and even more active role."

"We don't want that," said Meuhlnir as Sif returned to the circle of firelight. "How is she?" he asked.

"Shaken. She'll be fine."

"I'll take your word. We were discussing whether it does us harm for the Dark Queen to know we are aware of her involvement."

Sif shrugged. "She's not a stupid woman. If she's in communication with the demons behind us, then she will know that Yowrnsaxa saw them and what transpired next. Plus, there is no way of telling how much the demon could glean from Yowrnsaxa's mind. The Dark Queen may know our plans."

Meuhlnir nodded. "But what happens if we openly acknowledge that we see her plans?"

"She's always had the capacity to be several steps ahead of your thinking, you great lout. But then again, so do termites," said Mothi with a grin.

Meuhlnir held up his hand as if he were about to throw his hammer, but a grin split his face. "I knew it was a mistake to encourage your sense of humor."

"On the one hand, it might change nothing," said Sif oblivious to the banter of her husband and son. "On the other hand, she may come at us more directly. I'm not sure what that might mean, but I don't think it would be to our advantage."

"No doubt there," said Mothi, his grin fading away into a grim expression.

"What would it mean to let her know we are aware of her involvement?" I asked.

"It could be something as drastic as turning around and attacking that band of demons," said Mothi with a gleam in his eye.

"Or as minor as changing our plans," said Sif.

"And if we let her think we don't see it?"

Meuhlnir shrugged. "All we do in that case is let the demons herd us into whatever ambush they have planned. But, we'd go into it prepared."

Sif stared into the fire. "She's not stupid, though," she muttered. "She must know we might be playing the fool, so the ambush might not be the true thrust of her sword."

"Indeed, not," said Meuhlnir. "It may be nothing more than a feint to keep us from seeing the true danger she's laid in our path."

"Well, I don't think we will solve this tonight, and I couldn't be more tired if I'd carried the horse instead of the other way around," said Mothi failing to stifle a yawn.

"We should all sleep," said Sif. She turned her gaze to me. "Do you need more of the cream?"

She had an uncanny ability to know when the aches and pains were setting in. I stretched my legs out toward the fire, wincing at the stiffness in my knees and ankles. "Only if I want to get any sleep tonight," I said with a grin.

"So, no, then?"

"Well, I…" I stopped talking and just grinned as Sif's face broke into a sunny smile. "You got me again. You'd have made a great police woman. Or a second-grade teacher."

She chuckled and dug the pot of cream out of her bag. "Drop `em, Aylootr."

"Oh no! Not you, too."

She laughed at that and crawled toward me as I unzipped my pants.

"What is the plan anyway?" I asked Meuhlnir. "In the short term, I mean."

"We are heading to Veethar and Frikka's estates. They live just across the border of the province in a city called Trankastrantir. It's the southern-most city in the capital province of Suelhaym. Or what was the

captial province of Suelhaym, anyway. Things kind
of fell apart after we banished the queen."

"She married him?" I asked.

Meuhlnir looked at me with confusion, but Sif
grinned and said, "Indeed, and no one was more
surprised than Veethar."

I chuckled at that. "Why visit them? Why not go
straight to the closest *proo*?"

"Simple," said Meuhlnir. "The Vault of *Preer* is
located on Veethar's estate, if it's still intact. Plus, we
need them."

"We need their help?"

"There is no doubt," said Meuhlnir. "We need
everyone willing to help."

"Is she that powerful?"

"Yes," said Sif. "And she is not alone."

Suddenly, the prospect of getting Jane and Sig
back unharmed seemed quite remote. Sif patted my
hand in a mothering fashion. "Don't worry so, we
plan on doing more than retrieving your family." Her
mouth quirked in a half-grin. "Aylootr."

I smiled at her but felt very, very tired. Nothing
more was said as we all pulled our bedrolls out and
rolled into them. Despite how tired I felt, the fire
burned very low before my eyes drifted shut. It was
a long while after shutting my eyes that my mind
slowed down enough for me to drift to sleep.

THIRTY-ONE

Just before dawn the next morning, the air was rent with an eerie, wailing shriek. The sound was modulated by a chittering squeal and punctuated by a hooting sound that echoed through the forest. I sat up and looked around in the pre-dawn gloom. The others were also awake and staring in the direction Yowrnsaxa had on the previous evening, but to me, the sounds came from an arc that spanned about one hundred and eighty degrees of the compass—blocking any path back from the direction we had come.

"The demons?" I asked. "Are they talking?"

Meuhlnir shook his head, looking nonplussed. "No idea. That collection of sounds puts the nerves on edge, though, doesn't it?"

"It does," said Mothi through a yawn. "Couldn't they have waited until a decent hour?"

"What would be a decent hour to one such as you?" asked Sif, smiling to take the sting out of it. "Midafternoon?"

Mothi grinned and shrugged his big shoulders. "It would be preferable to now."

"Yes," said Yowrnsaxa, stretching her shoulders.

Sif scoffed. "If only the Nornir would take our wants and desires into account as they wove the skein of our lives."

"They are inconsiderate bitches, aren't they?" asked Mothi, climbing to his feet and peering into the darkness.

"Who? The Nornir or the demons?" asked Meuhlnir.

"Yes," said Mothi with a curt nod.

We all moved through our morning rituals with one eye scanning the forest behind us. Breakfast tasted like ashes in my mouth. No one spoke much—we were all too busy cramming food into our mouths to get it eaten as fast as possible. We saddled the nervous horses and rode away at a gallop, hoping to leave the caterwauling behind us.

Throughout the long day, however, the demons seemed to keep pace with the horses, always behind us, always blocking our retreat, always driving us north. That night, the cacophony of sound continued even after we made camp, ate dinner, and stared glumly at the fire. There was something about the quality of the sound that made talking seem like the least desirable thing in the world. We bedded down soon after eating, with little conversation, and I despaired that I'd never be able to sleep with all that direful racket, but about an hour after we turned in, the sound stopped.

The forest around us was as quiet as the grave—no night birds sang, no wolves howled in the distance, nothing—it seemed as if even the snow falling from the branches of the trees did so in silence. Without the ever-present ghoulish din, the silence of the night seemed somehow oppressive, and I worried I'd never be able to sleep in the utter stillness.

"A fellow gets kind of used to having that awful noise around," grunted Meuhlnir. "Now that there is a chance at sleep, however, I think we should set a watch."

"I know what that means," Mothi grumbled, as he shrugged out of his bedroll and stood. "Three hours?"

Meuhlnir grunted, already halfway to the dream realm.

"I'll take the next watch, Mothi," I said.

"I'll wake you when it is time for your watch," he promised, though he never did.

I woke with a start in utter darkness as the enigmatic wailing started again. I was fuzzy-headed and confused, but as I looked around, I saw everyone was already awake. Only Sif was not bleary-eyed, and she was standing at the edge of the camp, glaring into the woods behind us.

"They are closer," she whispered.

"Yes, I expected as much," grunted Meuhlnir.

"It is earlier than yesterday, too."

"Yes, I expected that, as well."

"Well, aren't you the smart one?" snapped Sif.

"I married both of you, didn't I?" Meuhlnir's grin split across his face like an axe wound.

"Don't try to flirt," said Sif, but with a certain fondness in her tone, "I'm on watch."

That day was much like the previous one—exhausting, nerve-rattling, annoying, and a touch scary. That evening, the shrieking lasted longer than the night before.

It seemed like we went on like that for weeks or even months, though it was only about ten days. We rode hard, trying to stay ahead of the demons as they got closer and closer to us, always herding us north. Each day I grew stiffer, needing more frequent applications of Sif's pain-blocking cream. I was also losing the battle to fatigue and outright exhaustion from the lack of sleep and increasing length of the day's ride. It was almost time for my next dose of methotrexate, and I hoped we'd get where we were going first.

The others were showing signs of fatigue and shattered nerves, as well—snapping at each other more, and joking and teasing less and less each day. Finally, we came to the crest of a huge, steep hill, and as we passed its crown, the cacophony of the demons behind us ceased. Below us was a plain on which the green of grass, not the white of snow, was the primary color.

Meuhlnir reined Sinir to a stop and stretched with a great sigh. "Now, we see what She-who-Waits has planned for us."

"How many nicknames for the Dark Queen do you guys have?" I muttered.

"Many," said Sif.

Mothi grunted and drew his paired axes from where he had tied them behind his saddle. He held them crossed on the saddle in front of him. As each of the others readied their weapons and tightened the straps of their armor, I reached into my pack and pulled out Bobby Timmens' .40 caliber HK and stuck it through my belt at the small of my back. Then I double-checked all spare magazines for both weapons and made sure that spare boxes of ammunition were at the top of my pack. I looked up and saw all of them watching me.

"No armor," said Sif.

"No," said Meuhlnir. "Nothing we can do about it here, however. We will outfit him in Trankastrantir. Veethar most likely has a smith in his karls, but if he doesn't, we will commission some armor from a local tradesman. Or maybe we'll take a trip to Nitavetlir."

"Perhaps I should teach him the iron skin?" Mothi raised an eyebrow at his father.

Meuhlnir looked me over. "Even if he can learn it in the time left to us, it would be unwise to count on the first attempt at *vefnathur strenki* during a battle."

"I will shield him," said Sif, tipping a wink at me. "He's cuter than you."

For some reason, that brought tears to my eyes, and I blinked them back, not trusting myself to speak.

"And I will guard his right flank," said Mothi. "No one will get past me. Not while I breathe, anyway." His face was smiling, but his tone was as serious as death.

"I don't want anyone to…to be hurt in my place," I said.

"Just don't hit me with those noisemakers," said Mothi with a chuckle.

"I won't. Meuhlnir, though…" I said.

"Am I always the butt of the joke?" asked Meuhlnir with a broad grin.

"Might as well ask if the morning follows night," I said, matching my grin to his.

"Ah, he's finally caught the knack," said Sif.

"Indeed," said Meuhlnir. "I knew he had the potential to be great. Like me."

Yowrnsaxa rolled her eyes to the heavens and shook her head.

"Is he always so modest?" I asked.

"Might as well ask if bears are always so fierce," said Meuhlnir.

"Ehh," said Sif, wagging her hand back and forth. "Aylootr might have surpassed you."

We sat on our horses, looking down at the grassy plain and laughed like idiots.

After we laughed ourselves out, Sif turned to me with a serious expression on her face. "If it comes to a fight, Hank, don't let distance open between us. It is my duty to stay with you, but you must do your part. You must stay with me in turn."

Yowrnsaxa nodded. "A *skyuldur vidnukona* follows the person she guards, but there are times when she may see something you may not. Also, she may step in front or behind you as the situation calls for, and you must be aware of her position."

"And be ready to duck behind my shield," said Sif. "I'll try to call to you, but sometimes it is difficult to hear during a battle and—"

"She forgets," said Meuhlnir. "She gets too busy watching everything and everyone, and plotting ways for enemies to end their days on the head of her axe."

"Do you talk just because you like the sound of your own voice?" asked Sif with a twinkle in her eye.

"Might as well ask if an eagle flies because he likes the feel of the wind under his wings. And besides, you know I love the sound of my own voice."

I grinned and then turned to Mothi. "What do I do for you?"

Mothi shook his head. "Watch my back swings. I'll take care of everything else. If I leave your side, I won't be far, and I will be back."

"Fair enough." I looked down at my saddle. "I meant what I said, earlier. Don't take risks to protect me."

"We will do what we must," said Mothi. He looked at me with hard eyes. "And, I will hear no more of that, Aylootr."

I shrugged a bit. "But I have to say this—"

"Come on," said Meuhlnir. "Let's get out of the chill and down there into the sunshine." He spurred his horse forward, and the others followed.

As we rode down the hill, I felt an itching, tingling between my shoulder blades—the hinky feeling I always got when I was expecting trouble but couldn't see where it would come from. I kept shrugging my shoulders and peering around behind us.

"Relax, if you can, until the danger presents itself," said Sif. "Being so tense will only tire you."

"Yes, I know," I said. "Unfortunately, I've never been good at making myself relax."

"Try," she said. "We can't have our secret weapon worn out before the fighting starts."

"And who knows when that will happen. It could be days from now. Relax, Aylootr. We can't have Father being the only one making ridiculous noises during the battle to come," said Mothi with a mischievous grin.

"Did I already promise not to shoot you in the upcoming battle?"

Mothi laughed and leaned over to clap me on the shoulder. "Yes, you did, so put that out of your mind."

"Drats," I said.

As the horses stepped from the bottom of the hill out on to the grassy plain, avoiding the patches of snow as if they could feel the cold stuff right through their hooves, the sun seemed warmer, and the sky more blue than gray.

The knotted muscles across my upper back eased a little, leaving an ache in their place.

"If we are attacked on this plain, we should remain mounted until one of us is unhorsed. We will ride north at a gallop until that happens. Once one of us is unhorsed, we all surround the one unhorsed and then dismount." Meuhlnir looked at me with a stern expression. "We will all stay together—no heroics. We fight as a unit and leverage the strengths of each other."

"Okay," I said.

"Repeat it back to me."

"We ride north at a gallop until one of us is unhorsed. Then we dismount and stay together. We fight as a unit."

"We first ride to surround the unhorsed person, *then* we dismount. And no heroics."

"Check," I said. "Assess, communicate, act."

"What?" asked Meuhlnir.

"Something we used to train new officers with," I said. "Assess the situation, communicate what you see to your fellow officers, act in concert."

Meuhlnir nodded. "A wise strategy."

The plains seemed to be vast and empty. There was a mountain range shimmering on the horizon to the west and nothing but flat to the east. It seemed like a horrible place for an ambush. I couldn't see how we could fail to see an ambush coming.

Mothi brought his horse beside mine and glanced over at me. "I'd like to try to teach you iron skin," he said. "Even if it fails, it doesn't hurt to try, yes?"

"Iron skin?" I asked.

He nodded. "In the battle with the group of harriers, you heard me call on *strenkir af krafti* twice."

"I remember," I said. I couldn't remember the words, but could almost remember the lilting sound of them.

"The first was to grant me the strength of the giants—and I get a little extra size as a side effect. With those noise machines, you have no need for that. The second *vefnathur* was iron skin. The first word in the *Gamla Toonkumowl* is '*Hooth*' which means 'skin.' You try it."

"*Hooth*," I said. It sounded close to me, but not quite right.

"Passable," said Mothi with a grin. "The next is *ow* which means *of*."

"*Ow*," I said. "I'm familiar with that sound, though it has a different meaning in my life."

Mothi grinned. "The last is *yowrni*, which means *iron*, of course. It's a harder word to get right."

He wasn't kidding. It sounded like he had a cat hidden underneath his tongue. "*Yow...yower...yowrni?*"

"Yes, that's it."

"*Hooth ow yowrni*," I said. Nothing happened.

Mothi laughed and slapped me on the back. "Such an eager pupil. But the words are only part of it. Your mind must be active as well. Think of what it feels like to wear a suit of mail, the weight of all that metal settling on your shoulders, the way it changes your balance and effects your momentum."

"Okay," I said without much confidence. I focused on what he had just said. "*Hooth ow yowrni.*" Again, nothing.

Meuhlnir had been watching out of the corner of his eye. "Have you ever worn chain mail, Hank?"

"No."

He grunted. "You have to be able to clearly imagine what you want to happen. After some practice, you can *vefa* things outside your direct experience—like a lightning bolt, for instance—but until then, we need something you have experienced and are quite familiar with."

"In your work, didn't you wear armor?" asked Mothi with a strange expression. "Your people ask your guardians to run around bare chested and susceptible to attack by anyone? Did they hate you?"

I grimaced and nodded. "We have some protections—tactical gear and the like, but most of our protection comes from psychology and presence."

"So, this tactical gear, it offers protection?"

"Yes," I said. "From some projectiles and stabbing weapons."

Meuhlnir grunted. "Use that then. Imagine wearing a full suit of tactical gear."

I did as he instructed, and I said the words. I felt a warm tightening sensation across my skin and a tingling feeling in my head.

"Ah, that's it," said Mothi, grinning.

I was amazed by how much the success pleased me. "That's almost easy," I said. The warmth left me, and the tingling faded. "What happened? It stopped."

Mothi shrugged. "It's no matter. You lost focus, is all. Practice, and you will gain more and more focus. You did it, though," he said in a pleased-sounding voice.

It was easier than I had expected it to be.

We left the patches of snow behind us, and the sun began to make our winter gear seem like a bad idea. We peeled off what we could while riding. The wind, which had been blowing from the west for what seemed like eons, shifted to blow from the south, bringing with it the most noxious odor I had ever smelled.

"What is that stench?" I asked.

"Something foul, whatever it is," said Yowrnsaxa.

"Yowrnsaxa the Understated," grunted Mothi.

"Look behind us," said Sif with urgency in her voice. "The top of the hill."

On the crest of the last hill behind us, stood a knot of dark gray forms. Though they had two arms, two legs, a head and a neck, they were clearly not human. The proportions were all wrong. Their arms and legs seemed far too long, and their torsos seemed hunched, crooked and too broad. Their necks were overly long, and their trapezius muscles formed broad, triangular shapes from their wide shoulders to the base of their skulls. Their heights varied as one would expect, but the distance and height of the hill made comparing their height to a human impossible.

"The demons?" I asked.

"Worse," said Sif.

"Svartalfar!" said Meuhlnir with disgust.

"Black elves?"

"Yes, the worst of the non-demons."

"Disgusting, cannibalistic creatures," said Yowrnsaxa with a wrinkled nose.

"But they aren't black," I muttered. "Why call them black elves?"

"Their souls are as black as pitch," said Sif.

As we stared at the dark gray figures on the top of the hill, the eerie shrieking noise began again, much louder than it had been before. Other dark humanoids came up the hill and joined the Svartalfar. These new forms had comically short arms and legs, and extremely thin, long torsos. Their heads appeared to rest on their shoulders without need of a neck. It was very hard to see any details due to the distance and elevation, but their faces appeared malformed— though maybe half-formed would be a better description.

They looked like fancy department store mannequins, the kind with a nose, but no eyes and flat plains for cheeks and foreheads. Their mouths weren't visible, but they were the creatures making the racket. When they reached the Svartalfar, they stopped walking and then they stopped shrieking. They were much shorter, and where the Svartalfar had dark gray skin that at least looked related to human skin, these new things had flat black skin that looked more like the black plastic used to make cheap dashes in American cars.

"What the hell are those things?" I asked.

Meuhlnir turned his horse and looked me in the eye. "I've no idea, and unless we want to see them up close, I suggest we move." He shot a glance up the hill. "Now."

We turned our horses and gave them the spurs. As the horses cantered across the plain, the creepy squalling started again. I looked over my shoulder, and what I saw sent shards of fear icing through my belly.

"Here they come!" I said.

"Svartalfar or the demons?" asked Meuhlnir in clipped tones.

"Both. Demons in front running fast, elves in the rear at a slower pace. My god, those demons move fast!"

Meuhlnir shot a worried glance behind us and then snapped his head forward again. "Faster!" he called, kicking Sinir to a gallop.

As we raced across the plain, all my attention was occupied with trying to stay on top of the galloping horse. The horse's hooves were drumming against the grassy ground, making a fast *clump-clump clump-clump* sound. Each step of the horse jarred me back and forth, each shift in the saddle slammed into my hips like a railroad spike driven by a trip-hammer. Soon, I was panting and then grunting as I rocked back and forth, knees pressed into the horse's ribs. I clung to the reins with white-knuckled desperation, grimacing at the pain in my knuckles. The horses were blowing breath through flared nostrils.

"How long can the horses keep this pace?"

"Five or six miles," grunted Mothi. "Not long enough."

"It's no matter," said Meuhlnir. "The trap closes." He nodded his head to the northeast.

Riders were racing toward us across the plain, intent on cutting off our escape. Men rode the horses—tall, well-built men, a very different sort than the harriers that attacked us first.

"Karls," said Sif. "Remember to stay close to me, Hank Jensen."

"I will," I said.

"This is as good a place as any," said Meuhlnir. "We stand here. Get what you need from the horses and drive them on."

We reined the horses in and dismounted. I moved the spare magazines for the Kimber into my back-right pocket and stuffed the HK magazines in the other pocket. I grabbed a box of .45 caliber rounds, ripped the box open and stuffed all fifty bullets into my right pants pocket. Rounds for the HK went into my left pocket. I wouldn't be moving with anything approaching stealth, but from the number of enemies charging at us across the plain, stealth wouldn't enter into it much. I swatted Slaypnir on the rump, and the horse swiveled his head around to look at me as if to tell me not to be such an idiot. Then he burst into a gallop to the west along with the other horses.

"How will we get them back?" I muttered.

"Don't worry," said Mothi, grinning. "We won't have to. You will see."

Sif strapped her shield to her left arm and drew her axe, bouncing it a few times in her hand. She glared at me. "Where will I be?"

"On my left. I will keep an eye out," I assured her.

"We will see," she grunted, stepping around me to be on my left side.

"You three deal with the karls as quickly as possible," said Meuhlnir, all business now. "Yowrnsaxa and I will keep the demons busy."

Mothi had both axes in his hands and stood a few paces to my right. Meuhlnir and Yowrnsaxa stood close together, him on the right with his hammer in his right hand, she with her shield and short sword on his left. She bounced on her toes as if she couldn't wait for the battle to start—and from the look of things, she wouldn't have long to wait.

I made both pistols ready, holding my Kimber in my right hand and the HK in my left. I let out a gust of a sigh and tried to look in every direction at once.

Mothi looked at me and winked. "Remember not to shoot me."

"You are no fun at all, Mothi Strongheart," I said. "Remember not to step in front of the bullets. That's a better plan, anyway."

He laughed and then turned to face the karls. "Come meet death," he yelled into the wind. "No, better yet, come meet my friend Aylootr! Then you will wish for death!" His roaring laughter echoed across the plain.

Then the karls were on us, weapons flashing in the sunlight, their horses' tackle jingling and rattling, hooves thundering. The Kimber, held low, almost by my hip, bucked twice in my hands, the reports echoing across the plain, and a man with flowing blonde hair and a long, braided beard flew off the back of his horse and crashed to the ground in the path of another charging karl. Hooves thudded into his head and chest, putting an end to any question I might have had about him getting back up. Horses shrieked and shied from the echoing boom of the .45.

Then they were through us and riding away toward the west. None of our party were hurt. Mothi was hopping from foot to foot in excitement, already glimmering with iron skin and swelling upwards like a magical body builder. He motioned to me with one of his axes and then whirled to track the course of the karls.

"*Vefa strenki*, if you're going to," said Sif.

I imagined putting on each piece of the tactical gear I'd wear going on a raid with S.W.A.T. and then muttered, "*Hooth ow yowrni*." I felt the warm tightening of my skin and the tingling in the middle of my forehead. "Thanks. Remind me again if I lose it."

Sif grunted, looking west with narrowed eyes.

I glanced in that direction. The karls were already charging back at us. I brought up both pistols. "Firing," I yelled. I squeezed off two rounds from each pistol, each aimed at a different rider. The .45 rounds hit a karl high in the chest, and I could see from how he slumped to the ground that I could ignore him from now on. One of the rounds from the HK hit another rider in the left thigh, making him cry out. The other round went through his left shin and slammed into the horse, making it whinny and veer away. The rider slapped a hand down on his thigh and tried to control the horse with his other hand, but the horse was done listening to him. The pair raced off across the plain toward the mountains to the west. Only a dozen or so karls remained to be dealt with.

Mothi bounced closer to me, smiling like a kid playing with his friends. "Leave some for me, Aylootr." He laughed.

"Firing," I shouted, not sure anyone could hear me over the caterwauling demons, the battle cries of the karls or the pounding of their horses' hooves. I fired the Kimber three times in rapid succession, thunderous reports echoing across the plain. Two of the big rounds tore through the chest of a karl bearing down on Yowrnsaxa and Meuhlnir, and the other boring a hole through the face of the man riding next to him—a lucky shot, to be sure. Both went down, flopping end-over-end like rag dolls. The two horses continued running straight through us and on toward the horizon to the east.

The slide of the .45 locked back, but the karls were too close now to deal with swapping magazines, so I dropped it into the holster and transferred the HK into my right hand. I could shoot ambidextrously, but I was far more accurate with my right hand.

The karls were among us then, horses milling around, snorting and pawing the ground. The karls grinned at each other, thinking they had the battle won. One pointed a hunting bow at me. He released the arrow, and the bow string thrummed. The arrow sped toward my chest. Sif stepped in front of me at the last moment and swatted the arrow with her shield. The arrow deflected up and over my head.

The HK boomed twice, the ejected brass bouncing in the lap of a karl to my right. The bowman sat up straight in the saddle and dropped his bow. He fumbled the reins and mumbled something unintelligible and then slid to his left, falling from his saddle. He had a small, black hole in his cheek and the eye above it was gone.

Mothi was a whirling dervish, dancing around the mounted karls, chopping viciously at their legs and feet, often leaving long, gaping wounds in the sides of their horses as well. Sif stayed to my left. She dismounted three karls by sweeping her axe from side to side under the bottom edge of her shield, thudding the glinting edge into the legs of the karl's horses.

I glanced over my shoulder. Meuhlnir and Yowrnsaxa stood ready, but the demons and black elves were not close enough to attack. They seemed to be holding back, waiting to see whether the karls would succeed before they risked their own skins.

"Eyes forward, Aylootr," panted Sif.

I snapped my gaze back to the karls in front of us. There were only seven karls still on horseback, only three of them were uninjured by Mothi's attacks, and three standing on their own two feet next to their fallen horses. Two of the dismounted karls were circling Sif and me in opposite directions, trying to open a flank. Mothi saw this and lifted both axes over his shoulders as he ran at the one circling to my right. He stepped up behind the karl, axes high and crashed them down into the man's shoulders. Both axe blades broke the karl's collarbones and came to rest in his upper chest. One of the mounted karls spurred his horse hard, intent on riding Mothi down while his back was turned.

"Duck!" I yelled at Mothi. He let go of his axes, and the karl he had just killed fell to his knees at Mothi's feet. Mothi dove to his right and I squeezed off four rounds, two into the karl, and two into his horse's broad chest. The reports boomed like thunder, and before the sound died, the mounted karl was sliding from the saddle, and his horse pitched forward, front legs buckling.

Mothi came back to the corpse he had just made and put his foot on the man's back and jerked his axes clear. He winked at me and then whirled back into the karls.

I turned to my left, but Sif was not there. She stood about ten paces away, exchanging blows in rapid succession with the other karl who had been trying to flank us. She caught his blows on her shield, and he did the same. They were circling each other, grimacing and snarling, neither seeming able to break the other's guard. I had no shot from where I was standing, so I moved toward Sif in a quick, shuffling trot, dodging left and then right, trying to find a clear shot.

Meuhlnir's hammer whistled past me to my right. The warhammer caught the karl low in the right side, and I heard ribs snapping like dry twigs before the hammer fell to the ground. "*Aftur*," shouted Meuhlnir, and his hammer jerked into the air and flew to his hand.

The karl facing Sif was panting now, his right arm clamped to his side and his face a grimace of pain. His movements were slow but was still able to catch Sif's attacks on his shield. Sif snarled and barged into him, trapping his shield between them. She chopped underneath the shield's rim, crashing her axe blade into his thigh. The blow was savage, crippling. Blood splattered the ground as the karl pushed her away. As she stumbled, my sight lines opened, and I snapped the HK into position and fired twice. The karl jerked to his left as the .40 caliber slugs ripped into the right side of his torso.

Sif recovered from her stumble and punched at the man as he tried to lurch out of her range. The iron rim of her shield thudded into his face, and bones snapped. The karl was wheezing and gasping, likely already dead without knowing it, but he looked at Sif with hatred. She followed the punch with a whistling, overhead blow of her axe. She chopped it into the side of his head, and the light left his eyes. He stood still for a moment, then melted to the ground. Sif gave me a brisk nod.

Only the three uninjured karls were still mounted. The others were limping and stumbling around in a circle, surrounding Mothi, doing their best to keep him off balance despite the wounds to their legs. The mounted karls looked ready to flee.

I glanced at Sif. "Your son needs you, *skyuldur vidnukona*," I said.

She shook her head and opened her mouth to speak, but I cut her off. "I have range; I have mobility. Mothi needs you more than I do right now. Go!" She looked torn between her promise to me and her duty to her son. "Go now!" I shouted.

She jumped and then ran toward the circle of men surrounding her son, screaming her battle cry.

I judged the distance between me and the mounted karls. It was less than fifty yards, but the shots were complicated by the karls milling around my friends. I didn't want to risk shots like that with a weapon I wasn't that familiar with. I pointed the HK up in the air and fired it until the slide locked back. Three loud booms swept across the plain and as the remaining horses reared and danced, I dropped the pistol to the ground at my feet.

I pulled my trusty Kimber, ejected the empty magazine and slapped a full one home. I released the slide and brought the gun up, pointing it at one of the mounted karls struggling to control the scared beast under him. I fired twice and saw bullets strike the karl's torso. He fell off the back of his horse, and the horse bolted forward, straight at the ring of circling karls, barging one of them to the ground and trampling him.

The other two mounted karls looked at me with frightened eyes. They were very young—boys, really—though I had no idea how to judge their age on Osgarthr. They looked scared and inexperienced, no matter what their age. I waved at them to run and then pointed the Kimber at the one on the left. He got the message and turned his horse, kicking the beast into a full gallop toward the western mountains. The other was already running when I pointed the pistol in his direction.

That left only the four remaining karls circling Mothi and Sif. I brought the pistol to bear on one of those limping karls, and something slammed into my back—hard. As I fell, the Kimber thundered, but the shot went wide. I slammed into the ground on my right side, barely keeping my grip on the pistol. Something smelly and quite heavy was on top of me—the last of the three karls Sif had forced to dismount. I'd forgotten him.

He grunted, spraying the side of my face with spit. His sword was trapped between us, and he had let go of it and was fishing for something at his right side.

"You'll not be killing anyone else with your vile, magic pipe," he snarled. His right hand came up holding a long dagger.

I struggled to twist around to my back to free my right arm, but he was straddling me now, trapping me with his legs. He rocked his weight back, coming up on his knees, and swept the dagger high above his head in both hands.

I twisted my wrist as far as I could and pulled the trigger. The gunshot rang in my ears and grass and dirt puffed into the air from the muzzle flash. The round took him high in his inner thigh. He made a kind of yelping scream, and his eyes popped open wide, but then they narrowed to slits, and he brought the dagger down.

It seemed to be falling toward me like a feather falling through honey. I had time to see the mottled texture of the steel and the gleaming cutting edges on both sides of the blade. Sweat was running down his face in rivulets. He snarled in slow motion, spit falling through the air toward me. Then his weight was gone, and he was no longer sitting on my stomach and hip.

I looked around in time to see Sif's axe thud into the man's neck again, and blood from the killing blow sprayed across me. "Ok?" she asked, her eyes darting across my body, looking for injuries. I nodded, and she leapt over me and sprinted back toward Mothi. He was whirling in the center of three circling men, with a dead man on the ground at his feet. His axes flashed in broad, sweeping slashes, keeping the three karls at bay.

I got to my knees and steadied my right hand on my knee, pointing the pistol at the man circling behind him. Before I could shoot, however, Mothi leapt into the air and whirled like a ballet dancer, axes glittering in the sun. The karls head slid from his neck and blood splattered down into the grass. I twisted my gun to one of the others, but Sif obscured my shot as she barged into one of them at a full sprint. Both *skyuldur vidnukona* and karl went down on the grassy plain, with a sound like a car wreck ringing through the air.

"They come!" yelled Yowrnsaxa.

I twisted around to look behind me and saw the demons sprinting at Meuhlnir and Yowrnsaxa, eerie in their silence. I slapped the Kimber into my holster and fished through the grass for the HK. I reloaded the gun and chambered a round. I pulled the Kimber with my right and got to my feet.

I turned my back on Sif and Mothi, knowing that between them the last two karls were doomed. Walking forward, both guns held ready, I yelled, "Get down!" Meuhlnir and Yowrnsaxa dropped into crouches, and I started squeezing off rounds from each pistol.

Thunder boomed as bullets from both guns smashed into the line of running demons, flipping their misshapen forms this way and that. When both guns were empty, I dumped the magazines and shifted my .45 to my left hand, holding both guns by their slides. With my right, I slammed fresh magazines into each pistol and then took the Kimber in my right. Both slides snapped shut with a metallic *snick*, and I was firing again.

By the time the magazines had emptied again, the demons were in retreat, running away from us as fast as their weird legs could carry them. Bodies of eighteen demons lay twitching and bleeding on the ground. Their blood was chartreuse in color and stank like a perverse mixture of skunk, blood, and bile.

"I'm out," I said. "Need to reload my magazines. I'll need cover."

Meuhlnir stared at me, and Yowrnsaxa's mouth hung open a little as she looked at the bodies, which were now starting to steam for some unexplainable reason, and shook her head. Mothi and Sif walked toward us as I started reloading the magazines for the Kimber. He was bleeding from a multitude of small cuts, and Sif was limping, her face screwed up with pain.

"That was..." started Mothi. "To be honest, I was impressed the other night. Now, I'm a little bit frightened." Even so, he winked and smiled.

I grinned at him. "Yeah, but I didn't shoot *you*, did I?"

That made him laugh, and the weird mood seemed to break for all of them.

"Impressive, Aylootr," said Meuhlnir, but now the nickname sounded like it was less of a joke to him.

"Indeed," said Sif, coming to stand next to me.

Yowrnsaxa was staring at the Svartalfar, and I glanced in that direction. The elves were as still as statues, staring in our direction. They didn't speak, they didn't cajole or taunt the demons as they ran past them toward the hill. They just stared at us, arms hanging limp.

"Why do they wait?" I asked.

"They are unpredictable. Craven," said Mothi. "But dangerous nonetheless. The most dangerous of the three."

"By far," whispered Yowrnsaxa.

"They just watched you kill almost all of the karls and enough demons to make the others run. Single-handedly, for the most part. They are trying to understand how, and decide if they have enough numbers to guarantee victory," said Meuhlnir. He turned to look at me. "I don't think they do."

I shoved reloaded magazines into my pockets. "Why don't they run then? Why are they just standing there?"

"There is no understanding the Svartalfar," muttered Yowrnsaxa. "To say they are strange is to call the sea wet."

As I slid the last of the reloaded magazines into the pistols and released the slides, the air split with a terrifying shriek, and the ground shook and rumbled with violence. The Svartalfar squatted but continued to stare at us like we were some interesting kind of bugs. The demons had reached the last hill and were running up toward the top with no sign of slowing.

"Looks like the demons have packed it in for the day," I said.

Meuhlnir grunted.

As the demons disappeared over the top of the hill, a rumbling, basso roar sundered the air. The demons reappeared, running back to the crown of the hill and then running around in a panic. Another roar ruptured the air, closer this time. The demons began to shriek and run away toward the east. The black elves stood and looked toward us with hateful smiles.

"Uh, what is that?" I asked.

"That is an indication that the Dark Queen is taking a more active role in this fight," said Sif.

"Looks like you might get to meet a dragon, after all," said Meuhlnir.

"What? A dragon? I thought you were kidding about that."

He looked at me from under his shaggy eyebrows, the worry evident on his face. "No. We may be in serious peril."

"A dragon," I said. "I hope its reality doesn't live up to the myth on my *klith*."

"If it's small enough, we might be able to face it," said Mothi in uncertain tones.

"How do you fight a dragon?"

"Usually, with an army of karls and a large number of *vefari*," said Sif.

The basso roar rent the air again, and the dragon moved to the top of the hill. It was an immense, pearly-white beast that looked to be as long as a football field from the tip of its bifurcated tail to the tip of its snout. It walked on four thick legs that had more in common with ancient Grecian pillars than any animal legs I had ever seen. The legs ended in paws equipped with two sets of opposed digits. Each of the digits was tipped with a long, tapering, black talon that dug deep into the dirt as it walked, turning the ground into a churned-up mess. Huge, leathery wings sprouted from its back, just behind its front shoulders, that were a silvery-white color and winked with reflected sunlight—like polished chrome on a hotrod. Its scales looked like the blade of a Roman pugio. The edges of the scales swept toward the tip with shallow S-shaped curves which looked sharp enough to provide a wicked laceration. The curves narrowed to a sharp point at the scale's tip. A triple line of ridge scales ran from the base of its skull, down the back of its torso, and out to the spade-shaped tips of its tail.

"So much for it being a small dragon," grunted Yowrnsaxa.

Meuhlnir looked grim. "It's just another thing to drive us in the direction the Black Queen wants us to go."

"Let us hope," said Sif.

"Lucky for us, it's the direction we want to go," said Mothi.

"That's what worries me," said Meuhlnir. "The horses, Mothi. Be quick!"

A look of intense concentration settled on Mothi's face. Power shimmered in the air around him as he pursed his lips and whistled at an ear-piercing pitch. The dragon shook its triangular head as if in irritation and then bellowed loud enough to make the ground beneath my feet thrum. Far to the west, I heard a series of shrieking whinnies as if in answer to the dragon's challenge, and then the thundering rumble of galloping horses.

"Will they get here in time?" I asked.

No one answered me.

We all stared as the dragon squatted with all four of its huge legs, muscles bunching and twitching like a bag full of fighting badgers, and then leapt high into the air, mighty wings stretching to catch the air before sweeping downwards. The graceful, sinuous flying beast looked like a completely different lizard than the plodding thing that had wallowed up the hill. On the ground, it had dragged its long tail behind it like a prisoner drags his chains, but in the air, its tail whipped left and right and up and down, providing a steadying counterbalance and a kind of crude rudder.

"My God," I muttered, half-entranced by its lissome flight and half-buffaloed by its venomous demeanor.

"Indeed," said Meuhlnir as he glanced to the west, looking for signs of the horses. "This plain offers us nothing but maximum exposure to the dragon's airborne weapons."

"Will the horses even help?" I asked.

"They should," he said. He sounded far from confident, however.

The dragon flew toward us without apparent effort, its wings slicing through the air in indolent beats. Its ebullient eyes seemed to stare into mine, and I began to feel lethargic and apathetic. As it flew over the clump of Svartalfar, it dipped its tail and let the two wide, shovel-shaped scales at the tips of its tail trail through the elves, slapping at them and knocking them to the ground.

My eyes burned, and I longed to blink, but my eyelids no longer responded to my desires. I could not tear my gaze away from the creature's magnificent eyes. The horses thundered toward us from out of the west, but still I stood, arms hanging limp at my sides, mouth slack, eyes riveted on the dragon's as if they were magnets and my eyes were iron filings.

"Get ready to mount," said Meuhlnir in a crisp voice. "We will ride hard, zigging and zagging across the plain. Our only hope is to either irritate the beast until it gives up or it tires out."

I felt a hand on my shoulder, but couldn't turn or even look in that direction. I wanted to cry for help, but my mouth seemed like it was cast from iron.

"Aylootr?" asked Mothi, shaking me by the shoulder. "Hank?" Alarm rang in his voice.

"He's mesmerized!" shouted Sif.

Mothi slammed me to the ground from behind, and I could no longer see the dragon's eyes. With agonizing slowness, the lethargy began to leave my limbs.

"What fool looks at a dragon's eyes?" muttered Mothi.

"One who doesn't know anything about dragons," snapped Sif. She shoved Mothi away from me. "We mustn't assume he knows the dangers of Osgarthr."

"Of course," said Mothi in a contrite voice.

"Are you recovered enough to ride?" asked Sif.

"I'll...I'll have to be," I said. "I don't think the dragon is inclined to wait for me to feel better. What else do I need to know about that big lizard? Does it breathe fire."

The horses swept up to us, shrieking their defiance at the dragon, which was flying in wide circles as if it were waiting for us to mount so the chase would be more sporting. I stumbled toward Slaypnir and fought my way into the saddle, keeping my eyes on the ground or the back of the horse's neck. I never wanted to feel the way I had looking into the dragon's eyes again.

"Not this kind," said Meuhlnir. "It's a white."

"And?" I snapped. "We have no dragons on my side, white or otherwise."

"Frost," said Sif, "and ice."

"Oh, joy," I said, through lips twisted and sour.

"Ride!" shouted Meuhlnir. "Zig and zag, but try to stay heading north. Keep each other in sight!"

We gave the horses the spurs and sped across the plain. We each twitched our reins from side to side without pattern, sometimes getting in each other's way, but avoiding any outright collisions.

The dragon roared in rage as it saw what we were doing, the oscillating sound sending shivers of fear across my shoulders. It veered back and forth, trying to keep me in front of it, but I kept pulling Slaypnir into tighter and tighter turns. As lithe as the dragon was in the air, the steed could turn much faster than it was able to follow. Slaypnir seemed to be enjoying the contest.

The dragon hissed and spit its anger down at us. There was a peculiar sound—something like a cheap

Styrofoam cooler rubbing against something made from leather—and then a torrent of white shot past us and splashed across the plains in front of us. Where the white stream hit, the grass froze and then shattered, tinkling like broken glass. Swatches of ice appeared as the beam of cold twitched across the plain.

"Jump them!" screamed Meuhlnir, kicking Sinir in the flanks.

"Don't touch the frozen ground," shouted Mothi. "It is death!"

I wasn't sure how I was supposed to communicate the need to jump to Slaypnir, but lucky for me, he seemed to know what to do. One moment, I was being jarred around like a bobble-head in a monster truck, and the next we were sliding through the air as if horses flew rather than ran. The impact of the landing rattled every joint in my body, and I lost my grip on the reins.

Slaypnir screamed a challenge at the dragon and tossed his head. I grabbed the leading edge of the saddle and held on for dear life. Slaypnir put on a burst of speed as the dragon veered toward us roaring and hissing.

The strange Styrofoam on leather sound came again, and Slaypnir darted to the left, hard and fast. I slid in the saddle, panic rubbing its cold, greasy hands across my insides. Slaypnir shrieked again as he leapt another patch of frost and ice and then bolted back to the right.

The temperature of the air around me dropped precipitously, and the dragon passed close over my head—close enough that I could feel the downdraft from its wings. I leaned close to Slaypnir's neck and stretched a hand back to my hip, pulling the Kimber out of my holster. Staying low, as close to the heaving neck of Slaypnir as I could, I raised my hand and snapped off two quick shots at the dragon.

Sparks flew from the scales on the dragon's side, just behind its shoulders, and the sound of bullets ricocheting away added to the din. Slaypnir shied a bit at the booming thunder of the large caliber gun, but otherwise took it all in stride. The dragon arched its neck and turned its head back to look at me from under its wing, its mouth open as if it were panting. I avoided its eyes by burying my face in Slaypnir's mane. The flying beast roared at me, and the subharmonics seemed to be boring holes into my guts.

"That won't do any good, Hank!" shrieked Yowrnsaxa over the buffeting wind of our flight across the plain. "The scales are too hard!"

The scales could deflect lead, and there was no way I was going to risk being frozen inside my own body by trying for a shot to the eyes, but the wings looked like skin rather than scales. I held my arm close to my side for support, bent at the elbow, gun raised above Slaypnir's neck. The horse grunted deep in his chest as if to say he didn't like the noise but understood the need for it.

I pointed the pistol at the huge wings and squeezed off a round. The dragon shrieked and veered away to the side and then landed heavily, holding its injured wing out away from its body. I pulled the trigger until the slide snapped back, each report followed closely by a shriek from the dragon. With the gun empty, I slapped it into the holster and made sure the strap was secure. I leaned forward and stretched my hand down to grab the reins, but there was no way I could retrieve them at this pace. I settled for lying against the horse's neck and holding on.

The dragon was shrieking and roaring in pain and with rage, it stomped after us in a clumsy, lurching sort of run. Slaypnir didn't slow, however, and neither did any of the others. After a short distance the white dragon gave up the chase.

We raced across the plain, leaving the screaming dragon behind us.

THIRTY-TWO

We cantered the horses all that afternoon, letting the horses rest when they needed to and urging them on when they were able. As dusk fell, the monotonous flatness of the prairie began to morph into small hills and gullies, slowing the pace. After dark, we slowed the horses to a walk out of necessity but rode late into the night. When we stopped to camp, we were all exhausted, and our nerves were jangled. Meuhlnir wouldn't risk a fire, so we had a cold supper.

"You said the dragon was the Black Queen's way of taking a more active role?" I asked, cringing at how loud my voice sounded after the silence of the meal.

Meuhlnir turned toward me, his eyes glinting in the light of the full moon. "Yes," he said.

"Was she… Was that her? Can she change into a dragon the way she and Luka changed into animals on my *klith*?"

"We call her the Dragon Queen because she has some kind of hold on the dragons of the air. Maybe the sea dragons, as well, I don't know."

He hadn't answered my question, but I was content to let it pass for now. "So that was an ordinary dragon? A natural dragon, I mean."

Meuhlnir nodded in the darkness.

I grunted and pulled out my guns and began to clean and oil them, which is difficult to do in the dark unless you've done it about eight billion times with the lights on. The smell of solvent and gun oil wafted through the air.

Mothi barked a sour laugh. "Is there anything those things can't do?"

"What do you mean?" I asked.

"Let's see, they can kill men with the speed of the Old Fart's lightning bolts, kill entire groups of demons, drive off attacking dragons… Did I miss anything?"

I shrugged in the gloom. "Guns don't kill people, people do."

"What?" he asked, bewildered.

I sighed. "Nothing. It's something that was said on my *klith*. It's meaningless here."

"I meant no offense," said Mothi.

"None taken," I said. "I'm just worn to the bone."

Mothi grinned, but his dominant expression was also one of exhaustion.

"Let's all get some sleep," said Sif in a voice that was raspy and hoarse.

I finished cleaning the two pistols and put the cleaning kit back in my pack. I laid back on my bedroll with a contented sigh, happy that it wasn't snowing in my face for once. I let my eyes drift shut, suffering through the aching, burning pains of my joints settling in silence.

THIRTY-
THREE

I was running across a bleak plain. Something
in the air, something flying with a sound like
creaking leather, chased me. I wanted to turn
and see what it was, but I couldn't do that, or
everything would be lost.

Ahead of me, there was a walled city where I could
find help, maybe, except nothing moved in the town.

I ran through the splintered and rent front gates. Dead men-at-arms lay scattered like broken, forgotten toys on a child's bedroom floor. Small fires burned, sprinkled hither and yon, and the smell of burning bodies was pervasive.

I was alone, except for the huge flying thing that was following me, and I knew I shouldn't be. I had friends somewhere. A family. People who cared about me and who were sworn to protect me with their lives if need be.

Maybe they were there, but just invisible.

I ran on, heedless of where I was going. Not caring about the burning houses I passed. Not even seeing the vast pools of blood gleaming in the late afternoon sun. I couldn't look around, or the flying thing would freeze me in midstride, and then, and then, everything would be for nothing. Everything would end in a flash of pearly white.

All of a sudden, howls, snarls and deep-throated growls erupted from the streets surrounding me. I could smell something now, something animal, something wild. Underneath the smell of wild animals, there was something else, an insidious odor, sickly-sweet and foul at the same time. The smell of corruption, but not the smell of death. It was the smell of suppurating sores, like those found on someone suffering from wet gangrene.

I knew what that meant. It was important. It was important, but I couldn't look around. No. I couldn't look for what was making that smell. If I did, I would be lost. What does it mean?

I knew what that meant, but I couldn't remember. I had to find out, to remember, but all I could think about was the damn flying thing chasing me and its creaky, leathery wings.

It was important. What does it mean?

I ran on, fear becoming terror, terror becoming panic, panic becoming hysteria. I knew better than to let the fear get the better of me, but that smell...that smell drove me like a cowboy drives cattle. Turning me left, then right, then left again. It was herding me, driving me where it wanted me to go, and behind me, ever behind me, the massive thing with creaking leather wings.

I rounded a corner and heard a terrific shriek from behind me. It sounded like a pissed-off bird-of-prey. One by one, the howls and snarls and growls fell silent, until only the tea-pot screams of the flying thing remained. I ran up the street, away from the shrieks.

The houses grew fat around me. Built from dry-stacked stone, they bore accent colors on the doors and shutters. Each house had at least one flower box beneath a window, but all the flowers were black and dead.

On my right, there was a house with live flowers in the flower box. It looked well cared for, safe and warm. The door was painted a bright red color, as were the shutters. The flower box was a garish shade of orange that clashed with the doors and shutters such that it hurt to look at it—a clear case of what I called 'winter-psychosis,' where after a long, white winter, people went out and bought the brightest color paints they could and painted their houses with them.

Fear froze me in front of a door...THE door.

Behind me, the shrieking tea-pot finally, finally stopped. I wanted to turn, to see the thing chasing me, but I was frozen, staring at the door.

"Turn and see me," boomed a voice from behind me.

"No," I mumbled. "I don't want to see."

"Then you must open the door and go in."

Icy terror wrapped its claws around my heart and squeezed, breaking my cardiac rhythm to pieces. Instead of my normal rhythm—ka-thump, ka-thump—my heart was making weak, squelching noises—ka-skish, ker-swossle.

"I-I-I—"

"I-I-I," mocked the thing behind me. "C'mon, Hank, you don't talk about things, you do. You just do."

I stood frozen, longing for the time I spent running with a flying thing chasing me.

"Open it," cajoled the thing behind me.

I reached out with a shaking hand and touched the blood-red door. As soon as my fingertips brushed the wooden door, there was a loud pop *from behind me, and I knew the flying thing was gone.*

But it could come back.

I pushed the door with my fingers, and it creaked open, sounding like old leather rubbing against bone. The interior of the house was dark—nothing but shadows—but I could see a female form and a smaller form tied to chairs facing the door. My heart crawled up into my throat without leaving a forwarding address and beat there so loudly I thought it would wake the dead men-at-arms littered around the city.

"I'm scared, Mommy," said a small voice.

"I know, Sigster. Think about Daddy. Okay? Think about how brave your daddy is."

I knew those voices as well as I knew my own. They belonged to my family. To Jane and to Siggy.

I moved forward on weak knees, unable to feel my feet. My heart had moved higher into my throat; I didn't imagine I'd ever be able to speak actual words again.

Something glinted behind and above the shadowed forms of my wife and son. Metal shrieked against leather, and the glint became a flash.

There was someone—no, something—standing behind Jane. There was a sound like a hammer splitting a rotten board, and then it came again.

"Jane? Sig?"

A rough, dry chuckle came at me from the darkness. "Too late," said the voice of a woman. A woman I knew.

"No!" I screamed.

I rushed forward, unseeing, to fall to my knees before my wife and child. I dreaded to touch them, fretting that they would be cold, dead.

And they were, they were.

Cold.

Dead.

THIRTY-
FOUR

I woke with a start, hearing the jingling of a
horse harness. It was daylight already, but I felt
like I hadn't slept at all. The nightmare swirled
around in my head like a cancerous, two-headed
snake. Everything it touched curled up, black and
dead.

It was one of those mornings I'd come to dread, where it seemed like there was no way I could move that didn't hurt, and no way to get comfortable. A black depression washed over me like seawater over the prow of a sinking ship.

I closed my eyes and lay there, thinking of Jane and how she'd take a day off from work on days like today—just to be with me and to try to keep my spirits up. She had called it "state of mind treatment." I thought about how she used to pour me into her German SUV and drive somewhere pretty—one of the Finger lakes like Keuka or maybe to Letchworth State Park.

We'd play a game—a guessing game—as we drove through rural areas. The game was to guess which farms we were passing were owned by an Amish family and which were not. We had all sorts of "rules" set up: if the barn was freshly painted and well-maintained, then it was Amish, if there was a bunch of trash in the yard, numerous old cars, engine blocks, and tires, then it was not; if there was a long clothes-line rigged from a window of the house to the top of a silo or barn, with a pulley system, then it was Amish; if the clothes on the line contained a lot of dresses (Jane had arbitrarily set a limit for non-Amish women of wearing no more than one dress per week), then it was Amish; if there was a buggy or two, well, duh, it was Amish. I remember being amazed at how often the barn rule proved correct.

The destination hadn't mattered, just spending time with her had reminded me that my life wasn't just a series of painful flares. It had reminded me that my life wasn't over and that there were plenty of things I could do and enjoy, even if I was doped to the gills with opiates.

I longed for her touch, for some of her smart-assed comments, for her laugh, for her silly jokes about political bumper-stickers, or the way she seemed to think she had to take corners like Mario Andretti with his pants on fire—all without breaking forty miles an hour.

Tears glistened behind my eyelids and a painful lump formed in my throat. The deep black depression tightened its grip. I rolled to my side, sighed, and opened my eyes, trying to wipe the tears away without looking like that was what I was doing. There was no use pining for the way things were. The only thing that would help was to find her and my son and take them back.

"Good morning," said Mothi, his eyes on the ground in front of him.

"Not a whole lot good about it," I muttered. I felt a cool hand on my shoulder and knew it was Sif, coming to check on her patient.

She squatted behind me and put her hand on my forehead. "You have a fever," she said with concern in her voice.

"It's nothing," I said. "All part of the joy of my disease. It'll go away."

She stood and dug into her bag. "Even so," she said. "I think willow bark tea will be a part of your breakfast."

"If you say so," I said. "I have to do a shot before breakfast."

"A shot?"

"An injection. Methotrexate."

"I don't know it," she said. "Shall we apply the cream?"

I sighed, keeping my eyes down. "I think it would be a wasted effort today, to be honest."

"Come now, no megrims," she groused.

"No, really," I said, sitting up with a groan. "Today is what I call a 'heavy' day. Nothing *really* helps, not even high-powered pain medicine, though it does take the edge of the brutality off of it."

She stood beside me, looking down at me. "Do you have this methotrexate with you? And this pain medicine?"

I nodded, wanting nothing more than to hear Jane's voice. "Both are in my pack."

"Let me see these medicines," she said.

"I don't know how that will help, but if you slide that behemoth of a pack closer, you are welcome to see them both."

She pushed my pack closer to me with her foot, and I fished the bottle of oxycodone out. I opened the bottle and poured one of the little white pills into her outstretched palm. She lifted her palm to her nose and sniffed the pill several times. Then she stuck out her tongue and tasted it with the tip of her tongue. "*Losa layntarmowl*," she said. She grunted and handed the pill back to me. "It is a form of Dragon's Kiss—a plant with red and black flowers that grows in the foothills of Kvia to the west—but yours tastes far more bitter."

"It's called an opium poppy on my side. It's been the root of many a war."

"We don't find much use for Dragon's Kiss," said Sif with a shrug. "I can do better, but I need ingredients I don't have here." She dusted off her hands. "And this methotricksah?"

"Methotrexate," I said without thinking. I rooted around and pulled out the little vial of chartreuse liquid. I fished out a syringe and filled it to my dosage and then added a little more.

Sif held out her hand, palm up.

I squirted a little of the yellow liquid in her hand. "Oh shit," I said. "You shouldn't be touching that. It's got black box warnings a mile long—"

"No matter," she said and licked her palm. Her face crumped, her nose wrinkled and she spit it to the ground. "Poison, Hank! It is nothing but poison."

"Yes," I said. "It's something called chemotherapy on my *klith*. Small doses of poison that are used to kill wayward cells. In my case, they kill back cells in my immune system. The theory—"

"Barbarism," she snapped. "Why do you knowingly poison yourself? Who told you to do this?"

I shrugged, a sour grin on my face. "It works. It's one of the only things that helps at all. If you've got something better, I'm all ears."

"I will come up with something better than that foul poison, I can promise you that. I need ingredients, that's all." She gazed down at me for a long moment before turning away. She went about packing up her bedroll as if she hadn't just promised to do better than modern medicine has been able to achieve with two thousand years of effort and fifteen million doctors practicing at any given time.

Mothi looked at me and squatted beside me, forearms on his knees, hands hanging limp at the wrist. "What can I do?"

I grimaced. It was the same thing in every culture. Everyone wants to help in some material way, even though there isn't a thing anyone can really do during the bad moments of the disease. "Help me up off this cold ground?"

He smiled and nodded, springing to his feet and holding out his hand.

I rolled onto my back and kicked the blankets aside. I grabbed his hand, and he pulled me to my feet as if I weighed nothing. While I stood there swaying, waiting for the stiffness and pain to let up the tiniest bit, Mothi gathered my bedroll under one arm and tied it.

I pulled up my shirt and jabbed the syringe into my skin near my belly button. I depressed the plunger. I'd done it so often it didn't even sting anymore. I'd skipped the alcohol wipes, but I doubted it would matter much.

"Need anything out of this?" he asked, holding up my pack.

I nodded and shuffled over to him. I shoved the bottle of oxycodone and the vial of methotrexate into the water proof pocket.

"You don't need to swallow one of the pills?" Mothi asked.

"If I take enough to help, I'll sleep most of the day. Riding would be out of the question, and there's no way I could shoot." I shook my head. "No, I can't take any today. Maybe when we get to Drinkga…"

"Trankastrantir," said Mothi. He tied my gear behind Slaypnir's saddle and then stooped and interlaced his fingers, making a stirrup of his hands.

I laid a hand on his shoulder and put one foot in his hands. He lifted me with no more effort than I would have used to lift Sig when he was six, and I swung into the saddle with a hiss and a grimace. I wasn't looking forward to another long day of riding, or fighting, or both.

We rode unmolested for half the day before we saw the smoke on the horizon to the north. I could tell, just by looking at my companions faces, that the smoke was coming from where Trankastrantir should be.

"Nithukkr's metal heart!" snapped Meuhlnir. "Does that Black Bitch have no propriety?"

Sif glared at him for a moment, but only sighed and shook her head. "Come on, then. Let's see how bad it is."

We rode in silence for another couple of hours before we started seeing the burnt-out farms. It was another fifteen minutes before we saw the first corpse, hanging from a tree branch that stuck out over the road. The young girl's body bore the marks of savage bites and was missing long strips of flesh and numerous bones.

I'd seen what Luka did to bodies, but in comparison, he was quite merciful.

"Svartalfar!" snapped Mothi. He leaned to the side and spit on the ground.

"It is similar to what Luka did to bodies on my *klith.*"

Meuhlnir glanced at me but didn't meet my gaze. "*Itla sem yetur,*" he mumbled and then walked Sinir forward.

We rode into the city—or what remained of the city. Broad swatches of street were still covered in frost, some of the buildings were sheathed in ice and yet other buildings still smoldered and smoked, burnt out husks. Karls of the city stood looking around in a vague, distracted sort of way, while thralls picked through rubble or moved among the karls, offering drinks or bread. Bodies were being laid out in the main square, many of them showing evidence that they had served as meals for the Svartalfar. Looking down one of the side streets, I saw several bodies hanging from ropes looped through second story windows.

Men looked at us with distrust, with no discernable expression, or in some cases, with expressions vacant of intelligence. The shock of the attack was still fresh for many of them.

"Did they pass us in the night?" I muttered.

"Seems so," said Mothi in clipped tones.

"Why?" I asked.

Meuhlnir looked at me with anger twisting his face. "Because they are cowards. They attacked us, and we stood them off, leaving them bloodied and hurt. They couldn't face us again, so they came here." His voice rose as he spoke and by the end of the sentence, he was almost shouting.

The karls of the village had fallen silent and still, and now just stared at us. The thralls kept their heads down and kept moving.

"We did fight them," snapped Meuhlnir, sweeping his arm about in a semi-circle. "We beat them." He glared at the karls, but none of them would meet his furious gaze.

One of the most beautiful women I'd ever seen in my life rode up on a magnificent dapple gray mare. She had long jet-black hair of the kind that would make supermodels on my *klith* drool with envy. Her skin was milky-white like porcelain, a perfect complement to her finely-chiseled features. She reminded me of Jane so much that my heart lurched, and a lump formed in my throat.

The woman wore armor of a shimmery, silver-blue metal, that was now splattered with blood, mud, and soot. "As did we, you big ox," she said. Her voice had a musical quality to it, but even so, it was ragged with exhaustion and pain.

"Greetings, Frikka. I wish we were visiting in better circumstances," said Yowrnsaxa.

Frikka sighed. "As do I, Yowrnsaxa," she said in a voice rimed with sadness. "Even after all these years, the Dark Queen still spits at us." Frikka's eyes were a sharp shade of blue that made me think of the color of the New England sky on the first day of spring. She sighed and turned her eyes back to the devastation of her city. "Welcome to Trankastrantir. Or what's left of it."

I looked at the destruction of the town, the dead lying on the ground, the frost and frozen spots, with despair. "I'm sorry this happened to your town," I said. The dark depression of the morning grew teeth.

"It is no matter," said Frikka. "We will rebuild. The Dark Queen will not defeat us." She was scanning the buildings surrounding the square. "It could have been much worse if that dreadful beast had been airborne."

"The dragon?"

She nodded. "For some reason, it was plodding around on foot. It seemed out of sorts. It kept stretching a wing out and shaking black blood all over the place."

Mothi nodded toward me. "That was Aylootr's handiwork."

Frikka arched a brow at me. "Aylootr, eh?"

I shook my head. "I'm Hank Jensen. Call me Hank."

"Oh, you'll call him Aylootr, too, after you've seen him fight," said Mothi.

Frikka sighed and rotated her shoulders to stretch her muscles. "There's nothing we can do here," she said. "We should leave so the karls feel more comfortable commanding the thralls."

"Perhaps I can help?" asked Sif.

Frikka shook her head. "I appreciate the offer, but the karls have a few healers they prefer. And you are still a yarl, even if you did marry so far beneath you." Her mouth turned up in a grin, and she winked at me.

"Well, someone had to keep Yowrnsaxa company," said Sif with a mischievous glint in her eye. We followed Frikka as she turned her horse and walked it away from the town square.

Meuhlnir looked at them with a hint of a grin and shook his head. "If I didn't know better, I'd think I was being insulted."

"Might as well ask a bear to *vefa strenki*, as ask a man to understand what two women are saying about him."

Meuhlnir scoffed. "Such a weak effort, Frikka. Didn't I teach you better than that?"

Frikka's laugh was charming.

We'd left the townsfolk behind us, except for a few solitary figures sifting through rumble or wandering around, aimless and in shock. I leaned across the space between Mothi and I and asked, "What's the difference between a thrall, a karl and a yarl?"

"We have a caste system here," he said. "Father told you of *Ragnaruechkr*, right?"

I nodded.

"The thralls are the lowest caste—the laborers. They descend from the lowest ranks of Isi's army.

Karls are the next caste. Their ancestors stood between the upper echelons and the thralls in Isi's army. Karls are now merchants, farmers, crafters, tradesmen, and the like. Yarls are the highest caste—the nobility and landowners. It is the caste all of us belong to. We descend from the leaders and scientists of Isi's army. The thinkers, the planners, and the strategists."

"Can no one rise up through achievement?"

Mothi shook his head. "No. You are born, live, and die as a member of the same caste."

"Huh," I said.

"You don't approve, Aylootr?" he asked.

"It's not that—I have no right to judge your culture. I know there are cultures on my *klith* that have used or still use a caste system, but I barely know anything about them. Still, what happens if a yarl is a miscreant with no talent and one of his thralls is a genius?"

"The yarl would become an *owsnertanleg*."

"A what?" I asked.

"He would be shunned—cast out of the caste system all together." He shrugged. "In practice, that means he would become someone lower than a thrall. He wouldn't be allowed to serve a karl or trade with one. He would have to become the property of some thrall in order to survive."

"And the thrall?" I asked.

"He would be a valued member of some yarl's household."

"But would still be a thrall?"

Mothi nodded. "Yes, it is so."

"Hmm. You and your father are taller and broader than the karls we fought. In general, is there a visible difference between the castes."

"Yes. Father told you about the Isi's plague?"

"Yeah, he said it killed the Vanir and ensured the health of the Isir."

"It did more than ensure the health of his army. Isi was always a paranoid leader. He never wanted his leaders and scientists—his chosen, you understand—to be displaced by the officers of the army. In the same vein, he didn't want the common fighters to displace his officers. His plague made certain changes to each group. To the thralls, he gave great endurance and the ability to heal quickly and resist pain. To the karls, he gave the gifts of the thralls, plus greater size and health, and increased intelligence and planning ability. To the yarls, he gave the gifts of the other two castes, but in greater amounts, plus the ability to *vefa strenkir af krafti*, increased creativity and the qualities of natural leadership. Plus, we have the longest life spans, living two or three times longer than karls. Karls live two or three times longer than thralls, who live about a century."

"Wait a second, here, Mothi. You said Isi gave the ability to become *vefari* only to the yarls?"

"Yes, that's right, only yarls can become *vefari*."

I shook my head. "But I am able to. How do you explain that?"

Mothi glanced over at me with a twinkle in his eye. "Not all men are monks," he said.

"What does that mean?"

"You are a descendant of the Viking people, yes?"

"I suppose you could say that, although how pure that lineage is I don't know."

"There's the answer, though. My people visited your ancestors. Many times. For long periods, sometimes."

"And? What does that have to do with me?"

Mothi grinned. "Some Viking women are quite beautiful."

I shook my head and scoffed. "You don't mean—"

"Yes," he said. "You have the blood of the Isir in your veins. You are a yarl."

That was not something I'd expected to hear, and I had no idea how to explain it. "So, technically speaking, we could be related? You could be my million-times-great-grandfather?"

He shrugged with a grin. "It's possible." He sobered. "You could also be related to the Dark Queen or Luka or none of the yarls we know."

"And you have all known this for how long?"

"You don't see the similarity? Think of the thralls you've seen, and then next the karls. Which caste do you seem the most like?"

It was obvious once he put me on the track. I nodded. "But still, many Scandinavians share similar characteristics."

"Ask Mother Yowrnsaxa if you want to hear more specifics of your lineage. She can use her gift to find more details."

"Yep," I grunted. I rode the rest of the trip to Veethar and Frikka's estate in silence, my mind awhirl with speculation.

The estate was a few miles northeast of the town square, smack dab in the center of a large woodland. The forest was chock-a-block with different species of trees, from alder to yew trees and everything in between. The road was well-traveled and well-maintained and threaded around clumps of trees as if the timber took precedence over the straightness of the road. Given that it was Veethar's wood, I decided that made a certain amount of sense. God of the Forest and all that.

Frikka led us around one such copse of timber, and the road opened up on both sides, widening to create a broad meadow. A ten-foot-high stone wall ringed the meadow, with gates standing open across the road. The road passed through the estate and then off through the trees to the north. Multiple buildings stood inside the gates, some given over to the breeding and raising of horses, others less obvious in their intent, but all were dwarfed by a massive stone-walled longhouse that was easily twice the length of a football field and stood at least three stories in height. Unlike the town, the compound showed no signs of a battle—no smoldering fires, no frost or ice, no blood.

"Welcome to our home," said Frikka.

"The raiders couldn't find you?" asked Meuhlnir with approval in his voice.

"No, the glamor has held, it seems. Veethar refreshed it just before his trip west." Frikka walked her horse up to a waiting groomsman and dismounted. "See to their horses," she said.

After I had dismounted and handed my reins to a diminutive man with dark hair, I walked over to Mothi and indicated the groomsmen. "Thralls?" I whispered.

He dipped his head and then jerked his chin toward the stable. A larger man stood there, watching the groomsmen gather the horses. He was perhaps half a head shorter than Mothi, and about fifty pounds lighter. "A karl," Mothi grunted. "The foreman, no doubt, serving under contract."

Sif stood next to Frikka, eyeing the way I was standing and walking. She grunted her approval and then turned to Frikka. "Veethar is not here?"

"No," said Frikka. "He went to Takmar's Horse Plains to capture new breeding stock. I swear he goes on these trips to avoid having to talk to anyone."

"What a time to be away," said Meuhlnir. "I bet he'd be on his way home if he knew what happened here today."

"Yes, but unless my premonition was false, you've come here for a bigger purpose than rebuilding Trankastrantir."

Meuhlnir bowed his head. "Your augury was true, Frikka."

"Then we will not speak of what happened today to Veethar."

"Do you think that is wise?" asked Yowrnsaxa in a restrained voice.

Frikka shrugged. "I know my husband and so do you. He would demand that we first seek revenge for this attack on our city. Why argue when we can avoid the issue?" She arched her eyebrow and gazed at Yowrnsaxa. "Now, tell me why you've come." She beckoned them inside the stone-walled longhouse and led them to a small, comfortable room. She snapped her fingers and waved the thralls out of the room.

"Luka has brought another to Osgarthr," said Meuhlnir.

Frikka looked at me, and I nodded.

"Luka has been very…active on Hank's *klith*. He and the Dark Queen have been living there for at least several centuries, and have been breaking the *Ayn Loug* there."

Frikka grimaced and looked away. "Is it time? You finally see the need?" she asked Meuhlnir.

"Yes," he said. "Luka has kidnapped Hank's wife and son and brought them to Osgarthr—hostages to ensure Hank would run the *Reknpokaprooin*."

"Luka, Vowli, or the Dragon Queen?" asked Frikka.

"I haven't run into Vowli yet, but Luka and the queen had quite a setup on my *klith*," I said.

"It doesn't matter if Luka did it on his own or not," said Sif. "They are all acting in concert now that Hank is here. Besides, it isn't as if we can do battle with one without doing battle with them all."

Frikka grunted and nodded. "I won't be involved with any more half-measures. Neither will Veethar."

"No, that we are at this junction yet again proves that half-measures are only a delaying tactic," said Yowrnsaxa. She shook her head, looking sad.

"Doesn't anyone believe that those three are worth rehabilitating? Shouldn't they be allowed to choose to abandon their dark ways?" asked Meuhlnir.

The room was silent for a few moments as the women looked back and forth between themselves.

"We can speak more of it later," said Sif. "Tell me, Frikka, what path to the Horse Plains does your husband travel? North to Suelhaym proper, across the pass through the Dragon's Spine and, finally, through the Great Wood of Suel?"

"I'd prefer not to travel north and encounter the Dark Queen's forces again," said Meuhlnir. "We've played her games long enough."

Frikka nodded in agreement. "Veethar has another route—a secret *proo* into Skalabrekka, known only to members of our house. He travels north onto the plains from there."

"And your collection of *preer* is unmolested?" asked Meuhlnir as if the answer held no importance.

"Yes," said Frikka. "I used one this morning to check on our breeding projects in Alfhaym. I assume yours is not since you're here on horseback."

Mothi's eyebrows shot upwards. "You are breeding horses with the Alfar?"

Frikka flashed a wicked little grin at him. "Yes, little Mothi. Can you guess our goals?"

Mothi boomed laughter. "Will the offspring have more than four legs? Maybe have a fiery disposition?"

Frikka winked at him. "They are such an interesting breed, the demon-horses of Muspetlshaymr."

"Any results?"

"Now that you ask, yes, one of the demon-mares will give birth in a week or so. That in itself is a triumph." Frikka laughed. "Then again, just getting one of our horses to mate with a demon-mare has been a trial beyond the limits of sanity."

Mothi gave an exaggerated sigh. "And what must I trade to have a chance at this demon-mare?"

Frikka looked at him, suddenly the shrewd trader. "Perhaps the use of one of your fine stallions as stud?"

"Not to interrupt the consummate demonstration of horse trading, but perhaps we can get back to the issue at hand?" asked Meuhlnir in a dry voice.

Frikka nodded and bowed, failing to hide a satiric grin. "Whatever you wish."

"Given that the queen is not shy about recruiting others to do her fighting, I wonder if we shouldn't consider the same," said Yowrnsaxa.

"I don't think so," said Meuhlnir. "We don't want to fight a war, not if we don't have to. A small group has a better chance of being overlooked, especially if we employ a bit of misdirection and stealth."

"What kind of misdirection?" asked Frikka.

"A glamor," said Meuhlnir. "We want the Dark Queen to see us traveling north toward Suel, while we use the *preer* in secret."

"A sound strategy," said Mothi.

"How would we keep such a glamor in place? How could we make it convincing enough that the Dark Queen would follow it instead of looking harder for us?" asked Yowrnsaxa.

"We would imbue the glamor onto an object—like I've done with my ring—and have a group of karls carrying it to Suel," said Meuhlnir in a matter of fact tone.

"Dangerous for the karls," I said.

"We could give them items that would help them battle the Dark Queen's troops," said Meuhlnir. "That would mitigate the danger."

"And require a trip to Nitavetlir," said Mothi with a pouting expression on his face. "I always get a crick in my neck."

"First, we would need to find the karls willing to do this for us," said Meuhlnir, glancing at Frikka.

"What would happen if we had Alfar do this instead?" asked Frikka.

"That could work as well," said Meuhlnir. "Why? Do you think it will be easier to convince the Alfar than your karls?"

Frikka looked at him as if he were the dumbest man alive. "Did you not see Trankastrantir?"

"Good point," he muttered. "Alfar it is then."

THIRTY-FIVE

Later that evening, after a big meal and a long soak in a tub full of near boiling water, I stood in a stone-lined room in the basement of Frikka and Veethar's longhouse. Each stone of the wall was inset with a strip of metal worked in the shape of a rune. The runes glowed with a subtle light of their own.

Frikka touched one, and an oval of shimmering silver expanded in the center of the room. "Each of these stones is anchored to a different *proo*," she said.

"Is there another *proo* to my *klith* hiding in one of these runes? Besides the *Kyatlerproo*?" I asked.

"Mithgarthr? Yes, there is a *proo* to there in our collection but not to your time." Frikka's voice was a silky contralto that reminded me of my first girlfriend and the summer I turned fourteen.

I swallowed hard. "More side trips to the Vikings?"

Meuhlnir glanced at me with irritation twitching in the muscles around his eyes. "This *proo* leads to Alfhaym," he said. "Before we go, you should know that the Alfar are nothing like their dark cousins, the Svartalfar. They are about as close in temperament as Luka and me. They are a wholesome, light-hearted people, but when provoked, they can be savage. Their laws are governed by the Law of Retaliation, so it is best not to run afoul of them."

"Law of Retaliation? Sounds ominous."

"I don't expect it to be an issue. Don't mention the Svartalfar—let me speak of that. They are inquisitive and love to learn new things. They will no doubt have many questions for you about your life and the interactions you had with the Dark Queen and my brother."

I nodded. Meuhlnir clapped me on the back and stepped through the *proo*. It was the first time I'd seen anyone use a *proo*—I'd used one, true enough, but I didn't see what happened. I'd expected something like you'd see in a science fiction movie—maybe the particles of his body being pulled forward at the speed of light, or the flashy transporter effects from Star Trek. Instead, as his skin made contact with the surface of the *proo*, everything about him froze—his expression, his eyes, the rise and fall of his chest as he breathed, even his nostrils froze mid-flair. Then he was gone, and the air popped, simple as that. No fading out, no flashes of light, no funny science fiction sounds, just gone.

I glanced at Mothi, who was looking at me with a slight grin on his face. "It's impressive, I know," he said and then reached forward to touch the *proo,* and he, too, disappeared.

I shrugged at the women and walked forward into the *proo*. One second I was in an underground vault lined with runed stones, and in the next, I was standing in the most beautiful wood I'd ever seen. A magnificent forest of redwood trees surrounded us like sentinels. Their thick trunks seemed to stretch forever upwards, and their canopies were shrouded in a gentle mist that seemed somehow warm and welcoming rather than cold and wet. A few small vines hugged close to the ground, but other than that, there was no underbrush. The bark of the trees looked like ropes that were stretched between the ground and the green-swathed branches high overhead. The air was filled with the music of undisturbed woodland.

"It's beautiful," I breathed. After a moment of staring, I realized that the pain I had worn like a mantle for the past seven years was gone. Not reduced, gone.

"You should see one of the protected glades," said Mothi in an awed tone. "Though, not many outsiders are permitted to."

"Greetings, Isir."

The voice seemed to come from all around us and from nowhere at the same time. I put my hand on the Kimber .45 hanging on my right hip.

"There's no need," whispered Meuhlnir. "The Alfar are friends."

"Indeed, Master of Thunder. Hello again, Mothi Strongheart. Have you more horses to trade?"

"Not this time," said Mothi.

An Alf stepped from behind a tree to our left and walked over to clasp forearms with Mothi. "It's no matter, Mothi. You are welcome any time." The Alf reminded me somewhat of the Svartalfar we'd seen on the plains. He had the same disproportionate length limbs, but where the Svartalfar were hunched and crooked, the Alf stood straight with his shoulders back—a proud stance. He had the same too-long neck bracketed by large triangular trapezius muscles, but his skin was light instead of dark. It looked like fine Grecian marble—bright white with striations of a very light gray. His eyes were fulvous in color, and his hair was ivory tinged with blue. His features were as sharp as if they were chiseled from shale. He was dressed in brown leathers and wore a thin bladed sword and matching dagger in his belt.

"Ah, Yowtgayrr, I thought that was you."

"If you aren't here to trade horses, are you here to see what Frikka and Veethar are creating?"

"I wish that were the reason for the visit," said Meuhlnir. "I regret that events in Osgarthr have prompted us to come to Alfhaym seeking help."

"Ah," said Yowtgayrr. "We no longer have a standing army, as you know Master of Thunder. Not since the Banishment of Suel."

Meuhlnir nodded. "I understand and respect your views on war. I've come to think you may be right over the past few centuries."

Yowtgayrr squinted at him for a moment, head cocked to the side. "Meaning no disrespect, your span is too short to understand our point of view. We sacrifice eons to give our lives in battle."

Meuhlnir bowed his head. "I do understand, Yowtgayrr, and if there were a way I could change what happened to your people in the last war, I would do so."

The Alf nodded. "Then we will speak no more of it, Master of Thunder." He turned his brownish-orange eyes to me. "Who is your guest?"

"This is a *kanka-ee* from Mithgarthr," said Mothi. "He calls himself Hank Jensen."

I glanced quickly at Mothi—he rarely missed an opportunity to call me Aylootr, and I wondered why he didn't call me that now. When I returned my gaze to Yowtgayrr, his gaze was intense, shrewd. His eyes seemed to spin like whirly-gigs in a light breeze. I didn't like looking into those eyes, and I looked away in a hurry. My experience with the dragon was still too close.

"Welcome, Hank Jensen," he said with an air of formality. He offered his left hand, and I clasped his forearm the way I'd seen Mothi do. He held on for a moment, and his eyes grew vague. "Isir…" His eyebrows shot upwards, wrinkling the skin of his forehead. "Cousin to Mothi?" he said, glancing at Meuhlnir who nodded. "Cursed by…" He released my hand with a sudden anger and turned to Meuhlnir, face filled with fury.

Meuhlnir held up his hands, palms outwards. "Yes, he has been cursed by the Dark Bitch. Hank has guest-right in my house, and I bear the responsibility."

The Alf seemed less than mollified. "Such a risk to take," he hissed.

"There is no risk," said Meuhlnir. "He isn't visible in that way. You've said yourself, he's Isir and blood of my house."

The Alf bowed from the waist. "As you say, then." He glanced at me askance. "No offense meant, Hank Jensen."

"None taken, and it's just Hank. Your realm is truly beautiful, Yowtgayrr," I said. "I've never seen anything like it."

The Alf smiled at me. "We do try to keep it healthy."

Meuhlnir cleared his throat. "Yowtgayrr, we need the help of a few of your brethren."

"As you said, Master of Thunder. If you will follow me, I'll assemble the Conclave of Elders and the Priesthood of Tiwaz." He turned and led us deeper into the forest, not seeming to follow any path, but very confident nonetheless.

I walked next to Mothi. "Cousins?" I asked.

Mothi grinned. "The Alfar are gifted with *syown*, like Yowrnsaxa. They can see things others cannot. They can see how all things are connected, including people. That means you are either a descendant of Paltr, Huthr, Father or…"

"Luka," I said. "That would be a trip, eh?" I was trying to make light of it, but no one smiled.

"No sense borrowing tomorrow's battles," said Mothi. "Nothing to be done in any case, is there?"

"No. Tell me about this Priesthood of…"

"Tiwaz," Mothi said, "the Priesthood of Tiwaz. Tiwaz is the god of the sky to the Alf. Priests of Tiwaz serve him by taking the role of protector, or guardian, as Tiwaz protects and guards Alfhaym according to their beliefs."

"Ah, I see. Warrior-priests."

Mothi nodded. "They are quite skilled. I wouldn't want to face one in anger."

We walked for hours through the magnificent forest of Alfhaym, but I never grew stiff or fatigued. Yowtgayrr set a fast pace, and we covered ground at a rapid rate. Though I could see shafts of brilliant golden light filtering down from above, we never seemed to walk through one, and the light was never in our eyes. The ambient light was always the same intensity—never dim.

"The light…" I whispered to Mothi.

"The Alfar are creatures of the light," he said as if that explained everything.

I shook my head at him and shrugged.

"There is no night in Alfhaym," he said. "No cloudy days, no darkness. The shadows you see from the trees is as dark as it ever gets here."

"Must be great for farming," I said.

"Yes," said Mothi. "The Alfar believe Tiwaz granted them life in order to have guardians and protectors for the *Skowkur Kuthadna*—the Forest of the Gods—which is what they call this realm amongst themselves. They are shepherds of the land itself."

"Like druids?" I asked.

"I don't know that word," said Mothi. "What is a druid?"

I waved my hand at the forest. "A religion that worships nature."

"I see," he said. "The Alfar don't worship nature, per se, it's more like they view the shepherding of the realm as a sacred duty, as a job given them by Tiwaz himself."

We came to a natural bowl-shaped depression in the forest floor. Trees grew undisturbed in the bowl, even when they were in the way. The bowl was brimming with Alfar of every shape and size: young and old, tall and short, skin like white marble, skin like beige marble. There must have been four or five hundred male Alfar in the bowl, with others standing around the edge.

"Wow," I said. "Big conclave."

"It isn't often we have Isir in our realm asking us for help," said Yowtgayrr, looking at me askance. "Let alone an Isir from Mithgarthr."

I wondered how he had summoned the conclave. He'd never left us from the moment he greeted us.

"Greetings, Isir," warbled a voice from the crowd.

The Alfar fell into a respectful silence, and the crowd split to reveal an Alf bent over a gnarled walking stick. His skin was a pale gray, and his hair, what little of it remained, was shock-white. His voice sounded like old papyrus rustling in the wind. Skin hung loose on his frame, and he had a withered, sick look.

Meuhlnir inclined his head. "I, Meuhlnir of the Thunder, greet you Master Freyr."

"Who are these others then?" he asked peering at me from under stringy white eyebrows.

"You know Mothi, of course," said Yowtgayrr. "This other one is Hank Jensen, a *kanka-ee* from Mithgarthr."

"Looks like an Isir to me," grunted Freyr.

"He has the blood," said Yowtgayrr. "He is related to the House of Meuhlnir, and also bears the guest-right from the same house."

"Ah, guest-right," said the old Alf. "Magic words, indeed." He cackled as if he'd just said the funniest thing in the world. "What do you want from us, Master of Thunder?" Freyr sank to the ground with obvious difficulty and waved everyone else down as well. Meuhlnir, Mothi, and I were the only ones left standing.

Meuhlnir cleared his throat and took a small step forward. "There is trouble in our realm. The Black Queen has returned to Osgarthr and is once again sending others out to do her bidding. Including dragons."

"Alfar?" asked Freyr.

"No, no Alfar," said Meuhlnir.

"Then why come to us?"

"The Black Bitch has spent most of her time over the past several centuries in Mithgarthr, doing what, I don't know. My brother accompanied her, where they came into contact with Hank." He waved his hand at me. "They've taken Hank's family hostage to force him to travel to Osgarthr."

Freyr glanced at me. "Sorrowful, indeed, but you haven't answered my question, Master of Thunder."

"We are set to rescue Hank's family, but do not wish an open confrontation at this time."

"No more wars, Master of Thunder," said Freyr in sad tones.

"No, Master Freyr. No more wars. Not if I have anything to say about it."

"Which you may not have." Freyr's voice was filled with an overwhelming sense of weariness.

"Granted," said Meuhlnir. "It is my wish, however, to encourage the Dark Queen, my brother Luka, and Vowli to repent their ways and rehabilitate themselves."

"Lofty goals, Master of Thunder. Lofty goals. Were not such goals the root of the problem in the last war?"

Meuhlnir looked at his feet. "I do not wish them to die," he said.

"Even now?"

"Even now."

"Wishes are like fishes," said Freyr. "They are slippery and tend to flop out of one's hands." The old Alf turned to stare at me for a long moment. "And you Hank Jensen, Isir of Mithgarthr? What is it you want from us?"

I cleared my throat. "I wish I could rescue my family without putting anyone at risk. I wish there were no reason for me to be here at all, but as you said, wishes are unreliable. I've been lucky enough to fall in with Meuhlnir and his family, and they have been gracious enough to offer to help me. Without them, I wouldn't be here—I'd be wandering around in the snow and ice of Snyowrlant, lost, alone, and without hope.

"We believe that by using decoys to distract the queen, we can avoid more bloodshed in the rescue of my family. We believe that a few brave men—or Alfar—may be able to reduce the cost of the rescue. I'm all for that, if it is possible."

Freyr looked at the gun on my hip, and his eyes narrowed to slits. "But you display these weapons of technology as if you are proud of them."

I glanced down at the pistol. "I'd happily throw them into the deepest ocean of the world if you can just show me they are no longer needed to defend the weak, myself, or the people I love."

"That is fairly spoken," said Freyr with reluctance. "Still, you've come here wearing a weapon of war, claiming to want to avoid war. The image is at odds with your words."

I shrugged and pursed my lips. "That may be, but we have a saying in the realm I'm from. Don't judge a book by its cover."

Freyr crinkled up his face as he tried to work that out.

"It means that appearances can be deceiving and shouldn't be used to judge a person or his motives."

Freyr scoffed without making a sound. "Why should we help you?"

"That's for you to decide. I don't know much about the Alfar, or any of the new peoples I've learned about since coming to Osgarthr, but what I do know is that you value the role of protector and guardian. I have devoted the majority of my life to protecting those who couldn't protect themselves. I've risked my life for others on countless occasions, and have saved many people from harm or worse.

"If it were just me, I wouldn't ask you for your help, but it isn't just me. Yes, I'm at risk in Osgarthr, and it seems I've put Meuhlnir, Sif, Yowrnsaxa, Mothi, Frikka, and Veethar, plus countless karls and thralls at risk just by being there. I understand I've put the Alfar at risk to some degree just by coming here. I'd bear that burden alone, and face whatever may come, but for one fact.

"My wife and son are innocent. They did not come into contact with Luka or the Dark Queen in Mithgarthr—their only crime was being my family, and I will do *anything* to ensure their freedom and safety. They are everything to me."

"I believe you," said the old Alf. "But even so, who are they to me?"

"I didn't ask to be brought here," I said, feeling the fury pounding away behind my eyes. "I didn't ask for Luka to commit random acts of violence, murder, and mayhem in Mithgarthr. I didn't ask for Luka to kill my partner." Mothi put his hand on my shoulder, but I shook it off. "I didn't ask for *any* of this—but it has happened. It happened because I believe in protecting others. If you don't, then to hell with you! If you can stand to sit in your beautiful forest when you could be helping others, then you are a worthless people who should be ashamed of yourselves." I stood there, glaring at Freyr, fighting the lump in my throat.

He looked back at me, eyes blazing at the words I had just hurled in his face. If his face was any indication of what he thought of my speech, it was a lost cause. I turned my back and stared past the Alfar looking at me in amazement and into the forest depths. Mothi put his hand on my shoulder, and this time I let it rest there.

Meuhlnir cleared his throat. "You can see why I have chosen to help him," he said. "I knew he was a relative to some degree, but even if that were not so, my brother Luka is at the heart of this good man's trouble. And Hank Jensen *is* a good man. It is plain to see."

"Yes," said Freyr. "No matter how impertinent he may be; it is obvious he is a good man who speaks the truth when he could lie."

Some of the tension drained out of me, and Mothi squeezed my shoulder.

"We have much to discuss," said Freyr. "You will take your rest and eat."

"This way, gentle Isir," said Yowtgayrr, holding up his hand to indicate the direction we should walk in. Once we had passed through the last of the Alfar standing around the edge of the bowl, he laid his hand on my arm. "That was well-spoken," he whispered. "You are a man I can respect."

"Thank you," I said. "I shouldn't have gotten angry, though."

"There is never anything wrong with expressing honest emotion among the Alfar," he said. "We value such honesty, and speaking your mind thus is a high compliment in light of what was at stake. It will not go unnoticed in this realm."

He turned and led us farther into the trees. We approached a very large redwood trunk and stopped in front of it. Yowtgayrr waved his hand in an elaborate pattern, and a door appeared in the bark. He opened the door and revealed a set of narrow stairs leading up the interior of the tree that encircled the heartwood of the tree. The stairs looked as if they were grown, not carved or cut from the wood of the tree.

"Delightful," said Meuhlnir.

Yowtgayrr smiled and led us up the stairs. There was another door at the top, and when Yowtgayrr opened it, we were in the canopy of the trees. Wide branches had been converted into walkways between various trunks.

"We will provide you with food and a place to sleep. The conclave makes few decisions without at least a day to argue and pout," said Yowtgayrr.

"Yes," said Meuhlnir. "I remember."

Yowtgayrr looked me in the eye. "No matter what the Conclave of Elders decides, I have a feeling you will not be disappointed."

"Really? I thought the conclave had the final say."

He shrugged and smiled. "So do they, but the simple truth is that the conclave merely advises the Priesthood of Tiwaz. In most cases, their advice is followed, but not in all."

Mothi raised his eyebrow at the Alf. "That is interesting information, Yowtgayrr. Why share it with us?"

Yowtgayrr placed his hand on my shoulder, his long fingers resting on my back. "Your cousin here has a worthy cause."

"Thank you," I said, the final bits of anger and frustration draining out of me.

After Yowtgayrr had left us in the small house that was grown inside the large trunk of a tree, we sank into chairs carved from wood that were as comfortable as anything I'd ever sat in—it was as if they were custom carved for our individual forms. Meuhlnir sighed and leaned back into the chair, wiggling his shoulders and advertising his pleasure with a broad grin.

"No one makes furniture like the Alfar," he said.

"It helps to be able to speak to the wood," said Mothi.

"There's that," said Meuhlnir. "That was a passionate speech, Hank. It was well spoken, though I might have resisted telling the entire race off."

I shrugged. "I wasn't talking to the entire race, just the arrogance embodied by Freyr."

"A bit of arrogance is to be expected once you've reached his age."

"Is he much older than you?" I asked.

"Oh yes. Much, much older. He is to me as I am to a thrall or one from your realm." Meuhlnir shrugged. "I'm not sure anyone knows how long the Alfar live. All I know is that Freyr has been alive since the Isir first visited Alfhaym millennia ago. He is used to being treated with deference and respect."

"You'd think he'd be ready to retire by now," I muttered.

Meuhlnir laughed, and Mothi grinned. "All of the Elders are 'retired' from the Priesthood of Tiwaz."

"Ah," I said. "Grumpy old men, then."

"Well, yes," said Meuhlnir. "Even so, I still say your impassioned speech was very nicely done. I think you won many allies with it."

I nodded. "Tell me about this Priesthood of Tiwaz. Will they help us?"

"You've spoken to their core beliefs, so I'd imagine you will get something out of it."

"Good," I said. We sat in companionable silence for a while and then we all turned in for the night.

When I woke the next morning, I dressed and went into the main room of the house. Neither Meuhlnir or Mothi were there, but Freyr was sitting in one of the chairs. He looked me over with a baleful manner, I thought, and then waved his hand at one of the chairs.

"The actions you are about to undertake are going to start a war," he said without preamble. "Many will die."

"I don't know about that," I said. "I'm only here to get my family back. What happens after that is not up to me."

The old Alf leaned his head back and looked at me over his steepled fingers, eyes narrowed into slits. "Yes," he said. "That is often the justification for war. My people have lived in peace for eons. We have no wars in Alfhaym. We are dragged into wars in other realms by people like you, Hank Jensen."

I shrugged. "You say you have no wars, but your religion is centered around the idea of protecting others and your land. Your priests act as guardians of this realm, yes?"

Freyr nodded, his eyes shrouded.

"Then tell me this: if your realm has no wars, why do you need protectors and guardians? Don't tell me it is for protection from people across the *preer*. If not for the Isir, there would be no *preer*. Can you honestly say that before the Isir came here, your people did not think they were alone in the universe?"

"Of course, we did," he said. "I wish we still did."

"You aren't," I snapped. "Believe me, I wish my people were as well, but instead, we share the universe with people who think we are playthings and others who think they are superior to us because we are more honest than they."

He bristled with anger and slid forward to the edge of his chair. "There you go again, lecturing me, who could be older than your entire line of ancestors added together. Do you think you have seen more of this universe than I?"

"As a matter of fact, I do," I said. "When trouble comes to my door, I don't pretend it doesn't affect me. I act. I've traveled through three different worlds counting yours. How many different suns have you seen?"

"Irrelevant," the old Alf snapped. "I've seen more in this realm during the years I've been alive than you will ever hope to see. I've seen brave Alfar go to fight in someone else's battles, never to return to Alfhaym. Never to see the sacred trees again. Never more to serve Tiwaz as a guardian and protector of the ancient groves. When one of us dies, child-who-thinks-he-is-a-man, he gives up thousands and thousands of years of experience. Think of the lives he might touch during that time."

I nodded. "Yes, it is a large sacrifice, but not one I want anyone—man, Isir, or Alf—to make."

Freyr scoffed and sank back in his chair. "What you want makes no difference. What will be has already been woven into the skein of fate."

"Then why are we here arguing this? If it's fate?"

Freyr scoffed and waved his hand at me. "I won't play word games with you, Isir."

"Then get on with it."

"You won't rescind your request?"

"No," I said.

"Even if it will cost the lives of beings older than your civilization?"

"No. You are free to refuse me, however. It's a free universe."

Freyr sat very still and just stared at me for what felt like a long time. Then, without a word, he got up and shuffled out the door.

I followed him, doing my own early-morning shuffle. Meuhlnir and Mothi were leaning against the trunk of the tree that contained the house we had slept in. Meuhlnir's face was impassive as he nodded to Freyr. As soon as Freyr was out of ear shot, Mothi turned to me and asked, "Good talk?"

I chuckled and shook my head. "More of the same, I'm afraid. My chances of convincing that Alf of anything are slim and none."

Mothi smiled. "Good thing it isn't really up to him, then."

Yowtgayrr approached us, giving us enough time to conclude any private conversations. "Gentle Isir," he said by way of a greeting. "The Priesthood of Tiwaz has made its decision."

"Without Freyr's input?" I asked.

"All things have been considered," he said. "If you will follow me?"

Yowtgayrr led us back to the tree with the staircase inside of it, and back down to the ground. His back was held stiffly straight, shoulders back and elbows slightly cocked out to the sides.

"Tell me, Yowtgayrr," I asked, "are you one of the Priests of Tiwaz?"

"Of course," he said without looking back. "Every male Alf is a priest."

It was then that I realized I hadn't seen a single female Alf for the entire time we'd been in Alfhaym. "What of your women?"

Meuhlnir coughed and touched my elbow with his hand.

"We don't speak of our females with outsiders," said Yowtgayrr with a touch of frost in his voice.

"Oh, I'm sorry," I said. "I meant no disrespect."

Yowtgayrr only nodded and kept walking. He led us to the small bowl-shaped depression in the floor of the forest. It was again packed with adult males, and ringed with male adolescents and male children. The Conclave of Elders was obvious in its absence.

The Alf led us to the center of the depression. "The Isir have come," he said in a formal, ritualistic tone.

An Alf stepped forward from the rest. His skin was cream-colored with light green striations running through it. He stood taller than Yowtgayrr and broader in the shoulder. "I am Roorik," he said simply. "I am the Voice of Tiwaz."

"Nice to meet you," I said, extending my hand.

He clasped it briefly and then let go. "You have requested the help of the Priesthood of Tiwaz. Do you still seek our aid?"

"Yes, I do," I said, nodding my head.

"We have considered your request and the advice of the Conclave of Elders," said Roorik. "We find merit in your motives and value in your arguments. We will help you."

Relief coursed through me and a smile creased my face. "Thank you. Thank you very much!"

"You should know that the Conclave of Elders was undecided when we last asked for their advice."

"Oh," I said.

"Five priests will travel back to Osgarthr with your party to act in your stead and try to misdirect the Dark Queen and her followers," said Roorik.

"Excellent," I said. "I appreciate your help. You've no idea how much this means to me."

Roorik held up his hand. "There is more, Hank Jensen of the Isir. The Priesthood of Tiwaz is sworn to act as guardians and protectors to those in need. Tiwaz himself gave us this mandate, and we strive to be worthy of his grace. The Priesthood has decided to exceed your request."

"Exceed my request? What does that mean?"

"We will provide you with a personal guard."

I looked at Meuhlnir and Mothi, unsure what was being offered, or if I could refuse. "I'm not sure what to say—"

"There is nothing to say, Hank Jensen of the Isir. It has been decided. Three Alfar will accompany you and will be your personal guard." Roorik motioned to Yowtgayrr and two other Alf standing in the front row. All three of them stepped forward. "These three have sworn to die before allowing you to fall into mortal peril."

"Uh," I said, looking back and forth between the three Alf. "I…I don't know what to say, except that I don't want anyone injured in my place. It's hard enough knowing Meuhlnir and his family feel that they must protect me at all costs. I am honored by your offer, truly I am, but I don't want—"

"Hank," said Yowtgayrr. "It doesn't matter what you want at this point. Your arguments touched many of us. You've awoken a sense of duty in our ranks that we did not know still existed. I will follow you back to Osgarthr, as will my brother priests, and we will strive to keep you from all harm."

"Yowtgayrr, I am honored by this, but I can't—"

"There is nothing for you to allow or forbid," said Yowtgayrr. "We will come even if you forbid us. If you will not have us in your party, we will follow your party and protect you as best we can from a distance."

I looked at Meuhlnir, who shrugged at me.

"Part of the reason the priesthood decides these things in seclusion is to remove any doubt as to who bears responsibility for what may happen," said Roorik. "In this case, we have decided, and no responsibility falls on your shoulders. We took this path because we know you are an honorable man, and because Yowtgayrr foresaw the quandary this would open before you. I only wish I was not the Voice, so that I, too, could accompany you."

That icy lump was back in my throat. I nodded my acceptance.

Yowtgayrr put his large hand on my shoulder and waved at the other two priests who were to act as my bodyguard. "This is Skowvithr," he said pointing at another white-skinned Alf. "And this is Urlikr." Urlikr's coloring was pale gray with light blue striations. Both looked capable of standing firm in a fight, and both met my eye without hesitation.

"I won't have any of you die in my place," I said.

"Then don't let it come to that," said Urlikr with a smile.

Yowtgayrr led the three of us followed by two of my bodyguards and our five decoys back through the forest to where the *proo* was anchored. Freyr waited in the clearing, his face a blank mask.

"So, you have what you wanted," he hurled at me as soon as I stepped into the circle.

"More," I said truthfully. "It is an honor and a responsibility I won't shirk."

"That's what everyone says," he spat.

"Father," said Skowvithr with a hint of reproach in his voice. "The priesthood has decided this matter. I am honored to take my place beside my brother priests and between this man and danger. Can't you respect that?"

"Ask your elder brother," said Freyr in a small, sad voice. "He never came back from helping this one."

He sneered and waved his hand at Meuhlnir. "Now you, too, go to waste your years."

Skowvithr stepped forward and laid a hand on each of his father's shoulders. "No, Father," he said. "I go to fulfill whatever Tiwaz has woven in the tapestry of my life. I go to earn a place in the sky kingdom next to my brother Fyuhlnir."

The old Alf clung to his son with white-knuckled desperation. "Don't do this, Skowvithr," he pleaded. "Stay, help manage the *Skowkur Kuthadna*. Take your place in the Conclave of Elders when it is your time."

"Father, you know all of those things would be empty for me if I did not take my proper place beside Hank Jensen of the Isir."

Freyr sniffed and then spat on the ground. His shoulders slumped, and he wouldn't meet anyone's gaze. "Go, then," he said in a defeated voice.

"If Tiwaz wills it, I will return, Father. If I don't, take solace that it is as Tiwaz wills and that I passed from this life with love for you in my heart."

Freyr nodded and half-turned away. "As your brother also said to me," he said, his voice as bitter as acid.

"Freyr," I said. "If I have anything to say about it, Skowvithr *will* return to you."

The old Alf didn't turn, and he didn't speak as the others used the *proo* back to Osgarthr. At last, it was just Freyr, Meuhlnir, and myself in the clearing. Meuhlnir gestured toward the *proo* with his head.

"Go on, Hank," he said. "I will have words with Freyr, and then I will follow."

I looked at him and then back at Freyr. I knew what it felt like to have a son ripped away from me by someone from another realm and my heart went out to him. "I'd tell him to stay if it would do any good, Freyr."

Again, the old Alf didn't respond.

I turned and walked to the *proo*.

THIRTY-SIX

When we returned to Osgarthr, it was midday. Pollen swam through the bright sunlight like tadpoles in a pond. If I didn't know that the village that supported the estate had been attacked two days earlier, I would have thought everything was copasetic.

The Vault of *Preer*, with its glowing runes set in the supporting stones of the walls and arched ceiling, had been empty as had the great hall above it. We went outside looking for the three Isir women and found a hive of bustling activity. Horses were being shifted from one corral to another or being put into the pastures that stood closest to the walls. The Alfar looked around with small smiles on their faces.

Meuhlnir stopped the karl that Mothi had pointed out to me the day we arrived. "What has happened?" he asked.

"Nothing, sir," said the karl. "The mistress has foretold that Master Veethar will return today with a large herd of new breeders. We are making ready."

"And where are my wives today?"

"They left for the village at first light with Mistress Frikka." The karl saw a thrall who was losing control of a large stallion and took a step in that direction, but then halted and looked at Meuhlnir.

"Go on," Meuhlnir said, clapping the man on the back. "I don't stand on ceremony."

With an apologetic smile, the man tugged the hair over his forehead and then strode away yelling at the thrall and sweeping his arms about in wild gestures.

"I had hoped for a hot meal, or at least a greeting, before we traveled to Nitavetlir," muttered Mothi.

"Life's rough," said Meuhlnir with a smile. "At any rate, I think you should stay and wait for Veethar. You know, since you always get a crick in your neck."

Mothi grinned and bowed his head. "As you wish it, Master of Thunderous Farts."

"Mothi, Mothi, Mothi," sighed Meuhlnir. "You are so grounded until you are four hundred."

"You already grounded me until I was five hundred, remember?"

Meuhlnir shook his head with pretended exasperation. "Shall we just say six hundred, then?"

It sounded so much like the bantering between Sig and I that I found that damn lump in my throat yet again.

Meuhlnir, my three new Alfar protectors, and I filed back into the longhouse and down the stairs to the Vault of *Preer*. The Alfar who had volunteered to serve as our decoys elected to stay in Osgarthr and see the new breeding stock as Veethar brought them in. It was surprising how much the Alfar seemed to like horses.

Meuhlnir activated the rune for Nitavetlir, and we watched as the *proo* to Alfhaym shrank and then faded into one of the runed stones. The new *proo* shimmered into being the size of a small dinner plate and then expanded like a balloon.

Meuhlnir put his hand on my arm. "Before we cross, I need to tell you a few things about the Tverkar."

"Okay," I said with a shrug.

He looked at the *proo* for a moment, choosing his words. "You've seen the Svartalfar."

"Yes."

Urlikr hawked up some phlegm and spit it into the corner.

Meuhlnir held up his hands, palms out. "I know, gentle Alfar. It is distasteful to you to hear of your so-called cousins, but Hank doesn't know our history. He needs to be prepared."

Urlikr looked disgusted but nodded.

"You could wait outside," suggest Meuhlnir.

"No," said Yowtgayrr. "As you say, Hank needs to know all of this. We will lend our knowledge where it is needed." He turned to Urlikr and Skowvithr and put a long-fingered hand on each Alf's shoulder. "We may have to do worse than hear stories of the Svartalfar before this is finished. We must be prepared as well."

"Very well," sighed Skowvithr. "Speak on, Master of Thunder."

Meuhlnir nodded once. "It is said that, once, long ago, the Alfar, the Svartalfar, and the Tverkar shared a single realm and a single set of ancestors. It is also said that the Tverkar were once part of the race of Svartalfar, but a schism arose between clans and the schism developed into a war."

"The war was much like *Ragnaruechkr* here on Osgarthr, the war between the Svartalfar and the Tverkar unleashed great devastation on the realm," said Yowtgayrr. "The initial power used twisted the bits of the *Plauinn* that defined them as a people."

"The *Plauinn* were your ancestors?" I asked.

Yowtgayrr nodded.

"As well as the Svartalfar and the Tverkar?"

"Yes," he said. "The *Plauinn* are the race from which we all descend, Isir included."

"They were the *Geumlu*?" I asked.

"No," said Skowvithr. "The so-called Old Ones of Osgarthr were also descended from the *Plauinn*."

"This was many, many millennia in the past," said Yowtgayrr. "We believe that the *Plauinn* were the

First People of the universe, and that at the time, all the realms were contained in a single domain, governed by one set of laws."

"I was not aware of this," said Meuhlnir.

"We don't often speak of it to *utanathkomanti*— to outsiders—if you will pardon the expression," said Urlikr.

"Fascinating," muttered Meuhlnir.

"Yes, well, this war you spoke of, we call it the First War. As I said, it twisted the bits that defined the *Plauinn* as a people, which only widened the schism between the warring factions over time. As the First People became the many, more and more powerful weapons were created and spent on the enemy factions. In the Sundering, weapons were developed that were so powerful that, when they were eventually fired all at once, split the fabric of the universe multifariously, creating the various realms that exist today, and ending the First War—each new race thought that it had obliterated the other 'impure' races. We learned this was a falsehood when Haymtatlr blew his mighty invention, the *Kyatlarhodn*.

"Many of the realms created by the First War had been further devastated by the Sundering, and the dominant races forgot the history of the *Plauinn* and the First War. Since the *preer* were opened by Haymtatlr, we've met only one other race which has preserved this knowledge."

"The Svartalfar?" I asked.

Urlikr scoffed. "Hardly. They are savages. It was the Tverkar."

"Ah," I said. "And this is what you wanted me to know?"

Meuhlnir shook his head. "I didn't know most of that story either. What I wanted to tell you was that the Tverkar are ugly—much like the Svartalfar are physically ugly—but that in temperament, you will find them to be much more like the Alfar, though they take great pains to appear otherwise. They are a wise and honorable people. Great craft- and tradesmen."

Yowtgayrr nodded. "We believe that either the Tverkar or the Alfar are the most closely related to the *Plauinn*."

Meuhlnir looked a little irritated at that, but he shrugged and said, "That may well be, but none of us are likely to ever know."

The Alf bowed his head—not agreeing with Meuhlnir, necessarily, but willing to allow him his own beliefs.

"Nitavetlir is a rocky, barren world," said Meuhlnir. "The Tverkar tunneled underground to survive. Their cities are elaborate, hand-carved caves, the grandeur of which most surface cities can't match. They have grown to fit their environment."

"As all races have," said Skowvithr.

"The Svartalfar and the Alfar seem a bit similar— did they evolve on similar worlds?" I asked without thinking.

Meuhlnir looked to the three Alfar and then glared at me.

Too late, I realized what I'd said. "My apologies," I blurted. "No offense meant, I spoke without thinking. I only meant the general similarity in musculature and skeleton—I didn't mean to compare you to Svartalfar on any other level."

The atmosphere in the room was chilly, and no one said anything for a long time. Finally, Yowtgayrr sighed. "It is true that we bear a distant resemblance on a purely anatomical level, but I believe that is simply a joke of fate, rather than an indication of any similar past history. Other than the relation to the *Plauinn*, of course."

"Of course," I said. I looked at each of them in turn. "I really do apologize. To each of you."

Skowvithr forced a smile on his face. "We are perhaps too sensitive to comparisons to our sworn enemies," he said. "And you are new to this."

"Still, it is better that you make such a mistake in the company of friends than in either Alfhaym or Nitavetlir," said Yowtgayrr.

"Or in any public place," snapped Meuhlnir.

I felt the heat in my cheeks as I nodded.

"Enthusiasm for learning should never be criticized," said Urlikr in soft tones. "It is one of the core beliefs of the Priesthood of Tiwaz, and yet we are eager to take offense when such eagerness challenges our belief in our own moral high-ground."

Skowvithr's forehead bunched and Yowtgayrr pursed his lips, looking at the ground.

"No, this was a mistake on my part," I said.

"Indeed," grumbled Meuhlnir.

"Yet it does bring to light a degree of hubris that is uncomfortable," said Yowtgayrr.

"Perhaps we should forget it happened," said Meuhlnir.

Yowtgayrr nodded but kept his gaze on the ground at his feet.

Meuhlnir grunted and pushed me through the *proo*. I arrived in Nitavetlir and hit my head on the ceiling. Meuhlnir came through next, already stooping and ducking his head.

Yowtgayrr came through next, also ducking his head, followed by Skowvithr and then Urlikr.

"One of you might have warned me about the roof," I said with a chuckle.

The room was dark and smelled a little musty, to be honest. Meuhlnir pointed at a small door, and I pushed on it, a bit too hard it turned out, and the door slammed open. The hall outside was bright, though there were no light sources visible.

"No need to slam the door," grumbled someone from the hall.

"Sorry," I said. "I expected it to be heavier."

"Do you not know you are in Nitavetlir?"

I stepped into the low-ceilinged hallway.

The person in front of me had to be a Tverkr. He came up to my solar plexus, and he was very ugly. His matted, stringy hair stood out at all angles, and looked brittle and dry, while his beard was long, braided and well-kept. His hair and beard were a combination of a honeydew green and laurel green color. His head was bulbous and misshapen and sat atop a short, stubby neck. His bushy eyebrows looked like fat caterpillars crouched over his malachite eyes, which were too small and too widely-placed in his wreck of a face. His torso was bent and twisted, and entirely too wide. Like both the Svartalfar and the Alfar, his trapezius muscles formed a broad triangle, but unlike the others, his short, stubby neck made the muscles look stunted and gnarled. His arms were too long for his torso, but his legs were too short—another example of stunted, contorted growth. His feet were too wide and too long for the length of his legs, giving the Tverkr an almost comedic look. His skin was mottled—Mikado yellow spots over a dark battleship gray—and pitted with what looked like burn scars.

"Well?" he asked me with spit flying from his thick lips. "Did you not know?"

"I knew we were coming to Nitavetlir, but this is my first trip, and I—"

The Tverkr waved a hand with long, slender fingers. "Yes, but you knew you were coming to Nitavetlir. Why would a door be made in such a shoddy manner as to be *heavy*?"

"Well, it is stone…"

Meuhlnir stepped around me. "He's a *kanka-ee*," he said in a matter of fact tone.

The short, misshapen man grunted and peered up at me with irritation on his face. "Why'd you not just say? You think I have time to stand around trading meaningless words?" With that, the Tverkr pushed past us and stomped off down the hall.

"Sorry," I called after him. When he was out of ear shot, I turned to Meuhlnir. "Maybe I'll just let you speak for me for the rest of the day."

Meuhlnir laughed. "Don't take it to heart, my friend. Tverkar are not known for gentle manners. All in all, that was an innocuous exchange for the race."

The Alfar were trying to hide their grins from me.

"Oh, laugh it up," I said and cracked a grin of my own, relieved to see them grinning at all.

We set off in the opposite direction than the Tverkr had gone, heading for what Meuhlnir called simply "the Smithy." After a walk of five or ten minutes, the hallway widened to about twice its previous width and about four times its previous crick-in-the-neck height. Instead of only being broken by featureless stone doors, we began to see wide glass windows displaying wares of various and sundry kinds. We also began to see more of the strange looking Tverkar, with hair colors drawn from the greenish-brown hue family and skin of various shades of dark gray with tinges of yellow and orange mottling. To a one, they looked at us, made a face and then looked away.

Meuhlnir walked forward like he owned the place, not looking at anyone and not speaking at all. We followed as he made turn after turn in the warren-like halls of Nitavetlir. When the hall ended, he led us out onto a balcony that extended to the right and left around a cavernous space. I stepped to the stone railing and looked down. Far below I could see firelight flickering. The ceiling of the vast chamber was lost in the distance and dimness.

The balcony was crowded with Tverkar, each hustling along on whatever business they had. They bumped and jostled each other, which ended with a cantankerous exchange of "pleasantries" and every once in a while, in a shoving match.

Meuhlnir waited while I took it all in and then led us away, pushing through the throng, his face set in stern, no-nonsense lines. We saw many a Tverkar open his or her mouth to bicker with Meuhlnir, but they never said a word once they saw who he was. Meuhlnir led us down stairways and along the balcony, but always to the left, and we found ourselves on the voluminous ground floor of the vast, bell-shaped chamber.

What I had taken to be firelight from the balconies above was, in fact, vast pools of molten stone that were being used as massive forges. The clanging of metal on anvils was enough to split my head. I couldn't see how the Tverkar could stand to work there in the heat and the noise, but work there they did—illimitable numbers of them stretching away into the haze and smoke.

Again, Meuhlnir waited until I met his gaze and then strode off again. I followed him through the smoke and sparks, trying to keep the incessant ringing of metal on metal from driving me insane. The Tverkar smiths around us pointed and glared at us, and though I could see their mouths moving, I couldn't hear a thing they shouted at us.

Meuhlnir walked up behind a tallish (for his kind) Tverkr and tapped on his shoulder in a rather forceful, rude manner. The Tverkr turned, his mouth open and his blackened face set in an ugly, glaring grimace of anger, but once he saw Meuhlnir standing in front of him, he swallowed whatever curses he had been about to fling in our faces and motioned for us to follow. From his expression, those curses tasted sour going down.

He led us to the side of the chamber and through a door that was covered with soot. He pushed through the door and waited for us to file through, then slammed it shut. "What do you want, Master of Thunder?" he all but snapped.

The office was large but had so much clutter in it that it felt claustrophobic.

"Greetings to you too, Master Prokkr," said Meuhlnir, his voice mild and light. "May I introduce my new friend, Hank Jensen from Mithgarthr? And these stalwart companions are Yowtgayrr, Urlikr, and Skowvithr."

Prokkr didn't even glance our way as he waved his hand at us, but whether it was in greeting or with impatience, I couldn't say. "Time, Master of Thunder, is important here, even if it is not in Osgarthr."

"Very well, Master Smith. I have need of a few items of Tverkar make."

"You don't say? Why I'd never have guessed you'd come to Nitavetlir and seek out the master smith to obtain anything. Are you sure you didn't come to invite me to a grand tea?"

Meuhlnir shook his head, suppressing a small smile. "I'm in a hurry."

"Doesn't seem much like it," snapped Prokkr. "Since you are Isir and know no better, I will ask you one more time to make your request or get out of my smithy."

Meuhlnir put his hand on my shoulder. "I need a set of armor for Hank, here. It must be as strong as granite while being as light as silk."

The master smith scoffed and sneered, scathing me with a glance. "Oh, is that all?"

"No, it isn't," said Meuhlnir with a trace of irritation. "I'll also need two small bucklers—one for each of his arms. Also, whatever these Alfar request, and I'll need five helmets to fit Alfar. All the items will need to be enchanted. By Althyof."

"Fine," grated Prokkr. "Return in three weeks." The Tverkr made to push past Meuhlnir and return to his smithy, but Meuhlnir put a hand, which looked huge by comparison, on the Tverkr's chest.

"No. I will need them today." Meuhlnir's voice crackled with command.

Prokkr's laugh was sardonic, and he slapped Meuhlnir's hand from his chest. "Shall I pull down the heavens for you as well?"

"No, but you will do as I ask, and without further theatrics," said Meuhlnir in an icy-cold voice and a dangerous glint in his eye. "I have no more patience for Tverkar manners today, Prokkr."

The master smith nodded his head, but couldn't wipe the sneer from his face. "It will cost more.

Significantly so. And the armor will have to come from premade stock, sized to fit." He came over to me and pushed my arms up and out to my side, while his eyes moved over me like a laser measuring device. With rough hands, he shoved me this way and that and then noticed the Kimber on my right hip. He looked up at me with wonder in his eyes. "A machine of war?" he asked.

I nodded and pulled the big pistol out of its holster. I ejected the magazine, cleared the chamber and then handed it to the Tverkr.

He smiled—the first genuine smile of delight I had seen in this strange realm—and ran his hands over the machined metal of the slide. He sussed out the locking mechanism for the slide and then took the gun apart as if he had been working with firearms all his life. He pulled every component-part out of the gun, examining each piece with eager eyes and then reassembled it without making a single error. "Chemical propellants?" he asked in the voice of a child on Christmas Eve.

I nodded and pressed one of the bullets out of the magazine and handed it to him. "Do you think you could craft replacements for this?"

"Can I keep this?" he asked, bouncing the bullet in one of his callused hands. "I'll need to pull it apart. Oh, and I'll need to examine this further," he said lifting the Kimber as if it were an afterthought.

"Sure," I said, figuring that one less bullet made very little difference one way or another.

"Then I will figure it out, Master Jensen," he said in a pleasant tone. "Is this why you require two bucklers?" He held up the gun, pointing it at the door. "You use it like this?"

"Yes, that's pretty close. I need to have plenty of freedom to move my arms, though."

"You have another of these?" asked Prokkr with wide eyes.

I shrugged and brought out the HK .40 caliber pistol, made it safe and then passed it Prokkr. He put the Kimber into a pouch of his work belt, as if it had already lost his interest, and then repeated the discovery process with the HK. He looked at the barrel and tsked. "Different," he muttered.

Trying to suppress a grin at how different his manner was now, I took out one of the .40 caliber bullets and passed it to him. "Smaller caliber," I said. "Same principle, though."

"Yes," he said. He had put both bullets into a different pouch of his belt and had both pistols out and was looking from one to the other with assessing eyes.

"You don't mind working on the bullets?" I asked, thinking of Freyr's reaction to seeing the Kimber on my hip.

"Why would I?" He glanced up at me, nonplussed, and then back down at the pistols. "So, this piece here is propelled backward on these rails when the chemical ignites?" He was moving the slide of the Kimber back and forth.

"Yes. You have a quick eye," I said.

"I am a master smith," he said with more than a little impatience.

"Of course," I said.

Meuhlnir cleared his throat. "Now, Prokkr, about these items—"

"Anything for you, Master of Thunder?" asked Master Prokkr.

"No, no." Meuhlnir patted his hammer. "The hammer you made for me so long ago is still more than sufficient."

"Come back in a few hours," said Prokkr in a dismissing tone. He grunted and opened the door to the smithy, bellowing at his subordinates before the door hit the jam. Then, he turned to Meuhlnir and made a mocking bow. "Is that sufficient, Master of Thunder?"

"Hank, you four wait for me outside a moment. I need a word with Master Prokkr in private."

Prokkr scoffed and rolled his eyes as we went out into the smithy.

"Come on," said Meuhlnir when he rejoined us. "We have time to kill, so we might as well find a tavern. I'll tell you another short tale of Luka—one from before he fell, and then I have to find a pair of equal, but different gifts for Sif and Yowrnsaxa." He looked at me with mirth dancing in his eyes. "I bet you thought having two wives was the best idea you'd ever heard."

Truth was, it sounded like a very bad idea, but I smiled and gestured for him to lead on.

The tavern was three levels above the smithy, and still, the noise level was like sitting inside the engine compartment of a big tractor, but at least it was cooler. Meuhlnir ordered mead for the table and then sprawled into a cramped booth that was considered large by the Tverkr barman. He sat with his arms crossed in front of him on the table and watched as the barmaid brought a large pitcher of mead and poured it into five flagons.

"Tell me this story about Luka," I said.

Meuhlnir grunted and looked down at the part of the table bracketed by his muscled arms. "It was a short time after the first assassination attempt on the queen, but after she'd gifted me the hammer. She wanted to get away from the politics for a while. A short holiday, you see? She was still trying to recover her voice—it was still very hoarse and shaky, and she couldn't maintain much volume.

"We traveled to a village we hadn't visited before— me, the queen, Luka, Veethar, Paltr, Sif, Yowrnsaxa, Frikka, and Freya. We rode Veethar's magnificent horses then, too. The village children ran along beside us as we walked the horses the last mile or so into the village square..."

THIRTY-SEVEN

The queen's party slowed their horses to a walk as village children began to appear on the sides of the road, running alongside and shouting the kinds of questions excited children shouted at extravagantly equipped strangers. The queen smiled at this and waved, but her voice was still too broken to shout answers back. She nodded her head at her sister Freya.

"Greetings, children of Hyatlanes," Freya called. "We are the Isir, and we've come in peace and friendship from across the *Kyatlerproo*. From another realm."

"Your horses are so pretty! How did you make them so tall and shiny?" shouted a tall, red-headed girl in her preteens.

"For that, young Miss, you'd have to ask my friend Veethar." Freya waved her hand at a terrified-looking Veethar. "But be warned, he doesn't talk much, unless you count grunts."

Veethar looked like he wanted to fade into the mists, like he'd rather wrestle a bear than talk to a young girl.

"How come their coats shine so much, Veethar?" asked the girl.

"Good feed. Brushed every day," said Veethar in a voice that was only just audible to Meuhlnir who was riding next to him.

"What?"

Veethar repeated his five-word sermon again, with a touch more volume, and then blushed and looked down at the mane of his horse.

Freya laughed, and Meuhlnir felt a pang of loss. Her voice sounded so much like Queen Suel's had before she had broken it saving his life. "I warned you, girl," she said with a touch of mischief in her voice. "Veethar is shy."

"Might as well ask a lamb to roar like a lion," said Meuhlnir as he leaned over to clap his friend on the back. "Although this lamb fights like a lion when cornered, so don't press him too much."

Veethar glanced at him, and then away, blushing.

"What's an Isir? What is the *Kyatlerproo*?" shouted a young teenage boy, who was having a hard time keeping his eyes off Freya's chest.

She caught him looking and unleashed another tinkling, musical laugh. "The Isir are a race of people. The *Kyatlerproo* is like a bridge made of rainbows that spans the void between our realm and yours."

"Who are you," asked the boy, in a crackling, breathless voice that only a boy in puberty can ever hope to imitate.

Freya smiled and batted her eyelashes at him. "You first. What is your name?"

"I'm Dilyar. You are very pretty," he said and then blushed as red as Veethar.

"Many thanks, Master Dilyar. I fear you are going to cause a lot of problems for the fathers of girls in this village."

Dilyar looked confused, and Freya laughed again.

"Pay her no mind, boy," said Paltr with a grin. "She is an unrepentant flirt."

The boy looked even more confused than ever and slowed a little to consider if he was being mocked or not.

"Is your realm in the branches of *Yggdrasil*?" asked another boy. "What is its name?"

"Its name is of no account. We told your ancestors of the World Tree, though, and our realm is at its peak," said Freya with a grin.

"You've come to Mithgarthr in peace and friendship, you said."

Freya nodded. "Indeed, we have."

"I heard my father talking about the Isir. He said you are gods of great power."

"How far to your village, boy?" grunted Meuhlnir.

The boy squinted up at him, his eyes roving across his armor and lingering on his shiny warhammer. "Are you the Thunder God?" he asked in an awestruck voice.

"Don't be rude, Ernir," said a teenage girl who looked a lot like the boy. "Our village is just around that bend ahead."

"And your name?" Meuhlnir asked.

"Forward of you, *Pror*," said Luka with a smirk.

"I am Erna," she said with evident pride. "Erinir and I are *spayl*."

Meuhlnir shook his head. "I don't understand that word."

She smiled. "We were born at the same time."

"Ah, *tveeburar*," said Paltr. "I am also a twin."

Her eyes widened. "Is your sister here?" She looked at each of the females in the queen's party, and then back at Paltr.

"My twin is a brother," said Paltr. "He no longer travels with us—he lost his sight, you see, and it makes traveling to unfamiliar places hard for him."

"You are a *leeta ayns*, then?" she asked in hushed tones.

"If that means that my brother and I look the same, then the answer is yes."

Erna nudged Ernir and whispered something in his ear. The boy sprinted into the woods.

"There's nothing to fear," said Paltr.

"No, sir," said Erna. "I've sent him to summon the *Veulva*. She will want to see you. I hope this does not offend you."

Paltr laughed. "I'd have to have pretty thin bark to be offended by meeting a wand carrier."

The girl smiled and bobbed her head.

The Isir walked their horses around a bend in the road, and the children quieted but continued running alongside the road. Hyatlanes was a small, poor looking village, overlooked by a yarl's longhouse set up on a hill to the west of the town. The village square was already filling with adults in various states of dress—some wore their daily clothes, some were half-dressed for battle and fumbling with straps of armor, and one old woman dressed in white woolen robes.

The old woman leaned on a carved staff and had a wand of yew looped through her belt. Her eyes were rheumy, and her hair was stringy and unwashed. Her skin had a jaundiced look. She squinted up at the mounted Isir, her eyes lingered on Freya but then coming to rest on Paltr. "Greetings, Isir," she said. "You are the *leeta ayns*."

Paltr smiled at her brusque manner but nodded. "As I've already said to young Erna and Ernir who stands behind you."

"I am Hildr, and I am a *Veulva*." Her eyes drifted to Freya. "I have the *syown*. I greet you, Goddess."

She bowed from the waist, looking stiff and uncomfortable, her hand holding the carved staff shaking with the effort of supporting herself in the unnatural pose.

"Well met, Hildr," said Freya in a light tone.

"Have you come to summon me to Fowlkvankr?" asked the old woman, an expression of hope wriggling across the loose skin of her face.

Freya's face twitched in a half smile. "Not yet, old mother," she said. "You know me, then."

The *Veulva* shrugged. "I said I had the *syown*. I also ensorcel and magick. If I'm to stay, then may I ask if you've come in your guise of war or wearing your fecundatory mantle?"

Freya tinkled a laugh. "Can I not come just to visit a village? Must I have a reason?"

Hildr bowed her head. "Who are we to say, your Grace?" She looked at Paltr again. "Be you Huthr or Paltr?"

Paltr's eyes widened. "I am Paltr, old mother."

"Ah," Hildr said. "I welcome the god of peace, love, and forgiveness. Please don't take offence, but I've always wanted to meet the god of darkness."

Paltr chuckled. "It's hard for him to travel to new places."

"Yes," said the old woman. "In any case, it is good that you've come. I have read dire portents in the mists."

The Isir looked at each other with faint smiles of amusement which seemed to annoy the ancient *Veulva*. Meuhlnir cleared his throat and bobbed his head in her direction. "I greet you, old mother," he said. "Where is your yarl?"

"Hello, Lord of Thunder." The old woman waved her hand toward the longhouse on the hill. "We don't see much of old yarl Varr. His son and heir died in a raid on Potnsa a few summers back and shortly thereafter, the yarl's woman followed him. Some say she died of grief, but I was not allowed to attend her toward the end. He has been…inconsolable."

"He is without other children?" asked Frikka.

"Yes, Lady Frikka, there were problems with his son's birth, and after that the field was barren." She nodded an apology at Sif.

"And how long has his woman been gone?" asked Freya.

"A few seasons, Goddess," said the *Veulva* with a shrug. "Time is slippery for me these days."

Freya looked at Frikka, and something passed between them. Frikka nodded and smiled. She pointed with her chin at a pretty girl standing to the side and then raised her eyebrows. Freya's only answer was her melodious laugh.

"What are you two caballing?" asked Meuhlnir with an amused chuckle.

"Never you mind, Thunder God," said Freya before laughing again.

The Isir dismounted and tried to look harmless, though they dwarfed the locals, as they handed the reins of their mounts to eager village children. The villagers crowded around as soon as the horses were out of the way. Some wanted only to pay their respects, and some wanted only to touch the arm of their favorite god or goddess, but some leaned close to whisper their heart's desires to one of the Isir.

Freya looked a question at her sister, Suel, who nodded her head. Freya took Hildr by the arm and led her to the side of the throng, signaling for Veethar and Meuhlnir to follow. "Dearest Hildr, when does your village expect its visitors?"

The old woman stared at her, face slack. "I've not shared the divining with the village as of yet, Goddess, though I am not surprised you've augured it yourself. I wanted to ask for the help of the Isir…"

"Yes, *Veulva*. How can the Isir help your village?"

"The Potnsar will raid before sunset. With the yarl in the state he is in, there will be no one to lead the karls in defense."

Everyone looked at Veethar, who blushed again and looked at his boots. He looked as if he wanted to disappear. Meuhlnir shrugged and took a half-step forward. "I would be honored to lead your karls, with my Queen's leave, of course."

Suel nodded regally, one hand to her throat.

"Isir, to me," Meuhlnir said the words with just enough volume to be heard over the crowd, and the rest of the party gathered around him.

Luka walked over, his face wrapped with a huge grin, and slapped Meuhlnir on the back. "Taking all the glory yet again, *Pror*?" he asked with laughter at the edges of his voice.

"Might as well ask the Sun to allow the cloud to take credit for daylight," said Meuhlnir, smiling. At the sound of horns in the distance, his smile faded, and he turned to Hildr. "Old mother, it's time to speak to your karls. Can we assume the yarl won't stir from his longhouse?"

"Oh, aye," said Hildr. "I have seen it in the leaves blowing in the wind."

"Very well, go talk to your people. Give us a moment to set our strategy and then send over your fighting men."

"As you command, Thunder Lord." The old woman shuffled into the center of the crowd, raising her hands for quiet. She began speaking, and the villagers gasped.

"Queen Suel," said Meuhlnir, "please allow Paltr and your *Trohtninkar Tumuhr* to escort you and Freya to the longhouse. They will remain with you and see to your safety. Veethar, Luka, and I should be able to handle the raid without much trouble."

"Shouldn't Paltr stay with you," croaked Suel in a hoarse, craggy voice.

"He's far too much of a dandy to risk any real work," said Luka with a teasing lilt to his voice.

"I'll dandy you into several pieces," growled Paltr before losing his battle to keep from smiling. "Besides, fighting humans isn't real work. Guarding all these beautiful women is more my style."

"Like a troll guarding butterflies," said Luka. "Only trolls smell better."

"If my younger brothers are finished showing off for the butterflies, perhaps we can get to it?" said Meuhlnir in droll tones.

Queen Suel smiled and patted his arm. "Might as well ask hounds to forgo fighting over sausages." Her voice was whisper-quiet, cracked and broken, full of craggy consonance and jangling tonality, but her face was filled with laughter.

Meuhlnir smiled and tried to keep how the sound of her new voice made him cringe. "Maybe you can teach Paltr how to knit while we're fighting."

Suel gave him a squinty-eyed look and shook her fist as if to tell him he'd be getting quite the tongue lashing if it didn't hurt her to speak. Then she chuckled, which sounded more like a rusty saw getting stuck in wet wood than an expression of joy and amusement. She looked at his face for a moment, and her own expression fell. She turned away, ducking her head, and started walking toward the longhouse.

Meuhlnir just stood there, his heart in his throat, and watched her go. He felt a warmth on his forearm and looked down to see Yowrnsaxa gazing up at him.

"It will get better," she said.

"Yes," he croaked. "It can't get any worse, can it?"

"And no matter what you think, it's not your fault." Yowrnsaxa patted his arm and then followed the others up the hill.

Veethar nudged his arm and jerked his chin toward the villagers. Meuhlnir turned toward them and tried to project his confidence at the gaggle of scared women, children, and old men looking back at him. "Do not worry," he said to them. "The Isir won't let you come to harm on this day."

Armored karls began appearing at the edge of the crowd, buckling their armor and loosening their weapons. They were a ragtag bunch—farmers and crafters, some with experience that showed in calm eyes and steady hands, and some fresh to the fields of battle, as shown by nervous ticks and nauseated faces. They looked like infantry.

"Will our opponents be ahorse?" Meuhlnir asked.

"No, Lord of Thunder," Hildr said. "They come afoot."

"Good. Here is our plan. We three Isir will go mounted. I want you karls to stay back, out of bow range and let us approach these Potnsar. Perhaps we can take the day without bloodshed."

Meuhlnir, Veethar, and Luka mounted and waited for the karls to form up behind them. With twenty men at their backs, the three Isir spurred their horses into a walk. The Potnsar were getting close to the village by the sound of the horns and were no doubt expecting little resistance. The war party from Hyatlanes found the raiding party in a meadow southwest of the village.

Meuhlnir signaled for the karls to halt as he, Luka, and Veethar rode toward the center of the meadow. He held up his right hand and stopped his horse. "Men of Potnsa!" he called. "You are expected."

The Potnsar looked at the three Isir, their eyes roving from the fine, large boned mounts, across the gleaming metal armor and finally to the exotic-looking weapons carried by the trio. "Who are you and why do you take the side of these dogs?" yelled the leader of the raiders.

"Meuhlnir!" he yelled, holding his hammer aloft. "*Ehlteenk*," he said under his breath and pointed with the warhammer. Bolts of lightning rained from the clear sky, splitting the air with thunder.

The Potnsar took a series of steps backward, each one looking involuntary and closer and closer to outright flight than the previous one. "Tor! It's Tor!" they cried.

Meuhlnir glowered at them. "You'd do well not to become our enemies. I've brought Luka and Veethar with me!"

Luka nudged his horse forward and sneered at the Potnsar. "*Huent elti*!" he shouted and held his right hand high above his head. His hand burst into bright yellow flames, which prompted another set of involuntary backward steps among the Potnsar.

Veethar sat on his horse, silent and staring at the raiding party. His lips moved, and his eyes changed from a pale, sky blue to a blazing yellow. He made a motion with his right hand, and the grass beneath the feet of the Potnsar withered and died. The raiders were close to flight, and their panicked cries echoed around the meadow. He made another gesture, and the branches of the trees behind them wove themselves into an impenetrable wall of greenery. When the Potnsar backed into the wall, they fell silent, and many of them dropped their weapons and shields to the ground.

"Lords of the Isir, what have we done to earn your wrath?" cried the leader of the raiding party.

"You come dressed for war with the intent of raiding Hyatlanes," roared Meuhlnir. "They are friends to the Isir!"

Luka smirked. "And it seems you are not," he said with a bestial snarl. "Plus, I haven't burned anyone in a long time." He balled his fist, forming the fire in his hand into a ball, which he then bounced in his palm.

"This is not a matter for the gods!" said the Potnsar leader. "This is but the actions of rival villages as it has been for all time. This is vengeance for an attack they made against us last season."

A low growling sound erupted from Veethar's throat, and he kneed his horse forward. He rode straight at the leader of the raiders and didn't stop until the man was pressed against the wall of branches and the horse's mouth was pressed against the man's cheek. "Shall I have him take *my* vengeance out of your face for assuming you had my blessing?" he hissed.

The man looked utterly terrified—not so much of the horse, but more that the God of Silence had decided to speak to him at such length. Legends had it that when Veethar finally chose to speak of vengeance, people died in hideous ways.

"No, Lord," the man whispered. "I meant no offense."

"You *have* caused offense, worm," shouted Veethar. Meuhlnir and Luka exchanged surprised glances. "Did the Thunder God not just tell you that the people of Hyatlanes are our friends? That they are protected under our aegis?" Veethar tapped his horse on the neck, and the great beast opened its mouth and peeled back its lips so that the horse's teeth now rested against the cheek of the Potnsa man.

"Steady, brother," said Meuhlnir. "I'm sure this man was caught up in the moment and spoke without thought."

"Yes! Yes, I did," said the raid leader. "I beg your forgiveness, mighty Veethar!"

Veethar stared down at the man whose near mind-blinding panic squirmed on his face. He clucked his tongue, and the horse took a step back and closed its mouth.

"I'm sure that is more comfortable," said Luka. "Just remember who it is that sits before you."

"Perhaps we can now put an end to this ill-advised raid?" asked Meuhlnir, the picture of reasonable calm. "Before your raiding party dies to the last man?"

The leader of the raiders gulped a breath and nodded.

"Good. It is our desire that the villages of Hyatlanes and Potnsa become allies, watching each other's borders and defending one another against invaders. Is that suitable to Potnsa?"

The man shot a suspicious look across the meadow at the karls from Hyatlanes. He nodded, not meeting anyone's eye.

"Good," said Luka. "Although I really wanted to burn one of you." He bounced the ball of fire in his palm and suddenly hurled it at one of the raiders. The man shrieked and turned to run, forgetting about the wall of branches behind him. When his feet didn't take him anywhere, he screamed and flailed at the branches with his fists. Just before the ball of fire hit him, Luka snapped his fingers, and there was a whooshing of air as the ball imploded. "Now, I feel better. Don't you?"

The man was panting in terror and eyeing Luka with distrust. "Trickster," he whispered and forked a sign against evil.

Luka grinned at him.

"You may return to your homes," said Meuhlnir with a wave in the direction of Potnsa. "But remember what I've said here today. If I must return to settle another fight, your village will suffer. If you do as you have promised, then you will prosper, and perhaps we will visit your town in due time."

Veethar made the deep-throated growling noise again, and Luka laughed aloud. Veethar waved his hand, and the branches returned to their normal shape.

"Run along home, now," said Luka with a sneer.

The men of Potnsa turned and began shuffling through the forest like children sent to their punishment. Veethar sat on his horse, still as if he were carved from granite, and glowered after them so that if any turned to look back, the last thing they would see of the Hyatlanes defenders was the God of Vengeance. When the raiders were no longer visible,

Veethar turned his horse to find Luka and Meuhlnir grinning at him.

"The lamb roars, eh, Veethar?" asked Meuhlnir.

Veethar blushed and averted his eyes, but his small, pleased smile could still be seen. He walked his horse toward the two brothers, ignoring the cheering of the Hyatlanes karls.

"Who knew you had all that in you," said Luka with a grin. "I might have to change my opinion of your furry friends."

Veethar shrugged and looked off into the woods, but his pleasure was still evident in his manner.

"That is one well-trained horse," said Meuhlnir.

Veethar shrugged his shoulders once again and looked down at the horse's mane. "I've worked a bit with him."

"I've never seen a horse more savage. How did you get him to do that thing on the man's cheek?"

Veethar met Meuhlnir's eye for a heartbeat, then his eyes danced away. "Well, he didn't like the thought of having a man's blood in his mouth, so I told him to make a good enough show, and he wouldn't have to actually bite."

Meuhlnir arched one of his eyebrows.

"We were trying to avoid bloodshed, right?" asked Veethar.

"Of course," said Luka. "The act you and your horse put on has won the day. We're just surprised you had such fierceness in you."

Veethar shrugged and spurred his horse back toward the village. As he passed through the rank of karls, they cheered him and patted the horse, even as they eyed it with fear.

The three Isir rode to the yarl's longhouse to share the news of the battle with Suel and the rest. The longhouse was well-built but had seen better days. The exterior of the building had been maintained with care, as that was something the villagers could do without disturbing the yarl, but the interior had fallen into a bit of disrepair.

The yarl was not to be seen but had left word that a celebratory feast would be held in their honor if they carried the day. The longhouse was bustling with the women of the village, giving the great hall a cursory cleaning and preparing the feast.

The yarl made his appearance just before the feast. He was an old man for the times, close to fifty, and looked broken and slump-shouldered. He gave them a curt smile and motioned for everyone to take their seats as the karls and their wives began to file into the room. He put Veethar on his right, and Meuhlnir on his left with Luka on the other side of his brother, as was the custom of the times—to seat the heroes of the day with the yarl at the head of the feasting table.

"Lord and Ladies of the Isir, honored karls, I greet you all. I am Yarl Varr, and I welcome you to my table."

Everyone made sounds of greeting and gratitude, except Veethar who sat in silence, looking like he'd rather be sitting in an anthill than at the head of the table.

"I understand from the *Veulva* that the battle was won without any injuries to my karls or to you, great lord," he said to Veethar.

Veethar grunted and looked at the table.

The yarl seemed confused by this behavior, so Meuhlnir put his hand on the yarl's forearm. "He prefers not to speak much and to a much smaller audience when he does."

Varr looked at Veethar for a moment, with questioning eyes. Then he turned to the table at large and gestured for everyone to eat.

"To be honest, he much prefers the solace of the forest to great halls or village squares," said Luka. "But he did have a lot to say to the raiders this afternoon. Didn't you, Veethar?" His smirk was not unkind.

Veethar glanced at him, and his nod was terse, but then his gaze found its way back to the plate in front of him.

"Hmm," muttered the yarl. "Tell me of the battle."

Meuhlnir cleared his throat and sat straighter in his chair. "We rode to confront the raiders and found them in a meadow not far to the southwest."

Yarl Varr nodded. "I know it."

"We asked your karls to wait at the edge of the meadow, and we three Isir rode into the center. I introduced myself, then Luka and Veethar. I, uh, expressed our friendship with your village. One of the Potnsar told us we were on the wrong side, and that their raid was one of vengeance. Veethar took exception to that."

Varr glanced in Veethar's direction but didn't seem to know how to respond to Veethar's introversion, so he took a long, gulping drink from the drinking horn on the table before him. "Indeed," he muttered.

"Veethar made it plain that they were not to seek out vengeance without his express approval," said Luka.

"Yes," said Meuhlnir. "I told them it was our desire for the two villages to become allies."

Yarl Varr stopped chewing the chunk of lamb he had in his mouth, and his face went red. He was glaring down at his plate, and he was gripping the table so hard the knuckles of his hands went white. "You did *what*?" he whispered in a broken, hoarse voice.

"My brother instructed the people of Potnsa to treat the people of Hyatlanes as allies—to guard one another and to come to each other's aid," said Luka, with far too much cheer for the mood at the head of the table.

"I know what the word ally means," snapped Varr. "What gives you the right to do this?"

Meuhlnir rolled his head until his gaze locked on the yarl's. "I am Isir," he said.

"Those animals murdered my son. They caused the death of my wife. I'll not be their ally. I will not rest until I have my vengeance!" The yarl had pushed back from the table and was glaring at Meuhlnir.

Everyone jumped as Veethar slammed his hand down on the table so hard that the plates and silverware jumped into the air. "Can it be that another mere man wants to usurp my domain?" he asked in civil voice, not much louder than a whisper.

Luka cackled and drummed his hands on the table. "This is great fun!" Meuhlnir slapped his hand heavily on his brother's thigh under the table and squeezed.

Veethar was looking Yarl Varr in the eye and looked as if he were doing nothing more than discussing the weather, but there was no doubt to anyone in the room, Yarl Varr included, that he was anything but apathetic. The sky-blue color of his irises began to thicken, to change.

Yarl Varr swallowed and made an effort to control his anger. "I assure you, Lord Veethar, that nothing could be further—"

"Good," snapped Veethar, his eyes glowing yellow and boring into the yarl's. "Because I would hate to think of what might happen otherwise. I've already fed my horse."

There were gasps at the other end of the table, but no one had shared the details of the day's events with the yarl, and he just looked confused by that seeming non-sequitur. "But they killed my son!" he managed to gasp.

"Yes," said Veethar, his eyes returning to their placid, blue state. "And you may take great comfort in the fact that those people must now defend your lands and die for you."

Meuhlnir nodded. "Two sets of karls will be quite a force in the field," he said. "Your two villages will prosper by this mutual defense, and your strength raiding villages in another land will be hard for any single village to match."

It was Yarl Varr's turn to looked down at his plate, avoiding everyone's eye. "And if they do not keep to the bargain?" he rasped.

Meuhlnir grinned at him. "After what they saw this afternoon, I doubt that will happen. Veethar can be quite convincing."

"And if they do fail to keep the bargain, I will visit them in wrath," said Luka.

"As will I," said Veethar.

"As will his horse," said Luka with a barbaric grin and a wink toward Veethar.

"What is this nonsense about a horse?" muttered Yarl Varr.

"Pray you never find out," snapped Luka, iron in his voice.

The yarl sat there and glowered at them for a long while and then pulled his chair back in to the table and set about finishing his meal. He didn't speak, he didn't look at any of them.

Meuhlnir glanced down the table to catch Suel's eye. She nodded her approval and favored him with a soft smile.

Freya glanced at Frikka and then stood and cleared her throat. "On this momentous occasion, we of the Isir would like to offer our favor to the village of Hyatlanes." She reached into her pack and brought out a horn she'd had the Tverkar craft for this trip. The sides of the horn were emblazoned with runes cast in silver. "If you have great need of the Isir, you may blow this horn, and we will be alerted. We will attend you as time permits."

Frikka stood and walked toward the kitchens.

Freya went to the head of the table and presented Yarl Varr with the horn, her walk as licentious as an expensive whore's. The old man looked up at her without gratitude, but took the horn and mumbled his thanks. He held the horn out toward Hildr. "The *Veulva* will have the honor of keeping the horn and blowing it in a time of need," he said in a voice devoid of emotion.

Freya nodded. "As you wish." She returned to her seat, her walk epicurean and seductive at the same time. She sank into her chair and grinned at Suel. Frikka returned to her seat and nodded to Freya with a small smile.

Three young women entered from the kitchens, but they were not dressed as drudges or as serving girls. Each wore a beautiful gown of Tverkar manufacture. Their hair was dressed in an elaborate manner with trinkets of silver and bone and stacked on top of their heads, exposing long, graceful necks. Each wore a fine golden chain around her neck that fit tightly so that a small ingot of gold nestled between their collarbones. Each ingot was engraved with Sif's sign—the rune for fertility.

Meuhlnir raised his brows at Sif, who grinned and tipped him a wink.

The three women approached Yarl Varr, who was staring at his plate and had not noticed them yet. It was obvious that he longed for the moment when he could excuse himself without giving offense. One by one, the women laid a hand on his shoulder and walked behind him, trailing their fingers across his shoulders. He looked up with surprise scrawled across his face. His gaze fell on Frikka, and her smile was as sweet as honey.

His head swung around, and he gazed at each of the young women in turn. He knew them, of course, they were from his village after all, but the way he looked at them was like he had never seen them before. It was an expression mirrored on the faces of many of the karls present.

"Yarl Varr," said Freya in dulcet tones. "We have asked a lot of you in a single afternoon. Our friendship is new to you and your village. We appreciate how malleable you've been to our needs. We appreciate your willingness to follow our lead with the politics of the region."

The yarl didn't say a thing, but his eyes drifted to Freya's face, and his expression was one of wonder.

"We've heard about your tragedy. It spoke to Frikka, Sif, and me. We can't have you pass from this realm without an heir. Your village needs the wise leadership of your line. We took it upon ourselves to ensure you will have an heir. And," she said with a significant pause, "companionship." She nodded to the three lovely young ladies standing behind him.

Frikka chuckled deep in her throat. "Never let it be said that we don't reward our friends."

Many of the karls present looked as if they wanted to find a way to become important to the Isir. Yarl

Varr couldn't keep his eyes from the three women, and for the first time, he smiled…

THIRTY-EIGHT

"The old man couldn't keep his eyes off the three beauties Frikka and Freya had caused to fall in love with him. He lived another thirty years, something that was unheard of at that time in Mithgarthr, and I believe it was because he couldn't bear the thought of leaving his three wives. They bore him many sons and daughters, and he had a happy life, despite its sad beginnings." Meuhlnir sighed and poured the dregs of the mead down his throat. "That woke my thirst."

"And what about the alliance?" I asked.

Meuhlnir grinned. "It was one of my more inspired moments. Hyatlanes and Potnsa became a powerhouse in the area. Varr married his son to the yarl of Potnsa's daughter, and their son became king of a large kingdom. Their descendants raided far and wide and gave birth to many legends of their own."

"And the horn? Did the Hyatlanes *Veulva* ever blow it?"

"Yes, many times over the years, though Hildr didn't live long after that initial visit. Erna became the next *Veulva* and served Hyatlanes with wisdom for many decades. That is how our visits started—we wanted to help the people on your *klith* to develop. We wanted to enable your people to avoid some of the mistakes the *Geumlu* made."

"Very noble," I said, trying to keep my voice neutral.

"The feeling of being so powerful was very hard to resist, though. It became...addictive." He shook his head. "Enough of Hyatlanes for now. We must see to the rest of our business."

Meuhlnir led us back down into the heat of Prokkr's smithy. We were met with dark glances of suspicion and outright hostility. One of the smiths even forked the sign of evil at us.

"Don't mind them," said Meuhlnir in a voice loud enough to be heard over the activity of the forge. "Some Tverkar are ignorant fools."

Shaking my head, I followed him into Prokkr's office.

"Hours, I said!" snapped Prokkr.

Meuhlnir sighed and made a place for himself to sit. "It's been hours, Tverkr. Show me what you have."

Grumbling, Prokkr, stepped away from his worktable, on which my pistols lay disassembled, and stuck his head out into the smithy proper. He bellowed at his underlings and, without another glance at us, returned to his worktable and began fiddling with the pistols again.

Two Tverkar came in, one carrying a box of helmets and one carrying a suit of mail and two bucklers, all made from the same bluish-white metal as Frikka's armor.

Meuhlnir inspected the items and then crooked an eyebrow at Prokkr. "And the rest?"

"Of course! I've had it all arranged. Get him fitted first."

The two smiths helped me into the suit of mail, which was so light it was like putting on cotton. The metal felt warm to the touch, almost as if it were alive. The two bucklers were about the size of dinner plates and clipped to custom mounts worked into the sleeves of the mail.

Meuhlnir looked it over with a critical eye and then smiled. "It will do, Master Smith. Now, those other items?"

I raised my eyebrows at him, but he just shook his head.

With a glare at Meuhlnir, the master smith stuck his head out the door and bellowed over the din. After a few minutes, another Tverkr came into the work room.

He was much shorter than Prokkr, but no less solidly built. He wore a sort of leather robe with runes embossed in the leather and stained with different colors. The handles for two daggers stuck from his belt.

"Master Althyof, I presume?" asked Meuhlnir.

"Yes. And you are Meuhlnir, He of the Thunder?"

Meuhlnir nodded. "Are you the same Althyof who slew the troll Fowrpauti?"

Althyof nodded gravely. "It is true."

"In single combat as the tale is told?"

Althyof nodded again.

"And you assisted in the binding of Friner?"

"What is this about?" asked Althyof with an air of impatience.

"I'll get to that when you answer my question," said Meuhlnir.

"Yes," snapped Althyof. "I bound the dragon Friner."

"Good," said Meuhlnir with a satisfied nod. "I'd like to hire you."

Althyof sneered. "I've spent all afternoon in your employ, Master of Thunder. What else can I do for you?"

"I don't want you as an enchanter. I want your service as a *runeskowld*."

"I don't travel anymore."

Meuhlnir pulled a bulging purse from his belt. "I bet we can come to an agreement."

Althyof looked at the purse with avarice. "Gold, not silver?"

"Of course," said Meuhlnir with a small smile. "One purse to enter my service, a quarter purse per week until the job is done."

"What is the job?"

"Does it matter?" Meuhlnir bounced the purse in his hand, making the gold inside clank together.

Althyof licked his lips. "Dangerous."

It wasn't really a question, but Meuhlnir nodded his head anyway. "A heroic task. Reputations will be made brighter, songs will be sung of it."

Althyof tried to look uninterested, but each bounce of the purse drew his eyes like moths to a flame. "One half purse per week."

"One quarter per week with an extra quarter every four weeks."

Althyof nodded. "Done." He looked at me, and his expression soured. "Weird weapons you wield, but Master Prokkr says they are no less deadly."

I nodded. "In the right hands, yes."

Althyof sniffed in vainglory. "We shall see," he said.

"Indeed, you will," said Meuhlnir.

Althyof looked at the three Alfar and smirked. "Don't worry, lads, I'll be there to protect you from now on."

Urlikr scoffed. Yowtgayrr met my eyes and then rolled his.

Althyof snickered and then looked at Meuhlnir. "Shall we see to your items, then?" He opened his satchel and pulled out a long leather cloak. "One cloak, enchanted as you asked." He turned to Master Prokkr. "And one belt, as you asked."

Meuhlnir took the cloak and spread it across my shoulders. He fastened it with a chain of the bluish-white metal. "This cloak, Hank, you will find to be of great use. I had Althyof enchant it to take the mantle of your pain."

"Within limits," said Althyof.

As the cloak settled on my shoulders, I felt energy flood my body and all the telltale little aches and pains that had become part of my everyday existence disappeared. I felt like I could run for miles. I laughed and shook my head in wonder.

Meuhlnir nodded. "Care to explain the rest?"

Althyof grunted. "Simple enough." He ran his hands down a series of runes embossed inside the front of the cloak. "This series here allows you to twist your fettle."

"Twist my fettle?"

"Yes, just twitch the edges of the cloak like so…" The Tverkr mimed pulling the cloak in front of him. "Or use the mnemonic: *vakt*."

"I'm still on the twisting my fettle part."

"It means to shift yourself slightly away. To become out of phase with reality. You will appear to have changed into smoke," said Meuhlnir.

"Okay." I twitched the cloak like Althyof had mimicked. Something crackled across my skin, a whisper of a touch, and then was gone.

"To reverse the process," said Althyof, "just repeat the activation."

I felt like I was floating in a sea of thick oil. The air seemed to clutch at me when I moved my arms. "Can I speak?" My voice sounded ethereal. "Too weird," I laughed.

"It will take getting used to," said the Tverkr. "Now, quit playing around and let me explain what I've done to your engines of war."

I twitched the edges of the cloak and felt the same whispery touch on my skin as I regained solid form. "What do you mean?"

Prokkr picked up the belt Althyof had brought and with deft movements, buckled it around my waist. It was equipped with two holsters, one above each hip, pouches for ammo and empty magazines, and funny little clips for full magazines. He had the pistols reassembled and, as he held them up, light glinted off the runes he'd etched into every flat surface.

Prokkr put the HK .40 into my left holster. "This one is named Krati. This part," he pointed to the plastic grip, "is an offensive material."

"Plastic," I said.

"Krati could only be enchanted for speed of use, because of it." He picked up the Kimber with a glowing expression. "This beauty, however, Althyof worked for speed, accuracy, and by replacing the wooden grips with grips carved from the talons of a *hrisvelgr*, augmented the penetrating power of the projectiles fired from it."

Prokkr handed the Kimber to me. The material of the grips felt smooth and cool against my palms. "What is a *hrisvelgr*?" I asked in a small voice.

"A large, predatory bird," said Althyof. "Your projectiles should be able to penetrate armor, shields, perhaps even dragon scales."

I stood there looking down at the etchings, wondering what each one meant.

"Kunknir is what I've named it. It means 'swaying one' in the *Gamla Toonkumowl*."

"Gungnir? Like Odin's spear?" I looked at Meuhlnir.

Meuhlnir shook his head. "I don't know this Odin."

"Your father?"

"My father was named Buri."

"Buri? Not Odin?"

"Buri. My mother was Bestla. Why?"

"Well, according to the Vikings, Odin was the son of Borr and Bestla and the father of Paltr, Huthr, Veethar, and Tor—well, you. Borr was Buri's son."

Meuhlnir shook his head. "I've never heard of Odin, but Borr was the father of the Black Queen and her sister Freya. No relation to my father. You already know Veethar is not my brother."

I grunted. "I guess they got more than your name wrong."

Meuhlnir shrugged. "They had an oral tradition and a ridiculously short life span. It's hard to maintain accurate information with those handicaps."

THIRTY-NINE

When we emerged from the Vault of *Preer,* we could hear bedlam above us. We crowded and jostled our way up the steps, out of the longhouse, and into chaos.

Horses whinnied and screamed. Smoke and the wails of thralls wafted through the air like pollen in the spring. There was a confusion of bodies running to and fro, yelling and, in some cases, howling their fear at the heavens.

Althyof pulled two long, thin daggers from the twin sheaths at his belt and started singing in a very strange tongue. A cadmium red aura faded into existence around the blades. The Tverkr nodded once to Meuhlnir and moved off into the smoke, seeming more to dance away than to walk. Meuhlnir grunted and walked in the other direction, his hammer out and his eyes sparkling with pent up lightning.

The three Alfar that had sworn to be my bodyguards drew their weapons and took up positions around me. Urlikr was to my left and a step behind. Skowvithr stood next to him on my right. Yowtgayrr stood between me and everything else, swinging his blades in small, experimental circles.

"No," I said. "That isn't going to work, Yowtgayrr. You are in my field of fire."

He shook his head. "My place is between you and whatever wants to harm you."

"No, trust me. I can take care of most of what I can see. I need protection for the directions I can't see."

Yowtgayrr looked me in the eye for a protracted moment and shrugged. "As you say."

"I will shout 'reloading' when my weapons need ammunition. At that point, feel free to step forward. I'll then shout 'ready' when I've reloaded, and you'll need to step back at that time. I'll try to remember to yell 'firing' before I shoot. These are loud, and it can be distracting at first."

"Understood," said Yowtgayrr.

"Okay. Since the others have taken the right and the left, we'll go straight forward." I put words to action, with the three Alfar close behind me, trying to see everything at once.

I pulled my pistols and made them ready. The small bucklers clipped to my forearms were a bit awkward, but didn't seem to affect my movement. I could hear the strange, shrieking howl of the demons that had pursued us across the plain. "Demons," I said to Yowtgayrr.

"And Svartalfar," he said with a scowl. "I can smell them."

"Then there is likely a dragon around, too. A big white one, but he might not be able to fly. I met him before."

Yowtgayrr nodded, face grave.

We pressed on through the smoke, seeing dark shadows of running men, but unable to tell who or what they were. We were moving toward the large stables. Flames licked at the sides of the wooden building.

Three neckless, matte black figures loomed at me from the smoke. "Firing!" I shouted pulling the triggers of both my weapons twice. The roar of the firearms added to the din, and two of the three demons spun in opposite directions and fell to the ground, their chartreuse ichor splattering across the ground.

The middle one let loose with one of those eerie wailing shrieks and then sprinted forward. Something was wrong with the way it moved—not just that its limbs were too short, but something insectile and twitchy in how its muscles bunched and relaxed. It held its stubby little arms out in front of its too long torso, hooking its three fingers into talons. Its mouth was just a straight slit in the middle of what passed for its face, and I fired Kunknir into that slit at point-blank range. The thing's head deflated like a popped balloon, and its ichor splashed over its shoulders as it fell to the ground.

The three Alfar stood staring—shifting their eyes between me and the bodies of the demons. Yowtgayrr nodded and pointed forward. I turned to meet the two Svartalfar menacing us. Their eyes tracked Kunknir and Krati as I spun toward them, and they began to circle in opposite directions—splitting up to keep me from targeting them both at the same time. Unlike the demons, their movements were graceful and showed an economy of movement like a trained dancer or master martial artist.

"Firing," I said. I snapped two shots with Krati at the one circling to the left—more to distract him than to do real damage—and he dove to the ground, impossibly fast. Giving my attention to the Svartalf circling to the right, I shot him once in the face with Kunknir.

"Behind us!" shouted Skowvithr. Steel clashed on steel as the Alfar met the threat.

I swung Kunknir across the front of my body and squeezed off a round at the remaining Svartalf. I didn't have a good shot, and it was more to make him keep his head down than anything else, but the bullet took him in the center of his chest, flinging him to the ground with a splatter of charcoal colored blood.

Behind me, my three Alfar protectors fought in a fierce battle with five other Svartalfar. Yowtgayrr spun in tight, graceful circles, keeping three of the Svartalfar busy, slashing at them and parrying their attacks. He made them look clumsy—like children fighting a master. Urlikr decapitated his opponent with a scissor-like motion of his longsword and dagger and then moved to help Yowtgayrr. Pale rose blood dripped from a shallow cut across Skowvithr's cheek.

The Svartalf facing Skowvithr held a black, single-edged short sword in each hand, and whirled them about, keeping them in constant motion, crouched low to the ground. With a cry, he sprang at Skowvithr, hacking at him with both blades. Skowvithr parried and fell back from the onslaught, eyes wide, mouth panting. I pointed Kunknir at the Svartalf and shot him in the chest. Skowvithr nodded his thanks and wiped at the blood streaming down his cheek.

Yowtgayrr and Urlikr were keeping the three remaining Svartalfar busy with feints and vicious, sweeping cuts with their longswords. The Svartalfar fell back into the swirling smoke, and we followed them in.

Subharmonics from a basso roar made our weapons vibrate in our hands. "Dragon!" I yelled. "We can't fight it in this smoke."

"Agreed," said Yowtgayrr.

We backed toward the corrals. The dragon roared somewhere in the smoke as it pounded toward us.

The beast was moving fast, and we were moving slow. We turned and sprinted toward the corral.

Thunder boomed, and lightning lit up the smoke on the other side of the paddock. Althyof wasn't visible, his glowing, cartoon daggers not withstanding, nor were any of the others, but the sounds of battle surrounded us.

We broke out of the smoke and leapt over the fence surrounding the closest corral. We ran toward the opposite side, hoping to put as much distance between the edge of the smoke and us. Behind us, the dragon let loose another deafening cry.

We reached the far edge of the corral and turned around, putting the corral fence to our backs. Yowtgayrr stood to my left, while Urlikr and Skowvithr took up positions on my right. I had nine or ten rounds left in Krati, but only two or three rounds left in Kunknir and didn't want to try reloading with a dragon charging at me, so I ejected the magazine into the pouch Prokkr had added to the belt.

As the weight of the magazine hit the pouch, one of the little clips holding the magazines for Kunknir rotated in a clever way, making the magazine stick forward at an angle, so I could just slide the gun down over it. As I did so, the clip released the magazine. Prokkr was a genius.

The dragon thundered, sounding very close, but I still couldn't see it. Seven Svartalfar edged out of the smoke on our far-right flank but didn't seem to see us, so I held my fire—I wanted all the rounds I had for the dragon.

The Svartalfar edged farther to the right, eyes glued to the smoke. I wasn't sure if they were stalking someone or trying to avoid a pissed-off dragon, but as long as they continued to ignore us, I was happy to leave them be.

The smoke seemed to solidify and bulge in front of us. Then there was a strange growling noise. It sounded like a big, pissed-off dog, only much louder and deeper in pitch.

The smoke swirled away and there the dragon stood. It had its long, sinuous neck arched so that its head was only eighteen inches from the ground, and it was glowering right at me. It didn't seem to notice the Alfar on either side, or if it did, it didn't care a whit about them. It opened its mouth.

I started pulling the triggers of each weapon as fast as I could. Bullets poured out of both guns, and I could see rounds from Krati ricocheting from the dragon's scales down the left side of its neck. At the same time, slugs from Kunknir were slamming into its open mouth, shattering its fangs and pulping its tongue and lower jaw. The dragon jerked its head up and to the left, trying to get its mouth and face out of the stream of lead I was throwing at it.

Rounds from Krati, which couldn't penetrate its scales, threw sparks into the dragon's right eye. I was still firing both pistols, intending to empty both magazines into the dragon's face if I could, and rounds from Kunknir seemed to curve in midflight to slam into the side of the beast's head. Unlike the lead slung from Krati, the Kunknir's bullets cut right through the dragon's scales as if they were tissue paper.

The dragon screamed in pain and hatred. It leapt upwards, its powerful hind legs propelling it about fifteen feet in the air, and then snapped its wings open and cupped them to catch as much air as possible. The gunshot wounds I'd inflicted a few days earlier were almost healed, but the fresh, baby-pink membrane wasn't strong enough yet for flight, and the new skin ruptured, tearing even bigger holes in the wing than the bullets had.

The dragon shrieked in pain and flopped on its opposite side in midair. It tucked its good wing close to its body and fell into the smoke. Wood splintered and tore, what I assumed was the stable being crushed under the dragon's weight, and then the air rent with screams of pain and rage from the beast.

"Hank, to the left!" screamed Yowtgayrr.

Four of the matte black demons had snuck up our left flank while we'd been focused on the dragon. Two of them swept their talon-like fingers at Yowtgayrr, and the other two came straight at me.

I pulled both triggers and screamed the activation word for my cloak in desperation. Slugs slammed into the demons, the ones from Krati going a little wild, but still probably fatal shots. The bullets from Kunknir slammed into the demon's center of mass, spraying its chartreuse ichor through the air. As the cloak started to "twist my fettle," the ichor started to fall on me, and searing pain erupted from the left side of my face.

I couldn't think, but I knew what to do from long practice at dealing with agony. I screamed.

Urlikr and Skowvithr leapt to Yowtgayrr's aid, passing right through me. The three Alfar dispatched the two remaining demons as my ethereal sounding cries of pain echoed across the corral.

As the two bodies fell, my cloak's enchantment wore off, my fettle untwisted, and I fell on top of the two bullet-riddled bodies at my feet. The pain was still there, but endorphins, dynorphins, and enkephalins had started doing their collective jobs of diminishing the pain. Sweat began to pour off me and vomit splattered across the ground and mixed with the demons' chartreuse ichor.

"Hank! Your eye!" panted Skowvithr.

Agony beat from my left eye socket in waves, and I staggered. Yowtgayrr took me by the arm and half-supported me, half drug me over to a trough filled with water. He started splashing water across the left side of my face.

Ichor, gooped in my left eye socket, reacted with the water, hissing and spitting flecks of acid in every direction. I gasped and tried to push Yowtgayrr's hands away, but his grip was like iron. I covered my eye with my hands.

"Hank! I must wash it out!" shouted Yowtgayrr. "Skowvithr, get his hands."

Skowvithr took both my wrists and wrested my hands clear of my face. I struggled as more water seemed to ignite in my eye socket. I shouldn't have been fighting them, but the lizard part of my brain insisted.

The water kept coming, as did the pain it caused. Skowvithr held on with a grip like iron. I was soaked through, but still, the water came. The pain decreased at last. I was exhausted by the time I regained my senses, and instead of holding me by the wrists, Skowvithr had me under the arms and was keeping me from falling on my face.

Urlikr was scrubbing something in the water trough, and eventually, my exhausted mind realized he was trying to clean the ichor off my cloak. Yowtgayrr was standing bent over, hands on his knees and taking big gulps of air.

"Leave it, Urlikr," said Yowtgayrr with exhaustion and worry in his voice. "We have to get Hank to cover."

Urlikr pulled the leather cloak out of the trough and flipped it around my shoulders. When it landed, more of the pain dissipated, and I sighed with relief.

Yowtgayrr picked up Skowvithr's weapons, put them in their sheaths and then retrieved his own longsword and dagger from where he'd dropped them. "Urlikr, you take the rear. I'll go ahead, and Skowvithr will help Hank. We are headed back to the longhouse, if it still stands, and will retreat down to the Vault of *Preer*. If necessary, we will take Hank to Alfhaym and then return to help what survivors there are."

"Krati and Kunknir," I whispered.

Skowvithr shifted me so that my left arm was across his shoulders. "In their sheath-things," he said. "Don't worry."

Some of my strength returned as my pain levels came closer to the threshold the cloak was able to handle, and I took more of my own weight on my own two feet. We set off toward the edge of the smoke, in the direction that would take us back to the longhouse.

"Dragon?" I asked.

"Don't worry about that now," said Skowvithr.

The Svartalfar I'd seen earlier were no longer visible, and we slipped into the smoke without incident. Yowtgayrr walked in front of us with the grace of a big cat hunting prey. I strained my ears but didn't really have the energy to distill the chaotic sounds I could hear into anything sensible. Horses galloped past us in the smoke, trumpeting their fear, but there was nothing we could do for them.

Yowtgayrr stopped short and pointed to our right. Something tall and ugly came at us from out of the smoke. It was taller than a man and had black horns coming out of the side of its head, and I decided it must be what Meuhlnir had called a fire demon in his tale about Muspetlshaymr.

The fire demon saw us and raised a sword that looked like it was more jagged scrap metal than the work of a smith. He opened his mouth and bellowed, and I could see the fiery glow dancing in the back of his throat.

Yowtgayrr set himself to meet the demon's charge, but I pulled Kunknir from its holster and fired four times. The reports rolled through the smoke like thunder, and the bullets slammed into the demon's head rather than center of mass, which is what I'd aimed at. The demon's head rocked back on his shoulders, and he stood up very straight and then stiffened before falling over backward like a felled tree.

The longhouse loomed out of the smoke ahead of us, and we started toward it.

The dragon roared from behind us, sounding close. Yowtgayrr whirled, his eyes scanning the smoke.

"Can we make it back to the longhouse?" I asked.

"If we don't meet any other demons or Svartalfar on the way," whispered Yowtgayrr. "I think it is a bad risk."

"You want to fight it?" asked Urlikr, sounding like that was the last thing he expected.

"Hank drove it off before," said Skowvithr. He pointed me at the ground and helped me down. His longsword made a hissing sound as he drew his weapon and stepped to the side.

I pulled Krati and made sure it was ready to fire. My hands shook with the weight of the pistols in my hands, so I bent my legs in front of me and rested my elbows on my knees. "I'll do my best," I said. "Just keep clear."

"I'm not sure we shouldn't engage the beast, at least to keep it distracted," said Yowtgayrr.

I shook my head and opened my mouth to speak but said nothing as the dragon's head snaked out of the smoke. It was dripping blood and chunks of gore from its mouth and the ruined left side of its face. Its eye beckoned, but I kept my gaze firmly on its snout. I raised my guns, but before I could fire, a strange song lilted from the smoke to my right.

Althyof whirled out of the smoke, daggers glowing red, and danced in front of us. When he met the dragon's gaze, he stopped and faced the great beast. His singing gained volume and seemed to take on an insistent note. The dragon made a strange mewling sound and tried to jerk its head away, but only twitched to the side a miniscule amount, unable to break eye contact with Althyof.

The Tverkr began to move, increasing the tempo of the cacophony of caterwauling clamor his song had become. The dragon's head seemed to weave back and forth as Althyof danced back and forth in front of it, weaving his daggers around in time to the ever-increasing cadence of his dance. The dragon made one more mewling sound, and its nostrils twitched.

Althyof stopped singing and began to chant—sounding all the world like a strange form of Gregorian chant in which the monks valued harsh sounds and discordant notes. The dragon's eyes seemed to lose focus but remained glued to the Tverkr. As the chant reached a tumultuous zenith, Althyof whirled forward, arms out straight at his sides, daggers held point-back in his fists, making him look like some kind of whirling saw blade.

The dagger blades seemed to stretch and morph until they formed long red blades. Althyof shouted a few more syllables and then leapt at the dragon's neck. The red blades chopped and sliced through the dragon's scales and flung dragon blood in great, blanketing arcs. He kept spinning and chopping and slicing, and the blood kept splattering and sloshing and splashing until the head of the great white beast fell to the ground with a muted *thud*. Off in the smoke, we heard a scream of anguish and then the crash of the dragon's body impacting the ground.

Covered in gore, Althyof turned and walked toward us. His daggers shrank back to their normal sizes, the red glow becoming more of a muted red outline again. He stopped and looked down at me and made a little moue. "Not to worry, Isir. All is not lost."

"We were taking him back to the longhouse," said Yowtgayrr.

"Of course, you were," sneered the Tverkr. "Shall I escort you and keep you safe?"

"How much gold would that cost us?" asked Yowtgayrr in acidic tones.

Althyof laughed. "I like you," he said. "Most Alfar don't know how to speak properly, but it seems you have the knack."

"Thanks," said Yowtgayrr.

"Oh, don't go and ruin it all now, Alf," snapped Althyof.

Skowvithr helped me to my feet again, and we all walked back to the longhouse without seeing another soul. We found Sif and Frikka inside the great hall. They'd set up a triage of sorts and were seeing to the wounds of about a dozen of the estate's thralls. The wounds ranged from stabs, slashes, and broken bones to cold and acid burns.

Skowvithr helped me to one of the empty benches that were serving as hospital beds and beckoned to Frikka. She came over and squinted at my face and eye. She shook her head and stood looking at me, arms akimbo.

"This is beyond my ken," she said at last. She turned on her heel and walked over to where Sif was ministering to a bloody thrall. She touched Sif on the elbow and whispered something in her ear, nodding her head in my direction. She looked over and nodded curtly, handing a roll of bandages to Frikka.

Sif came and squatted beside my bench. Disquiet danced across her features as she looked at my face. "Did you never learn to duck in Mithgarthr?" she asked. Her tone was light, but her manner expressed only gravitas. She leaned closer and used her thumb and finger to force my left eye wide open. She turned to Skowvithr, and her expression changed to one of anger. "I thought you three had sworn to protect him?" she demanded.

Skowvithr hung his head but didn't reply.

"Nothing they could have done," I said. "Four of those new demons flanked us while we were fighting the dragon. I shot two of them at point-blank range, and their ichor splattered all over me."

Sif grunted, but continued to stare at the Alf for a moment, making her displeasure quite clear. "What happened next?"

Yowtgayrr put his hand on my left shoulder, startling me. I have no idea if he'd been there the whole time or had just walked up. "He had activated his cloak and turned to smoke as he fired, so we didn't know this was happening. I was engaged with two other demons, and when Hank turned to smoke, Urlikr and Skowvithr came to my aid. As we put the two demons down, Hank started to scream, but his fettle was still twisted. When the enchantment wore off, his skin was smoking and bubbling like boiling stew. I grabbed him and started splashing water from the trough in his face to try to clear the gunk off him."

"And how did the ichor react to the water?" Sif asked.

"It seemed to resist the water," said Yowtgayrr. "And it seemed to cause Hank more pain."

"It burned," I grunted. "Acidic, I think."

"I had to restrain him so Yowtgayrr could finish getting the stuff off him," said Skowvithr.

"Eventually, we got all the ichor clear of his eye and washed off his skin," said Yowtgayrr. "I fear we weren't quick enough to save the eye."

Sif looked at me with compassion and took my hand in both of hers. "Your fear is justified, Alf. His eye is dead, and I fear for the skin around it."

The words hammered through me like an avalanche. Hearing that I had an incurable disease had been bad. Learning that the disease was a curse that had been inflicted on me had been upsetting. Nothing, however, had prepared me to be blinded. "Is there nothing you can do, Sif?"

"Nothing for the eye. I'm sorry, Hank, but the damage is beyond my power to heal. The skin, however, I might be able to stop any further damage, and minimize the scarring, but I'll have to get the eye out of there. It is poisoning the surrounding flesh, and the longer it remains, the smaller the chance of stopping the advance of the poison."

The words stunned me. Not only blind but disfigured. "Do what you must," I whispered.

Sif laid me back on the bench and walked away. She came back and held a drinking horn to my lips that contained a very foul-smelling tea inside. "Drink this, Hank."

I took huge gulps, fighting the urge to spit it out, and then fought the urge to vomit it up. When the worst of the urge to purge had passed, I was already feeling groggy. "You should bottle that and sell it," I slurred. "Make a killing."

Sif patted my shoulder. "Close your eyes, Hank."

I did what she told me.

When I awoke later, my right eye was gummed shut. I pried it open with my right hand. The three Alfar sat around me, looking dejected. Althyof was nowhere to be seen, but Sif, Frikka, and Yowrnsaxa were moving around the darkened hall, seeing to the needs of the wounded.

"He's awake," said Yowtgayrr.

"Good," boomed Meuhlnir, which earned him shushes from his wives and Frikka. "Sorry," he said at lower volume. "My ears still ring with thunder."

He came around my right side and squatted next to the bench. "Doing all right, Hank?" he asked.

I shrugged and gestured at my left eye socket.

"Yes. That's very unfortunate."

"The estate?" I asked.

"Don't worry, we repelled the attack. There is some damage—some burnt outbuildings and the stable was crushed somehow, but none of the attackers escaped. Veethar and his forest made sure of that."

"Good," I whispered. "Did Veethar lose many?"

"Horses? No. Just a few who were trapped in the stables. The attackers didn't seem much concerned with the herds."

"No, I mean people."

"Oh. Some thralls perished, but no karls. Of the Isir, your injuries were the worst. None of the Alfar took serious damage, and Althyof acquitted himself well."

I nodded and was rewarded for it with a splitting ache in the center of my forehead.

"Your battle with the dragon saved many lives. You should be proud," said someone standing behind my head.

"Yes," said Meuhlnir. "You did quite well there."

I shook my head and winced. "Althyof killed it."

"That may be, but your actions allowed the Tverkr the opening," said the man behind me.

"Veethar knows of what he speaks, Hank. And you should be honored he chooses to speak at such length."

"All this, the attack on Trankastrantir, the attack here, this is all because of me."

"No," said Veethar. "This all started centuries before you were born." Veethar stepped into my range of vision. His armor was covered in blood, and his face was still splattered with gore.

Meuhlnir nodded and grasped my forearm. "You've heard some of the stories already, Hank. You know that the Black Bitch has an agenda with us all."

"But still, she's left you all alone for centuries, as you say."

"That's because she was not here," said Meuhlnir. "She was on your *klith*, doing whatever she and my brother desired there."

"Today's events have just underscored to all concerned that we can no longer afford to ignore the Dragon Queen," said Frikka, who had walked over to the foot of my bed. She glanced at Veethar, who nodded. "Now, gentlemen, I'm under orders from Sif to drive you all away, with sticks if needs be, so that Hank can recover in peace."

"It's okay," I said.

She looked at me with an expression that I'd seen on Jane's face more than once. I knew better than to argue.

"I am also under orders to make you drink another horn of Sif's brew if you resist."

"Oh, good god, no," I said, and everyone laughed.

FORTY

O ur five Alfar body doubles left the next morning, each wearing a helm that had been glamored so that they looked, smelled, and appeared to move like one of the original five in our party. Althyof had tsked and muttered while Meuhlnir had cast the glamor and had then sneered at Meuhlnir's look of irritation.

Later that day, my head finally stopped spinning from whatever had been in that drinking horn, and Sif pronounced me fit to sit up and perhaps move around a little. Skowvithr set up a chair for me outside so that I could get some fresh air, and get away from the hustle and bustle of the makeshift hospital in the great hall.

I sat and watched the uninjured thralls and karls working the herd and integrating the new breeding stock Veethar had brought back with him. The stable was a mess of smashed timbers and broken beams. The dragon's talons had scored deep gouges in the ground. On the other side of the road, piles of Svartalfar and demons burned, casting a sickly-sweet odor over the compound.

The dragon lay where it had fallen and was now being butchered and harvested by a drove of Tverkar who had come from Nitavetlir for that express purpose. One of them was pulling what teeth and fangs remained from the beast's head, grumping and cursing all the while at the "utter waste of materials" my bullets had caused. Another was busy cutting scales from the dragon's body and casting black looks at the one harvesting the teeth. Another grumpy Tverkr was wading through the gore and flesh of the dragon, hunting for vital organs that could be used for some arcane purpose. Yet another took the beast's talons and nodded with glee as he extracted each one. Two more stood around and jeered at the rest, urging them to hurry up so the two could get at the bones.

Althyof approached me, pausing once or twice to mutter and curse at the Tverkar butchering the dragon's corpse. He wore his runed mail and his scuffed leather boots. His daggers were sheathed on either hip. He had what looked like an old leather strap in one hand. "Hello, lad," he said to me when he drew close. "How's the head?"

"Fair," I said. "The world seems a bit flat."

"This will help with that," he said, holding out the leather strap.

The leather looked well-worn, and I noticed that the strap was narrow on both ends but wider in the middle. "An eyepatch?"

Althyof puffed out his chest. "This is no mere eyepatch. You see only the comfortable old leather."

I peered at the strap, looking for runes decorating its surface.

"I am the best enchanter in all the realms," he said with pride. That drew him a black look from the Tverkr pulling the dragon's teeth, but Althyof either didn't see it or didn't care. Althyof smiled and showed me the back of the strap. Runes had been burned into it in the wider section. "It's nothing elaborate, but when you look at something while wearing this, your depth perception will be true." He glanced at the top of my head and then buckled the two ends together and slipped it over my hair.

The world lost the flat feel I had just been getting accustomed to. I turned my head back and forth, focusing on the near and then the far. Though it would take some getting used to, it worked. "Thank you, Althyof!" I said. "I would offer to pay you, but...well, I don't have any funds here."

"I've also made you these," he said, holding up a leather wrapped parcel. "These are to help your wife and son when we find them." He handed the package to me.

I untied the thin leather strap. Inside, there was a long, thin dagger and a platinum ring. Runes seemed to dance along the blade of the dagger, and I could see more runes inscribed on the inside of the ring's band. "Enchanted?"

"I *am* sort of known for it, you know," said Althyof with exasperation. "The dagger will allow your son to become invisible, so that he may avoid having to fight with it. The ring is...special. You must decide to give it to your wife or to keep it from her."

"Special?"

"Yes. The ring will cause the wearer to become something like a *filkya*—a spirit whose essence becomes entwined with the fate of a person. She will become entwined in *your* fate, Hank."

"Linked to my fate? What does that mean?"

"It means she will share what the Nornir have woven in the skein of fate for you. She will become tied to your life, she will live as long as you do, but *only* as long as you do."

I shook my head. "It sounds romantic in a teenager kind of way, but it sounds like there's tremendous risk to giving her the ring."

Althyof shrugged. "Yes. There are also tremendous benefits, both for you and your wife. She will be your *skyuldur vidnukona*—your shield maiden. She will share in the gifts of the Isir, but more than that, she will become very powerful. She will gain the power to sow confusion and doubt in battle, to intimidate opponents. She will be able to heal great injuries, and she will be able to cause death by the strength of her will alone. She will be granted the power to travel to your side on raven wings."

"That's... That's incredible, Althyof. A very powerful gift."

"Yes, but as I say, one you must decide to give or not to give. The responsibility is too great."

I pursed my lips and looked down at the ring. "Can it be given to someone else?"

Althyof shook his head. "No. It is for your wife and your wife alone. I've never met her, but it is within my power to focus an enchantment thus."

"I can't thank you enough, Althyof. Somehow, I will find a way to repay you." I said it knowing full well how a Tverkr might interpret such a statement.

The Tverkr looked down at me with a deliberate, thoughtful expression, and then tipped me a wink. "Don't tell anyone," he whispered, "but sometimes Tverkar do a thing simply because it's the right thing to do. We do like to keep up appearances, so I apologize in advance for how I'm about to act."

"What?" I said, a bit confused.

"Well!" he yelled. "You'd just better come up with a way, Mr. *Kanka-ee*. I don't work for free, and if you don't want to pay, then I'll just take the enchantment back and replace it with a curse! You have one week. You hear me, Isir?" His face was bunched in what looked like authentic anger, and no one would be able to tell from his tone that he didn't mean every word.

He glared at me for a moment, and then turned on his heel and stalked away. The Tverkar harvesting the dragon laughed and cast snide looks in my direction.

"What was that about?" asked Mothi, coming around the side of the longhouse. He had a bandage on his forehead and another on his left hand.

"It's nothing," I said. "The silly Tverkr did some work for me without getting payment up front." I made sure the Tverkar all heard.

Mothi squatted beside me. "Truly?" he whispered.

"No," I said matching his volume level. "He enchanted this ugly thing to give me back the depth perception from my left eye."

Mothi's eyebrows arched in surprise. "No one asked him to do so?"

"He said that even Tverkar sometimes do a thing just because it is the right thing to do."

"Then why the scene?"

I smiled. "He said he had to keep up appearances."

Mothi laughed long and loud.

"What happened?" I asked, pointing at his bandages when his laughs wound down to chuckles.

"It's nothing," he said with a shrug. "I really hate Svartalfar. Sometimes, I let my fury get the better of me."

"And that leads to bandages?"

He chuckled. "Yes, it does. When I'm furious, I tend to fight without a thought for defense." He gestured at his head. "I got this one by leaping into the middle of five of the swarthy bastards." He held up his bandaged hand. "This was just a bite from another one."

"It bit you?"

"Well, I was shoving my hand down his throat at the time. I guess it was a natural reflex."

"Oh," I said. I had no idea how to respond to that.

Mothi looked toward the bonfire of bodies. "He won't be biting anyone else, though."

It was hard for me to reconcile the jovial, friendly character I'd come to associate with Mothi, with the picture of a battle-mad warrior shoving his hand down someone's throat in order to kill them. "Why do you hate Svartalfar so much?"

Mothi shook his head. "That's a story for another time. But, tell me, Hank, how do you feel?"

I thought about that for a second, taking a quick mental inventory. "Pretty good, all things considered."

"And your head?"

I shrugged. "It seems to be okay. Why?"

Mothi plucked a stone from the ground and bounced it in his bandaged palm. "Mother Yowrnsaxa has news."

"Oh?" I arched my brows at him.

"She was trying to gather intelligence on Luka's location, and, well...we know where your family is being held, and it's much closer than we thought."

I lunged up straight in the chair. "Where, Mothi? Where are they?"

Mothi made placating gestures with his hands. "They are in the Pitra Empire, which is the northernmost country on the continent. It is bordered to the south by Takmar's Horse Plains and Kvia in the west."

"Takmar's Horse Plains was where Veethar was rounding up new stock?"

Mothi nodded. "Father has long suspected that Pitra was dealing with *Briethralak Oolfur* in Fankelsi. Now, it seems his suspicions are a certainty."

"So, the queen now has allies on this continent? Her exile hasn't held up very well."

Mothi looked grim. "No, it seems it hasn't." He sighed.

"How do we get there?"

"The Vault of *Preer* has several possibilities, but we don't know what kind of intelligence was gathered in the attack. It might be best to take a *proo* to somewhere somewhat far from your family's location and travel the rest of the way in secret."

"How long will the glamor on the Alfar fool her?" I asked.

"We have no way of guessing that." Mothi shrugged and tossed the rock away. "It may be eternal, and it might not fool her at all."

"In that case, it seems like we should take the *proo* closest to their location and just grab them and then get away."

Mothi shrugged again and stood. "Father and Veethar are discussing strategy as we speak. Perhaps we should join them?"

"Why didn't they come get me?" I groused, getting to my feet. I swayed a bit, and Mothi put out a hand to steady me.

"It won't do your family any good if you pass out in the middle of their rescue," he said.

"No," I said. "But then again, that will not happen." My tone was fierce.

Mothi's mouth twisted in a little moue of concern, but he kept his concerns to himself. "They are in Veethar's map room."

"Lead on, cousin," I said.

He squinted his eyes at me for a moment and then turned on his heel and led me into the longhouse. We crossed the great room, nodding to Sif and Yowrnsaxa who were tending to the remaining wounded. Mothi led me to a wide hallway that had doors sprouting off every thirty feet or so.

Veethar's map room was decorated with pictures of deep forest meadows and copses of trees unspoiled by human hands. Veethar, Meuhlnir, and Yowtgayrr were clustered around a hip-height oak table that was positioned in the center of the room. A tanned skin was unrolled on the table with a drawing of what I assumed was the continent of Suelhaym Eekier—Suelhaym of Yesterday.

Meuhlnir had his finger pressed on the map, pointing at a garrison town of the Pitra Empire. The garrison was located on cliffs overlooking a fjord on the western coast. The town was named Piltsfetl, and it seemed to be situated between a forest to the north that was named the Darks of Kruyn and another to the south called the Forest of Kvia.

"Is that where they are? Piltsfetl?"

Meuhlnir grunted and threw and accusatory look at Mothi. "Yes, Hank. Yowrnsaxa found them while trying to divine Luka's whereabouts. More of a side-effect than—"

"How do I get there?" I demanded.

"Hank, it's not quite that easy. We don't know what kind of force Luka has with him. We don't even know if the Black Queen is there with him, or if the Pitranar are in cahoots—"

"None of that matters! If they are being held there, it's time to go and get them away from Luka."

"I do understand the intensity of your feelings, Hank, but listen to reason a minute. We can't just charge in there in a head-on assault."

"Why not? We've stood them off several times. We are not a force to be dismissed out of hand."

"Hank," Veethar said in his quiet way.

I turned to look at him, and he dropped his eyes back to the map.

"First, no *proo* leads to Piltsfetl. Second, the Pitranar have a garrison there for solid strategic reasons. Take a look here," said Meuhlnir, pointing at the town and the fjord to the north of it. "The town is bordered on the east, west and north sides by sheer cliffs. And see this crossroads here?" He moved his finger east of Piltsfetl to a place where four roads came together. "There's another town here—it's not a garrison, but if the Pitranar are part of Luka's effort, there will be troops stationed there looking for us."

"Isn't the glamor supposed to trick them into thinking we are still on the way to Suelhaym?"

"Yes," said Veethar.

"But Luka is no fool. He won't be so utterly fooled that he will let his defensive plans lapse." Mothi looked down at the map and pursed his lips.

"Where is the closest *proo*?" I asked.

Veethar moved his finger to a place in Kvia, to the south of Piltsfetl, just on the eastern border of the Forest of Kvia.

"Then let's go there. We can hug the coast all the way to Piltsfetl."

"Luka will have the closest known *proo* guarded," said Mothi. "I would."

"Can't these *preer* be moved?"

Meuhlnir nodded. "But that would also alert my brother."

"Then what?" I asked, exasperation ringing in my voice.

Veethar moved his finger to a peninsula north of Piltsfetl that curled around like the letter C. The peninsula was covered in the markings for forest land and had a small range of mountains running up its center. "This is the Darks of Kruyn," he said in his whisper-quiet voice.

"The villages marked here are... They are marked more for historical purposes than to show areas of population," said Meuhlnir.

I shrugged at Meuhlnir in confusion.

"No one lives in the Darks of Kruyn anymore," said Mothi. "Not since Vowli conquered Ayiar Oolfur, the island south of Fankelsi, in the name of the queen, and then gave the land to his followers. Once they had a solid base of operations, *Briethralak Oolfur* began raiding across the Tempest Sea into the Darks. The thralls and karls who lived in the Darks have either been consumed or worse."

"Then the Darks of Kruyn are held by Vowli's troops?"

"Well, no," said Meuhlnir. "If only it were that simple."

"I don't understand," I said.

"*Truykar*," said Veethar.

"*Truykar*? What's that?"

"Revenants," said Meuhlnir. "Reanimated corpses."

"Zombies? You're kidding me." I raised my hands and let them drop in exasperation. "Wait, *draugr*? Hel's minions in Niflheim?"

"*Truykar* is the plural of *truykr*, but I don't know what zombies or *draugr* are, though it sounds like the latter is a Viking word for *truykr*," said Meuhlnir. "As far as Niflhaym goes, I don't see why the Dark Bitch would keep minions there. Awfully inconvenient for waging war here on Osgarthr."

I shook my head. "And it's better to face legions of *truykar* than try to sneak past any guards Luka might have seen fit to station in Kvia?"

"With any luck, we won't even see any *truykar*," said Meuhlnir.

"And how likely is that, Father?" asked Mothi. "The smell of your breath alone will draw them like gadflies to the stable."

"My breath? Why would that attract *truykar*?" asked Meuhlnir with an air of long-suffering.

Mothi shrugged, trying not to smile. "It does smell a bit of the grave."

Meuhlnir shook his head at his son and then turned back to me. "The very thing that makes you want to avoid the area is the advantage of it. No one would think of guarding the *proo* there because no one would choose to go there."

"But we will?"

"Yes," said Veethar. "It makes the most sense given our situation."

"If we can get into the area undetected, the number of options we have to mount a rescue increases. If we go in through Kvia, then our only option is likely to be an all-out assault against unknown forces. Plus, Luka will know we are there and will have plenty of time to put your family on a ship and set sail to who knows where." Meuhlnir tapped the point in the Darks of Kruyn that held the *proo*. "If we drop in here, all we have to do is avoid these former population centers and our chances of being discovered by *truykar* go down."

"Why is that?"

"*Truykar* live in their graves, or, lacking graves, at the place where they died. In the wilds, there will be small groups—former farmers or woodsmen and such—but no large concentrations. It has the added benefit that it will be unguarded, and that the approach to the fjord from the north will also be unguarded."

"How can you be sure of that?" I asked.

"Because only Luka's *oolfa* can travel the Darks without fear."

"*Oolfa*? Wolves?" I asked.

"Yes." Meuhlnir nodded, a grave expression settling over his face. "*Itla sem yetur.*"

"The evil that eats. I see," I said. "What are the chances of running into a wolfman on this little jaunt?"

"Wolfman?" asked Veethar.

Meuhlnir waved his hand. "*Oolfa.* I can't say for certain, of course, but to my mind, it is very unlikely. Luka will want most of his supporters close to hand."

It was beginning to make sense to me. It was a huge risk, but it was hardly the riskiest thing I'd done since following Bobby Timmens into that cave in Western New York. I mean, I did fight a dragon. Twice.

"How do we get from the *proo* to Piltsfetl? Looks like a long walk."

"Horses," said Veethar.

"They can travel with us?" I asked.

Veethar nodded.

"How do you get them down to the Vault?"

"Walk," said Veethar.

Veethar really didn't like to talk much. I turned to Meuhlnir. "When do we leave."

"Soon," he said. "I'll talk to Sif and Yowrnsaxa, and Veethar will tell Frikka and gather the horses. Mothi can track down the Tverkr, while Yowtgayrr gets the Alfar ready to move. Assuming Sif doesn't flat out refuse to let you travel so soon, we can leave by tonight."

"And how long will it take us to get to Piltsfetl?" I was already getting antsy—like I used to feel before boarding an airplane to go visit my folks in Florida.

"No more than two or three days to the inland end of the fjord, then another couple of days to the garrison—all of that depends on being able to move at speed and not running into trouble."

Since trouble, in this case, was a legion of undead, I wanted to take the best-case scenario and make it come true. "In four days, I might have them back," I mumbled.

Meuhlnir nodded. "If all goes well."

Yowtgayrr put his hand on my shoulder. "We will make it go well."

Once the women had given their approval, we all gathered our belongings and met in the Vault of *Preer*. "Mothi, Sif, Yowrnsaxa, Althyof, and I will travel first and make the other end of the *proo* secure if need be. Then Veethar and Frikka will move the horses through and then follow themselves. After that, I want the three Alfar to come through, which, Hank, leaves you for last. I don't want to see you step through before everyone else is through."

"Why?" I asked.

"You are the point of this exercise, and you are recovering from a very serious injury. It doesn't make much sense to risk you right at the cusp of getting your family back."

I shrugged. "I want you to go forward with their rescue whether I'm there or not,' I said.

"We will," promised Yowtgayrr. "But the Master of Thunder is right, there is no reason to risk yourself at this late point."

Again, I shrugged. "Okay, I'll do as you ask."

Meuhlnir's nod was curt. "Then, if everyone is ready?"

"Uh...I won't be going to the Darks of Kruyn with you," said Althyof,

Meuhlnir looked at him with a half-formed sneer twitching on his face. "Why not?" His body language was stiff and jerky, and his tone was as cold as ice.

"There is something I need to retrieve, first. I'll meet you at the tip of the fjord in a day and a half." He crossed his arms. "I'll need a *proo* to Kleymtlant, as close to the Forest of Fyalir as possible. Can you arrange that?"

"Why should we?" asked Meuhlnir.

"Because I can bring something of great power to the fight."

"What could you have in the Forgotten Land? An artifact?" asked Frikka.

"Something like that," said the Tverkr. "And besides, either you provide me with a *proo*, or I go on foot, in which case I won't be able to assist in the raid because I will still be walking to Kleymtlant. Or I could simply quit and go home, I suppose."

"I was under the impression that you were in my hire, Althyof," said Meuhlnir with anger in his face and voice.

The Tverkr nodded, keeping his face neutral, but the look in his eyes led me to believe he was struggling against his nature to do so. "That is so, Meuhlnir, but that doesn't mean I will act against my best interests."

Meuhlnir shook his head. "And if the other side of the *proo* to the Darks is swarming with *truykar*?"

"Then *kill* them," Althyof snapped. "You don't need me for that."

"Fine," snapped Meuhlnir. "Can you provide him with a *proo*, Veethar?"

Veethar nodded and began to study the runes inscribed on the walls of the Vault. After a few minutes, he activated one of the runes and invited Althyof to use it with a satirical flourish.

Althyof smirked at Veethar. "One and a half days," he said and stepped through the *proo*.

The Vault was silent a moment as everyone stared at the empty space where the Tverkr had just been. Then, Veethar grunted and activated the rune for the *proo* to the Darks of Kruyn. "Hope he gets lice," said Veethar with a smirk of his own.

Mothi barked a laugh and patted Veethar on the back.

"Right," said Meuhlnir. "Let's move."

The process was quick, except for leading the horses into the great hall and down the steps to the Vault. Veethar had no trouble getting the horses he led to do what he wanted, and Frikka and the Alfar fared better than I was able. Eventually, all the other horses were through, and I was still trying to convince Slaypnir to descend the steps. Veethar rolled his eyes and took Slaypnir by the bridle, gazing into the horse's eyes for a moment. After that, Slaypnir almost pulled me down the steps.

"Neat trick," I grumbled.

Veethar grinned, tipped me a wink, grabbed Frikka's hand and stepped through the *proo*. I was starting to feel that telltale pull—like gravity, or the pull of a very strong magnet—toward the *proo* as if my fate waited on the other side. The Alfar nodded to each other and then to me, and all three stepped through at the same time. I saw no reason to linger.

Stretching out my hand, I touched the rainbow-silvery surface of the *proo* and felt the instant of heat and cold before beings sucked through into the Darks of Kruyn.

FORTY-ONE

It had been late afternoon at Veethar and Frikka's estate, but when I emerged high up on a mountainside in the Darks of Kruyn, it was just after midday. The others were standing in a half-circle with the horses behind them, and me behind the horses.

We'd emerged above the tree line on a tall mountain. A dark forest stretched from the mountain to the sea shimmering in the west. The mountain top itself was steep, exposed granite from just above the tree line to the peak. To our left, the mountain fell away into the forest with evidence of frequent rock slides. The slope in front of us was littered with loose stone, but a faint foot path led down into the forest.

"No *truykar*?" I asked.

"Not yet. Let's get out of here before someone or something notices we are here," said Yowrnsaxa.

It was too steep to ride, so we all tied our packs to our mounts. We walked and slid down the path across the steep slope, leading the horses behind us.

It was very hot inside my new armor. My clothes under the mail were soaked through in short order, but everyone was sweating, and no one was taking off any armor. Mothi was wiping his brow about every thirty seconds, and Sif had bright splotches of red high up on her cheeks. Everyone suffered in silence.

We mounted up once we reached the tree line. The upper parts of the forest were dark and forbidding. Very little sunlight filtered through the heavy canopy of the trees. At the altitude we were descending through, there was little underbrush, just broken branches and a strange sort of green moss that hugged the ground. The moss released a choking cloud of spores when the horses stepped on it. An utter silence pervaded the wood like mist. Meuhlnir led us down the mountain side for hours, ever deeper into the dark rainforest that sprawled at the mountain's feet. The rainforest between the mountains and the sea was as black as midnight on the new moon, though it was still sweltering. Several forms of fern, creeping vines, and stunted Butia palms competed for soil and the almost non-existent sunlight. The forest felt bad, evil. Like an old, abandoned Victorian mansion, it felt haunted and set all of us on edge. I couldn't put my finger on any one thing that made it feel so malevolent.

Meuhlnir led us west until we were clear of the mountain's foothills and turned us south. He drew up and motioned us closer. "There is a village to the west," he said in hushed tones. "We shouldn't have any trouble, but let's keep things as quiet as possible anyway." He looked us each in the eye and then spurred Sinir forward, setting a brisk, but careful pace.

As we rode deeper into the pernicious and disquieting forest, the meaning behind the name of the region—the Darks of Kruyn—became clear. On the side of the mountain, it had been a bright, cheery day, but in the forest, it was as gloomy as a cloudy winter evening in New England. Shadows and tricks of the murk made us all uneasy and made the horses skittish. We rode the rest of the day in a kind of over-amped, jumpy state of alert. We saw nothing and no one. At dusk, the forest was as black as night, the trees became silhouettes against the mist that rolled in from seaward. Tree branches morphed into reaching, skeletal arms and the thorns of wild rose bushes became claws, grasping at our loose clothing. When we stumbled into a break in the trees just big enough to be called a glade, Meuhlnir called a halt. "We are close to the northern edge of the mouth of the fjord. If we could fly, we could be in Piltsfetl in a matter of hours."

Veethar swung down and stared into the forest with an intense focus. "Strange," he whispered.

"What?" asked Meuhlnir.

"Nothing," said Veethar, stroking the nose of his mount.

"Not 'nothing.' You said something was strange."

"I can sense nothing. No animals. No men."

"It *is* the Darks of Kruyn," said Mothi, as if that explained the unnatural stillness that was anything but tranquil.

"Even so, I expected small animals at least." Veethar shivered. "Unnatural."

Meuhlnir grunted and then swung his leg over Sinir's neck. "Mothi, some wood for a fire, if you please."

"No," said Frikka. "No fire. Not in the Darks."

Veethar frowned at his wife but, as usual, said nothing.

"You've seen something, Frikka?" asked Yowrnsaxa, staring into the dimness surrounding us and loosening her sword in its scabbard.

Frikka didn't answer. She turned to her horse and began to remove her gear from her pack. She paid special attention to her shield and her short fighting spear, making sure they were close to her bedroll.

"What is it," I whispered to Mothi.

"Frikka is gifted in foresight," he whispered back. "Perversely, she is rarely willing to share her prophecies. We just follow her lead in times like this."

"Why won't she explain?"

Mothi shrugged and rolled his eyes. "Women." He went about his business then, getting his weapons out and making sure his bedroll was in a comfortable hollow of the ground.

"We sleep in a circle tonight," said Meuhlnir. "Hank sleeps in the center."

"We sleep close to Hank," said Yowtgayrr.

Meuhlnir nodded. "As you wish. We will take watches in turn. I want two watchers awake at all times."

We bedded down without much conversation—the night didn't seem fit for talking, and with Frikka startling every couple of minutes, everyone was on edge. I hadn't thought it was possible, but as night fell, the already sinister-looking forest took on an even more apocalyptic look. What little light made it through the canopy took on a bluish cast, making everything seem darker rather than brightening the shadows. Sleep was long in coming, and from the noises of the others sleeping around me, I guessed that it wasn't a problem I suffered alone. When I did sleep, my dreams were dark and frightening—filled with animated corpses, dragons, and death.

Yowtgayrr woke me at what passed for dawn in the Darks. "We need to get moving," he whispered.

"No one woke me to take my turn at watch," I grumped. The dawn cast the forest with a golden light, although dim to the point of obscurity. As dusky as the dawn's light was, it painted golden highlights on the forest and washed some of the menace out of the shadows.

"There was no need," said the Alf. He waved his hand in an arc. "It was a restless night. Plenty of watchers."

We saddled the horses and packed up in a rush, eating a sparse, cold breakfast of bread and cheese. Meuhlnir pointed to the south. "The northern cliff of the fjord is there." He moved his hand so that he pointed south-southeast. "The largest city in the Darks is just there. That will be the largest concentration of *truykar*. Because of that, we ride east, deeper into the forest."

Veethar nodded in what seemed like satisfaction, but his wife looked pensive and wouldn't meet anyone's eye.

"If you have information that would change our route, Frikka, now would be a good time," said Meuhlnir with ill-concealed impatience.

Frikka just shook her head and walked her horse to stand next to Veethar.

Meuhlnir shrugged. "So be it, then." He turned and led us east at a trot.

Broken branches and stunted trees bordered the glade, all covered in a clinging cloak of green that we had to push through. The forest floor was greyish-black dirt, riddled with knobby roots and littered with old and decaying leaves. Creeping reddish-green vines a couple of inches in diameter ran between the ground, the fallen limbs, and the limbs still in the trees. Long, sharp thorns sprouted every inch or so from the ubiquitous vines, and some of them glistened with a viscous, opaque fluid. The horses seemed to abhor the vines and shied away from them when we moved them too close.

We covered a lot of ground, but after an hour and a half of travel, the underbrush of the forest thickened even more. Dark green vines snagged at the horse's hooves as they trotted, almost as if the vines were trying to trip the horses. The vines seemed to be cousins of the red monsters back at the glade, except these had no thorns.

"Can you not do something about this underbrush, Veethar?" demanded Meuhlnir.

Veethar looked around, muttering to himself. "*Fara til klithar*," he said, and the vines and underbrush started to withdraw but soon shuddered to a halt and reversed direction. Veethar shook his head. "*Svepn*!" he commanded. The vines shook with violence for a moment and then continued creeping forward.

Veethar looked up and met Meuhlnir's gaze. "No. They won't move aside, and they won't go dormant."

Meuhlnir grunted. "Can you not command them to wither, to die?"

Veethar looked as if he'd been slapped. "I won't."

Meuhlnir sighed with exasperation and shook his head. "Then we must move as best we can." He peered up at the tiny portion of the sky he could see through the canopy of the trees. "I think we must have passed the city to the south by this time."

As if that were the cue, the forest around them began to twist and surge. The ground shook, and the underbrush rustled as a rotten stench began to pervade the wood. Something crashed through the underbrush, sounding like it was headed straight toward us.

"Ride!" yelled Frikka, spurring her horse into the fastest pace the forest would allow.

Veethar rode after her. "*Fara til klithar*!" he yelled as he urged his horse to run faster. The underbrush began its slow withdrawal, and we all kicked our horses into a run and held on for dear life.

Veethar kept commanding the underbrush to move aside as we charged through the gloomy forest. The crashing behind us got louder and louder, and soon we could see the shape of something large, black, and hideous blazing a trail for man-shaped things behind us.

Frikka was riding to the northeast and kept shooting piercing glares at us over her shoulders as if we were not moving fast enough for her.

"*Truykar*?" I asked, yelling to be heard over the din.

"I don't know, but it seems likely! The stench!" yelled Meuhlnir.

"Why are we running?"

"No idea how many there are and with this forest, we'd never know until they were on us. We need space—a meadow, a field, anything."

We continued pushing the horses as the terrain grew more and more hilly. We rode for hours, fear brimming in our blood as foam began to sluff from our horses' nostrils and mouths. As the hills became rockier, the forest lost its chokehold on the soil, and we began to see bigger and bigger patches of sunlight penetrating the darkness.

We began to gain ground on whatever it was that was following us since the horses could run faster through the areas clear of the clinging, covetous underbrush, and our followers still waded through it. As the foothills petered out, the malignant forest began to give way to grassland, and we finally caught a glimpse of what was pursuing us.

A humongous dead reptile the size of an elephant led an army of *truykar*. The reptile was shaped like an enormous Komodo dragon, except it had a row of razor-sharp looking spines down its back. Its skin was black and rotting, and its eyes were filmed over and lifeless. The *truykar* were hideous. Their skin was peeling, black, and gangrenous. Gaping wounds festered and spewed maggots with each lurching, jarring step. Long, stringy hair fell unadorned from their heads and across the withered muscles of their shoulders and necks. Their nails were long and black. Disgusting, decayed meat drooped from their bones, and skin like wizened old, untanned leather hung from the meat. The stench as they broke from the forest was enough to make me want to vomit until my insides dropped on my shoes. It made my eyes tear and water, and my nose ran with snot,

"They shouldn't be following us!" yelled Sif. "Their unnatural life force is bound to their graves. Why are they chasing us so far?"

Meuhlnir shook his head, a grim expression covering his face. "Something is driving them to chase us. Or someone."

Frikka looked around with fear in her eyes. "*Illa sem yetur*!"

Meuhlnir cursed and shook his head, a grim expression on his face.

"Luka?" I asked.

Meuhlnir didn't pause from his effort to break the all-time record for continuous cursing.

"Turn and fight?"

Meuhlnir jerked his head back and forth without pausing his tirade.

"It's even more dangerous to stop now," yelled Mothi.

I threw glances over my shoulders, trying to catch a glimpse of the thing driving the *truykar*. All I could see was those hideous decayed corpses running, stumbling and, in some cases, crawling after us. "What do we do then? Hope they get tired?"

Still cursing, Meuhlnir shook his head again.

"What then?" I demanded.

Abruptly, Slaypnir shied and darted first to the left and then to the right. A large shadow covered us, and I stared up at the red underbelly of a dragon that seemed to be the size of a football stadium. I drew Kunknir.

"Stay your hand, Aylootr!" shouted a voice from above that sounded like Althyof.

I squinted up at the long, sleek dragon as it slid past in the air like a dolphin swimming through water. The dragon wheeled toward our pursuers, bellowing that basso roar, fraught with subharmonics that set my teeth on edge.

"Althyof! Watch for *Briethralak Oolfur*!" shouted Meuhlnir, reining Sinir in a tight turn to the right.

With a shrieking sound like a fighter jet on full afterburner, the dragon unleashed a billowing stream of reddish-orange fire onto the front ranks of *truykar*. Their desiccated bodies ignited, and they shuddered to one side or the other, trying to get away, but succeeding only in setting those next to them on fire. As the fire splashed onto the giant dead lizard thing, it shrieked—a sound that reminded me of a pissed-off infant—and then turned and bolted through the *truykar*, crushing whatever was in its path. Just before it made it to the forest, it collapsed in a charred, twitching mess.

A strange-sounding song rose above the din. The melody was hard to focus on, slipping around in my head like a snake in mud. The dragon roared again, followed by another shrieking jet of red-orange flames into the back of the *truykar* ranks. The cadence of the haunting melody increased, and the dragon wheeled on its wingtip to the right. It flew over the *truykar* army spitting flame and lashing its great tail. Every time the tail hit a *truykr*, a decomposing head flew up and away from the *truykr*'s decaying body.

The dragon made two more flaming passes and then landed amid the burning *truykar* with a savage fury. It began thrashing around, biting, and tearing at the revenants and slashing its tail through ranks of the undead. The haunting melody became more strident, and the dragon shrieked and hissed in response. The *truykar* didn't even seem to notice the dragon in their midst, they either thrashed around on fire or walked toward our party. The dragon decimated the *truykar* with ease, spitting fire and decapitating them with abandon. When all the *truykar* had died their second death, the dragon screamed and leapt into the air.

It twisted its neck back around its shoulder and snapped at the Tverkr riding between the great mounds of its shoulders. The direful diapason grew strident and insistent, disparate harmonies seeming to overlap and compete with one another. The dragon shook its great head and screamed a mournful cry, then leapt into the air. It flew close to the canopy of the forest, its great wedge-shaped head sweeping back and forth as if it were searching for something. Or someone. With an exultant shriek, and the explosive sound of trees being smashed to bits, the dragon slammed its rear talons toward the ground and then beat its wings, fighting for altitude. It looked very much like a hunting kite carrying away its prey. The dragon wheeled in midair and flew toward us, gaining altitude. As its shadow passed over us, it dropped its prey after a convulsive squeeze of its huge talons. A body fell through the air and cratered the ground behind us. The dragon wheeled back toward the forest, diving low toward the treetops again.

The body that lay crumpled in front of us was gangly and desperately lean, not to mention inhuman and strange. Where it had fur, its coat was either gray or brown, and where it didn't, its skin was pale pink, or rotted and black. Standing, he would have been incredibly tall—fifteen feet at least—and his legs had too many joints. The creature had the head and antlers of a decaying stag, though its teeth were that of a bear or wolf. The torso of the beast was patchy with lusterless fur and pale, diseased skin. Its arms stretched from its hunched shoulders to a three-fingered hand. Each of his fingers was tipped in a wicked-looking talon.

"A *wendigo*," I muttered.

Meuhlnir shook his head. "No, Hank, that is one of the many forms the *Briethralak Oolfur* can assume. Generally, this form is used to travel, but as you can see from the claws and fangs, it can still do quite a bit of damage."

"One of Luka's crowd, eh?"

No one wanted to answer that.

"Was this one driving the *truykar*?" I asked.

"Probably," said Meuhlnir. "I think Althyof is checking to see if he was the only one."

The dragon roared in anger and frustration and then wheeled toward us again. It slammed into the ground in the middle of the *truykar*, its great rear legs compressing to take up the shock of the hard landing. The strange music continued without pause as Althyof slid down the slick-looking red scales of the dragon's haunch. The dragon snaked its head around, lightning quick, and hissed at the Tverkr.

Althyof walked toward us, continuing the eerie chant, not seeming the least bit uncomfortable at having a dragon hissing at his back. He lifted a hand in greeting and then turned to face the dragon.

"*Thoo verthur owfram!*" he sang.

"*You will stay*," whispered Meuhlnir. "He's binding the dragon so that he can stop singing."

The dragon tensed and lunged half a step forward, jaws snapping. Its movements were slow and lackadaisical—as if it were trying to move through setting cement.

"*Thoo munt echki rowthast ow ochkur!*"

"*You will not attack us.*"

The dragon shook its massive head as if it were confused, but its anger-filled eyes never left Althyof.

"*Thoo verthur tholinmoeth ok bithur!*" chanted Althyof.

"*You will be patient and wait*," said Meuhlnir.

"*Ath oekleethnast myer er ath tayia!*"

"*To disobey me is to die.*"

The dragon hissed its hatred and despair, but settled down on its haunches, laying its belly against the still smoldering corpses of the *truykar* army. Althyof watched it for an intense moment, chanting that slippery song. The melody reached a crescendo of sorts and hung there in the air—sounding fragmentary and unconsummated as if it had ended in the middle of a phrase—and Althyof nodded and smiled.

"That should hold him here," he said. "For a while, anyway."

Meuhlnir looked at the dragon. "Friner, I assume?"

"Of course," said Althyof. "The Dragon Queen isn't the only one who can muster a dragon to the fight."

"Why didn't you just tell us?" demanded Sif with uncharacteristic irritation in her voice.

"And rob myself of such a dramatic entrance?" Althyof smiled and winked at me. "Thank you, Aylootr, for not putting hundreds of holes in Friner's flesh or mine."

"You're welcome," I said. "To tell you the truth, I wasn't looking forward to fighting another dragon anyway."

Althyof laughed as if that was the funniest thing he'd ever heard in his life. I didn't see what was so funny, but the Tverkar are a weird people. He walked to the small crater that contained the body of the *wendigo* or werestag or whatever it was. He kicked at the hoof resting on the edge of the crater and grunted

"This one was running away when we caught him. I think there may have been one other, but I couldn't spot him and neither could Friner, and that dragon has a gift for spotting living things it could set on fire."

"Why do you think there was another?" asked Meuhlnir.

"It's just a feeling, but that was a large group of *truykar* to be controlled by one man."

"True," grunted Meuhlnir.

"Why is this thing…this shapeshifter, why is it dead?" I blurted, kicking the hoof that was extended over the edge of the crater.

Althyof looked at me like I had a third eye. "He was pulped by a dragon and thrown down with enough force to embed his body in the ground. Why wouldn't he be dead?"

I looked Meuhlnir in the eye. "Your brother told me he was immortal."

"Well, you can hardly expect him to go around telling people how to kill him," scoffed Althyof.

Meuhlnir shot the Tverkr a dirty look. "The *oolfa* are not immortal. Their practices do grant them the ability to heal very, very quickly, however, which may grant the appearance of immortality."

"It is a straightforward matter to kill them," said Yowtgayrr. "You just have to outpace their healing abilities."

Althyof nodded. "Massive amounts of damage, done quickly, does the trick."

"Like getting pulped by a dragon," I said.

"Yes," said the Tverkr. "Fire can also work, or concentrated damage from a great number of people."

"And the more experienced the *oolfur*, the greater their ability to heal," said Yowtgayrr.

"Enough of this. It is pointless right now," snapped Meuhlnir. "If one has escaped, he will try to report to Luka in Piltsfetl."

"Meaning we need to move with speed or our diversion here to the Darks has been a wasted effort," said Frikka, who was staring at me with great intensity.

Panic began to gnaw at my guts. "It's still two days to the garrison?"

Meuhlnir nodded and glanced at Friner. "How fast can the beast fly, Althyof?"

The Tverkr shrugged. "I flew him here from Kleymtlant in the time it took you to ride this far."

Meuhlnir nodded. "A quarter of the world in two days. Impressive. Can it carry more than one?"

"The daft beast has much more capacity than it wants me to know about," said Althyof. "But the answer is easily yes...if it will permit it. And it will permit it while I sing."

"Right," said Meuhlnir. "We must split the party. If possible, we need Friner to fly Hank, Veethar, and I to as close to Piltsfetl as we can get without being detected. The rest of you make your way to the garrison as quickly as you can."

"No," said Yowtgayrr. "We go with Hank."

"And I'm not content to bring the baggage," said Sif. "What if one of you is hurt."

Meuhlnir blew an exasperated sigh through his lips. "Look, no matter how great the beast is, I don't think it will carry all of us and the horses."

"I'll bring the horses," muttered Veethar, looking at the huge dragon askance.

"We may need your help, Veethar," said Meuhlnir.

"Exactly what is this plan you've concocted in that head of yours?" demanded Yowrnsaxa.

Meuhlnir sighed again. "I simply think we need to get there before Luka's henchman. Maybe we can still win the day with guile and stealth, rather than with blood and iron.

"My thinking was that we'd take a small party and find the postern gate. Then, with Friner putting on a show at the main gate, we can make our way inside and find where his family is caged. Perhaps we can get them back out the postern and into the forest, where Friner can pick us up and return us to you and the horses."

"That plan is fraught with 'perhaps' and 'maybe.' I'm not sure you've thought it through," said Sif with her arms crossed and a stern look on her face. "For instance, what if you are spotted? You have no reserve forces. What if you are injured? What if Hank's child is injured? You have no healer."

Meuhlnir raised his hands in frustration. "What if Luka's henchman arrives before we can? What if the garrison is fortified? What if Luka takes Hank's family aboard a ship and sets sail?"

Sif shook her head. "It's better to stay together."

"No," Frikka snapped. "Not in this case." She was still looking at me. "Aylootr must certainly go on ahead with the Tverkr and his dragon. The Alfar have sworn to travel with him, and so should they."

"You've seen this in augury?" Meuhlnir demanded.

"Sif is otherwise right. The rest of us should stay together, and travel to Piltsfetl as fast as we can."

"Is this a foretelling, Frikka?" Meuhlnir asked again.

Frikka looked at her saddle and didn't reply.

"Sometimes this mystical seeress act grates on every fiber of my being," said Meuhlnir, eyes blazing.

"Hush, husband," said Yowrnsaxa.

"Why can't she just speak what she forecasts?" grumbled Meuhlnir. "What could possibly be different following my plan?"

Sif gave him such a look that even I felt abashed and chastened. "We will do as our sister says," she said in a tone that made it impossible to think of any other course of action. She turned her horse so that she could look at me. "I will bring Slaypnir myself. Leave your pack. Take your arms and armor and go save your family."

The clearing was silent for a moment, and then Althyof smacked his palms against his thighs. "No one will ever believe this tale," he said with a laugh. "If we are going, let's be off."

I glanced at Yowtgayrr, and as he nodded, I swung down from Slaypnir and passed the reins to Sif.

"Be careful," she whispered as she took the horse in tow.

I nodded and walked toward Althyof. "What do we do?"

Althyof looked at the Alfar with a critical eye. "Can you three do this?" he asked.

"So we've sworn, so we will," said Skowvithr. He cast his eyes toward the dragon. "No matter how distasteful it may be, it is what is required."

Althyof nodded. "You three may just change my mind about your race," he grunted. "You are hardly mambly-pambly at all."

Yowtgayrr favored him with a sour smile. "And you almost appear to be motivated by ideals other than greed, Tverkr."

"There's no need to be insulting," snapped Althyof, but I thought I could see him hiding a grin by tucking his chin into his beard. "This is what must happen," he said. "I will begin my runesong. When I wave you forward, all four of you run—*run*, mind—to Friner's flank and climb up his rear leg. Go to his forward shoulders and kneel between them. You must be forward of his wing joints. Once you are safely aboard, I will climb up. Don't try to talk to me. I won't be able to answer you and sing the dragon at the same time. In fact, try not to talk at all. It is best for the dragon to not even notice you are there. Especially you Alfar."

"Do we need to hang on or anything?" I asked.

"There is a wide leather strap around the beast's neck. I will secure you to it once I've mounted." Althyof broke eye contact to turn and look at the dragon. "He's a might pissed at me, so he occasionally tries a trick or two to kill me."

"What kind of tricks?" asked Urlikr.

"He tries to wheel sharply, hoping I will fall. He might also fly erratically. Nothing else is worth much notice—just be sure you remain fastened to the warded strap." He nodded to each of us in turn. "Once we arrive, wait for my signal again and then crawl down from the beast. I will not dismount. Instead, I will fly him toward Piltsfetl and begin to harry what troops I find there. Make your way to the town and find a way inside. When you have found your family, blow this." He paused to hand me what looked like a whistle that was carved from citrine. "When I hear your signal, I will attack the garrison in earnest. Once you are away, blow it again, and I will meet you where we land. If you get in trouble, blow it three times, and we will come, bringing fire and fury."

"Okay," I said.

"Land them to the west of the town," said Frikka. "Nowhere else."

With a nod in her direction, Althyof strode toward the dragon, beginning his runesong with a vocal flourish that seemed to pick up where the previous song had ended. Friner twitched its great head and hissed in our direction. Althyof sang louder, and the dragon shuddered. When he waved us forward, the four of us ran toward the dragon, leaping over smoking corpses of the revenants. When we were halfway to the beast's side, it lurched its head toward us and snapped its jaws. Althyof sang louder and with more insistence. Friner's head stopped moving, but its bright, blood-red-colored eyes focused on mine, and I felt an insistent tugging like it was coming from the center of my brain. Althyof chanted a series of sharp, discordant phrases and the feeling stopped as the dragon's eyes seemed to glaze.

Climbing a dragon's leg sounds a lot easier than it is. First off, dragon scales are slick and slippery. Also, dragons have a tendency toward ticklishness and are constantly shaking the leg to make you fall off. Or at least Friner did.

We made it to the dragon's back and began to pick our way forward between its great wings. We crouched next to the broad leather strap, that looked enough like a large version of the kind of belt powerlifters use to protect their lower backs that I had to stifle a chuckle. The belt was inscribed with runes along its length—I assumed it had something to do with what Meuhlnir called "the binding of Friner."

Althyof continued to chant and sing as he climbed up behind us. When he reached us, he drew a thin-looking cord from his pack and tied it around my waist. He looped it through the belt around Friner's neck and then moved to do the same for the Alfar. The cord looked flimsy. It was goldish in color and had a kind of rainbow-sheen that danced along its length as I moved the cord. I didn't think it would be of much use if the dragon decided to unseat me, but Althyof seemed confident in its strength.

The runesong changed, with subtlety at first, and then grew more insistent. Beneath my feet, Friner grumbled deep in its chest and then sprang into the air. Its great wings beat against the air, propelling us upwards at a surprising rate of ascent. The dragon veered to the southwest, alternating between beating its great wings in a flurry and gliding gracefully through the air. The land dropped away from us quickly, and I could see the Darks of Kruyn stretched out to my right and the Empire of Pitra to my left. In front of us, like a great tear in the land, was the fjord. The sun glinted off the water in its depths like jewels.

Without warning, the dragon dove toward the water with a neck-breaking suddenness. As my stomach dropped away, I was glad of the golden cord Althyof had used to tie me to the dragon—regardless of how flimsy it might have looked. The dragon held its dive long after the point I thought was prudent. As it angled its wings to pull out of the dive, I could see fish swimming in the fjord. Friner pulled level so low that its wingtips skimmed the tops of the waves pounding into the cliffs of the fjord. A weird rhythmic sound came from deep in the dragon's chest, and I could have sworn the beast was laughing at us.

We flew at the level of the wave tops the length of the fjord and then out to sea before the dragon made a lazy turn to the left and began to gain altitude. Friner flew straight toward the tip of the cliff that made the south side of the fjord. It skimmed over the edge, putting down its rear legs and stretching its talons wide. The shock of the abrupt landing transmitted itself through the dragon and into the soles of our feet. Althyof nodded and made a "hurry up" gesture, though he never broke the tempo of his song. Yowtgayrr, Urlikr, Skowvithr, and I hurried to climb down the dragon's leg and raced away from the beast. Once we were clear, Althyof nodded to me and then the dragon sprang into the air with a teeth-rattling roar.

"Let's go," I whispered and strode forward to the trees that stood between us and the walls of Piltsfetl. We moved at a slow pace through the boscage, pausing often and trying to move without any regular tempo in case there were watchers on the back wall. Squatting behind the last row of trees, we stared across a small clearing at the stone wall of Piltsfetl. We were in luck. Not only was the rear wall unmanned, but the postern gate—which was more of a large door than a gate—was right in front of us. Weeds grew at its base, and from the heavy oxidation on the hinges, it wasn't used much.

Yowtgayrr put his lips to my ear and whispered, "I don't like the looks of that door."

"I can find a window or grate or something and use my cloak to get inside as smoke, but those hinges will make a bucket-full of noise if I open the door to let you three inside."

"Let Urlikr or Skowvithr climb the wall and check to be sure it's clear. Then use your cloak to gain the wall top," whispered Yowtgayrr.

I shook my head. "We can't risk being seen. I should go in first."

"No, Hank. Let us do what we've pledged." Yowtgayrr nodded at Urlikr, and the Alf started moving his hands about as if he were writing in thin air. I began to see a tail of silvery light stretching out behind his finger, and I raised my eyebrows at them.

"He's writing in the language of the stars," whispered Yowtgayrr. "The Isir aren't the only ones with access to the *strenkir af krafti*."

As I watched, Urlikr finished whatever phrase he was writing, and the color seemed to leech out of him, and he faded away. "Invisibility?" I asked.

Yowtgayrr nodded. "Of a limited form. If he is far away, or remains still, he will be almost impossible to spot. Go, Urlikr."

I heard Urlikr moving toward the wall with stealth. After a few moments, I heard a strange sound like a bird being strangled.

"The signal," Yowtgayrr grunted. "It is clear."

We ran to the base of the wall, trying to keep our footfalls light and soundless. Yowtgayrr and Skowvithr raced up the rough-hewn rock wall like spiders running on water. They hesitated right below the top edge of the wall, and Yowtgayrr waved to me.

I activated my cloak and vanished into smoke. I had no idea how to fly, so I just pretended to climb a ladder to the top. It was easy, since I didn't have any mass to speak of. When I got to the top, I stepped over the crenulations and stood on the wooden platform attached to the inside of the wall.

No one was visible, but I made my way to the steps leading down to the courtyard below and hurried down them. I moved into the shadows under the stairs just in time for my fettle to untwist and make me solid again. I wondered where the three Alfar were, until I felt an invisible hand on my shoulder.

"I go to scout," whispered Urlikr in my ear.

He brushed past me, and concentrating on the area I knew he must be moving through, I could see a faint blurriness moving away. The area the rest of us waited in was kind of a cross between a back alley and a midden. It seemed few people ventured between the last row of houses and the back wall. The houses themselves were constructed of plaster-covered wooden lathe and had thatch rooves. The architecture reminded me of small villages in the country-side of Great Britain.

As we stood there, waiting for Urlikr's return, Friner roared and flew low over Piltsfetl, from the back wall toward the front. I looked up in time to see the dragon's tail whipping back and forth over the rooftops. The dragon roared as it passed over the front side of the village, accompanied by a pandemonium of screams, shouted orders, and general uproar from the villagers and garrisoned troops.

The town wasn't large. I guessed that the population was less than three hundred people, counting the garrison, but I was willing to bet Luka had brought a few friends with him.

The dragon roared somewhere to the east, the bass notes of its cries rattling around in my gut. Doors slammed shut in the row of houses between us and the rest of the town, and I could hear mothers scolding wayward children to get away from the windows. From deeper toward the center of the village came the sounds of an organized military response.

"I went as far as the village square," whispered Urlikr. "The town is overflowing—troops are billeted everywhere, and I've seen a few that must be *Briethralak Oolfur*. Tall, gaunt, and mean-looking."

"That sounds about right," I said. "Any sign of my family?"

Urlikr hesitated, and my stomach fell into a churning mass of fear. "Yes. There is an iron cage in the center of the square. Thick black iron bars and a big lock. A woman and a boy child were inside."

"Are they all right?" I asked with my heart in my throat.

"They appear to be in perfect health, though they look exhausted and scared."

"Can we approach unseen?" asked Yowtgayrr.

"We can get to the edge of the square in relative safety, but the square seems to be where the troops are being marshalled to meet the dragon." I could hear Urlikr fidgeting somewhere to my right.

"Will it be safe for Hank?"

"I think so. There is a sort of alley way between the blacksmith's shop and the stables. It is swathed in shadows. He will have to use the cloak several times to get there unseen, but once there—"

"Fine," I said. "Lead on, Urlikr." I held out my hand, and the Alf grasped it and guided it to his belt.

I grabbed his belt and followed him as he advanced through the back streets of the town.

As we approached an intersection, Urlikr turned, and his lips brushed my ear. "Smoke now," he whispered. "Go around the corner to the right, and there will be an alcove protecting a door. Wait for me there."

I activated my cloak and wafted around the corner of the intersection, which was bathed in full sunlight. Off to the east, Friner was knocking trees about in front of the village gates and the troops now lining the front walls screamed and taunted the great beast. I found the alcove Urlikr mentioned with ease and ducked into its shadows and deactivated my cloak.

Footsteps came toward my position, and the invisible Alfar pressed me tight against the walls of the alcove. I couldn't reactivate my cloak yet, so I hoped the shadows were deep enough to hide me from casual observation. A young man in the uniform of the Pitra Empire's martial forces strolled down the center of the lane. His eyes darted over me and away, searching the shadows but not seeing past them. It was obvious that something had spooked him—he held his right hand across his body on the hilt of his sword and was moving slow, trying to minimize the noise of his passage. I held my breath as his eyes turned toward the alcove I was hiding in for the second time. He peered into the shadows that hid me and took half a step toward me. I put my hand on the butt of Kunknir, but one of the Alfar's hands covered mine. The soldier took another step toward us, and his eyes widened.

"Smoke," hissed Urlikr in my ear. I activated the cloak. The soldier stepped into the alcove and stepped right through me. I could hear the faint rustling of the Alfar moving out of the alcove, and I followed suit. I darted toward the next alley between the houses and ducked around the corner, just as the enchantment on the cloak wore off. I was hoping the Alfar could follow me but couldn't hear any of them moving around me. Just as I was about to panic, a commotion broke out in the street behind me.

The unconscious soldier floated, face down and limp, around the corner into the darkened alley, and I had to suppress a chuckle at the sight of it. He slumped against the wall and slid to the cobbled passageway. His arms arranged themselves in a pose as if he were napping and an invisible hand pushed me away down the alley.

We made it to the alley between the blacksmith's shop and the stables without any other incidents. Friner was putting on quite a show in front of the village gates by the sounds of its roars and the shouts of the troops guarding the town. I skulked toward the mouth of the alley that opened on to the village square, trying not to make a sound, keeping the cloak wrapped in my hands, ready to snap it up and activate the smoke if necessary. The Alfar followed behind me.

When I saw Sig and Jane, it was all I could do to stop myself from running to them. A warning hand squeezed my shoulder.

The square was on the small side—perhaps one hundred feet across. A large, black iron cage crouched in its center. The bars were rough and thick, and the large lock on the gates looked crude but effective. Troops were formed up surrounding the cage and our position. The men shifted nervously, looking to the sky. They seemed to be waiting for something.

I fingered the whistle Althyof had given me and pulled it out of my pocket.

"Wait," hissed Yowtgayrr into my ear. He pulled on my shoulder, and I let him pull me back into the deepest shadows of the alley. "We need a plan."

I nodded once. "I'm going to shift to smoke, run over there, and free my family. All I need is to scatter those troops."

"No, Hank. Think it through. How will they get out of the cage? We need a key for that lock."

"That's got to be pig iron," I said. "I can use my pistol butt to pop that lock right off. All we need is for Althyof to distract or scatter this rabble."

Yowtgayrr shook his head. "I don't know about this, Hank."

I drew the citrine whistle to my lips and blew it as hard as I could. Nothing happened. No whistle, no sound, nothing. "Great, the Tverkr gave me a broken whistle," I muttered.

Yowtgayrr opened his mouth to speak, but whatever he was going to say was lost in the din that exploded from the front gate. The racket was loud and chaotic as I raced toward the mouth of the alley. The jet engine sound of the dragon breathing fire shrieked, and then the beast's front claws slammed into the gate like battering rams. The troops that had been standing in the village square ran toward the gates, drawing their swords or waving spears, as if those paltry weapons would do anything against a pissed-off dragon. I turned to smoke and dashed across the square. As I reached the rough iron bars, the enchantment faded, and I solidified.

Neither Jane nor Sig reacted at all when I appeared beside the cage. They didn't look up, they didn't startle, they just sat in the same positions they'd been in since I'd started watching them. My stomach did flip-flops.

They weren't there at all. I reached for one of the iron bars, and my hand passed right through it. It was as much a part of the glamor as the image of Jane or Sig was.

I turned and ran back to the alley, fighting desperation and a mean, dark depression. I was halfway back when I heard *him* laughing. It was the same sickening laughter I had heard in the safe house while I shot him over and over. I whirled, looking for the man I'd known as Chris Hatton. Luka. Meuhlnir's brother. I didn't see a soul, but his laughter was louder than ever.

"Where are they, you son of a bitch?" I yelled. "Why not come out? I brought my pistol!"

I was standing there, glaring around me when the troops started pouring back into the square. Frustration and anger were pounding through me like nitromethane through a dragster engine. I wasn't surprised to feel the pistols in my palms.

"Hank, run!" screamed Yowtgayrr.

He was right, of course, but running was the last thing I wanted to do. The depression of a moment ago had been trampled by a dark fury. All I wanted to do was to fight.

To kill.

I forced myself to holster my guns instead of setting them free to chew their chaotic way through the men pouring into the square—into the trap Luka had set for me. I muttered the activation word for my cloak and ran toward the alley. As I entered it, I dispelled the cloak's enchantment and ran toward the other end, feeling the invisible Alfar running with me. I pulled the citrine whistle back out of my pocket and blew sharply into it three times in rapid succession.

Luka's laughter boomed, seeming like it was coming from all around us, as we sprinted toward the back of Piltsfetl. Snarls and howls rent the air from every direction. It sounded like *oolfa* were all around us. My heart thudded in my chest, and I could feel it all the way to my wrists. *Ka-thud, ka-thud, ka-thud.* "I'm sorry," I whispered, but whether it was to the Alfar at my side or to my family, I couldn't have said.

"It isn't over yet, Hank," said Yowtgayrr.

"Run and hide," I whispered. "Let them think I was here alone. Get away—tell Meuhlnir and the rest that I thank them."

Yowtgayrr answered me with silence, but I could still feel them running with me.

Friner began to roar and smash things in earnest. I could hear the Pitra regulars screaming in terror as the gates of the garrison splintered and then exploded inwards. The snarls and growls were getting closer, and it became clear that they were herding us away from the back corner where the stairs had been. I couldn't tell how many *oolfa* were out there stalking us, but Luka was not alone. I was running blind, getting farther and farther from where I wanted to go—reacting to snarls or yips from around corners or at the end of streets we were racing down. We were being herded toward the southern wall of the garrison. "Can't go where he wants!" I panted. I turned west, heading away from the open route I was supposed to follow.

Almost instantly, the snarling in that direction grew more savage. I kept on, though, refusing to go where Luka wanted me. To the east, I heard Friner growling and hissing flame into the village. No doubt that Piltsfetl was going to be devastated by this ill-thought plan, but there was nothing I could do about that now.

We were running full tilt toward the back wall of the garrison when we saw the *oolfur*. Nearly twelve-feet tall and as thin as a winter bear, he stood, arms raised to his sides. His reach was so wide that his talons scrapped along the plaster walls of two houses facing each other across the lane. He looked like a man with a bear trapped beneath his skin. He was either wearing a bear pelt, or his suppurating skin was sprouting rough fur. His smell was foul, and I had to fight to keep from vomiting. He roared and snarled at us, but didn't move to engage us.

This time, when I felt the weight of my pistols in my palms, I let them have their way. I remembered Yowtgayrr saying I had to outpace their healing abilities to kill them, and I began to fire Kunknir and Krati as fast as I could pull the triggers and maintain any kind of accuracy. The *oolfur* jerked and thrashed his arms as the bullets smashed into his torso. Wounds gaped in his flesh, and black blood drained down his body, mixing with the purulence already running across his skin. His snarls turned into howls of pain and rage. I roared my own rage, frustration, and disappointment as I poured lead into his bent and twisted form. I'd expected him to leap to the attack, but instead, he turned and ran—using his superior speed to escape us, rather than using his superior strength to end us. I kept firing at his retreating back until the slides of both pistols locked back, empty. The immediate area was very quiet in the aftermath of all that shooting. The only sounds came from Althyof and Friner, who were fighting their way toward us. The path to the back wall, and subsequent escape from Piltsfetl, was clear of threats. We could escape to the promontory to the west of the garrison, blow Althyof's whistle, and be airborne in a matter of minutes, but the thought that the long ride through the Darks of Kruyn, evading an army of *truykar*, everything that had happened in the past two days, had been for nothing was loathsome and repugnant to me. The thought of just chucking it all and running away burnt the anger out of me.

I stood there amidst the screams of the villagers, the snarls and howls of the *oolfa*, the roars of Friner, and felt nothing but dejection and despair. My hands fell to my sides, still holding my weapons, but in a weak, loose grip.

"Hank? We should get out of here," said Yowtgayrr, as the three Alfar became visible again.

I opened my mouth to speak, but then just stood there, not knowing what to say. I should have been saying "yes" and putting words to action, but I had a sense that if I left, I'd never find Jane or Sig. That if I ran away, I'd live the rest of my life, no matter how long or short that was to be, under the cloud of the Dark Queen's curse.

"Hank?" asked Yowtgayrr, putting his hand on my shoulder.

Suddenly, mist swirled in the air in front of me. It had no source, no telltale steam from a convenient puddle of water. It thickened and began to coalesce into the vague form of a man. "Do you see that?" I croaked, pointing at the mist with Kunknir, its slide still locked back and empty.

The Alfar looked where I was pointing and then exchanged concerned looks with one another. "See what, Hank?" asked Urlikr.

The mist congealed into a white, statue-still form that was about my height. As I watched, the misty-form began to animate—seeming to breathe and swallow. Then he looked me in the eye, and I took a slow step backward, having no idea what to expect next. The form lifted its arm and pointed west, then shook its head. Color was bleeding into the misty form. His gaze was fixed and keen, and his face clarified. It was Veethar looking back at me. Veethar's mist-double opened his mouth to speak, but I couldn't hear anything it said.

"I can't hear you," I said.

"Hear who?" asked Skowvithr, coming to stand at my left side, brandishing his sword and dagger. "Is it some kind of attack, Yowtgayrr?"

I shook my head. "It's Veethar, I think."

"We see nothing, Hank," said Yowtgayrr, his mouth drawn up into an intense frown.

Veethar's form now looked solid and was rendered in full color. With a gasp, he drew air into himself. "Don't leave!" The words seemed to explode into the air around me.

"It was a glamor, Veethar," I said. "They weren't in the iron cage."

"They *are* there, Hank. Frikka has seen it. Even if your Alfar were fooled by the glamor, Frikka was not. Your family is being held in a small dwelling on the south side of the garrison. Look for a flower box with old, dead flowers in it, under a window to the left side of the door. Your family waits inside. Go!

Save them!" Veethar said the last two phrases with such intensity that I seemed to feel them in my bones.

I didn't want to believe Jane and Sig were in Piltsfetl only to have my hopes dashed again. "How do I know you aren't another kind of glamor? How can you be so sure?"

Veethar looked to the side—at nothing but air. "Frikka says to tell you to choke back your despair and marshal your faith once more. She says that..." He looked to the side again, his facial expression the picture of dubiety. "Frikka says that Supergirl needs you, and she needs you now. *Run*!"

The rosy promise of hope blossomed within me, right alongside the bête noire of fear that we would be too late. "Okay," I said. "Okay." Color began to drain from Veethar's form, washing out of his image like sand from a river bed. He raised his hand and pointed to the southeast. His form was getting soft around the edges, like a Hollywood special effect. He opened his mouth to speak, but his form was already too soft to hold enough air for speech. It was clear that he wanted me to hurry, though.

I turned my back on the form as it lost more coherence and looked Yowtgayrr in the eye. "I'm going back. I don't expect any of you to come with me. You didn't see it, but I was just in communication with Veethar and Frikka. My wife and son are here. I'm going to them."

Yowtgayrr put his hand on my forearm. "We've sworn to protect you, Hank."

"Yes, and I release you from your oath. I have to do this, but you three don't."

"Yes, we do," said Urlikr in a tone that didn't allow for dissent.

"We go where you go, Hank," said Yowtgayrr.

"Now, let's go save your family," said Urlikr. "No matter what the cost."

I turned back toward the east and marched toward the sound of Friner wreaking havoc. Snarls and savage cries sounded from every direction now, like the sound of a noose sliding ever tighter. I reloaded my guns and, holding them ready, started steering toward the south, moving in a kind of zigzag through the streets of Piltsfetl. The *oolfa* were getting closer, content to drive us south, but not yet ready to show themselves and risk our wrath. Excitement and fear boiled through me. I felt like I was going home. Somewhere along the walk, I developed a spring in my step and even caught myself whistling a time or two.

The sun was on the verge of setting, and the shadows lengthened around us. We never saw a single person—not an *oolfur*, not a villager, not a legionnaire from Pitra. We never saw a door creak open to allow a villager a glimpse of the strangers attacking their town, but I could hear them whispering behind their doors and shutters.

The houses near the southern wall were different from the ones to the west, more opulent. In the west, the houses had been small, plaster-over-wooden-lathe affairs, but in the south, they were made of dry-stacked stone. Color was painted on the doors and shutters, flower boxes rested under windows, and planters stood guard beside the doors. Then I saw it, the house Veethar had told me about. The door was painted a bright red color, as were the shutters. The flower box was a garish shade of orange that clashed with the doors and shutters such that it hurt to look at it—the clear result of 'winter-psychosis' like back home.

Fear froze me in front of the door. The house was a duplicate of the one in my nightmare. It was identical in every detail right down to the garish colors. In my dream, this moment was my last few seconds of peace and hope, the last chance to make things work out right. The fear of opening the door and finding the house empty was bad, but the fear of opening the door to find Jane or Siggy—or both—dead was debilitating hideous. "I...I can't," I mumbled.

"I understand." Yowtgayrr took two quick steps forward, and before I could say anything to stop him, he kicked the door open and rushed inside, sword and dagger flashing.

It was all inky-black shadows inside, but a female form and a smaller form were tied to chairs facing the door. My heart beat so loudly that I was sure it could be heard over the sounds of the dragon destroying Piltsfetl behind us.

"Who is it, Mommy? Who are those people?" said a small voice.

"I don't know, Sigster, but whoever they are, we have to be brave like Daddy. Okay?"

It was her voice. The keystone of the universe as far as I was concerned. It was the woman I love more than anything else in the world. It was Supergirl.

It was Jane.

I stumbled forward on numb legs. Light flashed off the pistols I held in both hands, and I thrust them savagely into the holsters on my hips. My heart beat like it was going to explode in my chest. I tried to speak, but what came out was a kind of croaking rustle—like a frog eating leaves. I saw four glints as both people in the house turned at the sounds coming from my throat. I am not ashamed to say that tears covered my cheeks, nor am I ashamed to say that in that moment I felt the love of my wife and son like a physical force. I forgot about everything else and just rushed forward, unseeing, to fall to my knees before them. I dreaded to touch them, fretting that they would be insubstantial, another glamor, but their eyes were tracking my face, and I saw matching tears on two sets of cheeks.

"Daddy?" asked Sig in the little voice he reserved for hope.

"Hank?" asked Jane at the same time.

"Yes," I croaked. "I've finally found you." I brought my hands up to caress one cheek each— Jane's left and Siggy's right.

In real time, it hadn't been that long—not even a month. But it felt longer. It felt like an age had passed, and I realized that deep down inside me, in that place so deep that it is impossible to lie to yourself, that I hadn't really expected to see them again. Not alive in any case. A strange feeling was running through me like a greyhound chasing a rabbit. It was something fluttery and golden; it was elusive and yet ubiquitous. It was relief. It was joy. It was love.

"Daddy, who are those men?" Sig asked.

"Friends," I said. "Good friends. I'll tell you all about them later. Now, we have to get you and Mommy out of here." My voice cracked with emotion.

"We have to be brave, Daddy," whispered Sig.

"Yes, Siggy, we do." I bent myself to finding all the knots that were holding my family in that little house. I got their hands free and untied the ropes that were wrapped around their waists. I bent down in front of Jane, gazing into her face like a love-struck buffoon, I'm sure. I began fiddling with the ropes that held her feet to the legs of the chair.

"Oh, Hank," she breathed in relief.

"Has it been terrible?" I asked in the same tone.

She didn't speak, but she nodded slightly. "But we made it through, didn't we, Sigster?"

Pride swelled inside me as my son nodded and looked me in the eye. "We were brave like you, Daddy."

"Yes, I'm sure you were," I said, fighting to keep my voice even, steady. Having freed them both, we stood for a moment and just looked at one another before crushing into a group hug, Sig pressed between us—what we used to call a Sig-sandwich. "We are a family again," I said.

"We were always that," said Jane around her sniffles. She stared at my face—it was a moment I had been avoiding thinking about. She touched the eye patch Althyof had enchanted for me, her fingers light and gentle. "Oh, Hank," she said in a tiny, hurt voice. "Your eye. What happened to your eye?"

I trapped her hand in my own and pulled it away from the leather patch. "Time for that later," I said with a meaningful glance at our son. She leaned into my arms and squeezed hard, but I could still feel her trembling. It felt great to be there in that warm huddle, but the world outside was still full of howling monsters. It sounded...it sounded as if they believed they had won.

"Oh," I said, pulling away. "I brought you a present, Sig." I fished the dagger Althyof had made for him out of my belt. Jane's eyebrows shot up when she saw me hand the runed dagger to our twelve-year-old son.

"A knife, Hank?" she whispered.

"This isn't Western New York," I said. "There are things here... He needs this. It's been enchanted to allow him to avoid having to fight."

"Okay," she said in a small voice, looking down at Siggy.

"Remember our talk about firearms, Sig?" I asked.

"Yes," he said with the simplicity reserved for the young.

"This dagger demands respect as much as any firearm. It is not a toy, and it should not be used for anything but defending yourself as a last resort."

"Okay."

"This dagger is very special," I said. "It was made by the Tverkar, and—"

"What's that?" he asked.

"It's what our ancestors called a race of beings that lived in a place called Nitavetlir. They are very skilled craftsmen—"

"Oh, a dwarf? Like in J.R.R. Tolkien?"

I nodded. "Yes. Tolkien got his inspiration from the Norse Sagas. That's a group of stories that tell the myths and legends about Norse mythology."

"Yeah, I know, Dad. We had a unit on all that last year in ELA."

I glanced at Jane in time to catch that special little smile she reserved for moments when Sig was being especially cute. "Okay. The Tverkar made this dagger and have given it special powers."

"A *magic* dagger? Cool!"

I told him what the dagger could do, and how to activate the invisibility enchantment. "Whenever there is any kind of danger, Sig, I want this dagger in your right hand, and I want you to activate it. Don't wait for me or Mommy to tell you to do it, just activate it and get away from the danger. Can you do that?"

Sig looked down at his feet. "I want to be brave. Like you, Daddy. I want to fight and protect you and Mommy."

"You can do all that when you are older. For right now, I need to know you will be safe so I can be brave. Will you do that?"

"Well… Okay, I guess."

"Promise me, Sigster."

"I promise."

"Go ahead and try it out," I said. "Stay in this room, though, please."

Immediately, Sig was gone. He laughed from the far corner of the room behind me. "That was neat," he said.

"Good. See how you can always get away from anything that threatens you?"

He nodded. "Like school."

I laughed. "Yes, like school." I turned back to Jane. "Althyof made something for you, too. But it's… It will tie you to my fate, in exchange for a set of powers. We need to decide if I give it to your or not."

"Tied to your fate? I'm already that," she said with a small shrug.

"When someone uses that phrase here, it means far more than back on Mithgarthr."

"Mithgarthr?" she asked.

"Home." I waved my hand around and then shrugged. "It's how they say 'Midgard.'"

She shrugged again. "Okay. What's it mean, tied to your fate?"

I told her that her life span would become linked to mine. I told her about being an Isir and what it meant. I told her about the powers it would grant her.

"So, I get to turn into a bird?"

I shrugged. "If we decide you should have it, you will have to try it out and see what you turn into. I am betting it will be a rabbit."

"No," laughed Sig. "Mommy's too cool to be a rabbit, unless it's the Monty Python kind."

"Just a wee little bunny rabbit," I said mimicking a Scottish accent.

"One, two, five!" laughed Siggy.

"Three, sir," said Jane, on cue.

"The Holy Hand Grenade of Antioch!" I said. "How does it work?"

"Armaments chapter two, verses nine to twenty-one," said Jane with a smile.

"Blow thy enemies to tiny bits, in thy mercy!" Sig was laughing so hard it was almost impossible to understand him, but we all knew it by heart anyway.

"Feast on lambs," I prompted.

"And sloths," said Jane.

"And breakfast cereals!" squealed Sig with laugh-tears running down his cheeks.

We laughed together for a short while, and I was almost able to pretend we were back at home. I was smiling at them, looking back and forth between them when Yowtgayrr cleared his throat.

"We should be moving, Hank. We are not safe here."

"Yes, just one more minute." I turned to Jane. "So, willing to risk it?" I held up the platinum ring.

"You always knew how to treat a girl," she said and gave me a peck on the cheek.

I smiled and slid the ring on her finger, just above her wedding ring. "Twice linked."

"Yeah, you are stuck with me now," she laughed.

"Come on," I said. "I have new friends for you to meet." I shepherded my family out of the house and introduced them to the Alfar. Sig seemed enthralled to learn that they were "real live elves," which seemed to amuse my three protectors to no end.

"Daddy?" asked Sig and something in his voice made a trickle of fear go racing down my spine.

"What is it, Sigster?"

"I think...I think that man is here."

Dread ripped through me, and suddenly, I could feel his eyes on me. My mind snapped back to that night in the safe house. It was Luka, I was sure. "Use your dagger, Sig." He disappeared. Jane twisted her new ring around her finger, as she peered into the shadows between the houses across from us. "Do you feel it, too?" I whispered, easing both pistols out of their holsters.

"Ah, more guns," said a voice from the darkness. I recognized it, of course. It was Jax's voice. "Why do you always bring guns, Hank?" He sounded irritated but also amused. The voice came from the shadows to the west.

"Jax is dead, leave his voice out of this."

Luka laughed, and it sounded like it was coming from the south this time. "I think if you're going to bring your guns, that I should be able to bring out my best, too. Fair enough?"

"I don't understand why you are doing this. Why you did *any* of this. Who am I to you?" I didn't really care, but I wanted to keep him talking so I could figure out where he was.

"I've explained that." He sounded irritated again, but this time his voice sounded like Yowtgayrr and came from the north. "At the diner and in my note." He cackled.

I was spinning around like a whirly-gig, and he was getting off on it. He was playing with me—once again. "I didn't understand it then, and I don't understand it now. You'd already ruined my life with this curse, why take it farther? Why bring me here?"

"Put your guns away, and I'll tell you everything." Meuhlnir's voice came from the east this time.

"I know it's you, why play around with the stupid voices? I mean, Yowtgayrr is standing right next to me. Who are you supposed to be fooling?"

"Oh, I'm not trying to fool anyone, Hank. If I were, you'd be fooled." It sounded like a whisper from right behind me, but I was standing in the middle of the street, surrounded by my friends. "Go on, Hank, put your guns down. *Join me*. I promise to let Jane and Sig go. Or they can stay here and live with you forever."

If the Norse god Loki was inspired by this man, then Luka's character wasn't concerned with honesty or keeping promises. "You first," I said. "Go ahead and put your shape-shifting abilities down."

Luka chuckled from my right. "See? *This* is why I brought you here. You are funny."

"Yeah, I'm a laugh a second. Why don't you step out of the shadows so we can start laughing together?" My voice had gone as cold and empty as the space between the stars in the night sky.

"That doesn't sound very friendly at all, Hank. Maybe I'll let my underlings feast on your boy." His voice had turned nasty.

Fury surged through me like a tsunami. "Touch him ever again, and I'll bring such wrath down on you that you will never have a moment's peace. You won't be able to eat, sleep or even shit without having to look around and make sure I'm not there. *With my guns.*"

"Does this mean we can't be friends?" Luka's tone was mocking, but it had an edge of anger to it.

"I think that came off the table when you killed Jax. Before, maybe. All those bodies in your little cave of horrors."

"What is it they say? What happens in Vegas, stays in Vegas? Nothing that happens on Mithgarthr really matters, Hank. Can't you see that now?" His voice had stopped moving around—it was coming from the roof of the house to the north. "Those were *thralls*, Hank. Meaningless people with meaningless lives."

"That's where you're wrong, Luka. What you did there brought me here, for whatever obscure reason you and the Dark Queen want me here." I turned toward the northeast, not wanting him to know I had a good idea where he was.

"Don't call her that," he snapped. "You have the blood of the Isir, Hank. You belong here."

"And Jane?"

"As I understand it, you sort of like her around. You wouldn't come here without her. Or your little guy." His tone was light, friendly.

"So, things on Mithgarthr *do* matter?" I eased the hammers back on my pistols and raised my arms to my most comfortable firing position.

"No, not in the least. Any descendants of the Isir trapped on your *klith* are ignorant of their roots, their powers, their *privileges*. Plus, people on your world have no respect for racial boundaries. Blacks mate with whites, Indians mate with Hispanics. The people of Mithgarthr are a muddle." He was creeping toward the edge of the roof.

I backed toward the house on the south side, hoping to see something on the opposite roof. "You're an ignorant racist, too? Over there, we realize that racial boundaries are arbitrary and stupid. I mean, who can honestly believe their ethnic heritage is superior to another because their ancestors moved north and someone else's stayed where life began? It's a stupid thought."

"I don't think so. *Your* ancestors are superior to the other races of Mithgarthr." I was sure Luka was moving back and forth on the roof, just out of sight. "It matters that they moved to the north. You are Isir because of it."

I settled into a combat stance. It sounded like Luka was opposite me now. "So, because some ancestor of yours did some fiddling with your genetics, that makes you superior? Have you had your eyes closed for the last five hundred years? You are an evil man, Luka."

"I transcend the silly ideas of good and evil, Hank. Surely, you can see that? And besides, the fiddling with my genetics *does* make me superior, just as your genetics make you superior."

"More nonsense," I said, letting a trace of irritation leak into my voice. "You're nothing but a common thug. A murd—"

"Hank! Look out!" screamed Jane and something roared from the roof above and behind me.

I dove to my left, activating the cloak as I fell, but I still felt something hot as a poker sliding across my cheek. In smoke form, I twisted around, and I aimed Kunknir at the center of mass of a large thing with the skin and features of a man, but what looked like the bone structure of a wolf. He had sores all over his body, and they were dripping a putrid-smelling, foul-looking pus.

Luka. My nemesis, all dressed up in his werewolf outfit.

I deactivated my cloak, and Kunknir barked, sounding strange. Luka yelped as the rounds tore into the muscles of his torso. Hatred burned in his eyes, and he crouched over me where I lay. Jane slammed into Luka from the side, knocking him sideways and against the wall despite his superior size and strength.

She jumped, her leap carrying her to the roof of the house across the lane. She stood straight, and a set of huge black wings unfurled from her shoulders. Raven's wings. Luka screamed in rage and stepped by me. A strange grunting sound came from his misshapen mouth, and I thought he was trying to laugh. He flexed his overlong toes, and his too-long thighs bunched like an Olympic speed skater's.

"Jane! Get away!" I screamed. I leapt to my feet and tried to catch Luka, but it was too late

Luka sprang up at her, growling deep in his throat. His clawed fingers raked down the side of Jane's left leg, splattering blood across the cobblestoned street. He cuffed her hard, and she flew to the side, landing hard. Jane bunched the muscles of her back and flapped those huge black wings. She shot off the roof but fell to the cobbles. Luka made his weird chuffing laugh and jumped to the ground. He bent toward her, his eyes locked on hers, and he snarled with hatred and savagery. Saliva dripped from his long canine teeth.

I tracked Luka with both weapons, but with him standing over my wife, I couldn't let myself fire. "No shot!" I yelled, hoping someone could help somehow. I took a rapid step forward, but Urlikr whirled by me. He was spinning like a dancer, his arms extended, longsword in one hand and that long, barbaric-looking dagger in the other. As he reached Luka's side, he snapped both wrists, and long, gaping wounds appeared across Luka's back and down one side. Without pausing, Urlikr leapt into the air, whirled, and lashed out with his back leg, like some kung fu master in a cheap martial arts movie. His foot thudded into Luka's neck, just below his left ear and Luka sprawled on top of Jane. Urlikr bent at the waist and scoured Luka's back with both blades before jumping away. Growling, Luka pushed away from my wife and whirled into a crouch, tracking Urlikr with vicious eyes.

Kunknir and Krati snapped up into firing position, and I started squeezing the triggers. Reports boomed and echoed back and forth across the cobbles, bouncing between the stone walls of the houses on either side. The distinctive smell of burnt gunpowder filled my nose like the perfume of a long-lost lover. Luka screeched and snarled and howled, shaking his head savagely from side to side. He pointed a long finger from a long hand at the end of a gangling arm at me and barked like an angry dog.

I didn't stop firing, but I shuffled toward Jane. She lay on the ground, panting and making a mewling noise deep in her throat. "You can heal yourself," I said. She looked at me, startled, and then smiled. She ran a hand down the cruel gash in her thigh. As her palm covered the part of the wound, the skin on either side of the cut knit together neatly, not even leaving a scar. "Remember what else you can do."

Jane blanched and looked up at me with wide eyes. "I...I can't do that," she cried.

Luka rose to his full height, which must have been fifteen feet, towering above the eaves of the houses on either side of the street and glared at me, and then

Urlikr was there, slashing across his midsection with a longsword. Without breaking eye contact with me, Luka pistoned his arm forward like a striking snake, and he caught Urlikr by the neck. He jerked the Alf forward, off his feet and three feet into the air, and snarled into Urlikr's face, spraying spittle and a greenish-brown pus all over the Alf. He shook Urlikr ferociously, back and forth, and back and forth, like a Rottweiler playing tug of war, and then threw Urlikr to the ground. The Alf's head bounced from the cobbles with a sickening *crack*. Thick, black blood splattered across the stones. Urlikr lay crumpled into an unnatural position—maybe alive, maybe dead.

With a whimper, Jane's face filled with the pain of seeing Urlikr lying all rimpled up on the ground. She looked at me and mouthed the words, "My fault."

Yowtgayrr stooped by Urlikr's crumpled form, and Skowvithr leapt to stand over them both.

With a savage shriek, I began firing both pistols again, pausing only long enough to eject spent magazines and slam full ones into the guns as needed. I don't know how many rounds I fired, I just remember seeing Luka's body dancing and jinking as the lead slugs bit into his flesh from close range. He was alternating between howling and making a strangely human-sounding scream as the bullets slammed into him. I was causing him pain, but despair began to settle around me like a fog as I saw that I wasn't causing enough damage to put him down.

"Run!" I shouted, but I knew there was nowhere to go, and even if there had been, Urlikr wasn't going anywhere. I hoped Sig was hiding out of sight because I could tell from the insane rage scrawled across Luka's face, that this time, no quarter would be given to my family.

Luka crouched as if he were about to leap at me. Jane muttered something under her breath, and Luka glanced at her and then shook his head as if to clear it. He looked back at me and tilted his head to the side. He took a hesitant step away from me and shook his head again. I shoved Kunknir into its holster and fished in my pockets for the whistle. Maybe Althyof could get them to safety. I tossed the citrine whistle to Jane and stepped closer to Luka. I was praying—to whom I had no idea—that if I had to die, then let it be that I died saving my family and friends. Kunknir was back in my hand and seemed eager to point itself at Luka's heart. Jane looked at me in confusion, holding the whistle carved from a precious gem.

"Just blow it! Long and hard!" I yelled.

She gave me the strangest look—a small crook of a smile under hurt eyes streaming tears—but raised the whistled to her lips and blew it. It would have been a loud shriek if the whistle made noise. She looked at me in confusion. "Broken," she muttered. From the north, Friner made his basso roar that set my teeth on edge. Jane's gaze drifted up and toward the sound, and her eyes opened very, very wide. "What in god's name is that?"

"The cavalry."

Luka jerked his head from side to side and his eyes cleared. He snarled and slashed at me, but Skowvithr stepped forward, longsword and dagger swinging with a vengeance, and Luka backed away, growling and snarling. He kept us all in sight, but his head darted to the left and the right, looking for somewhere to run. He tilted his head back and made a strange, ululating kind of howl.

Oolfa from all over the small garrison town howled or roared in response. It sounded like there were quite a few of them out there in the shadows.

"Give it up, Luka," I said with a bravado I didn't feel. "Even you can't stand up to a dragon."

"Dragon?" Jane whispered, sounding like a lost little girl.

He sneered at me—an expression that was hideous on his distorted wolf-face—and made the ululating call a second time. Again, the *oolfa* howled and roared in response, but this time, they sounded closer. Much closer. I ejected my empty magazines and fed my pistols full ones. I had no idea what was about to happen, but I had the feeling that the time it took me to reload, even with the elaborate setup Prokkr had outfitted me with, was going to cost me in blood.

A new kind of howling sounded from the west. I'd been scared before, but when I glanced down the lane and saw ten or twelve *oolfa* sprinting toward us, I learned the real meaning of terror. Each one of the beast-men was covered in blackened, necrotic sores, and looked like a creepy cross between a demon, and either a wolf or a bear. Luka howled, and it sounded like a shout of victory. The smell washed over us first. I've been to a lot of crime scenes and have smelled some cadavers in a decayed and fouled state, but the stench coming off the *oolfa* was enough to make me want to hold my breath forever. I didn't even want to breathe through my mouth because the foul odor was so strong, the air tasted of corruption and doom.

Luka made that strange barking laugh of a sound and stood straight. The *oolfa* swaggered and strutted toward us, assured of their victory. I turned back to Luka and smirked at him—though the only thing I felt was terror. "You are supposed to be immortal, right?" I forced myself to laugh. "So immortal that you need fifteen other immortals to kill little old Hank from New York?" Luka growled and took a menacing half-step toward me. Skowvithr slashed at his side, and Luka batted at his blade, snarling and spitting. The *oolfa* coming up the street snarled and roared and began to come at us faster.

I had no plan for escape. Worse yet, I had no plan for any kind of credible defense against sixteen werewolves and werebears. The only thought I had was to get everyone inside the house that Jane and Sig had been held captive in. "We have to get inside," I said. "We can use the door as a bottleneck. Maybe." Jane looked up at me and opened her mouth to speak, but whatever she'd been planning to say was washed out by the painful squealing jet engine sound of Friner spitting fire. Her head snapped toward the end of the lane, and her eyes opened very wide, while her mouth made an almost perfect O of surprise.

Sorrowful shrieks and woeful wailing filled the night air. A conflagration of red-orange liquid fire splashed across the rank of *oolfa* coming up the lane at us. A languishing lament tore from Luka's throat. Friner leapt into the air from the next lane over and slammed down on top of the house across from me, spraying us with shards of glass and splinters of wood. Its eyes were windows of hate, and thick blood dripped from the exposed fangs in its great maw of a mouth. Friner's massive head darted forward as quick and as sinuous as a snake, and its massive jaws snicked shut, missing Luka by fractions of an inch. Luka yelped as he twisted away and reeled into the wall of a house. He cast such a look of hatred and fury at me that I had to fight to keep from taking a step backward. Then fear filled his face as Friner sucked in a puissant gulp of air in preparation for another blast of fire, and Luka turned and raced to the east as fast as his stretched and contorted legs could carry him.

"Althyof!" I screamed, fearing that Friner was about to unleash a jet of fire that would burn us all. The dragon looked at me with a hint of reproach and then squatted, getting ready to leap into the air to pursue Luka. "No! Althyof, we need to get out of here! Urlikr's down, hurt! Get my family to the others!"

The sinuous, silky song Althyof was singing mutated and meandered into a fractious inflection that was at once both imperious and surrendering. The song seemed to cajole and command as it twisted and twined around dissonant harmony that set my teeth on edge like fingernails sliding down a blackboard. Friner hissed in frustration and looked at me, baleful and angry, but its massive rear legs relaxed back into a squat. Althyof leaned forward and waved at us. I glanced at Yowtgayrr, but the Alf was staring down at Urlikr's broken form, who hadn't moved throughout the rest of the battle. Skowvithr put his hand on the Alf's shoulder and whispered something that made Yowtgayrr nod. Skowvithr came to stand by my side.

"Urlikr?" I asked.

Skowvithr jerked his chin back and forth. "Yowtgayrr is seeing to his remains."

"I'm sorry, Skowvithr." I had that lead balloon feeling in my gut again. I decided, then and there, that Luka was not going to be allowed to go on killing the good people around me, and Meuhlnir would just have to get with the program. "I wish—"

"I know, Hank," said the Alf. "We all knew the risks. We all knew who—what—we were going to face. Let's not diminish Urlikr's sacrifice with despair."

"Fair enough," I said. Sig put his hand on my arm, and I marveled that he was no longer child-sized.

"Is he dead, Dad?" Sig asked.

"Yes, Son. Urlikr died protecting your Mommy."

Sig made an odd sound deep in the back of his throat and glanced in the direction Luka had run. "What about—"

"Don't worry," I said. "We'll catch up to him later. I promise."

"What now, then?"

"Now, we ride a dragon."

His eyes were very wide as I led him to Friner's flank.

FORTY-TWO

The dragon landed in a small break in the foliage, a bit ahead of Meuhlnir's party. I helped Jane and Sig climb down the beast's back leg and then turned to help Yowtgayrr and Skowvithr with Urlikr's broken body. Althyof's song was a twisting, undulating thing, squirming in a harmonic minor packed with dissonance and counter-harmony. Friner stood twitching its great head back and forth like a metronome and alternating between hissing and a weird crooning sound. The tip of the dragon's tail was jiggling and trembling. Sig stood shock-still, staring up at the great beast.

We got Urlikr's body down and away from the dragon, and then Althyof slid down the dragon's flank without breaking his melody. He backed away from Friner, keeping his eyes locked on the dragon's. The dragon began to hiss louder and with more vehemence.

Jane shot me a questioning look, and I tried to smile, but between the great beast of a dragon hissing at us and the squirming, vellicating runesong, my smile wasn't very reassuring. Althyof stopped singing mid-phrase but had his hand held up and his eyes locked on Friner's. The big red beast lurched half a step to the left and shook its great wings. The dragon narrowed its eyes at Althyof and hissed with a seething hatred. Althyof seemed unconcerned, standing there like an insane school crossing guard. With his left hand, he began to shoo the dragon away like you might chase away a pesky cat. I doubt anyone can read a dragon's expression, but I got the feeling that Friner was not amused. Its hissing grew more insistent, though its eyes remained locked on the Tverkr's in front of it. Althyof pointed to the north and uttered a sharp word that made me want to get away from him. Sig stood next to me and took my hand in his sweaty palm. Friner roared, almost in Althyof's face, and I'm not ashamed to say that my first instinct was to run, and to run fast. The Tverkr seemed unfazed, he pointed to the north with one hand and made the shooing gesture again with the other. The dragon hissed and broke eye contact, and then shuffled away, shooting venomous glances at us over its shoulder. It looked like a recalcitrant child being sent to its room. With a parting shriek, the dragon launched itself into the sky and battered us with the wind of its departure.

Althyof stared, watching the dragon flying north and away from us. He kept staring long after I had lost the speck of the dragon to distance and altitude. Finally, his shoulders slumped, and the Tverkr sighed. "Every time, it takes more and more out of me," he breathed.

"He fights you," said Yowtgayrr.

It wasn't a question, but Althyof nodded anyway. "He tries to break the binding every time I call him and every time I send him away. He's getting stronger."

"Was that a real live dragon?" asked Sig.

"Yes, one of the largest ones I know of," said Althyof.

Sig gave me a hard look. "You said that monsters were made up. You said monsters were for fun."

"Where we are from, they are," I said. "At least non-human monsters." I turned to Yowtgayrr. "Do you need help with…the burial?"

"I couldn't leave him there to be eaten by—" He stopped talking, and his eyes darted in Sig's direction.

"Of course not."

Meuhlnir and the others galloped into the clearing, sending even more dust up into the atmosphere. When Meuhlnir saw Urlikr's remains, his face fell, and he cursed under his breath. "Another death on my brother's tally sheet?"

No one spoke until Sif dismounted. "Is anyone else injured? Hank? Your family?"

"Bruises and scrapes," said Skowvithr.

"Urlikr saved us from worse. And Friner and Althyof, of course."

"And Luka?" asked Meuhlnir, his voice tight.

"Gone," I said in a gruff voice. "He ran when Friner took care of his minions."

"Of course, he did," said Yowrnsaxa. "He's good at running away." Her scowl was intense.

The silence stretched between us.

I looked away from Urlikr's body and stared into the woods around us. "What do we do now?"

Meuhlnir looked at the Alf's corpse for a long moment. "We should take a *proo* back to Trankastrantir and regroup. But, first, I think, we should bury Urlikr."

We buried him under a stately elm at the edge of the clearing.

"He should be in *Skowkur Kuthadna*, but I guess Tiwaz can find him here as well as there," said Yowtgayrr. He began to speak in a language I did not comprehend, but the words had a ritualistic feel to them, so we all stood with heads bowed. When he'd finished, he and Skowvithr began moving dirt back into the grave, covering the body. I bent to assist them, but Yowtgayrr shook his head. "This is a matter for Priests of Tiwaz, Hank, though we appreciate your offer to help."

I nodded and followed the others to the center of the clearing to give the Alfar space to grieve.

Meuhlnir put his hands on his knees and bent to look Sig in the eye. "And who's this mighty warrior, Hank?" he asked.

"Meuhlnir, meet my son Sig. Sig this is my friend, Meuhlnir."

Sig was looking at his feet when Yowrnsaxa pushed Meuhlnir to the side, muttering something about great oafs standing in the road. She curtseyed in front of Sig and smiled. "I'm your Auntie Yowrnsaxa," she said. "I bet you are hungry. All boys are always hungry. Would you eat something, Sig?"

Sig looked up at me with uncertainty splashed across his face like paint. I tousled his hair. "She is a very good cook," I said. "I bet she has something sweet tucked away." Yowrnsaxa winked at me and led Sig off toward the horses. Mothi put his hand on my son's shoulder and walked with them, telling some joke that made them all laugh.

When the Alfar rejoined us, we mounted. Jane rode behind me, her arms wrapped around my waist and her cheek on my shoulder blade. Having her so close was like balm on a third-degree burn. Sig found a place in front of Yowrnsaxa, smiling at her with sweet shyness.

Meuhlnir led us southeast, toward the closest *proo* in Kvia. It was a long, dusty trip that led us out of the Forest of Kvia and into the hills on the eastern edge of the country. We camped, and the Isir spent the evening getting to know my family. The Alfar were withdrawn and quiet, though they spared small smiles for Sig.

On the second day, we rode into the afternoon before Meuhlnir and Veethar stiffened in their saddles at the same moment and drew up. Veethar looked at Meuhlnir with a stricken expression and something passed between them.

"What is it?" I asked.

"Could be nothing," muttered Meuhlnir. "I don't want to speculate."

Two days later, we reached the barrow that contained the *proo*. The sun was low in the sky, and we were all tired and looking forward to the comfort of Frikka and Veethar's home. Meuhlnir jumped down from Sinir's back and trotted inside the barrow. He stomped back out, his face a mask of irritation and disappointment. "We should set up camp," he groused. "The *proo* is gone." He and Veethar shared another look.

"What's going on?" I asked.

Meuhlnir shook his head. "Luka must have closed this *proo*."

Everyone stopped what they were doing and turned to look at Meuhlnir. Veethar was looking at the ground beneath his feet.

"And what about earlier? When you both tensed up?"

Meuhlnir sighed and looked down at his feet. "There was some kind of event."

"Well, I'd gathered that," I said. Jane put her hand on my arm, and I patted it.

"Something happened," said Veethar. "Something big."

"Was it the closing of this *proo*?" asked Jane. Veethar couldn't meet her gaze, and Meuhlnir was suddenly busy rooting through his packs.

"Tell us," I demanded.

Meuhlnir stopped rooting and glanced up to meet my eye. "I think you might be with us a while longer."

"Why?" asked Jane.

Meuhlnir shook his head. "We don't know anything for sure," he said. "All we know is that this one *proo* is gone."

"Fine, you are absolved from being wrong in your guesses," said Jane with a touch of impatience.

"Veethar?" I asked.

Veethar looked me in the eye. "We think Luka has traveled to Herperty af Roostum—the Rooms of Ruin." He glanced away when my expression showed bewilderment instead of understanding. "Pilrust," he whispered.

"Why would he go there?"

"Haymtatlr created a—"

"Yes," I snapped. "Haymtatlr created *Kyatlarhodn* and blew it, opening the first *proo*."

"*At Pilrust*," murmured Veethar.

"And?"

"Hank, if there is anywhere in Osgarthr that one could control the *preer*, it would be at Pilrust," said Meuhlnir. "In the Rooms of Ruin."

I shook my head.

"*All* of them," whispered Veethar. "This *proo*..."

"This *proo* was ours," said Meuhlnir. "Veethar's and mine—the other end is in the Vault of *Preer* below Veethar's longhouse. Luka had no access to it. He didn't know where it was."

What they were getting at dawned on me, and I closed my eyes and groaned.

"What is it, Hank?" asked Jane.

"They think Luka closed *all* of the *preer*. Including the one that leads to your home."

Neither Veethar or Meuhlnir would meet Jane's eyes. Sif came to stand near us and put her hand on Jane's shoulder. Jane just stood there, shifting her gaze between Veethar and Meuhlnir. "Open them again," she said.

"Yes," said Veethar. "We must."

"How long will it take?" Jane asked.

"Pilrust is very far away," said Meuhlnir. "We are used to calculating distances from where we are to the closest *proo* and then from its terminus to the destination."

"How far?" asked Jane with an edge to her voice.

"Thousands of miles," said Mothi. "We are on the southern continent." He drew the rough shape of the continent in the dirt and then another above it to the north. A land bridge similar to Central America back home connected the two continents. He made a point in the center of the northern land mass. "Pilrust is on the northern continent, about here. It is in a sheltered valley—surrounded by mountains."

"That looks like more than five thousand miles if your continents are the same size as the America's in Mithgarthr," I muttered.

Mothi shrugged. "I don't know."

"We are not provisioned or equipped for a trip like that," said Meuhlnir. "We need more gear, more horses, more food and water. Perhaps a ship."

"And the Pitra Empire may not be disposed to help us," I said.

"Indeed, they will not be," said Mothi. "They are, at best, friendly to the Dark Queen, and at worst, they are her pawns."

"Can we outfit ourselves here?" asked Jane. "In Kvia?"

"Perhaps," said Sif. "*After* we try another *proo*."

No one said anything after that, but I had the feeling we were all sharing the same certainty that the *preer* were closed and that we were all trapped in Kvia. The trip to Pilrust was long either way, and even the shortest, most direct route was a massive undertaking. Even if we rode directly to Pilrust, riding hard every day and took no days off to rest or to rest the horses, the trip was likely to take more than half a year. My face hardened in a grimace.

Jane wormed her hand into mine. I looked down into her face, and a warmth suffused me like I was stepping in from the cold of winter and directly into a sauna. She smiled up at me. "It's not ideal," she said. "But we *are* together, and you haven't taken us on vacation in a long time."

"And you have friends to share the road with you," said Sif.

"Together, we will face this trial," said Veethar. "We will overcome this."

Frikka stood next to her husband and grinned. "Who knows? Veethar may even start speaking in paragraphs instead of single words or short sentences." Even Veethar grinned at that.

"You will be able to return to your *klith*, Hank," said Meuhlnir. "I promise that you will."

"If you still want to return, after all this is over," said Frikka with a small grin. "I think I know several places that might have you, if you no longer do."

FORTY-
THREE

Fury.

The woman named Hel, who used to think of herself as Liz, opened the rusty metal door and frowned. The room in which Luka had chosen to live was filled with the detritus of lost ages. He stood from a squat and smiled at her. His smile made her want to choke him.

"*What have you done?*" she screamed. She took three quick steps into the ruin of a room Luka had chosen to live in. She slammed the door as hard as she could. Her hands went automatically to smooth her wind-swept hair. She hated looking like a tatterdemalion—in front of Luka *or* Vowli. She didn't understand why the two men had to compete for her attentions, when, despite minor dalliances with Vowli since their return, Luka had already won. Truth to tell, though, Hel found she didn't really mind their competition all that much. What she did mind was incompetence.

Luka's smile faded. "I-I...my Queen, I closed the *preer* to stop my brother and his friends from—"

She sneered at the weakness in his voice. The way he pretended at innocence infuriated her. The actions he'd taken at and after the fiasco at Piltsfetl smacked of his disregard for her needs. The stakes were too high for the level of incompetence he had shown. She wondered if he had outlived his usefulness.

"Who stands before me? Luka *Oolfhyethidn* or some lost, petulant child?" Her eyes lingered on Luka's lean form. He looked so much healthier now that the meat was plentiful, and he didn't have to sacrifice to make sure she had enough. He looked like a tatterdemalion, though, and she hated that. Her eyes, hardening and burning with rage, slid down his torn clothing, noting the half-healed injuries and abraded skin.

"My Queen, I—"

Hel whirled away, fearing that if she continued to look at him while he groveled her rage monster would loose its chains. In the tunnels behind the rusty door—the tunnel where Vowli waited—the wind howled and shrieked, burying the Ruins of Pilrust with the dust of lost ages. Luka had acted at the worst possible time. Vowli had called Luka befuddled and lost. Hel scoffed at the thought.

"What have I done, my Queen?"

Her expression hardened as she thought again of the reason that had forced her to come to this dusty, decayed tomb. She turned until she could look at Luka askance. Hel's eyes blazed, making her look like a demon of ice and fire.

Luka shrank away from her gaze.

She felt the words that would set him alight tickling her tongue, and she forced herself to think of the time they had spent together in Mithgarthr. After all he had done for her, all the mayhem he had wrought in her name, she owed him a better death than the agony of fire. Memories flashed through her mind, reminding her of the man Luka could be when properly motivated. She put her back to the rusty metal doors and squinted at the ground beneath his feet. The ghoulish, terrible expression that had been on her face for so long that it felt as if it were cast in iron, grew even colder.

His knees buckled, and he fell to the ground, head down, arms held out in supplication. It cooled her fury a small degree to see him act with such respect. She understood the power he had over her. She understood that his loyalty and fealty had sunk long fangs into her heart. She understood the reasons she loved him and regretted that her love made what had to come next so difficult. Her mouth narrowed to a brutal, unforgiving slit. *Vowli was right*, she thought.

Her gaze drifted around the small room, lingering on all the things that offended her—the rotted ruins of ages-old furniture, the colored dust that had once been carpeting and the boxes littered helter-skelter around the room that her time in Mithgarthr had taught her were computers of some kind. She gritted her teeth and blew out her breath in angry frustration. "Thou art mad now, Luka, and reft of mind," she snapped, and he recoiled as if she'd slapped him. Hel's smile was vicious, and she pointed at him with her chin. She sighed, knowing she didn't want to do what she must, and it was a grim, sad sound. The destructive powers she'd refined over the years were known to him, and she could see that knowledge twisting fear into him.

Her lips writhed as she fought to keep from saying the words that would end his life in a blaze of emerald green flame. "You promised to take care of him, Luka." Her voice was far from bland, and the glare she gave him from under her long lashes was hateful and a touch insane. Her love for him was absent in her expression but evident in how hard she fought to keep herself from burning him where he stood.

Luka pushed himself into a proper kneeling bow and set his jaw. "My Queen, if I have offended you,

my life is yours. It always has been. You know that."
He looked her in the eye, the very picture of calm
acceptance.

"Just tell me *why*, Luka. Why did you flee from
him *again*?" Her face convulsed with a fresh wave of
rage. "And why did you close the *preer*?"

"I'm sorry, Queen Hel. That little pretender
brought—"

Like some wild beast, her rage leapt out of her with
its claws extended. "*You left me trapped in Pitra! I had
to ride here on a damn horse!*"

The muscles in his torso spasmed and his upper
body jerked away from her. His eyes were large and
shiny with the hint of tears before he turned his gaze
away from the madness and acrimony in her
expression. "He had... My brother, Meuhlnir, was
helping him. They had a dwarf... I think it was
Althyof... a-and he had a dragon. F-Fafnir or maybe
Friner. I think it was—"

"Do you think I *care*, Luka?" Her tone was
suddenly silky soft and smooth.

"I... The dragon flamed the *oolfa* I had with me.
The forces from Pitra had been distracted by an attack
on the gates, so it—"

"*I know the circumstances*!" she screamed. In a
flash, she took three quick steps across the room and
shoved her face toward his. "Your little games with
your many-times-great-grandson have cost me quite
a lot, Luka."

Luka's jaw dropped open, and his eyes opened very
wide. "Grandson? What do you—"

"Don't pretend at innocence, Luka."

"My Queen, I don't know what you are talking about."

She looked at him with hard eyes for a protracted moment. Finally, with twitching eyelids, her expression softened a small amount. "How can you not know?" she asked. "It's plain to see."

Luka shook his head as if by doing so he could stop the knowledge from coming.

"He's your blood, Luka. That annoying cop. He's your descendant. So is the *other* one."

"But... How..."

She laughed, and a bit more of the anger left her face. "Oh, dear one, if, after all this time, you don't know how to make children..."

He flashed a small smile at her. "No, I mean how can he be—"

"The blessed act must have occurred on one of our trips to visit the Vikings, playing at being gods. I've never been jealous of your flings with the girls in Mithgarthr. After all, they are gone in such a short time."

He nodded in a way that suggested he hadn't been listening to what she said. "But if Jensen is my kin, then that means—"

"Now, he's starting to see it," said Hel with a sour grin. "Yes, slow one, he's like the other one."

Luka dropped his eyes. "This changes everything, my Queen," he whispered.

"No, Luka, this changes *nothing*." The sentence sounded flat and terrible in the small, ugly space, even to her.

He looked up at her with a pleading expression. "No, my Queen. This changes *everything*."

She looked at him through slitted eyes, and she wondered if he was about to stand up to her at long last. She almost hoped he would but, in the end, didn't think he would. After all, Luka knew his place. "Why, Luka, lea'vst thou not off?" she demanded.

His gaze hardened, and he stood, mouth set in a grim, defiant line. "No, my Queen."

"Take me home, Luka, then we will deal with your grandson. Turn on the *preer*."

He looked at her, and a crafty expression stole over his face like a thief in the night. "No, my Queen. Let me explain."

A large, furious frown spread across Hel's face. "Are you standing up to me, my Champion?"

"I am standing up *for* you, my Queen, as I always have. Killing him now would be a mistake."

She scoffed and shook her head, a dark, deadly expression on her face. "You can't convert him, Trickster. He won't be converted."

"With all due respect, my Queen, I can and I will. I have an idea."

She looked at him for a long, hard moment, reassessing him for the first time in centuries. Her frown faded, and her tense muscles relaxed. "You always knew how to convince me, sweet Luka."

"I think we should set a trap of sorts. Here." Luka grinned like the mischievous trickster he was. "One which severs his ties with my brother's family and leaves him adrift in this land—which he knows nothing about. Maybe we can finally be rid of Meuhlnir, Sif, and all the others at the same time."

Hel laughed. "Oh, excellent, Luka. Your wickedness inspires me, yet again. For that, I'm willing to put up with this wretched place for a while longer."

She offered him her hand with a smile and pulled him into her embrace. "Inspire me a bit more, my Champion," she purred.

FORTY-FOUR

The second *proo* had been closed, of course. It took eleven weeks and a handful of days to get back to Veethar's estates—even using his secret tunnel through the mountains. We must have made a grim picture, riding through the streets of Trankastrantir, judging from the stir we caused in the karls and thralls who lived there.

Siggy had enjoyed every square inch of the journey and had developed a close relationship with "Cousin Mouthy" and "Auntie Yarns." From what I could tell, everyone enjoyed seeing Sig marveling at the horses, Mothi's weapons, the Alfar, the Tverkr, the Takmar's Horse Plains, the tunnel between Takirnia and Suelhaym, campfires, sleeping under the stars—everything a thirteen-year-old should love. I was a bit amazed that he didn't seem to miss his electronics, and I was proud that he took everything in stride and did what was asked of him with very little grumbling.

I don't think I'd ever felt so much relief as when we rode through the gates to Veethar's estate. I was surprised at how much it felt like coming home. Supergirl squeezed me tight around the waist with a sharply indrawn breath as she saw what little that the Tverkar had left of the white dragon. "You fought that?" she whispered.

"He harried that beast until it wanted to commit suicide," laughed Althyof.

I grinned and shook my head. "It was your singing and dancing that did that."

We had decided to rest a while before we made the journey to Pilrust. We needed time to decompress— to come to terms with the costs of getting Jane and Sig back. I think the other Isir needed time to figure out what they were going to do about Luka.

Veethar showed us maps. The ruins of Pilrust were roughly in the center of Kleymtlant, which literally meant "the forgotten land." The name didn't inspire much confidence that the journey would be easy. Just getting to Kleymtlant was going to be difficult. The map showed the obstacles we'd have to get past if we took the land route: a very long mountain range that stretched from south of Trankastrantir to well north of Pilrust, the Great Wood of Suel—a forest that seemed to run over half the length of the continent of Suelhaym Eekier, something that was called the Jungles of Fyalir, and we'd have to travel through the Pitra Empire. The sea route wasn't spoken of much. Veethar just grimaced and shook his head when I asked about it. Adding to that, none of the maps had much detail about Kleymtlant itself, other than the mountain range, the coast line, and the location of the ruins of Pilrust. It was a logistical nightmare, especially given that the Isir were so used to traveling by *proo* that they could hardly comprehend a journey of such magnitude.

I knew Yowtgayrr and Skowvithr were glued to me, and it seemed sure that Meuhlnir, Veethar, and Mothi were going. I didn't like the idea of asking Jane to stay behind with Sig, but I liked the idea of risking them again even less. To be honest, I wasn't sure I would have anything to say about whether Jane came along or not, and I doubted whether Sif, Yowrnsaxa, and Frikka could be convinced to stay behind. Althyof would follow the gold, of course. Even so, the party seemed comically small given what we'd seen Luka and the Dragon Queen muster.

One day shortly after we'd arrived, Jane and I were sitting on a fence, looking at the impressive herd of horses Veethar owned. It was hot, and the leather of the eye patch chaffed and itched, so I'd pulled it off and hung it around my wrist.

"Too hot?" asked Althyof from behind me.

The last thing I wanted was to sound ungrateful. "I'm just not quite used to it yet. And it's such a hot day."

"Yes," he said. "I've brought you this hat to shield your face from the sun."

He put the hat on my head, and I gasped in surprise. It was like I had opened my left eye and could see from it again. The *runeskowld* laughed, but not unkindly.

"What in the world?"

"Well," he said, "I *am* the best enchanter in the known universe as I believe I have already told you once." He looked about as pleased with himself and smug as any one person could. "Close your eye."

I did and gasped again. With my right eye closed, I could see in a 360-degree arc around my body. I opened my eye, and the effect faded back to normal vision. I spent a few moments opening and closing my eye, marveling at the enchantment.

"I wanted to give you the ability to see remotely the way the *syown* sometimes works with the Isir, but alas, I haven't quite worked out the runes to inscribe and the runes to sing to make that happen. I'll keep working on it, though."

"You do that," I said with a grin. "After all, I'm paying you good money."

The Tverkr looked at me with a sparkle in his eyes and then turned and walked away.

"I don't think I will ever get used to that," whispered Jane.

"What?" I peered at her from under my new floppy hat.

She smiled and made a vague gesture with her hand. "Elves. Dwarves. *Dragons.*"

"But being accepted as one of the Isir makes perfect sense to you?"

She swatted me on the arm. "Shaddap, you." She smiled at me in a way that made me want to melt into a puddle.

"You really are the best, you know," I murmured.

"Yes, I know. You are lucky to have me."

I was. I am. I hope I always will be.

If you enjoyed this novel, I hope you will consider joining my No-Spam™ email list. You can sign up at the link below.

https://erikhenryvick.com/book-updates-mailing-list/

As a thank you for signing up, you will receive a free copy of Devils, my #1 bestselling horror anthology.

AUTHOR'S NOTE

I have always been an avid reader. In fact, I can't remember a time when I wasn't reading a book. I wore out books by my favorite authors, reading them until the pages fell out, and then bought another copy.

When I was disabled by my Personal Monster™ I turned to fiction for solace, although in ebook form (and now, I can read them as much as I want and the pages do not fall out). It was a bleak and dark time for me—I was lonely. I was depressed.

I felt…useless.

I needed to do something that mattered to me, and I wanted to do something that mattered to others as well. People have a hard time understanding chronic illness, and I can't say I blame them—I have one that I can't understand at all. It's a so called "invisible disability." When you see someone with a wheelchair or a prosthetic, you immediately recognize what's wrong and can imagine the limitations that person faces. Imagining what goes on when someone is disabled by a chronic illness is much harder. You can't see the pain, the exhaustion, the isolation, the mental toll.

I began writing this novel out of desperation. As I said, I needed to do something, and I needed to keep my mind working. I also wanted to provide a peek into the life my Personal Monster™ allowed me. I decided to write about a guy with rheumatoid arthritis, to describe the pain, the darkness, the hopelessness.

Years before, I'd written as a hobby, but always with the idea of publishing "at some point." Supergirl (the real one) encouraged me to write again (and as usual, she was right. And super). In the face of my illness, I knew it would be hard. There are stretches of time in which I can't do much more than watch the clock—waiting for the next time I can take pain meds. I knew I'd spend weeks or even months NOT working on this novel, and that's A Very Bad Thing for a writer. The story evaporates. Characters change into potted plants. I also knew I could never meet a traditional publishing deadline.

I didn't care. I wanted to try anyway, and in the beginning, the novel suffered because of my illness. Then, I read about "next notes" in *Bag of Bones* by Stephen King, and it was like being struck by lightning. Suddenly, I knew how to overcome the problems of not working on a schedule. The simple act of leaving a next note for myself at the end of a writing session allowed me to develop the ideas that were bouncing around in my head, and the simple story of a guy chasing a serial killer grew beyond its bounds.

The first draft of this novel was over 215,000 words (about 900 8.5 x 11 pages, double spaced). By contrast, the version you just read is 159,000 words—what I cut is long enough to be considered a novel on its own. Part of that was because I like to talk. A lot. Part of it was because of the way the book developed (around page 300 of the original draft, the story became something new, and suddenly there were a bunch of Norse gods running around casting lightning bolts and such). But also, part of it was because I'd started with the idea of telling everyone what it was like to be disabled by RA. I wanted to explain how stupid some laws and policies of insurance companies are. That's a bad idea. I've always said that when you want to get up on your soap box and right wrongs with your fiction, you should go write an essay and get all that out of your system so you can get back to writing a story. Plus, a lot of what I wrote in the beginning was just plain bad.

After I cut the bad, reworked the mediocre, and finished the novel, I think I still painted a picture of what it's like to battle a Personal Monster™ on a daily basis, and I think I did it without too much preaching. I also had a lot of fun running around the universe with Hank. I hope you did, too.

ABOUT THE AUTHOR

Erik Henry Vick is an author who happens to be disabled by an autoimmune disease (also known as his Personal Monster™). He writes to hang on to the few remaining shreds of his sanity. His current favorite genres to write are dark fantasy and horror.

He lives in Western New York with his wife, Supergirl; their son; a Rottweiler named after a god of thunder; and two extremely psychotic cats. He fights his Personal Monster™ daily with humor, pain medicine, and funny T-shirts.

Erik has a B.A. in Psychology, an M.S.C.S., and a Ph.D. in Artificial Intelligence. He has worked as a criminal investigator for a state agency, a college professor, a C.T.O. for an international software company, and a video game developer.

He'd love to hear from you on social media:

Blog: https://erikhenryvick.com

Twitter: https://twitter.com/BerserkErik

Facebook: https://fb.me/erikhenryvick

Amazon author pages:

USA: https://bit.ly/4ehvusa

UK: https://bit.ly/4ehvuk

Goodreads Author Page: https://bit.ly/4ehvgr